MW00414624

LOST ANGELS

By
John Galt Robinson

KCM PUBLISHING
A DIVISION OF KCM DIGITAL MEDIA, LLC

CREDITS

Copyright © 2022 by John Galt Robinson
Published by KCM Publishing
A Division of KCM Digital Media, LLC

All Rights Reserved.

This content may not be reproduced in whole or in part, in any form or by any means, electronic or mechanical, including photocopying, recording, or by any information storage and retrieval system now known or hereafter invented, without written permission from the publisher.

This is a work of fiction. Names, characters, businesses, places, events, and incidents are either the products of the author's imagination or used in a fictitious manner. Any resemblance to actual persons, living or dead, or actual events is purely coincidental.

Lost Angels by John Galt Robinson

ISBN-13:978-1-955620-07-9
ISBN-eBook: 978-1-955620-08-6

First Edition

Publisher: Michael Fabiano
KCM Publishing
www.kcmpublishing.com

To our sister and one of my first readers, Kathy "Beeb"
Robinson Houck;
Ballerina, US Marine, ER Nurse, mother, sister,
wife and friend.
We hope you and Wayne are riding the streets
of gold on your Harley's.
How about a ride when we meet again?

Acknowledgements

My Lord and Savior, Jesus Christ. Phil 4:13 "For I can do all things through Christ who strengthens me."

My wife and inspiration, Pam Robinson, the women who encourages me, provides honest criticism and who endures hours of writing sessions. We are in this together!

My adult children, Jenna, Luke and Jordan for your encouragement and support.

My outstanding publisher, Michael Fabiano, and his team at KCM Publishing. Thank you for taking a chance, standing with and guiding me through these endeavors. Here's to many more!

My beta readers, James Blake, David Smith, John Cunningham and Mac Ogburn. Thank you for your honest criticism and helping shape these stories.

Josh Rogers for the aviation expertise. Blue skies my friend.

My brother Tom Robinson for the computer and IT expertise.

The always accessible MJ for the criminal and federal law enforcement insight. Our nation is grateful for your selfless dedication and service.

Gary Blackard and the amazing staff and volunteers at Adult and Teen Challenge. Thank you for your continued support and for all that you do to change lives.

Founder Joseph Travers, Master Chief Kirby Horrell, Ms. Stephanie Brown and all of the selfless and dedicated volunteers at Saved In America. Thank you for finding and rescuing our lost angels. I have enjoyed meeting and getting to know you. Thank you for the background information on the cartels and human trafficking.

Contents

Prologue

Durham, North Carolina

Traces of gray began to illuminate the campus of Duke University in the pre-dawn calm. In a little over an hour, the campus would be bustling with cars and pedestrians as students made their way to Friday morning class. For now, the peaceful silence was only broken up by the musical interlude of chirping birds and the soft, rhythmic pacing of a small pair of running shoes.

Tracy Courtnall, a freshman mechanical engineering major, floated along Towerview Road at a seemingly effortless eight-minute mile pace. A gymnast and cheerleader in high school, Tracy had always kept in top shape as evidenced by her petite frame that barely made a sound as her feet touched the road. Tracy was well aware of the dreaded "freshman fifteen" and was determined to fight it off. A quick check in the mirror before she left her dorm this morning reassured her that she had managed well, so far. It had only been a little over a month. Her long blond hair was pulled back into a ponytail which danced side to side, matching her perky personality, as she ran.

It was late September, but the days were still reaching into the eighties. The mornings were in the low sixties making for perfect running weather. Tracy actually preferred running in the morning. She had purposefully taken on eighteen credit hours which burdened her with a heavy amount of studying. It was easier having her run out of the way, leaving her afternoons and evenings free to study. In contrast to the stereotype of her cheerleader looks, Tracy was actually quite studious and intelligent. The fact that she was an engineering major with an academic scholarship at Duke underscored that. Today was actually filled with tests and quizzes, but she was ready. When you know the material so well you actually look forward to taking the test, you're ready. With her run out of the way and no new material to cover, Tracy would have a rare night off. The football team was home against Wake Forest tomorrow, so there would be a lot of activity in the fraternity houses tonight. Tracy looked forward to a night of fun with her new sorority sisters as they made the rounds. She promised herself she wouldn't be out too late. Her parents were both Duke alumni and huge Blue Devils fans. They lived in Charlotte but had a luxury box at the stadium and never missed a game. Tracy would be expected to drop by for an early lunch before kickoff and she didn't want to show up a hungover mess. Not that she would. She wanted to experience all that college had to offer but she didn't want to lose control and place herself in a compromising situation. She was one of the few girls who had kept her virginity through high school, and she was not about to lose it by allowing herself to get drunk and stupid.

Tracy crossed Circuit Drive and, warm up completed, picked up her pace. The turn into a running path that circled a small lake was just up ahead. It was more wooded along this stretch of road and the fresh morning air invigorated her as she began to breathe harder. She swerved out into the empty street to avoid a van parked along the side. Suddenly, a man darted out from where he was crouched down in front of the van. He wore a dark t-shirt and black denim jeans. Before Tracy could scream, he had a hand over her mouth while he wrapped his other arm around her and carried her, kicking and flailing, to the open sliding door on the passenger side. She was violently thrown onto the carpeted floor and he landed on top of her. He reeked of sweat and cigarettes. The door slid shut and the van began to move. The man held her down while another man and woman bound her with duct tape and then placed a gag over her mouth. The woman then searched Tracy and only found her student ID. The trio then straightened Tracy out on the carpet's edge and rolled her up inside. They wrapped tape around the roll of carpet and laid it alongside a similar roll as the van picked up speed, leaving the quiet campus behind.

LOST ANGELS

"Let not anyone pacify his conscience by the delusion that he can do no harm if he takes no part, and forms no opinion. Bad men need nothing more to compass their ends, than that good men should look on and do nothing."

- John Stuart Mill

Chapter 1

Chattanooga, Tennessee

A clustered mass of people stretched along the bike path in a line measuring well over half a mile. The serpentine line led to a temporary dock where, for the past ten minutes, people had been jumping off the end, like lemmings, into the Tennessee River. Some of the women wore swimsuits, some of the men were clad only in bike shorts, while most of the competitors wore traditional triathlon jerseys with matching bike shorts. All wore swimming goggles and bright colored swim caps.

"Ooooh, let's light this candle!" Dr. Wendy Conlan exclaimed with nervous excitement as she and her friend spotted the entrance to the dock. It loomed, just up ahead, over the mass of competitors walking toward it.

Dr. Christine "Christy" Tabrizi smiled remembering the phrase Wendy always spoke aloud during medical school, minutes before beginning a major exam. Wendy, a practicing OB/GYN, here in Chattanooga, had talked Christy into this race over a year ago. Despite her schedule as a night shift ER physician, Christy had trained faithfully and, fully aware of her palpable nervousness, was now eager to jump in the water and start her first Ironman Triathlon. Christy, a tall, slender, yet shapely brunette, looked down at her petite blond friend.

"I just want to remind you that this was your idea!"

"That's right, Dork! We've got this!" Wendy smiled with excitement as she and Christy fist bumped...

1

"Where else would you rather be..." Christy began.

"Than right here, right now!" They finished in unison.

"Here we go!" Christy announced as they stepped onto the dock and pulled their goggles down onto their eyes. Christy nervously checked her ponytail to ensure it was still tucked up under her swim cap. The pace picked up markedly as they hurried to the end of the dock. Christy quickly put aside any thoughts of jumping on top of the competitor before her as well as thoughts of being jumped on from behind upon entering the water. And there it was. An opening in the dock space as a race volunteer waved her on. Without another thought, Christy drew a breath and jumped in. The dark green water of the Tennessee River was 76.2 degrees this morning. Just a tenth of a degree too warm for the race to be wetsuit legal but cool enough to greet Christy with a jolt. Eager to vacate the entry area, Christy stretched out into a form-perfect freestyle and began to swim downriver.

Christy's reach and form gave her a speed advantage and she quickly began to work her way around slower swimmers as she searched for open space. A telltale trail of bubbles appeared just ahead in the dark water, warning Christy that she was swimming up on the kicking feet of a slower swimmer. Christy veered right and was greeted by an elbow to her forehead, unintentionally struck by an adjacent swimmer stroking through the water. Christy took it in stride as she smoothly stroked her way between and past the two swimmers. Another swimmer angled into Christy's side before passing behind. She hoped the congestion would soon clear as she continued to angle toward the center of the river. Her hope was that the current would be faster out there and that there would be fewer swimmers. Through the dark green water, Christy could just make out the lighter shade of kicking legs as she began to overtake another swimmer. The form drew closer as the two converged. Christy's right arm lightly bushed the other swimmer's left arm as she passed but not before the other swimmer accidentally swatted Christy's face as she rolled to her right for a breath. The jarring blow stunned Christy, but she powered on and moved past.

Realizing she was passing many swimmers while not being passed by others, Christy began to wonder if she was swimming too fast. Was the adrenaline surge causing her to exceed her long-distance pace? She didn't think so. This felt like her race pace, something she had developed to the point of comfort over the past year of training. She wished she could glance at her Garmin watch to see her actual pace, but that would break her stroke efficiency and she knew better than to do that.

Trust your training.

Joe's words echoed those of Wendy's and several seasoned triathletes she had trained with. Christy knew she was fast in the water, but the swim portion of the race, although 2.4 miles, was, by measurement of time spent, less than ten percent of the race. The few minutes that might be gained pushing for a faster swim could sap her endurance and cost her dearly in the bike and run portions. As the swimmers began to spread out, she sensed she had more space. She settled into her pattern of long comfortable strokes, elbow high, efficient entry, good body roll, and a comfortable kick. Without breaking her stroke, she would gently raise her eyes above water in what is known as an "alligator peak" every minute or so to get a position fix. Her breathing was relaxed, and she was in her zone. This was her "forever pace." Her body went into autopilot and her thoughts began to wander as her mind was able to separate from her body.

Inevitably, her thoughts turned back to Joe. Lieutenant Commander Joseph O'Shanick, United States Navy, was a Navy SEAL platoon leader whom fate had thrust into her life a year ago in Honduras. Christy had been serving on a medical missions trip along with Wendy and two other doctor friends when the women's shelter they were serving was taken captive by a violent gang. Joe's platoon had been sent in to rescue them, but a cartel ambushed them. Half of Joe's teammates were killed in a helicopter crash while Wendy had been shot, nearly fatally. Meanwhile, Christy had been carried away by one of the cartel members. Joe had taken off after Christy but was also ambushed resulting in his capture as well. Always resilient and resourceful, Joe ultimately helped Christy escape. She wouldn't be here today were it not for him.

At first, they seemed like total opposites, he an atheist, Christy a devout Christian. Were it not for their mutual peril at the time, they likely would have gone their separate ways; however, their shared ordeal had created a mutual respect that evolved into a friendship. Despite living hundreds of miles apart, Joe in Virginia Beach and Christy in the Atlanta area, they kept in touch and grew closer. They shared another brush with death three months ago which brought them even closer and brought Christy close to Joe's family as well. Now, nearly a year after their first encounter, they were finding their way through the early stages of a relationship. Christy smiled in the water as she recalled describing to Wendy her new relationship with Joe as "awkwardly exciting." Awkward in that, despite both being early thirty-something professionals, neither had ever been in a serious relationship before. Exciting because they both brought out strong qualities in each other and, well, it was a new relationship. One that was quickly becoming serious. Christy already knew this was the man she was going to marry. She just didn't know if Joe knew that. Joe was growing in his faith as a new Christian, a journey Christy was pleased to have walked Joe through. His SEAL training had instilled a discipline of excellence that led him to amazing growth over a short time. She had never met a man like him. Nevertheless, his life was rapidly moving through several changes at once.

Not the least of which was he stood at a crossroads in his career. A recent mission resulted in a shoulder injury that took him out of the training rotation. He was supposed to have already begun training with Green Team, the selection pool for DEVGRU, the elite counterterrorism team more commonly referred to as SEAL Team Six. Joe had already stepped down from his previous billet as the commanding officer of Echo Platoon. He hated to leave his team but, after completing his two deployments as the CO, he was forced to move on and make room for the next CO. His injury resulted in losing his Green Team slot and his chances of getting that back were poor. Joe openly confided with Christy that he did not want to become a desk polisher in operations. He would still be a SEAL and the job would be important, but he didn't see himself as anything but an active combat operator. If he couldn't do that, he wasn't sure he wanted to stay in the Teams.

He had been given two months to rehab his shoulder, which, thankfully, did not require surgery. A visit with Christy's brother, a highly regarded orthopaedic surgeon back home in Nashville, revealed that

Joe's rotator cuff and labrum were partially torn but would likely heal with good rehabilitation. Joe would soon have to choose what he would do after the two months were up. Among his options were remaining in Virginia Beach to work in operations, shipping out to Coronado to train recruits in BUDS, the arduous training and selection program employed by the SEAL teams, or taking a non-SEAL assignment handed out by the Navy. Door number three was *not* an option according to Joe. That left either Virginia Beach or Coronado.

Christy felt her Garmin vibrate, informing her that she was a half mile into the swim. A quick alligator peak above the water reassured her she was in good position without disrupting her comfortable stroke. She quickly returned to her thoughts.

Christy was very happy with her current job in Duluth, Georgia. She worked in a busy but well-run emergency room and lived in a cozy house on Lake Lanier. She didn't want to give that up but she was ready to live minutes from Joe, rather than hours. She sensed Joe was ready for that as well. The Navy afforded Joe very little flexibility in where he lived, whereas Christy could get a job anywhere. Unfortunately, not all emergency departments were the same and she doubted she would find a setup as good as her current gig; nevertheless, she would do so if it meant living near Joe. She had already hinted at it with him but he expressed regret over her giving up a good job on his account. Regardless, the issue would have to be decided soon. She didn't want this to go on undecided for much longer. Christy was ready to start thinking about their future.

Without warning, a foot appeared out of nowhere heading straight for Christy's face as she rolled right for a breath. She instinctively ducked her head at the last second and took the kick to her forehead. The jolt made her gasp after already having exhaled her breath. Christy quickly popped up choking as she gasped for air while her head throbbed. She treaded water for a few seconds until she recovered enough to start swimming again. She angrily looked around and spotted the other swimmer. She then took a quick position fix and started off being sure to give the breast stroker a wide berth as she passed. Breaststroke was legal in triathlons but frowned upon by other competitors. The kicking style was hazardous to other swimmers as

5

the sidekick Christy just received illustrated. Christy shook off her anger and refocused on her race. She hoped her headache would go away soon but, if not, she had some Ibuprofen in her transition bag, just in case.

Shake it off, Christy. The only easy day was yesterday. Joe's reassuring voice spoke clearly in her mind.

Chapter 2

Atlanta, Georgia

The pain was intense. Tracy felt like her head was tightly clamped in a vice. A lone ceiling light cast a dim glow that still seemed to penetrate Tracy's eyelids as if a spotlight were directed directly at her. She tried to open her eyes, but it only intensified her headache. She lay there for a few minutes with a bruised forearm draped across her eyes as she tried to recall the nightmarish events of the past two days.

She remembered untold hours of claustrophobic terror wrapped up in that carpet. She counted three more girls abducted in similar fashion over the course of the day before they were delivered to wherever they were now. It took nearly an hour after being cut out of the carpet and tape, before Tracy and the other girls were able to adequately regain the ability to move their limbs. Their clothes had been drenched in their own urine after their prolonged time wrapped up. Several men and the same woman reappeared and ordered them out of their clothes and into a small bathroom down the hall where they were told to quickly clean up. The girls must not have responded quickly enough as one of the men snatched a redhead up by her hair and slammed her into the wall before backhanding her several times. The woman then told the rest of the girls this would happen to all of them if they didn't do as they were told. Tracy perceived they singled out the redhead as an example to exact compliance out of the rest of them. It worked. All the girls, Tracy included, quickly cleaned up, applied cheap makeup per instructions and then donned the skimpy lingerie handed to them.

Each was then brought into a larger room where several men and women were scattered about slaving over various laptop computers. The room reeked of body odor, marijuana, and cigarettes. Other girls, wearing little or nothing at all moved about, in a trance-like state, from an adjacent room and through a beaded curtain that covered a make-shift door roughly cut through a wall in the eat-in kitchen. Each of the new girls was forced to stand in front of a green screen set up on one wall while a raven-haired older woman took their pictures. Once their pictures were taken, they had been forced to disrobe and sent back into this room where they each had a small black exercise mat laying on a concrete floor. The only other "furnishing" was a five-gallon bucket in the corner for answering the call of nature. Two men remained in the room. Both men wielded electric cords, which an athletic looking brunette painfully learned were used to enforce a strict code of silence.

The redhead and one other girl had wept while the others had lain here in shock as they faced their new reality. A short while later two men came in, selected one of the other girls, a blond, like Tracy, and escorted her out. They returned ten minutes later and exchanged her for the redhead. Ten minutes later and it was Tracy's turn. She was walked back into the main room where she was weighed, measured for height, and then placed on a folding table where another woman performed a very crude exam of her pelvic region.

"Sergei!" The women had yelled as she looked into and adjacent room.

"Da?" A male voice answered.

The women had excitedly yelled something in what Tracy guessed was Russian. Several of the men and women looked up from their laptops and stared at Tracy. A tall, muscular male with closely shaved brown hair and a beard had appeared from the other room. He had icy blue eyes and a sharp nose that appeared to have been broken once or twice. He walked over to the table and eyed Tracy as the woman spoke to him. He appeared to ask the women a question which she promptly answered. He had then spoken over his shoulder to a man and woman who were hovering over one of the laptops. He stroked Tracy's left cheek with the back of a calloused hand and then walked out. Tracy was then hoisted to her feet and taken back to the room with the other girls.

Over the next twenty-four hours, the other four girls had each been taken out of the room for hours at a time. Each had returned bruised, disheveled, and emotionally broken. By their slow painful gait, Tracy surmised that each had been excessively raped and abused. Each minute had slowly ticked by with Tracy dreading her turn but, so far, it hadn't happened. Due to her fear, sleep had been evasive but her exhaustion eventually won out.

Tracy had never experienced a migraine before, but she assumed the headache she was now experiencing was just that. It must have been caused by the intense fear and stress she was experiencing. Finally able to open her eyes, Tracy sat up and looked around the room. The men were gone but the door was shut. Presumably locked from the outside but she couldn't tell for sure. She thought about trying the door but was afraid that would result in unwanted attention. The spartan room, in which they lay, had a solitary window which, unfortunately, was boarded up from the outside. The only other way out was through the door which led out into the large room where the computer people worked. Not an option.

Tracy picked up the plastic bottle of water next to her and looked at the contents. There was a trace amount left. She unscrewed the cap and drank the last remaining sip. In the past two days, she had been given a total of two bottles of water and one McDonald's hamburger each day. Tears welled up in her eyes. Tracy was hungry, she was thirsty, she was suffering a migraine, and she lay in fear waiting her turn when the men would come take her to be sexually molested and abused. She lay back down on her side, curled up in the fetal position, and began to cry. It was only a matter of time before she would lose her carefully preserved virginity in a painful and brutal manner. Through her tears, Tracy saw the almond-shaped brown eyes of the brunette, also laying down just a few feet away, looking right at her. The brunette's cracked and swollen lips barely moved as her dry, scratchy voice croaked out.

"Welcome to hell."

Chapter 3

Chattanooga, Tennessee

A s Christy angled into the swim exit, the forms of other swimmers began to appear through the water as they all converged.
Christy took another sight and saw she was probably fifty yards from
the well-marked exit. She fought off the urge to sprint and continued
her smooth stroke as other swimmers closed in. Another sight and
she saw people climbing up the swim exit stairs just ten yards away.
She swam in until the AstroTurf carpeted steps appeared underneath.
Christy placed her hands and feet down and climbed up onto the wide
concrete walkway that flanked the river. A quick glance at her Garmin
Fenix 3 watch revealed that her swim split was just under fifty-two
minutes. *Yes!* She exclaimed to herself as she pressed the button to
change her watch into the Transition 1 mode. With a gleeful spring
in her step, Christy pulled off her swim cap and goggles and began to
jog with the other competitors down the walkway which would lead
them to the transition area. Throngs of cheering spectators lined the
barricade separating them from the triathletes. Hands were held out
for congratulatory high-fives while cowbells and other noise making
devices added a festive ring to the crowd. The crowd was packed
shoulder to shoulder and appeared at least five deep.

Up ahead, a familiar and pleasant face stood out from the rest of
the crowd. Close-cropped, dark brown hair and a chiseled jawline underscored strong Irish facial bones that framed a ruggedly handsome
face. Joe's green eyes lit up with delight when he spotted Christy.

Standing with Joe were her parents, Sami and Shannon Tabrizi, her brothers Jason and Peter, Jason's wife, Lynn, and Christy's younger sister Caitlyn. Absent was Christy's brother, Jamie, a Marine Corps officer currently deployed in Central America. With a beaming smile, Christy ran up to the barricade, grabbed Joe's face and excitedly kissed him.

"Fifty-two minutes! Best swim ever!" She exclaimed to Joe before kissing him again. She then noticed the man standing next to Joe. Almost as tall and muscular as Joe, Master Chief Petty Officer Matt Ramsey was Joe's right hand man in their SEAL Platoon and one of his closest friends.

"Matt, it's so good to see you! I had no idea you were coming!"

"You think I'd miss this?" he smiled through his goatee as Christy gave him a quick hug that left his shirt wet.

Christy moved on to hug her mom and dad and then resumed her run as she high-fived her brothers and sister in law.

"We'll see you out on the bike course, Christy!" Jason yelled.

Christy waved back as she ran off. The exuberant crowd lined the entire shoreline giving the triathletes an emotional lift as they ran by. Christy reached the turn and jogged uphill with the rest of the competitors. Reaching the road, they were directed into a chute lined with volunteers handling the transition bags. Christy gave her number to a young woman who relayed it, by radio, back to another volunteer. Christy ran down the chute and was met by another woman who handed over her bag as she ran by. She was then directed into the female tent where there were dozens of volunteers helping the triathletes change into their biking gear. Christy found an open folding chair and sat down. She opened her bag, pulled out her socks and quickly put them on, followed by her sunglasses. She then removed a tube of Chamois Butt'r, untied her bike shorts and applied a handful of the lubricant in her groin area. Not exactly glamorous but quite necessary. Any significant time in a bicycle saddle was sure to cause chaffing. She quickly dried her hands with a disposable surgical towel, threw her swim cap and goggles into the bag, and put on her bike gloves. On her way out she handed the bag off to another volunteer and then stopped at a table for an energy gel and a cup of water. That done, Christy ran out of the tent where several volunteers met her and sprayed her down with sunscreen. Then she was off to her bike.

Like most of the triathletes, Christy came by during the pre-dawn hours before the race started to set up her bike. This involved topping off the air in her tires as well as stocking the bike with energy gels, water bottles, and two frozen bottles of Infinit, a custom-made blend of carbohydrates and electrolytes to keep her properly fueled over the bike course. They would be thawed by now but still cold. She had two replacements bottles waiting for her in a special needs bag at mile 56. Additionally, there were aid stations every eighteen miles offering water, flat cola, Gatorade, energy gels, bananas, and more. Keeping properly fueled throughout the ultimate endurance event was crucial for anyone wanting to cross the finish line. Christy had no idea if she could really make it to the finish line. She had extensively trained over the past year, but never all three distances in the same day. She felt great coming out of the 2.4 mile swim and, barring an accident, was sure she would make it through the 116 mile bike (the Chattanooga bike course is four miles longer than the standard 112 miles of most Ironman races) but didn't know if she would have the legs or the time to make it to the finish line by midnight in order to count as an official finisher.

Only one way to find out, Christy thought to herself. *Trust your training.*

Christy located her bike, a secondhand Cervelo P2 she found on eBay, grabbed her bike helmet she had positioned on the handlebars, and strapped it on her head. She and Wendy had French braided each other's hair in the wee hours before the race which allowed the helmet to fit perfectly while keeping her long dark hair from flying around. She removed her bike from the rack and, with one hand on the saddle, pushed it out to the bike start as she ran next to it. She had pre-clipped her shoes to the pedals this morning allowing her to run in her socks. This gave her a speed advantage over those running in their clunky bike shoes and, as a result, she passed many people on her way out of the transition zone. She reached the bike start and, with practiced ease, mounted her bike in a flying start. She clicked her watch into the bike split as she placed her feet on top of her bike shoes and began to pedal. Upon reaching adequate speed, Christy smoothly reached down with her left hand, slipped her left foot into its shoe, and secured the Velcro strap. She pedaled back up to speed and then repeated the process with her right foot. Once this was done, she settled down into her aero-bars and began to pedal in in earnest. She worked her way up into a comfortable gear and began to fly through the streets of Chattanooga amongst a long line of triathletes, all colorfully clad in their various racing apparel. They coasted up and over several sets of train tracks made smooth by the racing staff who had placed carpeting over the tracks.

That was thoughtful, Christy thought to herself as she marveled over the details the race committee went through to make these races great events.

More cowbells and noisemakers rang out as the spectators lined the streets that led the racers out of the city. The celebratory sounds began to diminish as the crowd thinned and the urban landscape gave way to a rural landscape. They were soon on a long stretch of a four-lane highway heading south out of Tennessee. As they crossed into Georgia, Christy could see an endless train of triathletes on their bikes and marveled at the sight. She and Wendy had ridden this course many times over the past year, as part of their training. It was a spectacularly beautiful course, looping through northern Georgia over rolling hills, but it normally seemed quite remote and quiet. Conversely, today, it seemed to teem with life crowded with miles of bikers as well as the spectators randomly scattered about the course. Many sat in lawn chairs or in the back of pickup trucks and cheered as the triathletes cycled by. At one point, there was a group of shirtless men, wearing hillbilly hats and dressed in denim bib overalls playing rock music on bluegrass instruments. Christy recognized AC/DC's "Thunderstruck" as she rode by. The crowds were a pleasant diversion and, before she knew it, Christy was approaching the aid station at the eighteen-mile mark.

Christy dropped into a lower gear and slowed down as she entered the aid chute. Dozens of volunteers in bright yellow t-shirts held out water bottles, Gatorade, gels, and other snack items. Christy reached out and snatched a water bottle from a volunteer as she rode by. She flipped it upside down and poured it into her aero-bottle, an insulated bottle mounted between her aero-bars that had a large straw which allowed her to take sips without using her hands as she rode. Upon filling up her aero-bottle, Christy squeezed the last of the water into her mouth and then flung the empty disposable bottle into a designated trash collection area as she rode by. She settled back into the aero position and peddled back up to pace. Only 98 more miles to go.

Chapter 4

Durham, North Carolina

C harles Courtnall III sat with his legs crossed in a leather, padded wing back chair. He was middle aged with an average build but his tailored suit and short, prematurely gray hair gave him a stately appearance of wealth and importance. Next to him, in an identical chair, sat the Dean of Students, Robert Westerkam, a personal friend and fraternity brother of Courtnall's from when they were undergrads here at Duke in the early nineties. They sat across from the University President, Dennis Kettering, who sat behind the desk of his private study. Also in the room were the Campus Safety Director and the Chief of the Durham City Police.

"Charles, let me say again how devastated Cecilia and I are over the disappearance of your beautiful daughter. As the president of this university I take full responsibility over the welfare of every student and staff member. Moreover, as your friend and fellow alumni, I want to assure you that I have put every resource into finding her as soon as possible."

"Thank you, Dennis. I know you have."

"I asked Director Kemp and Chief Taylor to come by and present what they know so far as well as to help us try to piece this all together. Director Kemp," Kettering said as he looked at his security director, "would you care to start off, please."

"Yes, sir," Kemp said as he stepped away from the wall behind Kettering's desk.

Kemp was in his upper forties, stocky with close-cropped gray hair. He was a retired North Carolina State Trooper who was now double dipping as the director of Campus Safety. He maintained a fit appearance with a barrel chest and just the beginning of a slight paunch above his waistline. He wore khaki pants and a black polo shirt with the campus safety emblem embroidered over the heart.

"Mr. Courtnall, we have conducted a thorough investigation into your daughter's disappearance and here's what we know so far." He cleared his throat before continuing. "Our records show that your daughter used her card to enter the dorm at exactly 8:04pm Thursday night. Now, our locks only require the students to use their ID to enter the building; therefore, students can leave the building simply by pushing open any door and there will be no record of their leaving."

"Understood," Courtnall nodded.

"Your daughter had a Calculus test at 8:00am Friday, but she never showed up for it or any of the other tests she was scheduled for on Friday. Her roommate tells us that Tracy was asleep, in her bed, before 10:00 on Thursday night and that Tracy was still sleeping when the roommate hit the rack an hour later. Tracy was gone when she woke up the next morning but that wasn't unusual for her. The roommate says Tracy routinely left early every morning to go for a run but was always back before 7:30 to shower and get ready for class. She said Tracy never missed class," Kemp looked over at Courtnall as he finished this sentence.

Courtnall nodded in response.

"Continuing, sir, a search of their room revealed your daughter's cell phone, wallet, and purse were still in the room. The only thing that wasn't found was her student ID. Now it's possible she could have left the dorm at any time after she was last seen at eleven; however, we think it's reasonable to assume she left in the morning for her morning run like she always does."

Courtnall again nodded silently.

"Her roommate said Tracy was gone when she woke up, she didn't have class until 10:00 and, as such, she didn't wake up until 9:00. She said she didn't think anything of it because Tracy is always gone when she wakes up. This leads us to believe that Tracy likely left to go for a run and never returned. That would put her time of disappearance between 11:00pm and 8:00am but our best guess is sometime between 6:30 and 7:30am, sir."

"Any ideas as to the cause of Tracy's disappearance?" Courtnall asked.

"We can only speculate at this point, sir, but the circumstances do not paint a pretty picture. A preliminary canvassing of the campus has not turned up anything nor has an exhaustive search of our security cameras. The fact that several important items were still in her room and that she had a calculus test at 8:00am tells us she had every intention of returning to her room. My best guess, sir," Kemp hesitated before continuing with a pained expression, "is your daughter was abducted. I'm so sorry, sir."

Courtnall briefly closed his eyes but otherwise remained stoic. He was an incredibly intelligent man. A brilliant financial analyst and investor. A math and computer major as an undergrad who had later developed investment software that predicted market trends which helped him make a fortune for his clients as well as himself. He prided himself on his logical mind which was not driven by emotion. He had come to the same conclusion over the past twenty-four hours. Hearing it from someone else was painful but not a surprise at this point.

"I see," Courtnall answered solemnly. "Do you have any leads as to who may have taken my daughter or where she might be?"

"No, sir. At this time, we do not. However, we are doing everything we can to track her down."

"Has anybody stepped forward who may have seen or heard anything?"

"No, sir. Not at this time. I'm sorry."

"Charles," President Kettering spoke up, "this is Durham Police Chief, Amelia Taylor. She has been leading her department in investigating this matter. I'd like her to go next."

"Thank you, President Kettering," Chief Taylor spoke as she stepped closer to the desk.

Chief Taylor was a medium height, solidly built, but not overweight, black woman with an authoritative presence. She wore the full uniform of a police chief and stood ramrod straight as she spoke.

"Our investigation has given us no insight as to the disappearance of your daughter beyond that which Director Kemp has already told you; however, we are looking into a similar disappearance of a female co-ed which happened across town at NC State that morning as well. We have no idea if the two are related, but we are coordinating with the Raleigh Police Department to share resources and information should there be a link. In their case, a canine search led them to two clumps of hair near on the side of a street that is a popular running route among the students. One of the hair samples may belong to the missing student in question, a Lindsay Meehan, who is a sophomore mechanical engineering student on a Navy ROTC scholarship. It appears to match a hair sample taken from her hairbrush. We are awaiting DNA confirmation."

"And the other sample?" Kettering asked.

"It has been sent for DNA testing and will be submitted to a known criminal DNA base to see if it matches. From what we have learned, Ms. Meehan is very proficient in Mixed Martial Arts. Her father is an active duty Marine. She may have had the wherewithal to have purposefully pulled out a clump of her hair as well as that of her assailant, if that's indeed what happened, in attempt to leave a trail for the authorities."

"I'd say that's quite the remarkable young lady," Kettering said in admiration.

Courtnall slumped as if deflated. Kettering noticed this immediately.

"Charles, I'm so sorry. I didn't mean that to imply anything regarding your Tracy. She is an amazingly talented and intelligent young lady in her own right. If something terrible happened, she may very well be leaving a trail as well. I hope you understand I am just trying to glean any bit of hope we can get."

"No, Dennis, I'm not upset with you. I'm upset with myself. I should have equipped her better to know how to handle herself, how to defend herself, and how to avoid danger. This is on me," Courtnall said with a glance out the glass-paned French doors.

Across the foyer, he could see his wife, Jane, seated in the living room with Kettering and Westerkam's wives. How could he even begin to comfort Jane with this information? Of all his amassed wealth, nothing could replace their Tracy. Nothing. He would trade it all in a second to get her back safely. Courtnall had been confident that he could provide anything his family needed. How deceived he had been. The one thing Tracy needed more than anything else, he had failed to provide. What she needed now, he couldn't provide. He turned back to face the others.

"Where do we go from here?" He asked.

"My department will continue to investigate this and search for the whereabouts of your daughter. As I stated, we are coordinating with Raleigh PD and State Police to increase our resources and manpower."

"Has an Amber Alert been put out?" Courtnall asked.

"No, sir..."

"Why not?" He asked sharply.

"Amber Alerts are for children under the age of seventeen," Taylor finished.

"What about alerting the FBI?" Kettering asked.

"We can't right now, sir," Taylor answered. "So far, this is a missing persons case. We have no evidence there was a kidnapping or state-to-state transportation of Ms. Courtnall. The moment we have such evidence, we will notify the FBI. Of that, I can assure you; although, I hope it is something much simpler and she is found safe and sound before the day is over."

"We all hope for that. Thank you, Chief Taylor," Kettering finished as he turned his attention back to Courtnall.

"Charles, we are at your disposal. As president of this university, I will put every resource on this and we will not rest until Tracy is returned safely in your care."

Courtnall nodded grimly in acknowledgment. Nobody dared speak what they were all thinking. They were all intelligent and learned. They had all read the crime reports of what happens to most abducted women. They're rarely, if ever, found alive again. More often than not, if they were found, it was the decayed and battered remains of a women who had been violated and snuffed out for the temporary satisfaction of the animal or animals who had taken them. Jane knew that. There would be no consoling her.

Chapter 5

Chattanooga, Tennessee

The Chickamauga Battlefield was eerily quiet the second pass through. The bike course included a forty-seven-mile loop around North Georgia that was ridden twice before turning north for the final stretch leading back to Chattanooga. The small charming town of Chickamauga was located near race mile 55, close to the traditional midway portion of the bike split. The town had been the sight of a famous Civil War battle fought in 1863. At least a thousand cheering spectators, Joe, and Christy's family among them, had lined the street of Chickamauga and greeted the triathletes as they sped by on their bikes. Many competitors had stopped at a designated location where their special needs bags were kept. In Christy's case, her bag had contained a small tube of skin lubricant, two additional bottles of Infinit, two previously frozen peanut butter and strawberry jelly *Uncrustable* sandwiches, a small container of Pringles, a small towel, and four ibuprofen tablets. A volunteer had held her bike upright after she hopped off to replace her Infinit bottles and wolf down her sandwiches. She had been too cotton-mouthed to eat and the excitement of being halfway through the bike led her to get right back on her bike and keep riding. The cheering crowd had been a major lift as she rode north, out of town surrounded by fellow triathletes, most of whom were in a similarly jovial mood. A long stretch of downhill course had given a brief rest to their legs before they turned left to start the second loop around the course.

The first time through the course, Christy had seemed to effort-lessly work her way up and down the scenic rolling hills that stretched on for dozens of miles. The second time through, the hills had seemed to have grown significantly. It had required far greater effort to climb them, yet, as a cruel bit of irony, the downhill coasts seemed shorter. Absent the second time around was the comical band of hillbillies playing their unique brand of heavy metal bluegrass. Little delights like that made the ride more bearable. Christy had looked forward to the emotional boost of the cheering crowd upon reaching Chicka-mauga for the second time, but, save for a few stragglers, the crowd was gone. *Probably back in Chattanooga for the run,* Christy thought disappointedly.

She was just short of mile 100 of the bike. Roughly sixteen more to go. The fatigue was setting in. Her shoulders ached from hours spent hunched over in the aero position. Her neck ached from hold-ing up her head. Her pelvis was numb and chaffed from hours in the bike saddle and her legs felt like rubber. Nevertheless, she pedaled on. On a positive note, she was now passing many people on this second loop who had previously passed her during the first loop. Wendy had coached her to keep to her pace early on and accept that she would get passed but that it would even out later in the course. She was right.

Wendy had yet to catch up to Christy. Christy was the faster swim-mer but thought Wendy would have caught her on the bike. Christy hoped everything was alright with her friend. Bike accidents happened as did flat tires, chains derailing, and other mishaps that could delay one's progress if not take them out of the race. Christy hoped it was something minor and fully expected Wendy to pedal by at any moment. If not, she would surely catch Christy on the run. Wendy's strong suit was the run. An avid runner, she ran several full and half marathons every year. Conversely, Christy didn't care for running and was dread-ing the run portion looming ahead. As such, she hoped to finish the bike by 5:00 which would allow her seven hours to get through the 26.2 miles of the run. If her legs fell apart, she figured she might have a chance to walk, or more likely crawl, the distance in time to finish.

They soon left Chickamauga behind and began a slow steady climb that went on for two miles before being rewarded with that pleasant downhill stretch. Christy dropped gears and pedaled. She checked to make sure her cadence was above 90 RPM's and settled in for the climb. The climb seemed to stretch on forever. Despite the no drafting rules, the climb led to many bikers clumping up into groups. Not wanting a costly penalty, Christy tried to get around the packs which wasn't always easy. Passing required bursts of speed that could quickly sap one's endurance. It was like a box of matches. Every time one used a burst of speed, a match was burnt. There were only a limited number of matches in the box. More sage advice from Wendy. She finally passed another large group and then a lone female biker out in front of them.

"On your left!" Christy called as she began her pass.

"This climb seemed much shorter last time around!" The fit looking woman jokingly yelled as Christy rode by.

"I know!" Christy answered. "I swear I remember there being a nice downhill stretch somewhere around here!"

A few minutes later and they reached the downhill. Finally, a leg rest. Christy opened a gel pack and squeezed the syrupy contents into her mouth. Strawberry-banana, her favorite. Christy took a few sips of water from her aero-bottle, settled into the aero-position, and began to build speed. She shifted up into the highest gear, pedaled up to a high rate of speed and then let gravity take over while she gave her legs a rest. She glanced at her Garmin watch. She was traveling at thirty-six miles per hour! The exhilaration of flying down a rural two-lane road nearing the final stretch of the bike course in her first Ironman was incomparable. Christy let out a loud *whoop* of excitement as she rounded a bend and more downhill appeared before her. The descent eventually bottomed out and she began to pedal up a slight upgrade which ended on the main highway leading back to Chattanooga. Two hours ago, she had to turn left to start the second loop. This time it was a right hand turn into the final stretch. Just eleven miles to go! Still no sign of Wendy. Christy prayed her friend was alright.

She pedaled on in a semi-state of cruise-control as her thoughts wandered about from, Joe, his sister, Marina, whom had nearly been killed a few months ago when she and Christy were abducted by a mafia organization trying to kill Joe, and the rest of Joe's family. Christy didn't want to look too far ahead but she couldn't think of a better family to one day call her in-laws. She texted or talked to Joe's mother several times a week. They acted more like sisters but she was very motherly to Christy at the same time.

Christy's thoughts returned to the race when, up ahead, she saw the large blue sign marking the Tennessee border. She smiled with delight. This was her home state. Born and raised in Franklin, Tennessee, just south of Nashville, Christy went on to play volleyball for the University of Tennessee followed by medical school at East Tennessee State University. She would have gladly moved back home for work but found a great job in Duluth and couldn't turn it down. It took less than four hours to drive home, and that wasn't too bad. Living in Buford allowed her a cozy little house on Lake Lanier where she could swim and sail. Being close to Hartsfield International Airport, she could book a direct flight to just about anywhere. Very convenient. Nevertheless, no state could compare to Tennessee and Christy felt compelled to sing "Rocky Top" as she crossed the border. She continued to sing as she passed another female triathlete which caused them both to laugh.

"We just hit mile 112!" The other triathlete growled in mock anger. "Any other race and we would finally be off these bikes but NOOOOO! Four more miles to go!"

"I know!" Christy chortled back over her shoulder. "I hate running but, right now, I'll gladly go run a marathon if it means getting off this bike!"

"Me too!" The other woman answered. "Good job! Finish strong!"

Even just a little social interaction was uplifting at this point. There really was a strong sense of community among triathletes, especially at this level. Nearly everyone was very friendly and encouraging to one another. The last four miles passed quickly as Christy weaved through the city streets on her way back to the transition zone. She spotted the bike finish up ahead and, in preparation for dismount, reached down and opened the Velcro strap on each bike shoe. She then slid her feet out of the shoes and pedaled the last hundred yards with her feet on top of the shoes. Approaching the dismount area, she placed her weight on her left foot and swung her right leg over the saddle to the left side as she balanced the bike with her weight and coasted into a stop, finishing with a flying dismount. She clicked her Garmin into T2 (second transition) mode as a volunteer took her bike, allowing Christy to jog back into the transition zone as the volunteers returned her bike to the rack. Christy and Wendy had performed the same task as volunteers last year. Doing so allowed them priority registration which guaranteed them a slot in this race which typically sells out within hours of registration opening. The thousands of volunteers underwent extensive training and worked a long day to make a sensational event for the triathletes. Christy made it a point to thank them all throughout the day.

Her legs protested the slow jog. That was to be expected after a 116-mile bike. Her training included many "brick" workouts, where one immediately follows a bike ride with a run. This trains the legs to adapt to running after biking, but it couldn't completely hide the shock of the new motion. Her fatigued legs now had to handle her full body weight for the remaining marathon distance run. Christy hoped they would loosen up.

Another volunteer handed Christy her T2 bag as she neared the tent. Once again, Christy found an empty chair among the several rows and sat down. She quickly removed her well cushioned Hoka One One running shoes from the bag along with a fresh pair of socks. She changed out her socks and slipped on her shoes. She removed her bike helmet and replaced it with a yellow and black *Team Endurance* visor which matched her sleeveless top and her bike shorts. Sitting in the chair felt so good that she was tempted to rest for just a few minutes. Christy quickly pushed that thought out of her mind. She knew she had to keep moving or her legs would tighten up and her momentum would be gone. A line from the song "Half the World" by Joe's favorite band, Rush, came to mind.

Half the world waits, while half gets on with it anyway.

With that, Christy stood to her feet, clipped on an elastic belt that held her running bib displaying her name and competitor number and she was ready to go. A volunteer took her bag as Christy jogged out of the tent. She stopped for more sunscreen and decided on some flat cola. She then ran to the run start, clicking her watch into the run mode as she passed through.

The thought of the next 26.2 miles was overwhelming but she had a plan. There would be an aid station every mile providing drinks and snacks. A while back, Christy had talked to Joe about his experience at BUDs, the twenty-seven-week grueling training and selection course SEAL recruits must pass in order to become Navy SEALs. Christy remembered watching a documentary about BUDs with her father and brothers that had aired for weeks on The Discovery Channel when she was younger. The recruits were subjected to unending strenuous exercise, cold water immersion, and psychological abuse all aimed to identify the few recruits who had the mental fortitude to never give up. Joe related his experience to her in detail and stated that he quickly learned to focus on the task at hand. He said he took it one evolution at a time. The goal was to survive the evolution and not think about the next evolution. Once he trained his mind to think along those lines, he was able to see each evolution as a painful but temporary challenge to overcome. The days blurred together and before he knew it, he had made it through the course. That was Christy's plan. She would consider each mile as its own evolution. Each evolution would end with an aid station where she would walk through, rehydrate, and grab a cookie or a banana. She was told there would be hot chicken broth available but she couldn't see wanting that.

The path out of transition took the runners back down to the waterfront. They ran upriver along the same concrete walkway they had run down after the swim. Similar to after the swim, the barricade was packed with spectators holding signs and ringing cowbells. It was a welcome sight and Christy felt her legs loosen up in response.

"Hey, beautiful! What's a nice girl like you doing in a suffer fest like this?"

Christy instantly recognized Joe's voice. She looked to her right and saw him grinning in her direction as he effortlessly ran alongside her.

"I'm asking myself the same thing!" Christy replied with a laugh.

"Oh yeah?" Joe asked. "Well look up there," Joe said pointing to a spot in the crowd where Christy's family stood cheering as she approached.

Her brother, Peter held up a large sign that read:

Just remember, you paid to do this!

Christy laughed and moved closer to the barricade to high-five her family and Chief Ramsey as she ran by. Joe stayed with her.

"We've been monitoring your splits, you're crushing it!"

"I am?" She asked. I've had my Garmin on but I've hardly looked at my times.

"You finished the bike in just under five and a half hours! You're way ahead of schedule. Just keep to your plan on the run and you've got this!"

"Really?!" Christy exclaimed. "That's awesome! What time is it?"

Joe glanced at his watch, "It's 2:30."

"Yes!" Christy responded joyfully. "I was just hoping to hit the run by 5:00. This gives me a much better chance of finishing."

"Stick to your plan. One evolution at a time, Christy, and enjoy every minute of it! I'll see you out there," Joe said clapping her back as he broke off and vaulted the barricade back to the spectator's side.

Chapter 6

Atlanta, Georgia

" *P*ut the new *shlyukhas* to work tonight, Elena. All except the blond."

"There are two blonds, Sergei," Elena responded.

"The virgin," Sergei said in exasperation. "You know who I'm talking about. We will auction her to the highest bidder on the dark web. A beautiful girl like that, who's still a virgin? She will fetch a good price. Much more than these other *shlyukhas* could get us in three months."

Sergei Petrenko placed a cigarette in his mouth and lit it. He took a deep pull and exhaled the smoke up the ceiling as he mentally ran through his operation. A former Russian spetsnaz sniper, Sergei had built a legendary reputation as a ruthless killer with many useful skills. Several years ago, a Russian oligarch hired Sergei away from the military with a high-paying, delicate operation. Sergei removed a rival oligarch in a manner pleasing to his benefactor and was rewarded with a United States visa and the promise of a fast track to citizenship. Sergei was set up with a light contracting company that performed carpet installation, drywall, painting, and insulation which served as a front for a small division of a larger Russian criminal organization. Sergei was occasionally asked to employ his previous skills neutralizing various people in the U.S.; rivals in other crime syndicates, public officials, and trial witnesses to name a few. In exchange, he was allowed to use the front for a profitable prostitution ring. Locally, Sergei answered to only one person, Victor Tupolev, the head of the Russian organization. Tupolev, however, answered to the oligarch. Sergei had never met the oligarch nor did he even know his name. His initial hiring had been arranged by several cutouts. Not that Sergei didn't want to know. Knowledge is power, after all, and Sergei was all about power. The issue was no one was allowed to know and anyone who seemed to be inquiring was never heard from again. Sergei was in this for the long haul. His prostitution ring was extremely profitable and he lacked for nothing other than greater power. That would come in time. Sergei was relatively young, whereas Tupolev was aging and his health was failing. Sergei knew how to play the game and would be sure he was seen as the wise pick to succeed Tupolev when the inevitable happened. In the meantime, he would play his role while using his prostitution ring to amass wealth and resources.

The *shlyukhas* (whores) were easy to obtain, low overhead, and ultimately disposable. They could be worked round the clock and brought in good money. Sergei actually had several operations throughout the International Village area of Atlanta. This was his main center of operations. It was a quad-plex set up of second floor apartments located above the contracting company. The girls could be moved in and out through the garage bays where prying eyes could not see. They were kept in the main apartment where they slept on mats five or more to a room. The other three apartments were used for entertaining the clientele.

Sergei quickly learned that obtaining prettier girls and advertising them under a special moniker would catch more eyes online and allow him to charge double and sometimes triple the normal street price. This current batch of *shlyukhas* would be his priciest to date. He would use them as long as they were profitable and then trade them off to another street gang that was lower on the pecking order. They were easily replaceable. His crew had proven adept at finding new ponies for his stables.

Sergei sat at the head of the table, contented, as he savored the American Marlboro. Much better than those nasty smokes back home. He leaned back with his eyes closed as he listened to the quiet goings on of his crew around him. Their activity meant money. Lots of it. He paid them well. They were handpicked from Russia and knew that by performing well and keeping their mouths shut they would be able to write their tickets anywhere in America after five years of service. Their benefactor in Russia had an arrangement with a high-ranking United States senator who was able to arrange their visas and fast track their citizenship. The senator was adequately compensated for his cooperation and no one was the wiser.

"Excuse me, Sergei?"

Sergei's thoughts were interrupted by his main computer guru, Petr Orlov. Petr stood over Sergei holding his laptop. He was tall and thin with dark eyes and medium length dark hair that hung down in his face. Although deferent to Sergei, Petr was no shrinking violet. He had grown up in a poor section of Moscow. At a young age, he learned to handle himself on the streets but knew the only way out of the sewer he lived in was to use his intellect. A self-taught computer hacker, he had amassed a small fortune until one day running afoul of the government. While in jail, he received a visit from another cutout for the oligarch, acting in the interest of building a crew for Sergei. Faced with an indefinite amount of time in a cold, damp cell or the opportunity to re-amass his wealth by putting his skills to work in America, he jumped at the offer and was stateside two days later.

"Yes, Petr?" Sergei asked.

"It's all set. My best work yet," Petr said with pride.

"Let's have a look," Sergei said as he sat up and stabbed out his cigarette.

"I titled it *Girls of the ACC,* like you asked," Petr said as he set his laptop down in front of Sergei.

Sergei manipulated the curser and worked his way through the website. Using green screen technology, Petr was able to create images of each girl posing in front of various campus imagery and university logos. Petr had the ability to create an image to look like a girl was seductively posing on a red satin sheet bed or on the school logo in the middle of the football stadium. Using the latest software, Petr filtered their skin and faces to cover blemishes and, if need be, bruises. He also manipulated eyes and facial features to enhance their looks as well as create seductive facial expressions.

"This is indeed good, Petr Petrovich," Sergei complemented as he reviewed each girl's photo array.

"I would like you to remove this one and create a separate website for her on the dark web," Sergei said pointing to Tracy Courtnall's page.

"Already done, Sergei. Her pictures won't show on this website until after you have auctioned her off. I just wanted you to see her photo shoot as well."

"How soon will you have her auction page up on the dark web?"

"I will have a secure webpage that is untraceable in about an hour," Petr said confidently.

"Excellent, Petr. See to it that it is flagged worldwide. I want every Middle Eastern sheikh, every oligarch, every head of state, and any pervert with deep pockets bidding on her. She will be a goldmine for us."

"*Da*," Petr nodded as he scooped up his laptop.

"Oh, and Petr? Please include a delivery option for the *Girls of the ACC* page. Triple the in-house rate."

"*Da,* Sergei," Petr nodded as he walked back to his folding table.

Most of the clients availed themselves of the *shlyukhas* here in the apartments. It allowed them anonymity and a lower rate. Conversely, Sergei could work the girls more frequently by keeping them in house which made for a better bottom line. The new college girls would command a higher rate which would attract a different clientele. Many of the clients were wealthy businessmen and politicians who preferred to be serviced in a hotel rather than take an Uber to a cheap apartment complex in The International Village. Sergei was happy to meet this demand but found he could ask three times the hourly rate and would have no trouble getting it.

He smiled as he lit another cigarette. Escalating up to a higher class of clientele could be a financially lucrative move. Better pay for less exposure. If it didn't work, he would still have a more attractive group of *shlyukhas* and that would always be profitable. It was a win-win.

Chapter 7

Chattanooga, Tennessee

A welcome breeze greeted the runners as they exited off the Riverfront Walkway onto the Veterans Bridge. The air temperature was still in the low 80's as the sun began to set off to the west. The gentle breeze carried cool air off the river providing a brief respite from the heat. For some of the runners, it was their first trip across the bridge. This was Christy's second trip. She recently passed run mile twenty. Six miles stood between her and the finish line. Six miles of steep hills.

The run course was a 13.1-mile course that straddled the Tennessee River which each triathlete had to complete twice. The first eight miles were relatively flat. Across the River lay five miles of steep hills, the longest was a climb up Barton Avenue. Christy found her first trip through the notorious hills difficult yet entertaining. The hillbilly band reappeared on Veterans Bridge where the runners were crossing into the hill portion. The first time Christy ran across, they were appropriately playing a bluegrass version of Iron Maiden's "Run to the Hills." As Christy crossed this second time, they were playing "Carry on My Wayward Son." She smiled at the boys and blew them a kiss as she ran by. A shirtless, thin, bearded man in overalls and a hillbilly hat, playing a banjo, smiled, and pretended to nearly fall off his stool. That gave Christy a good laugh.

The bridge ended and the gentle rise to Barton Avenue began. Her legs were beginning to scream in protest. Christy was in the middle of what is referred to as "The Pain Cave." This mythical cave of torture is found on the run course between miles sixteen and twenty-three. The physician exhaustion at this point causes intense physical and mental pain causing many competitors to question whether or not they can make it to the finish. Many consider dropping out during this portion. Christy was fine. Her legs were heavy and sore but her plan was working and the miles were slowly ticking by. She had a little over five miles to go and plenty of time to complete them. The excitement of knowing she would likely finish overrode any discomfort she was feeling.

The climb up Barton Avenue began in earnest. Christy tried to run it like she had before but quickly realized her slow shuffle was no faster than those who were walking. She decided to call an audible. For the duration of the run, she would walk up the long steep hills and run down them. At least there was a lively crowd over here. Barton Avenue and the streets that followed were lined with large shade trees and beautiful older homes. Nearly every house had a lively crowd on the front lawn and lining the sidewalks. Christy could smell charcoal grills cooking and heard loud music emanating from every yard she passed. One house had a live band playing. As she neared the crest of the hill, someone dressed in a Gumby outfit, was dancing in the street, and giving high-fives to runners as they passed by.

She reached the next aid station and immediately sought out the hot chicken broth. Yep, she had found herself craving the salty brew since around mile six. The volunteers at this station were all dressed as the *Despicable Me* minions, Christy's personal favorite. It was unbelievable how much the volunteers got into the race. An unmatchable experience. She followed the broth with some flat cola and then dumped a cup of ice water over her head. She grabbed a couple of sponges soaked in ice water and placed them under her jersey allowing the cold water to trickle down her chest and back. She picked back up to a jog and began to work her way downhill. Mile 22 was behind her.

Over the next forty minutes she wound her way through the residential streets, around a golf course and back up the Barton Avenue hill heading the opposite direction. As she crested the hill, she realized that it was all behind her. A little over a mile to go and it was all downhill or flat. Christy quickly made her way down the hill and began to run the short stretch along Frazier Avenue that would take her to the pedestrian bridge leading back across the river.

"Dork alert!" Came a familiar voice from behind.

Christy looked over her shoulder and was thrilled to see Wendy running up alongside her.

"Where have you been?!" Christy asked. "I figured you must have passed me on the bike and I just didn't see you."

"I wish," Wendy said as she matched her pace with Christy. "I was run off the road during the bike!"

"What? How?"

"Some Fred tried to take a drink from his water bottle while he was passing me. He wasn't paying close attention and he veered into my lane. I was in aero and couldn't brake. I had to run off the road to avoid a collision."

"Oh, Wendy, that bites. I'm so sorry. Are you alright?"

"I'm fine but I ended up with two flat tires. I burned a lot of time changing them."

"What about the other guy?'

"Oh, *he's* fine! Nothing happened to him. He just kept on riding as if nothing happened."

"You have got to be kidding me?"

"Nope, but that's alright." Wendy said between breaths as they ran side by side. "I'm still in the race. Could've been worse. My cousin Stephanie had a similar incident happen to her a few years back at Ironman Arizona. She ended up with a fractured clavicle and was out of the race. She was furious. That was her first Ironman."

"That would suck," Christy agreed as they turned left onto the Walnut Street Bridge.

They ran for a minute in silence as they crossed the wood-planked pedestrian bridge. The river looked spectacular but both of their eyes were locked onto the finish area just down river in front of the Tennessee Aquarium. They could hear the crowd and the upbeat music but what they really noticed was the popular announcer, the "Voice of Ironman" calling out the names of each participant as they crossed the finish line followed by that iconic line; "You are an Ironman!"

Christy looked over at her friend and smiled. It would be the first time for both of them.

"Wendy, don't let me slow you down. Speed on up and I'll see you down there."

"No way, Dork!" Wendy said using the nickname she had bestowed upon Christy their first year of medical school. "You and I were both nearly killed last year. We've trained for this together, and we are finishing this together!"

"I'm good with that," Christy answered as they descended off the bridge and down onto the final quarter mile leading to the finish. "But what if I bonk?"

"If you bonk, I will kick your sorry rear end across the finish line, myself!"

The final quarter mile was a blur as the street was lined on both sides with cheering spectators offering hands to slap in congratulating fashion.

"Savor it, Christy. Savor every minute!" Wendy said as they approached the carpeted runway leading to the finish line.

The crowd grew larger and louder. Christy and Wendy grinned widely in elation. The Voice of Ironman was standing in front of the finish line holding a microphone on his left hand and wildly swinging a towel overhead with the other.

"How 'bout this!" His voice boomed over the PA system. "We've got two doctors, folks! An OB/GYN and an ER doctor! Wendy Conlan and Christy Tabrizi, YOU ARE AN IRONMAN!"

Chapter 8

Atlanta, Georgia

The dull light crept through Tracy's eyelids. She stirred as the sanctuary of sleep ceded to wakefulness. She had survived another night, but her back and hips ached from laying on the thin mat. She sat up and leaned against the wall. A water bottle lay next to her. She opened the top and held it up to her chapped lips. She took a long drink of the tepid water as she realized the cap had not been sealed. She figured the men were probably reusing the same bottles by filling them in a sink. How thoughtful. Looking around, Tracy saw three of the other girls were sprawled out and sound asleep. Each in various states of semi undress. Tracy was the only one still without clothes. The only one missing was the brunette. Lindsay was her name. That was all Tracy knew. The room nearly always had a guard. Conversation was strictly forbidden. The other four young women had been intermittently taken from and returned to the room all night. No one spoke, but it was obvious what was happening. Each girl wore a look of fear as they were forcefully taken out of their prison of a room. They returned defeated with a look of despair.

They hadn't come for Tracy yet. The dreadful anticipation battled with the fleeting sensation of relief every time another girl was chosen. The guilt she experienced over feeling this way, weighed heavily on her. The unspeakable horrors the other girls were experiencing were her likely future. Did she prepare herself to accept it or did she keep hoping it wouldn't happen to her?

The door opened and Lindsay entered. She was dressed like a Catholic school girl, wearing a short plaid skirt with a light blue button-down oxford shirt tied at her navel. Her gait was slow and had a stiffness about it revealing her soreness. Her left eye was swollen and bruised. She and Tracy briefly made eye contact before each looked down. She sat down close to Tracy, leaning against the adjoining wall with her knees pulled to her chest. She leaned her head forward and rested it on her arms. Tracy watched as Lindsay's shoulders sagged in resignation. Lindsay seemed to have an athletic toughness to her but only a brokenness could be seen now.

Tracy looked at the man guarding them. He was younger, like the others with whom he shared the duty. This one had short blond hair, a youthful athletic build, and cold, blue eyes. Normally, he would be considered good looking, but Tracy could only see an evil-induced ugliness. He sat hunched over his cell phone, seemingly oblivious to the tortured souls around him. Did he not have a conscience?

As she looked at him hunched over his phone, an idea began to form. What if she was able to get ahold of his phone and call for help? Could 911 trace the call? Maybe even a text to her father would be effective.

Her father. Her parents had to know she was missing by now. Her dad was a kind and gentle man, but he was also protective and likely kicking every hornet nest he could find to get the right people looking for her. What she wouldn't give to be in Daddy's protective arms right now. She had never taken it for granted. Quite the contrary, Tracy and her father had always been close. Her earliest memories were sitting on his lap as a toddler as he read bedtime stories to her. He may have become wealthy but he never stopped being a dad to Tracy and her two older brothers. The type of dad who got in the pool and played Marco Polo or launched all the kids across the water. He never missed a game Tracy cheered at and, as much of a football fan as he is, his eyes were glued on his little girl for every cheer, every pyramid, and every fly. Her mother was just as loving and committed. Her brothers too for that matter. Tracy never felt the need to seek love and acceptance elsewhere. She always knew the time would come when a good man would enter her life but was content with her family and her life as it has always been. The need for a romantic relationship had never been a priority. Would she ever get that chance now? Conversely, would her innocence be ruthlessly taken from her by these animals? Did she just sit here and hope Daddy, or someone, came to her rescue if did she try to do something about it?

The guy watching their room suddenly stood up. Tracy placed her head down on her arms and tried to appear small and unnoticeable. Out of the corner of her eye, she saw the man stretch and step out the door. She heard the deadbolt slide shut locking them in. She assumed he was making a trip to the bathroom which would give her just a couple of minutes. Tracy slid closer to Lindsay to where their knees touched. Lindsay looked up, her eyes a mix of despair and anger.

"Are you okay?" Tracy whispered.

"Not really," she answered.

"How bad was it?"

"Which time?" Lindsay answered bitterly. "Earlier last night when I was marched to the other side where I was beaten and then forced to have sex for hours with who knows how many disgusting men? Or later when I was driven to a house and four college guys took their turns on me?"

Tracy started to say something but the words weren't there and she could only stare at Lindsay open mouthed.

"Yeah, it was bad. How was your night?" Lindsay asked sarcastically.

"That's just it," Tracy replied. "They haven't touched me yet."

"Lucky you," Lindsay said with a shrug of nonchalance.

"Well, I don't want to just lay around waiting for my turn. I have an idea."

"What's that?" Lindsay replied with a mixture of disbelief and curiosity.

"A way we might be able to get out of here."

"Really?" Lindsay replied sounding annoyed. "In case you weren't aware, there are at least half a dozen Russian thugs between this room and the exit. And what are you going to do? Run down the street naked like you are now?"

"If that will get me into the safety of a police car, yes!" Tracy whispered harshly. "It can't be more degrading than this. Anything is better than this hell hole! But, no, that's not my plan. Not exactly."

"Then just what is your plan?"

"I was thinking we could try to overwhelm our guard and get his cell phone away from him long enough to make a 911 call or even send a text."

"Sounds like a long shot to me. Even if we got it away from him, there are armed men right outside that door that would be in here within seconds. You'd never get a call off in time. Besides, do you even know where we are?"

"No," Tracy confessed. "Do you?"

"We're somewhere in Atlanta."

"How do you know?"

"Because the house I was at this morning were four college guys who go to Emory."

"So we're near Emory?"

"I don't think so. We drove for over twenty minutes."

"Well did you see anything that gave you an idea of where we are?"

"No. They had a cloth sack over my head."

"What if we dialed 911? Couldn't they find our location using GPS?"

"That's a thought. Wait!" Lindsay's face suddenly lit up. "We could ping our location using one of the map APPs."

"We could, but that might take a minute. We may not have that kind of time."

"We would have to get everyone in on it. Two to handle the guard and two to barricade the door while one of us dials."

"They'll make us pay something terrible," Tracy said.

"What are they gonna do? Beat us and rape us? They're already doing that," Lindsay countered. "It's worth the risk."

They both heard the sound of footsteps approaching the door. Tracy slid away and both woman put their heads back down, just as the guard opened the door.

Chapter 9

Buford, Georgia

A flavorful aroma emanated from the grill as Joe flipped several thick ribeyes and doused them with Worcestershire sauce. The grill responded with a loud sizzle. Joe stood at the grill, barefoot, wearing shorts and a gray t-shirt that read *Navy Lacrosse*. He sensed Christy's presence before she opened the screen door from her porch and stepped down onto the patio.

"Perfect timing, Sleeping Beauty! Dinner's almost ready," Joe said smiling.

Christy gingerly walked towards him. Joe extended his arm and she stepped in, wrapped her arms around him and kissed him. She rested her head on his shoulder as she continued to hug.

"I'll bet that nap felt good," Joe spoke into her hair. "You look sore."

"Mmmh, I feel sore," she mumbled sleepily. "But, yes, that nap was just what I needed. Thank you. What are you making, anyway? It smells heavenly."

"Salad, corn on the cob, and my world famous ribeyes."

"Oh, that sounds so good!" Christy said as she disengaged from Joe and placed a foot on the back of an Adirondack chair and began to stretch. "Where's Chief?"

"He's over at your neighbor's house getting a quick shower," Joe said pointing next door. "That's really nice of him letting us stay there."

"Are you kidding?" Christy said while switching to her other leg. "As soon as he heard my SEAL boyfriend was coming to town and needed a place to stay, he insisted. Is he home?"

"No, not yet. He gave me a spare key before Rammer and I left for Chattanooga yesterday morning. He said he'd be home around 6:30 so I timed dinner for his arrival."

"That was thoughtful. And what a pleasant surprise that Rammer drove in for my race! What did you guys do while I was asleep?"

"We went for a swim."

Christy shot Joe a menacing stare. "Joe O'Shanick?!"

"*He* went for a swim," Joe clarified. "I followed him in your kayak."

"You didn't swim?" Christy asked making a pouty face.

"No, I didn't swim." Joe said shaking his head. "I wanted to, but I was good."

"You better be good, Joe O'Shanick!" Christy said as she stepped closer and playfully poked a finger in his chest. "No swimming until next week if you want to get your shoulder better for a shot at DEV-GRU. Doctor's orders!"

"I know," Joe said smiling with his hands held high in surrender. "I'm doing everything your brother said."

"I wasn't talking about him. Those are *my* orders!" Christy said giving Joe another kiss.

"Hey, hey, hey! Break it up you two!" Chief Ramsey said as he and Christy's neighbor, Tom Crittendon, walked over.

"Don't listen to him, Joe! Get it while you can!" Crittendon said with a gravelly voice.

"I like your advice, Mr. Crittendon!" Joe said as the two shook hands.

"Call me Critter, Joe. All my friends do."

Thomas Crittendon at six feet four inches stood as tall as Joe and Chief Ramsey but easily outweighed them both by a good forty or more pounds. Whereas Joe and Ramsey had a wiry muscular build with broad shoulders and narrow waists, Crittendon looked more like a defensive end. His hair was mostly gray and close cropped as was the goatee he sported under a bulbous nose and mischievous blue eyes.

"Critter it is then and thank you, again, for allowing me and Chief to rack at your place."

"Well, if your steaks are half as good as Chief tells me, we'll call it a fair trade," Critter smiled and then turned his attention to Christy. "Congrats to you Ironlady! How're you feeling?"

"A bit sore, but good. Thank you, Tom."

Critter turned back to Joe and Ramsey and grinned. "Now you see, only pretty ladies like the good doctor here, are allowed to call me Tom. Y'all two froggy rascals can call me Critter."

"Works for us, Critter. They call me *Rammer* and the Lieutenant Commander here goes by *Joey-O*."

"How long have you two been in the teams?"

"I just hit my twentieth year in the Navy," Ramsey said. "Went to BUDs straight from Great Lakes."

"I'm in my tenth," Joe answered.

"Naval Academy?" Crittendon asked.

"That's right."

"We don't hold that against him, Critter. Joey-O here is an enlisted man's CO and a solid operator," Ramsey said, sticking up for his friend and CO. "Who'd you serve with?"

"Army. 82nd Airborne and Rangers. Did my twenty and got out."

"I'm guessing you saw some time in the sandbox?" Joe asked.

"That's right. First Gulf War in '91 then returned in '03 to finish the job. Didn't think it would take us so long."

"It wouldn't if we could keep the politicians and media from telling us how to fight every friggin' conflict we enter," Ramsey opined. "We haven't fought a war with the intent to win at all costs since World War Two."

"What about what we have going on down in Central America?" Crittendon asked. "It seems like President Galan has given you boys a fairly unrestricted hunting license."

"That he has," Joe spoke with a nod as he quickly gave the steaks another turn. "But we still have to watch that we don't hurt the civilians, which blurs the line since the cartels are everywhere. It's still better than the sandbox. And you're right, President Galan has had our backs. That's for sure."

President Galan, a former career enlisted Marine was from San Diego. He and his wife were first generation American citizens, both born in the United States to Mexican migrant parents. Border security was an ongoing hot button issue. President Galan was sympathetic to the plight of the Central American refugees seeking asylum and a better life in America; however, he was also a proponent of border security. Having grown up in San Diego's inner city, President Galan was well aware that not everyone crossing the southern border was well intentioned. There was no way to allow all persons in without risk of some being criminals, particularly those of the drug and human trafficking trades but also terrorists seeking entry through a porous border.

The dilemma led President Galan to pursue a different solution. This solution involved declaring the Central and South American cartels terrorist organizations. Using promises of foreign aid and trade deals, Galan formed a coalition with Central and South American governments to root out and eliminate the cartels. This required large scale involvement of United States naval and military forces, special forces in particular. Joe and Chief Ramsey's platoon had been heavily involved during their last deployment. Significant progress had been made, but the work was ongoing, as was the effort to restore industry and farmlands to the people of Central and South America. In contrast to most campaigns waged since World War Two, President Galan, himself a fighting Marine, had bestowed tactical planning and rules of engagement upon the military leaders. He gave one caveat, to win at all costs. Many in the media as well as the opposition party took exception to President Galan's operation but he knew that would be the case and willingly caught the spears while allowing his commanders to run the operations. As long as they produced good results, President Galan would stand by them and let them do what they did best. By and large, the men and women of the armed forces, appreciated their Commander in Chief. Joe, Ramsey and, apparently, Crittendon, were equally on board.

"Where's the Irongirl?!" Sang out an excited female voice.

Everyone looked to the source of the voice. A petite, smiling woman with blond hair appeared from around the side. She was carrying a cookie cake box and wearing a black, mid-thigh golfing skirt with a red University of Georgia polo shirt. Spotting Christy, she ran up, set the box down on the table and gave her a big hug.

"You did it, girl! How do you feel?"

"A bit stiff and sore but quite accomplished," Christy replied humbly. "Guys, this is my friend, Stacy Morgan. We work together. Stacy, you remember Joe..."

"Of course! We met last year at The White House. Hello, Joe," Stacy said as she gave Joe a hug in greeting. "I've heard so much about you since last year. I'm so glad you were finally able to come down here."

"Christy has told me a lot about you too, Stacy. It's great to see you again."

"And I know Critter," Stacy said giving the big man a hug before stepping back and assessing Ramsey. "But I don't believe I've had the pleasure of meeting this handsome fella."

"Matt Ramsey, ma'am," Ramsey said extending his hand in greeting.

"Matt is Joe's most trusted teammate and friend, Stacy. He was at the Rose Garden Ceremony too." Christy said by way of introduction.

"Yes! That's right. I'm sorry, I didn't recognize you out of uniform."

"Not a problem ma'am," Ramsey replied. "Are you an ER physician too?"

"Who, me? Heavens, no. I'm OB/GYN."

"Did you and Christy go to medical school together?" Joe asked as he began transferring the steaks to a platter.

"No, I'm pure Georgia girl. UGA undergrad, Medical School of Georgia, and I did my residency here in Atlanta."

"My kind of girl, Dr. Morgan," Crittendon smiled as he turned and looked appreciatively at the thick ribeyes. "You're not gonna make us waste time with a salad first are you, Joe? I know how you Navy officers can be; cloth napkins, salad forks, manners, and what not."

"Strictly optional, Critter," Joe said smiling. "But we are ready, if everyone wants to fix a plate."

The orange flames danced in a mesmerizing fashion as Joe listened to the conversation and savored the time. The evening was still warm but the fire provided a focal point of comfort. They sat around a fire pit on the deck Critter had built onto his dock. Lake Lanier was tranquil as it reflected the bright moon on a cloudless night. Christy's head lay in Joe's lap as she sprawled on the bench beside him. Joe looked down as he gently massaged her shoulder, and noticed her face was a picture of serenity as she lay there with her eyes closing. Stacy sat across from them as she talked to Crittendon, Ramsey, and a new arrival, Chris Stubbs aka "Stubber." Stubber was an old Army buddy of Critter's who lived up in Dawsonville, where Stacy grew up. Stubber and Critter met in jump school at Fort Benning and had pretty much served together ever since. Both served in the 82nd Airborne followed by Rangers and retired after finishing their twenty years. Stubber was just a hair shorter than Critter but much lighter. He had a slender, wiry build compared to Critter's defensive end build. Stubber wore his salt and pepper hair slightly long along with a droopy mustache that, along with his deep drawl, gave him a stunning resemblance to the actor Sam Elliot.

"Well, I have a full schedule in the morning," Stacy said while pushing herself out of an Adirondack chair. "I really need to be on my way. It was nice meeting you, Mr. Stubbs. I've driven by your farm countless times, but never knew who lived there. That's so cool that my daddy is your veterinarian!"

"And a good one at that, young lady. Nice to have met you."

"Hold up, Stacy," Christy said as she slowly sat up. "I'll walk with you. I'm ready to turn in, myself."

"I thought you were dozing off," Joe said knowingly as he rubbed her back.

Christy turned to Joe. "Thanks for looking after me today. Dinner was great. I promise I'll be more fun tomorrow."

"What are you talking about?" Joe asked dismissively. "You just competed in an Ironman. I expect you to be sore and tired. You'll be even more sore tomorrow. You should have seen us after Hell Week. We were zombies for an entire weekend. Isn't that right, Rammer?"

"Shoot, Joe, I still haven't recovered," Ramsey shot back.

"Well, sore or not, I still want to show you around tomorrow. If the weather's good, we could even go for a sail," Christy said as she slowly stood and stretched her arms high overhead.

"I'd think twice about that, Christy," Ramsey teased. "Joey-O here tends to sail over waterfalls."

"Wait a minute!" Stubber started. "O'Shanick? Now I know why that name sounds so familiar! You're the guy that went over Niagara Falls earlier this year. Aren't you?"

"Yeah," Joe said sheepishly.

"Shut the front door!" Critter exclaimed. "That was you?"

"That was him," Ramsey said with a nod. "Ol' Joe here showed the world just how drown proof SEALs really are."

"Oh, I've got to hear about this!" Critter proclaimed.

"I'm outta here!" Christy said as she bent down and kissed Joe goodnight.

"I'll walk with you," Joe as he started to rise.

"Oh no," Christy said with a smirk, gently pushing him back down. "Critter and Stubber want to hear your story. Have fun with that," she said, kissing him one more time. "C'mon, Stacy. Let's let the boys have their story time."

"My word. Are they really doctors?" Stubber asked as he watched Christy and Stacy walk away.

"Hard to believe isn't it?" Critter answered.

"Never seen me no doctor that looks like either of those two," Stubber said, shaking his head. "How'd you meet her, Joe?"

"That's another story," Joe said as he watched Christy's silhouette disappear around her house.

"Sounds like a story I need to hear," Stubber said as he reached into a small backpack sitting next to his chair.

He pulled out a small humidor opened it up and took out a large cigar. He passed the box around. Joe declined but Ramsey and Critter each selected one. Stubber pulled out a cigar cutter and expertly cut off the end before lighting up. He blew out a cloud of smoke and handed the implements to Critter before nodding at Joe to proceed.

Joe and Ramsey spent the next half hour retelling the events of their platoon's involvement in Central America, leading up to Christy's capture by a cartel, while she was in Honduras on a missions trip along with Stacy, Wendy, and another friend. Joe gave pursuit to rescue Christy and was captured as well. They eventually escaped together and an unlikely friendship was born.

"So that was you guys that President Galan honored in that Rose Garden ceremony last fall?" Stubber asked astounded.

"Along with a few others, yes," Joe answered.

"And didn't Senator Fowler get some kind of bee in his bonnet about you this summer and try to use that against the president?"

"He sure did," Ramsey answered. "Before all the facts came out."

"What actually happened?" Critter asked as he took another puff on his cigar. "All the press ever reported was you killed some mafia guys under some shady circumstances. Never did hear all the rest."

"There was a lot more to it than that. They went after me and my family." Joe leaned his head toward Christy's house. "Christy actually killed two of them. I *did* shoot a mafia thug, but he was about to shoot Christy, and his partner had just shot my sister. Once the truth came out, the press moved on to another story," Joe answered.

"What Joe is diplomatically trying to say is: Fowler and the press jumped to conclusions and, as usual, put out a false narrative. Once the facts emerged, they moved on. No retraction, no mea culpa, and certainly no holding that hack Fowler accountable," Ramsey stated.

"Wait! Christy shot two mobsters?!" Critter asked incredulously. "She didn't tell me that! Holy moly that is one amazing lady. Nothing but pure smoke there, Joe."

Joe smiled and nodded his agreement.

"So I take it you're not voting for Fowler for president this fall?" Stubber chuckled.

"I wouldn't vote for anyone over Galan, least of all that traitor," Ramsey answered.

"Okay, so what actually did happen with the mafia?"

Joe spent some time filling in the details of his run in with a Western New York mafia organization while up visiting his family. It began with a near brush with death at Niagara Falls and continued with several more close calls, including his sister and one of his fellow SEALs.

"That's a much different story than what the press and Fowler were spinning. That's pretty low, trampling on the reputation of a decorated

Navy SEAL and then letting the narrative float like that," Stubber commented in his mellow drawl.

"It is what it is," Joe said with a shrug. "Nothing they didn't do to you guys in Iraq once the press turned on Bush."

"And that can't compare to what they did to our Vietnam vets," Critter added.

"So are you boys going back to Central America anytime soon?" Stubber asked.

Joe looked at Ramsey before answering. "I would, but my time as an operator is probably over. I was just forced to step down as platoon leader..."

"Because of what went down in Niagara Falls?" Stubber asked in outrage.

"No. Nothing like that. My time was up. Two training cycles, two deployments as CO, and then it's time to step aside and let the next guy have a swing at command. I'm also sidelined with a shoulder injury but will have to decide my fate soon."

"What do you want to do?" Critter asked.

"I *had* a slot in DEVGRU's Green Team but I lost it when I injured my shoulder during an op. I can qualify for another slot once I'm cleared hot but there's no guarantee. I can also stay on with our current team and move up into operations."

"You don't sound too excited about that," Stubber commented.

"I don't know," Joe sighed. "I'd still be a SEAL and it could lead to a command billet but I would never operate downrange again. I'm just not looking forward to operating a computer. You know what I mean?"

"You should have enlisted if you wanted to keep operating that much. I've heard that even the DEVGRU officers don't operate a whole lot," Stubber said.

"That's true but they do get to get their hands dirty once in a while."

"Any other options?"

"I could head out to Coronado and help train new SEALs, or I can work a non SPECOPS billet."

"That sounds worse, Joe," Critter commented. "Let me ask you this: Are you wanting to stay in the Navy until you get your twenty?"

"I thought I did, once upon a time, and it would make sense in many ways. Having a full pension at the age of forty-two would be nice."

"Life ain't all about money, son," Critter said. "How serious are you and my neighbor?"

"We're still fairly early in this relationship but I can see it getting quite serious."

"Do you see yourself marrying her one day?"

"Yeah," Joe said nodding in contemplation. "I've actually thought about that. Christy's one in a million. I just don't know if she's thinking along those lines."

"Son, a woman like that ain't playing the field. If she's with you, she's serious. She certainly sounds serious when I talk to her. Now how serious do you think this can get if you're living out of town, serving at the pleasure of the Navy?"

"I know, I've thought about that. Christy has mentioned possibly finding a job closer to where I am."

"See what I'm saying? She's thinking long term. She's serious. Now, I once had a good woman. Nothing like that goddess over there," Critter said pointing his thumb over his shoulder toward Christy's house, "but a lot better than what I deserved. Problem was, I was already married to the Army. I would be gone on deployment for a year and then clam up when I was home because I couldn't leave the war behind. It got to where I was more comfortable in the sandbox and was rarely ever home. One day, I came home and she was gone. Looking back, I can't say as I blame her. Even when I was home, I wasn't home. Not a day goes by I don't regret that, Joe. Ten more years for that Navy pension ain't worth losing your life over, son. Not when you've got a promising life with a woman like that."

Joe nodded quietly.

"Joe, have you considered that a man with your skills and resume could make enough money as a civilian to eclipse what you could make if you stayed in the Navy?" Stubber spoke up.

"Not really. I haven't really considered life outside the Teams. All of this is still relatively new."

"I'm not gonna try to talk you out of the Navy, but it sounds to me like you're at a crossroads and you need to consider all your options. You could be a private contractor handling security for rich folks, you could be a security consultant, or you could even run one of those tactical training camps for rich yuppies who want to pretend they're Rambo. People pay good money to go to those. Teach em' how to shoot and make em' crawl through mud in fatigues; they'll drop good money if they know it's a SEAL running the course," Stubber paused and puffed on his cigar with a contemplative look. "Or go back to school and become a doctor like your girlfriend. All I'm saying is you have a lot more options and plenty of them are right here."

"He's right," Critter jumped in. "This is Atlanta, there are corporations everywhere. Probably lots of opportunities for a new security firm. Or get you some land a little ways out in the country and start one of those tactical courses. There are all kinds of preppers and survivalists who are looking for that kind of thing."

"What do you guys do?" Joe asked.

"I own and operate an indoor gun range. We've got a store as well. Teach shooting courses and concealed permit courses as well. I'd tell you to get into that but I'm afraid you'd cut into my business if you were to open one up around here."

"What about you, Stubber?" Ramsey asked.

"I've got me a cattle farm just north of here up in Dawsonville. I've actually thought about using part of my land to run one of those tactical courses, but I'm getting too old and the cattle keep me busy enough as it is."

"Do you have the land to do that if you wanted to?" Ramsey asked.

"Plenty. Only about half of it's been cleared. Lots of wooded hills with trails and creeks. I've even built an outdoor shooting range."

"Would you consider leasing some of it out to a couple of frogmen to run just such a course?"

"Rammer?" Joe asked in surprise.

"Yeah, I think we could work us a deal," Stubber said with a slow nod. "What you got in mind there, Master Chief?"

"Yeah, Master Chief," Joe added. "I'm curious as well."

"Well, Joe, as you know, I just hit my twenty. I'm thinking it might be time to cash out as well."

"Are you serious?" Joe asked astonished. "I was under the impression you were staying in until they threw you out."

"I thought so too but command has decided that this Master Chief needs to move up into admin. I'm like you. If I can't operate, I don't think I want to stay in. The pogue life isn't for me."

"But what about Echo Platoon? They need you to help break in Lieutenant Berenson and train up the new squad."

"Kowalski just made Chief and they're bringing Senior Chief Cooper over from Delta."

"Cooper is a fine operator and I personally put Kowalski up for chief but that's a lot of new blood at the top, Rammer. Wow!" Joe said shaking his head. "Don't get me wrong, I trust Lieutenant Commander Harrison but that just seems like too much change."

"I said the same thing, Joe, but considering we lost half the squad on our last deployment, Harrison wants to rebuild the entire platoon. I wanted to stay on. Believe me. I begged Harrison to let me stay on but he wants to raise up a new platoon and believes this is what's best for Echo. Berenson seems capable, as does Cooper, and we know Kowalski will be a natural at chief. Echo will have some growing pains, but they'll be ready to deploy when their turn comes."

"So are you really thinking of hanging up your Trident and getting out?"

"Yeah, Joe, if they won't let me operate, then I would rather cash in and do something else. That tactical course sounds like a good idea and you're gonna need your chief to help you run things."

"Just like always, huh?" Joe smiled nodding.

"You know it, brother." Ramsey said with a fist bump.

Chapter 10

Charlotte, North Carolina

The Courtnall, Clark and Leeman Financial Group was located on the top two floors of a modern skyscraper in downtown Charlotte. Twenty years ago, it was simply Charles Courtnall Financial located in a small rented office. Now, Courtnall and his two partners owned the forty-story building in which their army of investors, financial advisors, and accountants worked.

Charles Courtnall III looked out the floor to ceiling windows of his palatial corner office. Tracy could be anywhere. Even here in Charlotte. Courtnall couldn't concentrate on his work. His partners understood and were picking up the slack, but he couldn't help but feel he was letting his investors down. Courtnall quickly dismissed the thought. His Tracy was missing. His only instinct was to go find her, but he didn't have the first idea where to look.

Courtnall prided himself on being almost completely left brained. Pure logic and reason with just a nod to emotion. It had served him quite well over the years. The logical part of his mind led him to trust the experts who were looking for his daughter; consequently, he returned to work this morning. Jane was frantic. She was barely sleeping and had been on the phone with friends and family seemingly round the clock. Courtnall had offered to stay home with her, but even Jane knew there was little that would accomplish, and she told him to head in. She knew he would be meeting with the lead investigator of the private investigator firm Courtnall had hired, which partly assuaged his guilt over leaving Jane at home.

The desk phone intercom trilled and his personal assistant's voice came through.

"Clay Whitmore of Whitmore Investigative Services is here."

"Thank you, Beth. Please send him in."

Courtnall took a standing position behind his expansive mahogany desk. The door opened and his assistant led in a sharply dressed, middle-aged man. What was left of his sandy blond hair was closely shaved. He was of average height but appeared physically fit. Were it not for his well-tailored, Brooks Brothers charcoal gray suit, he would have easily blended into any crowd.

"Mr. Courtnall, I'm Clay Whitmore," he announced as he quickly crossed the room, reaching across Courtnall's desk for a firm handshake.

"Charles Courtnall, Mr. Whitmore. Thank you for coming. Please have a seat."

"Thank you, sir. Please call me Clay," Whitmore said as he sat down in one of two padded, leather wing chairs facing the desk.

"And I'm Charles. Can I offer you something to drink? Coffee perhaps?"

"No thank you, sir. I know your time is quite valuable, so if it's alright with you, I'd prefer to get right to the matter of your daughter."

"I appreciate that, Clay. What have you learned?"

"We've been in touch with the Durham and Raleigh police departments as well as the State Police. The hair sample DNA does match that of Lindsay Meehan, the girl who went missing the same day as Tracy. The other hair sample hasn't turned up a match yet."

Courtnall's face soured at that revelation.

"I know," Whitmore sympathized. "But that's just using a national criminal database. I spent sixteen years in the FBI and have amassed a lengthy list of contacts. I have them running the DNA through the FBI's database as well as through Interpol. If there is a match, we will find it. Moving on, sir. I apologize in advance as this will be extremely painful to discuss. We are working with the assumption that Tracy was taken against her will. That leaves one of three likely scenarios. Again, this will be difficult for you but we have to deal with the reality. Tracy may have been abducted by an individual for his own personal pleasure, may have been kidnapped for ransom, or she has been forced into a human trafficking ring."

Whitmore paused and looked at Courtnall who solemnly nodded his understanding.

"Since there has been no demand for ransom as of yet, we are operating under the other two possibilities. If she was taken by some sicko with a perversion, then she is likely close to the Raleigh-Durham area and we have a team combing the area along with the various police agencies. Personally, I don't think this is the case but we are pursuing the possibility with vigor. Based on our experience and statistical probability, she has most likely been abducted for prostitution. Again, Mr. Courtnall, I'm sorry to be so blunt but I want you to understand what we are facing and what we are doing about it."

"I'm aware, Clay. Proceed please," Courtnall voiced flatly.

"If this is the case, then she was likely taken to a larger city where the prostitution business is bigger. Usually somewhere within driving distance but not too close where she could be recognized. Cities with a lot of transient visitors and money. Convention cities like Atlanta, Charlotte, Baltimore, Orlando, Miami, Nashville, Memphis, and New Orleans would be most likely, along with Washington D.C. I have already placed teams in these cities. They know where and how to look but, even then, it's like looking for a needle in a haystack; nevertheless, my people are all professionals and they get results."

"Do you really have that many people working for you?" Courtnall asked.

"The short answer is no. I have roughly two dozen people working full time for me but this kind of a search requires a whole lot more manpower. In cases like this, I have a network of people I can contract to do the legwork when needed. They aren't cheap but you told me money was no object and to find her at all costs, so I took the liberty of activating my contacts. I trust that was in order?"

"Absolutely, Clay. I know enough to know that every minute counts if we want Tracy returned safely. Leave no stone unturned."

"Indeed, sir," Whitmore nodded. "That brings us to the next action being taken. Many prostitution rings use the internet to advertise their services. Most post pictures of their girls online. I have a team working through the internet to see if your daughter turns up. This is rather tedious as, sadly, there are many prostitution rings and literally hundreds of thousands of human trafficking victims but we are conducting a thorough search."

"Has anything turned up so far?"

"No, sir. I'm sorry, but we haven't been at it for even twenty-four hours. We are fully online and searching. Your daughter is our number one priority."

"Thank you," Courtnall spoke numbly.

Courtnall looked out the window. An intelligent man, well read and knowledgeable, he knew the statistics. The first seventy-two hours were crucial for recovering a missing person alive. The chances dwindled every hour they remained missing. They were well past that. Whitmore had an impeccable reputation and, if Tracy was to be found, Whitmore was the person who could find her; nevertheless, the realist in Courtnall knew they faced long odds. Perhaps it was time to dangle a carrot.

"What if I were to post a sizable reward for her safe return?" He asked.

"You can do that, Mr. Courtnall, but I don't recommend it."

Courtnall lowered his head slightly while raising his eyebrows in a questioning manner.

"The reason being, is once you let it be known who you are, your vast financial resources, and your willingness to pay, it would essentially be sending up a flag that could open your entire family up to kidnapping and extortion. It could endanger your entire family. I'm not telling you no. This is your family, and you alone can decide what to do, but I strongly recommend against it. Tracy's kidnappers would likely see this as an open door to exploit your family while they continue to exploit her. They are also very unlikely to ever risk being identified and would be much more unlikely to ever return her alive. It pains me to even speak that, sir, but I am obligated to inform you of all the risks and benefits."

"No apologies, Clay. I'm a pragmatic man and I need your candor regarding this manner. This is killing me inside but getting emotional is not going to bring our baby girl back home to us. You're doing exactly what I'm paying you to do, and I appreciate it."

"Thank you, Mr. Courtnall. That's all I have for now. I will keep you updated regularly. Is there anything else I can do for you while I'm here?"

"Just please get her back," Courtnall's voice began to crack. "A million-dollar bonus each to you and to the team that finds her if she's returned alive."

"That's not necessary, Mr. Courtnall. This is our job and we are adequately compensated for what we do."

"I appreciate that, Clay, but my offer stands. Tracy is priceless to us. I'll do anything to get her back."

Chapter 11

Atlanta, Georgia

Tracy leaned against the wall with her knees drawn up to her chest. She had yet to be taken out of the room, let alone sold out to service men. She was the only one who hadn't. She was also the only one who had not been given even a shred of clothing. She desperately clung to her self-respect which was difficult in her current situation. She was confined to a room full of other woman, all victims. Each forced to relieve herself into a bucket in front of everyone else including whichever guard was in the room with them. Her conflicting emotions were raging within her. She felt relieved over having not been molested, yet guilty for that as well. She ranged from apprehensive to terrified. Lonely and depressed, while anxious over the seemingly accusing eyes of the other girls who were being subjected to round the clock prostitution. It seemed like they were all feeling bitter toward her. All except for Lindsay.

Lindsay had recently awakened and now sat nearby. The guard, Aleksey was his name, either didn't notice or didn't care. Like the others, he passed his time staring into his cell phone. Tracy and Lindsay stole glances at each other. Each weighing the risk of trying to silently communicate. Any social interaction and companionship would be welcome to Tracy right now. Tracy cleared her throat. Aleksey didn't seem to notice. He was seated by the door on the opposite side of the room. He turned to glance out the door allowing Tracy to see an ear bud in his left ear. It was the ear opposite the door. Perhaps he didn't want his bosses to see he had an ear bud in. Could it be he was listening to something? Tracy chanced a quick whisper to Lindsay.

"I think he has an ear bud and is listening to something."

Lindsay spent the next dozen seconds cautiously inspecting Aleksey. She subtly nodded in agreement.

"How are you holding up?" Tracy asked.

"See for yourself," Lindsay said as she cradled her knees and leaned forward.

As she did so, she pulled her shirt up slightly, revealing several large red stripes across her back.

"What did they do?" Tracy whispered.

"Beat me with some kind of strap. I think it was a fan belt from a car."

"Why?"

"As if they need a reason? These creeps get off on it. This time, though, it was because I put up a fight over letting some pervert perform a certain sex act on me."

"And they did *that* to you?"

"They'll beat you if you don't smile and act as if you like it," Lindsay said dejectedly. "I didn't think I would break that quickly, but I did. Then they upped the game."

"What's that mean?" Tracey asked.

Lindsay pointed to her left forearm. Tracy looked and saw a small puncture mark.

"They injected me with something. It might have been heroin. I don't know. All I know is I was numb and then out of it for a while. Later, I woke up with some fat hairy guy on top of me. I was too numb to care. I think I just laid there all night and let one guy after another do what he wanted. I was hoping it was just a nightmare but you can see that it wasn't."

"Heroin?"

"Probably, or something like it. Fentanyl maybe? I don't know. It sure wasn't meth or coke. Whatever it was put me out. I've heard heroin is cheaper than prescription drugs so that's my guess. They sure don't seem to want to spend much money on us," Lindsay said looking around the room.

"That stuff's addictive!"

"I didn't ask for it. They forced it on me. That's how they control you. Get you addicted and then you'll do whatever they say to get your next fix. Probably their plan with all of us. You saw the girls in the other room they day we got here?"

Tracy nodded.

"They looked like zombies. That'll be us unless we figure a way out of here."

Tracy stole a glance at Aleksey. Satisfied that he was oblivious to their conversation she turned back to Lindsay.

"How do we do that?"

"If they take me away from here to another house, I could try to escape. Your idea of jumping a guard and stealing his phone might work too. If we could get one text out with our location, it could give us a chance."

"I'll do anything, Lindsay. I can't stay here like this and wait for them to turn me into an addicted prostitute. I'd rather die."

"Well, if we're gonna jump the guard, we have to get everyone in on it. It will take all of us to have any hope of pulling it off. Next time he leaves us alone, we need to get everyone up and tell them the plan. You and I will jump the guard and get his phone. We'll have to get the others to barricade the door. Once you get his phone, I'll try to hold him back while you text someone and call 911. Try to pull up our location if you have time. We will only get one shot at it."

"Do you think you can hold the guard that long?" Tracy asked.

"I can handle the guard," Lindsay said confidently.

"It's a shot in the dark and there's going to be hell to pay. I hope it works."

"A shot in the dark is better than no shot at all."

Chapter 12

Buford, Georgia

$\mathcal{T}$he mid-morning sun rose above the trees as they gently swayed to a mild breeze. The early day serenity was mildly disrupted by the rhythmic footfalls of a runner. Joe took in the beauty of Lake Lanier as he ran along the shore on Buford Dam Road. He was on the return leg of an out and back nine-mile run. The sun and sweat blurred his vision but this was a mild inconvenience. In BUD/S training, they ran in boots and fatigues along a sandy beach. And *they* were sandy. First Phase runs often were conducted as "sugar cookies." The recruits were frequently ordered to get "wet and sandy" which required them to submerge themselves in the frigid waters of the Pacific Ocean followed by a roll on the beach until they were covered in sand, head to toe. The end result was referred to as a sugar cookie. Many drills and training evolutions were performed in this state resulting in painful chapping and abrasions, not to mention sweat running sand into one's eyes. *You don't have to like it; you just have to do it.*

Today, however, Joe was shirtless, clad in gym shorts, shod in running shoes, and listening to music. The music of the day was what Joe referred to as his *Canadian Mix.* His favorite band is Toronto's own Rush; however, Joe found Canada had many other great bands to offer. Most of whom had been overlooked if not ignored by the classic rock stations in the U.S. The mix included Triumph, Red Rider, April Wine, Honeymoon Suite, Max Webster, and several others. The fast-paced "Go for a Soda" by Kim Mitchell was currently moving him along the shoreline on this perfect day.

He had slept surprisingly well. Joe still had mixed feelings about his future in the SEAL Teams. It would be extremely difficult to hand in his rifle in exchange for a desk. Even more difficult would be hanging up his Trident and walking away completely; nevertheless, last night's fireside discussion opened his eyes to other possibilities. And realities. The discussion went on at length as they actually began to discuss specifics of opening a tactical course on Stubber's property. So much so that Ramsey decided to take a drive out this morning to see it. Joe opted to stay behind. Christy would start back working her night shifts tomorrow which would require a day nap to get ready followed by sleeping through the day after her shift. Not wanting to miss any time with her today, Joe told Ramsey he would take a look when she was sleeping.

Christy was still out on her bike. She took yesterday off to recover but wanted to get an hour in on the bike this morning to loosen up her legs. Joe was medically cleared to run and decided he would match her bike with an equal amount of time running. With a little over a mile to go, he was feeling good and running on all cylinders. Like many runs, the past fifty minutes helped him work out his thoughts. On paper, resigning from the Navy made sense. He was still conflicted but going into business with Rammer and building a future with Christy were tipping the scales. Aside from being a combat operator, the other big draw the SEALs offered was the brotherhood. Whether he stayed in or not, he was losing that bond he had with his teammates. Lost was more like it. They had a new commanding officer and Joe was moving on. Now might be the opportune time to resign and pursue the next chapter in his life. Joe knew he still had an outside shot at DEVGRU which was his only hesitation at this point. It was a slim chance, but a major honor that would be tough for any SEAL operator to turn down. Were it not for that, he was ready to move on.

Crittendon made sense. Christy might be thinking long term and, as such, she might be amiable to Joe moving on to a new chapter as well. One where she is a major player. He still couldn't believe a successful and beautiful woman like Christy was interested in a door-kicking Navy SEAL like him. A woman like that could have any man she wanted, yet here they were. Joe knew a good thing when he saw it. If there was a future with Christy, he would *not* let anything get in the way. It had nothing to do with her career or stunning beauty. Christy was a remarkable person; intelligent, reasonable, driven, modest, and strong. The only thing about Christy that had ever annoyed him was her Christian faith, but that was a distant issue. Back then, Joe was a self-declared atheist. Christy had patiently and gently assisted him on his own truth quest and now, after a comprehensive examination of the evidence, he now embraced that same faith. What once annoyed Joe, now made Christy all the more attractive.

It was a big decision and time was running out. He would have to decide soon. *No that's not right. We will have to decide soon.* Joe was so used to being the one who made all the decisions. A lifelong bachelor, CO of his platoon, Joe bounced ideas off of people but, in the end, the decision was his. Not this time. This was a decision he *and* Christy would discuss and decide together. If she wanted a future together, she would be honest about it as well as her thoughts about what Joe should do. He trusted her completely. They would decide this together.

Joe tuned off Buford Dam Road onto Christy's street and picked up his pace. Just under a mile to go. Triumph's *Allied Forces* played in his earbuds as he gradually lengthened his stride and turned on the jets for the sprint home. His arms pumped in proper form with no protest from his injured shoulder. Joe's future was filled with several good options and he felt alive. He looked at his Garmin, a quarter mile to go. Joe kicked it up into overdrive, nearly a full sprint. A neighbor's sprinkler was errantly spraying into the left side of the road. Joe checked his six and angled over to run through the cool mist. The shock of the spray quickly gave way as his Gamin chimed the completion of nine miles. Joe slowed to a brisk walk and circled around in front of Christy's driveway. He looked back and saw her pedaling in his direction. Just the sight of her made Joe smile. He turned off his music and stepped into her driveway.

"Hey, sailor!" she said by way of greeting as she unclipped her shoes and braked to a stop.

"You say that to every guy you meet?" Joe teased.

"Only the tall, dark, and handsome ones," Christy said with a mischievous wink as she dismounted her bike. "Which, considering

I'm five foot eleven, makes for a short list. In fact, you're the only one on it, so consider yourself lucky," Christy said as she stood on her toes and gave Joe a quick kiss.

"Mmm, I am lucky," Joe said as he wrapped his arms around Christy and pulled her in tight.

"Ugh! You're all sweaty!" Christy protested with a laugh.

"So are you!" Joe said in retort as he held on and laughed.

"Alright, let me go so I can hang up my bike and get changed."

"Oh I doth protest!" Joe said as he let her go. "I think you look perfectly fine in that bike outfit."

"Well this bike outfit is going to be traded in for a swimsuit so we can go sailing."

"Um, yeah, I'm good with that," Joe answered enthusiastically as they walked toward the garage.

Christy punched in the code for the door opener and one of the twin bay doors quietly opened. She replaced her bike in the rack, hung up her helmet, and removed her shoes. Joe followed her into the house.

"I have water, Body Armor, and Bai coconut drinks," she offered.

"Body Armor, please."

Christy fished a couple of bottles out of the refrigerator and handed one to Joe.

"You want to head out to the porch for a stretch and cool down?" Christy asked.

"Sure."

They stepped onto her screened in porch. It was tastefully decorated in a beach-like theme with white wicker furniture, turquoise cushions, and light gray outdoor carpeting. Christy turned on a ceiling fan with palm leaf-shaped, white blades and handed Joe an exercise mat. She unrolled another mat and sat down.

"So where did Rammer go? His truck isn't over at Tom's."

"He drove up to Dawsonville to see Stubber's farm."

"Those two must have really hit it off," Christy said as she seemed to effortlessly stretch her hamstrings, her head nearly touching her knee. "I didn't take Rammer for someone who would be interested in a farm."

"They did hit it off. Stubber and your neighbor are great guys. True patriots. Our kind of people."

"That's great. I'm not surprised though. I knew you'd like Tom. So were they doing anything specific?"

"They're thinking about a business idea."

"A business idea?" Christy asked in surprise. "What kind of business idea?"

"Rammer is considering setting up and running an outdoor range and tactical course. One of those courses where we train law enforcement and civilians to shoot and conduct basic tactical shooting and woodcraft."

"Oh yes, I know what those are. Some of the doctors I work with have gone to those courses. Wait. How can he do that while he's active duty at Virginia Beach?"

"His twenty is up and he's thinking about getting out."

"Are you serious? You thought he was a lifer."

"Times change. Rammer's facing the same thing I am; being taken off operator status and put out to pasture, so to speak. He's thinking he'd rather do something other than man a desk."

"So is he for sure getting out or just thinking about it?"

"Depends,"

"On what?" Christy asked.

"On what I do," Joe said making eye contact.

Christy sat up straight. "Okay, you guys had some kind of serious talk around the fire last night after Stacy and I left. What are you talking about?"

"Nothing you and I haven't discussed. Stubber and Critter have a lot of experience and wisdom. We talked about all my options and moving on from the Navy was one of them."

"Because, like Rammer, if you can't operate, you're not keen on staying in."

"Right."

"But what about DEVGRU? I know you said it's a long shot but you were still keeping that option open."

"That's true, but it is a long shot and there are bigger things to consider."

"Like what?" Christy asked, tilting her head in curiosity.

"Like what I'll be doing if I don't get a DEVGRU slot, what I could be doing if I got out and...you."

Christy's mouth dropped open and her eyes went wide with shock. "Joe, what are you saying?"

"I'm saying a lot has changed over the past year and you're now a central part of everything. I don't want to put any pressure on you but, in all honesty, I can really see a future with you as the starring role and my priorities are changing. While I can't, for the life of me, figure out why an amazing woman like you would be interested in a pipe-hitter like me, I'm sensing that you may be thinking about us in a long-term plan as well. If that's the case, then I don't want to jeopardize things by keeping this a long-distance relationship."

Christy continued to stare at Joe, speechless.

"I'm sorry if this is too much, too soon. I know we've only known each other a year and have only been a couple for roughly two months," Joe said as his heart began to beat out of his chest with increasing nervousness. "Like I said, I don't mean to pressure you, but I have to make some career decisions soon and knowing where we stand will play a big role in that."

Christy stared back at Joe.

"What?" Joe said as close to a worried state that his training would allow.

He had never been serious with any woman before. He had no idea how to proceed. Honesty was his only course and he now worried he may have just lobbed a grenade into a great beginning.

"Did I jump the gun with this?" He asked.

"No, Joe. You didn't jump anything. I've been thinking these same things myself but didn't want to pressure you with your big career decisions. You've been a SEAL for most of your adult life. It's a part of who you are. I'm proud of what you do, and I will do anything to keep you doing that, *if* that's what you want to do. But I *do* see a future for us. So much so, that I am willing to move to wherever the Navy takes you, if you want to stay in. And to what you said about how long we've been together? I believe our being taken captive by the cartel in Honduras was a divine encounter. God began weaving you and I together that very day."

"So," Joe began with a look of puzzlement, "what you're saying is..."

"What I'm saying, Joe O'Shanick, is I am officially all in. I think we should pray about this together but, if you decide to stay in the Navy, then I will sell this house follow you wherever you go. If you decide to get out and want to move close to here and start up a business with Rammer, then I say I will be counting down the days. Whatever you decide, we are in this together."

"You mean whatever *we* decide," Joe corrected.

"Exactly. What *we* decide." Christy smiled back. "So this business you mentioned with Rammer. What's your plan?"

"We're working on it," Joe said with a grin.

Chapter 13

Atlanta, Georgia

Sergei Petrenko looked down at the red head sprawled on the bed. Her performance was adequate, but she was attractive enough to bring in good money. That's all that really mattered. Darcy was her name. At least he thought that's what it was. It didn't really matter. Her internet name was "Little Tiger" in reference to having been taken from the Clemson area. This "Girls of the ACC" idea was already proving to be quite profitable. Sergei originally was unsure how easy it would be to manipulate the girls. Like most pimps, he typically preyed on young teenage girls. Show a little attention, dangle the trinkets of the fast-paced adult world, and enough of them would follow him or his men all the way home. Runaways were especially easy. Sergei thought college girls may have a little more fight in them. They certainly couldn't be lured like younger teenagers. In the end, they cowered in fear from his men. A beating would do that.

Nevertheless, beatings left marks. That wasn't a problem with his cheaper *shlyukhas*. The average john off the street didn't pay much. They would get what they pay for; however, Sergei was trying to attract customers who would pay better money for attractive girls. Bruising and welts would not be good for business. The college girls he would control with drugs. They began with the heroin last night. A few hits a day and they would be hooked in no time. Once that was accomplished, they would do whatever they were told to do in order to earn their next hit. Withdrawal was a more powerful motivator than a beating. Track marks would not be good for business, but they were only temporary. Once the girls were hooked, he would give them powdered heroin which they would gratefully snort. They just wouldn't voluntarily do that now, so it was easier to have them injected by his men for a few days until they were craving more. Once they were in the routine, Sergei would mix cocaine into their heroin at the beginning of the night to liven them up for his customers.

Sergei had a crew under him that distributed drugs to the local street gangs and dealers. The drugs came directly from his boss, Victor Makarov, at wholesale prices. Sergei used some of the drugs to control his *shlyukhas* while the bulk was cut and sold to the dealers at a hefty mark up. The amount he used on the girls was minimal compared to what he sold. The upside was having several dozen girls who could be worked round the clock at huge profit.

Sergei buttoned his designer jeans and walked out of the room. He nodded at the guard overseeing this apartment as he cut back to the main apartment. Several men were lined up in the connecting hallway. It was mid-afternoon on a Tuesday and business was good. Petr Orlov and Elena were waiting for him when he returned.

"The bidding on our auction is starting to go up, Sergei," Elena informed him

"Is that so?" Sergei responded coolly. "Let's have a look."

Petr set his laptop down at the head of the table where Sergei took his customary seat.

"As you know, Mr. Petrenko, we went online yesterday at noon," Petr began. His crude Russian accent belied his high degree of intelligence and computer savvy. "I set the auction to run until noon on Thursday. I want to give good time for the word to get out and for the regulars to log in and find it. Many are heads of state, politicians, and corporate big shots with busy schedules. They aren't always sitting at their computers monitoring the internet. Even though it is only Tuesday, the bidding has already gone over one million U.S. dollars. The latest offer is currently 1.3 million dollars. I want to show you this in case you want close the auction early. It is good price, and by closing early, we run less risk of detection."

"Petr, are you using all your encryption and firewalls?"

"Yes, sir."

"I hired you precisely because I was led to believe you could conduct my business online without detection," Sergei said as he removed a cigarette from his pack lying on the table and lit up. "Are you telling me that your skills are not as good as I was led to believe?"

"No, sir. I stand by my work, but nothing is foolproof. The FBI and CIA have excellent hackers and it is good to limit exposure."

Sergei blew a cloud of smoke in Petr's direction as he studied his IT guru for a moment. "Petr, I pay you good money. You will not allow my operation to be exposed. If it ever is exposed, by the time the authorities raid this building, I will be gone, and you will be found in a room full of dead *shlyukhas* with your throat cut. Is that understood?"

"Y-yes, Mr. Petrenko."

"Good. Then you will keep the auction up until Thursday. If there are no new bids before..." Sergei glanced at a Rolex watch on his left wrist, "nine o'clock, then you are to stoke the bidding with a two-million-dollar bid."

"Two million?" Elena asked.

"Yes, Elena. This is a beautiful woman, blond no less, and a virgin. A rarity that will command a high price. There are sultans and sheikhs who will pay well to add such a woman to their harem. I think we can get ten million for her, if we play this right. Once we do that, we will have announced ourselves on the world stage as serious players. It will generate more business and open more doors. This will be only the beginning. Then we can leave this filthy rathole and take up residence in high-priced hotels with high-priced *shlyukhas.* Or would you prefer we stay here with the street rats?"

"No, Sergei. Your plan is good."

"Good. Now how is tonight looking?"

"We have a full schedule through the night."

"Any house calls?"

"Yes, a hotel downtown. They're requesting the blond from Wake Forest and the girl from Chapel Hill."

"Will that work?"

"Yes, it's only for an hour. I can make it work," Elena said confidently.

"Good. Go with them and find out if these are people we can compromise," Sergei ordered as he stabbed a finger through another cloud of smoke. "Anything else?"

"That's it for tonight, but the Senator's son requested another house call for tomorrow night. He is requesting the same girl again. I told him she will be available at midnight. He was not happy with that. Wants nine pm."

"For how long?"

"All night."

"Did you offer to let him try one of the other ACC girls?"

"Yes, but I know him. He has a thing for dark-haired girls. Lindsay is the only brunette of the group."

Sergei ran the math in his head. This was a college student son of a wealthy, high-ranking senator. He was an ideal customer; a frequent flyer with plenty of daddy's money and lots of friends. It wouldn't do to upset him, lest he take his business elsewhere. Furthermore, his repeat business made the senator vulnerable for blackmail. A compromised high-ranking politician was always a good thing to have if Sergei ever ran afoul of the law.

"Make it happen, Elena. He is the kind of customer we want long term. I want you to accompany her. Have Vitaly drive, but you take the girl into the house and supervise. Take more pictures for his file."

Chapter 14

Duluth, Georgia

S aigon Fusion was a very popular Vietnamese restaurant in the north Atlanta area. The owners, Kim and Ai-Van Nguyen were Vietnamese refugees. Their families were from South Vietnam which had been taken over by the North Vietnamese communists in 1975, after America pulled out of the war. Ai-Van's father had been forced into a communist re-education camp shortly after Ai-Van was born that same year. After two years of forced labor and deprivation, he was released back to his family. A year later, in response to not catching his quota of fish for the government, her father learned he was going to be sent back to re-education camp. He loaded his wife and only child into his small fishing boat and fled that very night. Eight days later, they landed in Bataan of The Philippines after a treacherous journey across the South China Sea. A year later, they were granted work visas in the United States and eventually settled in Atlanta's International Village. Kim and Ai-Van met when they were teenagers attending the same school in the International Village. They married out of high school and lived with Kim's family while they both worked two jobs until they had saved enough money to open their restaurant. Ai-Van had learned to cook as a child and possessed great skill that many would consider gourmet. As a result, their restaurant was considered the best Vietnamese and Asian Fusion in the Atlanta area.

Christy and Stacy were regulars at Saigon Fusion. They knew Ai-Van's family well and even went to the same church. Joe, having a

Filipino mother, was well accustomed to Asian fare. Christy had been telling him about Ai-Van's restaurant and insisted they dine there the first time Joe visited. Since Ramsey was coming with them, Christy took it upon herself to invite Stacy, who was just walking in the entrance now. True to their training, Joe and Ramsey had requested a table near the back and sat facing the entrance after having checked all points of entry and egress. They both waved to Stacy as she entered the restaurant. Smiling, Stacy waved back and started in their direction. She wore black slacks, black heels, and a white, sleeveless blouse. Christy smiled at Joe as she discreetly signaled for him to look over at Ramsey who seemed mesmerized by Stacy as she approached. Joe returned her grin with a slight shake of his head.

"Hello, hello!" Stacy greeted as Joe and Ramsey both stood.

"Oh, please don't get up on my account, guys!"

"Can't help it ma'am," Ramsey began. "Navy etiquette. We stand in the presence of a lady. Especially ladies as enchanting as the two of you."

"Oh, stop it! I just rushed over here from a delivery and my hair's a mess!" Stacy said as she gave Joe and Ramsey each a hug and peck on the cheek before doing the same for Christy.

The four sat down and Ai-Van's teenage daughter, Lin, came over to take Stacy's drink order. She ordered an unsweetened iced tea and, checking to see if anyone had ordered, asked for a tray of spring rolls.

"I'm sorry I'm late," Stacy apologized. "I had a patient show up in labor this afternoon and I had to sprint over from my afternoon clinic."

"Everything go okay?" Christy asked.

"She had a postpartum hemorrhage, but I was able to manage it with Oxytocin and intrauterine massage. She did fine."

"Do I dare ask what that is?" Ramsey smiled as he took a sip from his beer.

Stacy looked at Christy with a smirk.

"They're SEALs, Stace. They eat snakes," Christy egged her friend on.

"After the baby is delivered, the uterus normally starts to contract which stops it from bleeding. Sometimes it decides it doesn't want to contract which can lead to extensive bleeding, possibly even fatal. We give medicine to make it contract but I also reach up into the uterus, with one hand, while placing my other hand on the mother's lower abdomen and massage the uterus from both sides. It helps it contract which slows the bleeding."

Ramsey tipped his head down while looking across the table at Stacy with his eyes wide and eyebrows raised. "You're able to get your whole hand up there?"

"A baby just came out of there, Matt. Believe me, there's room."

"Gadzooks! You're hardcore, ma'am." Ramsey stated with awe.

"Matt," Stacy began, looking at Ramsey with a menacing stare, "if you don't start calling me *Stacy,* I'm going to show you just how hardcore I really am."

This drew a good laugh around the table. Ramsey leaned back with his hands up in surrender.

"Yes, ma'am."

Stacy kicked him under the table to the amusement of everyone.

"I mean Stacy!" He urgently corrected himself.

"That's better," Stacy smiled mischievously. "Rumor has it you two may be around here a lot more in the near future, and I prefer my friends call me Stacy."

"How does *she* know *that?*" Joe asked looking at Christy with suspicion.

Christy shrugged her shoulders with a mirthful smile. Earlier, she and Joe had discussed and prayed over the situation. Both felt peaceful and excited about Joe moving to the area with Ramsey. Christy actually seemed overjoyed by the idea. The fact that Stacy already knew confirmed that. Joe continued to stare back while smiling in a teasing manner.

"Oh look!" Christy exclaimed to change the subject. "The spring rolls are here."

Ai-Van stood at the table holding a large tray of spring rolls. She was in her mid-forties but looked twenty years younger with long dark hair, a slender build, and soft Asian features.

"Hello Doctor Christy, Doctor Stacy. Lin told me you were here with two handsome gentlemen. I had to come out and see for myself. Who do we have here?"

"This handsome fella is Joe O'Shanick," Christy said as she laid a hand upon his.

"Oh! You're the famous Joe! I've heard so much about you! It's so nice to finally meet you."

"Very nice to meet you too, ma'am," Joe said as he stood and shook Ai-Van's hand.

"And this is his good friend, Matt Ramsey," Christy added.

"It's nice to meet you too, Mr. Ramsey."

"Pleasure's all mine ma'am. You can call me Matt."

"Are you guys all having Pho tonight?" Ai-Van asked.

"Absolutely!" Christy answered. Stacy and I have been telling them how good it is here.

"Are they familiar with Vietnamese cuisine?"

"Joe is. His mother is Filipino and a great cook of everything Asian including Vietnamese. You actually look a lot like her. You both look a lot younger than you actually are."

"You're too kind, Dr. Christy. Well, if you will allow me, I want to bring out a few other Vietnamese dishes for you to try before the Pho. This is a special dinner now that your Joe is here, and I want to do something special. Enjoy the spring rolls. I'll be back soon," Ai-Van said as she rushed back off to the kitchen.

"That sounds good," Stacy commented. "I wonder what she is going to make."

"I don't know," Christy replied as she selected a spring roll. "But her spring rolls are to die for. Everyone dig in."

Ramsey took a bite of his spring roll and chewed appreciatively.

"Good night, these are good!" He commented. "I've never had Vietnamese before. I've only heard what the Vietnam veterans used to say about it."

"And what was that?" Christy asked.

"Nothing good. They said that, back then, the Vietnamese soldiers carried rice balls in their ruck sacks with something the vets referred to as *armpit sauce* which the Vietnamese would pour over their rice."

"Armpit sauce?" Stacy said raising an eyebrow.

"Yeah," Ramsey said with a chuckle. "The real name sounded like *nuke mom* but the vets all said it stunk to high heaven. Apparently, it's made by grinding up anchovies, mixing them with salt, and then putting it all in a barrel to ferment for months. What they drained out was used as their sauce. The vets wouldn't go near it."

"Do you think you could?" Stacy asked.

"Negative on that," he answered shaking his head. "But if the rest of Vietnamese food is half as good as these spring rolls, then we're doing alright."

"It's all good, Matt," Stacy said. "It's lighter but more flavorful than Chinese."

"Well, I'm with Chief on these spring rolls. They're fantastic," Joe said as he reached for another one.

"You guys need to try dipping your spring roll in this sauce," Stacy said as she dipped hers into a small bowl of an amber colored sauce and took a bite.

Christy made eye contact with Stacy while trying to hide a smile.

Following Stacy's advice, Ramsey selected another spring roll. He and Joe both dipped their spring rolls in the sauce and took a bite. After tasting the combination, they both looked at each other and nodded appreciatively.

"Um, yeah, that's killer," Joe agreed.

"Here, have some more," Christy said handing a small bowl of sauce around to each of them. "There's a dipping bowl for each of us."

Joe and Rammer went to work on the tray of spring rolls and outpaced the girls by three to one. They finished and returned their dipping bowls to the tray.

"That was out of this world," Joe said as he took a long drink of his tea.

"Vietnamese spring rolls, huh?" Ramsey asked looking at Stacy.

"That's right," she answered.

"And what do you call that sauce?"

"Well, the Vietnamese spelling is N-u-a-c M-a-m, which sounds like *nuke mom*."

Ramsey and Joe stared dumbfounded as Christy and Stacy laughed heartily at their expense.

"You're kidding me, right?" Ramsey asked.

"Nope," Stacy said shaking her head with a mirthful smile.

"Alright," Ramsey shrugged. "You won me over. I'd have never tried it had you not hornswoggled me like that."

"My mom has served this stuff to us for years," Joe commented. "I had no clue that's how this stuff is made!"

"That's because your mom knew you wouldn't have tried it had you known how it's made," Christy chided playfully.

"Enough about that," Stacy jumped in. "Christy tells me you two might be moving here? What's that all about?"

"The Lieutenant Commander and I are being put out to pasture, so to speak," Ramsey said gesturing toward Joe. "We can stay in the Navy, but if we can't play in the sand and go downrange, staying in doesn't look all that appealing."

"Earth speak, please?" Stacy asked.

"Rammer's saying that we are both being promoted out of operator status. The powers that be would make us become desk jockeys rather than shooters and looters."

"So your saying if you can't go to war and get shot at, it won't be fun anymore?" Stacy asked in disbelief.

Joe and Ramsey looked at each other, shrugged their shoulders, nodded, and said, "Yeah."

"It's not that it's *fun*," Joe explained. "It's more like it's what we are trained and wired to do. Let me put it another way. Do you consider an emergency c-section fun?"

"No. It's potentially tragic but necessary."

"Exactly. So is combat. Now how would you feel if you were told you had to move up into administration and could no longer perform surgery?"

"I would hate that," Stacy said nodding in understanding. "Okay, good point, but at least I'm not getting shot at."

"True, but you're vulnerable in many other ways. You have the responsibility of your patient's health and lives, along with that of their babies. Am I right?"

"Yes."

"And you may not get shot at but you're always at risk of being sued."

"That's true," she nodded.

"Yet, despite all your risks, you not only willingly step up for the job, you run to it. Don't you?"

"Every time," Stacy answered. "Okay, I get what you're saying. I've always respected what guys like you do even if I didn't always understand why you wanted to do it. What you're saying rings home with me, and I admire you all the more for it. So what will you do if you don't stay in?"

"We're tossing around a couple of ideas," Joe answered. "Your friend Stubber offered to lease us some of his land to open up a tactical and shooting course."

"Really?"

"Yes. In fact, Rammer here, drove up to Dawsonville this morning to check it out."

"So what'd you think, Matt?" Stacy asked, intrigued.

"I like what I saw," Ramsey answered thoughtfully. "There's plenty of wooded land with trails, gullies, and creeks for a good tactical course. Stubber already has a nice outdoor range set up. We could actually add on a sniper's course and even build an obstacle course if we thought it was worth it. There's plenty to work with. I'd really like Joe to come up and see it with me while Christy is sleeping tomorrow."

"And Christy and I were talking this afternoon about a few other possibilities we could do in *addition* to this course," Joe spoke looking at Ramsey.

"Like what?"

"We are close enough to Atlanta; we could still do security work on the side. I'm talking consultant work, personal protection for VIP's, even protection abroad. Shoot, Atlanta is a direct flight away from virtually any airport in the world. We could base our operations here but work anywhere on short notice. We could also start a podcast and a YouTube channel with short instructional videos. If we generate enough hits, we can pick up sponsors but, even if we don't, we can use them to promote the course and our services.

"That's actually pretty good, Joe," Ramsey said. "I'm shocked an officer came up with all that without his Chief Petty Officer's input."

"Most of those were Christy's ideas," Joe confessed.

"That explains it. I always knew you'd make a fine chief, Christy."

"Thank you, Matt," Christy said with a mock sneer aimed at Joe.

"So is this looking like a real possibility?" Stacy asked in an excited manner.

"It's starting to look that way," Joe said looking at Ramsey and then nodding at Stacy.

"I'm in, if you're in," Ramsey said looking at Joe.

Under the table, Christy grabbed Stacy's hand and the two silently squeezed each other's hand in excitement.

Chapter 15

Atlanta, Georgia

Tracy's heart began to beat rapidly as she recognized the stately trees lining the street. It was a street she knew well; it led to her parents' house. For the first time in days she was now wearing clothing. A pair of gym shorts and a t-shirt but they were clothes. The unmarked police car she was riding in began to slow as they approached her house. The gates were open as if in welcome. They turned into the long winding driveway and her house appeared. An elegant light sandy gray brick exterior with dark brown accents, beautifully lit up with landscape lighting. Home.

Tracy felt tears begin to well up as they neared the home she began to think she may never see again. A place of warm family memories was now a place of sanctuary. The car rolled to a stop under the portico. The large double doors stood open, inviting her in. Her two older brothers, Charles IV and Scott stood on each side of her parents in the doorway. They all smiled excitedly. The officer got out of the vehicle, walked around, and opened her door. Tracy emerged and slowly walked toward her family standing in the doorway. The surreal moment eclipsing the horror she had just left behind. Suddenly the door slammed shut.

The noise of the door shutting jolted Tracy out of her dream. In a cruel irony, she had awakened from a pleasant dream only to face the nightmarish reality of her prison. Tracy looked around as she sat up. She was still without clothes. Darcy, the red head, walked to the far corner and slunk down against the wall. The look of despair and anger she had earlier was replaced with a drugged look of resignation.

A new guard had replaced Aleksey. This one was named Erik. He had sandy blond hair, a stocky build, and pale, lifeless eyes. Like the others, he was passing his time staring at his phone. His presence kept the girls at bay and silent. Lindsay rolled over and looked up at Tracy. She then sat up and leaned against the wall in close proximity to Tracy. Erik looked up briefly but became disinterested when Tracy and Lindsay buried their heads into their knees. He quickly returned to whatever he found more interesting on his phone. Tracy turned her head away from Erik and focused on Lindsay, who kept her head resting on her arms but had her face turned toward Tracy.

"They haven't left us alone for a minute," Tracy spoke with barely a whisper.

"We'll get our chance," Lindsay answered. "I hope it's this guy. He slapped me around and held me down the night we got here. Let three other guys rape me before he took his turn. While you're on his phone, I'm going to go to town on his face."

"Are you sure that's a good idea?" Tracy asked with concern. "They'll kill you!"

"No, they won't. They're making money off of us."

"Well they'll make you pay, one way or the other."

"What are they going to do? Beat me? Rape me? They're already doing that. I'll risk it. Just make sure you get his phone and call for help. Find out where we are too."

"I will. Believe me, I will. I want out of this nightmare."

"We all do, sister. If this doesn't happen soon, we're all gonna be addicts."

"That's the part I don't get. They haven't done any of that to me."

"What? Do you feel left out?" Lindsay asked sarcastically with a cold stare. "Cuz I'll trade with you."

"I'm sorry," Tracy replied shamefully. "I didn't mean that like it sounded. I'm just wondering what they've got planned for me. I'm just scared. That's all."

"I get it," Lindsay said softening her features. "I'm sorry I snapped at you. I'm scared too. Scared, angry, hungry and sore."

"Yeah, but you seem a lot tougher than the rest of us,"

"I thought I *was* tough. I grew up in a military house. My dad is a Marine and was gone a lot. Mom was gone a lot for work. Had to fend for myself and my younger brother and sister. I've been competing in Mixed Martial Arts for years, Navy ROTC at NC State, all on my own. But this," Lindsay shook her head. "I don't know. I'm to the point where if we don't bust out, I'd rather they just kill me. I really don't care anymore."

The guard, Erik, stood up and stretched. Tracy and Lindsay stopped talking and just leaned back against the wall with blank stares. They watched as Erik, looked around yawning. Tracy willed him to leave the room. Erik scratched himself and then glanced at his watch. Finally, he opened the door and stepped out, closing the door behind him. The sound of the dead bolt sliding home was heard a second later.

Tracy and Lindsay sprang into action. They motioned for Darcy to join them as they woke the two blond haired girls up. They took a minute to rouse. Lindsay figured they were drugged up as was Darcy. Not the best scenario but it was the best they had to work with. Lindsay and Tracy explained the plan. The other girls groggily agreed. Tracy and Lindsay hoped they were up to it. It would take all five of them.

"Hey, since he's not back yet, everyone give Tracy your names. Tracy, if you get enough time, put all of our names out there. It should help."

"I'm Darcy Kerrigan," the red head spoke first.

"Chelsea Hammond," the first blond girl spoke.

"Rebecca King," the other blond girl answered.

"I'm Lindsay Meehan, and this is Tracy Courtnall. We all need to learn each other's names in case any of us gets away. Now remember, act normal and wait for me to act. I'm going to give him a few minutes to get lost in whatever he's looking at on his phone. Is everyone clear?"

A round of solemn nods went around the room.

"Okay then get to looking like you normally do."

All the girls moved their mats closer to Erik's vacated chair. Lindsay also took up position closer to where Erik would be. She laid down on her side facing his chair and waited. Erik returned within seconds of everyone laying down. He surveyed the room and, seemingly satisfied, sat back down. He leaned forward, elbows on knees as he began to scroll through his phone. Tracy saw, with slight satisfaction, that he had his earbuds in. She shifted her attention to Lindsay and waited. The minutes seemed like hours to Tracy as her anxiety levels increased to fever pitch. Lindsay continued to lay there, seemingly dead to the world.

Tracy watched as Lindsay began to scratch her knee, slowly drawing it up to her chest. Suddenly, she lashed out with a vicious heel strike to Erik's nose. Erik let out a howl, dropped his phone and reflexively covered his face with his hands. Tracy dove for the phone while Lindsay sprang to her feet, punched Erik's throat and jumped on him. She wrapped her legs around his torso and applied a rear choke hold to silence him.

"Hurry, Tracy!" She yelled. "The rest of you get the door!"

The other girls moved to block the door, while Lindsay continued to subdue Erik. Tracy picked up his phone, swiped the screen to get out of the porn site Erik was on and swiped to the home screen. She opened the phone setting, dialed 911, minimized the screen and opened up the map function. A pounding came from the door followed by a man shouting in Russian. The pounding became loud thuds as the men began to try to break down the door.

"Hurry!" Lindsay grunted, as she continued to hold on.

The map came into focus as the number began to ring. Tracy studied the map as she willed the dispatcher to answer. She memorized their location and switched to the texting app. She punched the icon to start a new text. She could hear the door begin to splinter as the men outside continued to ram it. Tracy froze, dumbfounded when she didn't recognize the keyboard characters. Realizing it was in Cyrillic, Tracy frantically tried to open the settings app to change the language. Suddenly, two gunshots rang out and the room froze. Chelsea collapsed to the floor and was swept aside when the door burst open. The man with the pockmarked face appeared.

"Stop!" He yelled pointing his gun at Lindsay, while he stepped over to her.

"911, what's your emergency?" The dispatcher's voice sounded from the phone.

"Please help! We're being held..."

Tracy was cut off mid-sentence when the man struck her in the head with the pistol grip. Stunned, she fell over, dropping the phone. The man stomped on the phone with the heel of his work boot. The phone went dead.

Chapter 16

Atlanta, Georgia

Tracy trembled in fear. The large pockmarked man pointed his gun at her while he shouted for the other girls to stand against the wall. Lindsay lay next to her, curled up in the fetal position and moaning in pain. The pockmarked man forced her to let Erik up who, in raging vengeance, proceeded to kick Lindsay's left side, several times. Against the far wall, Chelsea, the blond from Wake Forest, labored to breathe as she lay in an expanding pool of blood. Pockmark yelled at Lindsay and Tracy to join the other girls standing against the wall. Lindsay delicately crawled and had to be helped up by Tracy and Darcy.

Sergei appeared in the doorway and surveyed the room. He spoke to Pockmark in Russian and received a lengthy reply. His eyes narrowed as he zeroed in on Lindsay and Tracy, while Pockmark continued to ramble on. He slowly approached and then viciously struck Lindsay with a backhand before turning his attention to Tracy. Still without even a shred of clothing, Tracy felt completely exposed and vulnerable as Sergei stared at her with his icy blue eyes. The trembling increased as Tracy fought back fearful tears.

"Who did you call?" he asked in a cold measured tone.

Tracy panicked as she tried to think up the best answer. Did she tell him she got through to 911? Would that make them flee, leaving the girls behind? Doubtful. Did she tell him that Pockmark broke the phone before she could talk to anyone? With the phone smashed, he couldn't possibly know the truth but was desperate for Tracy to tell him. If she told him that she learned their location and told 911, would that force the issue and make them bolt? On the other hand, Sergei and his goons might move all the girls to another location, and they would be back to not knowing their location. Sergei's back hand struck Tracy's right face and jolted her out of her panicked deliberation.

"Don't stand there thinking up a lie, little *shlyukha!*" Sergei shouted, with spit flying into Tracy's face. "You will tell the truth!"

"I...I...I don't know!" Tracy stammered as tears began to flow. "He hit me with his gun, and I dropped the phone."

"What did you say? I will know if you are lying to me!"

"I only had time to ask for help. I didn't get a chance to tell them who I was. I...I swear!"

"You swear, eh?" Sergei said quietly with narrowed eyes.

He walked over to where Chelsea lay on the floor, bleeding and struggling to breathe from her two gunshot wounds and pointed the gun at her head.

"One last chance to tell the truth," he said calmly.

"I did! I swear!"

Sergei pulled the trigger. The ear-piercing gunshot rang out loud, resulting in the shocked screams of the remaining four girls. Sergei walked up to Tracy and leveled the barrel on her forehead.

"Now, think harder, blondie. What did you tell 911?" He spoke with his thick Russian accent.

Fear driven tears ran down Tracy's face as she desperately tried to speak through her panicked breathing.

"That's it. Ask him," Tracy said pointing to the pockmarked man. "I dropped the phone when he hit me. I swear."

"Igor?" Sergei asked the pockmarked man standing nearby. "Is this true?"

"Da," Igor nodded.

"Okay, blondie." Sergei said, as he slowly nodded to Tracy. "I believe you."

Sergei then turned and pointed his weapon at Erik, who lay propped up against the wall, holding his throat as he tried to regain his breath. Sergei fired a shot into Erik's forehead, causing the back of his head to explode into a pink spray. Darcy and Rebecca screamed out in horror, while Lindsay simply stared at Erik's lifeless form. Tracy began to feel faint with fear and lowered herself to the floor.

"You *shlyukhas* belong to me. There will be no escaping. What you tried today was foolish and you will all be sorry."

He turned and looked at Chelsea's dead body. Her face frozen in a mask of fear.

"Your *friend* got off easy," Sergei said with a diabolical sneer before turning and walking out of the room.

Lindsay lowered herself down next to Tracy. The other two girls, Darcy and Rebecca, did the same while the pockmarked man, Igor, stood by the door. Tracy could feel his probing eyes on her still naked body. In reaction, she pulled her knees to her chest and hunched forward. Between Igor and the lifeless bodies of Chelsea and Erik, there was nothing but reminders of the hell she was in. Not wanting to look at any of it, she leaned her head down into her drawn up knees. No sooner did she do this, when she heard a commotion at the door. Looking up, she saw Aleksey standing beside Igor and speaking quietly in Russian. Igor scanned over Tracy and the others before turning and walking out. Aleksey took Igor's place in the doorway.

Tracy immediately noticed that Aleksey eschewed his chair for the door, where he seemed nervously alert. Her fear rose a notch. If Sergei's working stiffs were scared, that couldn't be good for Tracy and the others. She chanced a look at the others. Darcy and Rebecca were quietly sobbing, while Lindsay blankly stared at the far wall. Aside from the muffled sobs of Rebecca and Darcy, the room was quiet. Tracy swore she could still hear the resonating sounds of the gunshots. They sat on in silent dread for what seemed like an eternity before Sergei marched through the door trailed by Igor and another man.

"Vitaly, Igor, start with the raven haired one," Sergei spoke to his minions.

Igor and the other man, Vitaly, walked over and grabbed Lindsay by the arms and hair. They violently dragged her to the center of the room and placed her face down on the floor. Igor placed a knee on Lindsay's upper back, while Vitaly knelt on the floor and held her legs. Sergei slowly stepped up wielding what Tracy thought was probably a fan belt from a car engine. The loop was cut making the belt into a long, narrow, but heavy strap. He held one end in his right hand as he slowly and dramatically slapped the other end into the palm of his left hand. Sergei knelt down and nodded to Vitaly, who dutifully pulled down the short plaid "prep school" skirt Lindsay was wearing.

"You are all now my slave-whores. My *shlyukhas*." Sergei said, looking at the girls with disdain. "The sooner you learn that and learn to do as I say, the better it will be for you. You have not learned that yet. You tried to cross me today. That was a mistake. You will learn now."

Sergei's eyes narrowed as he raised the fan belt over his head. An audible whistle was heard as he rapidly swung the belt down, violently striking Lindsay across her exposed buttocks. Tracy cringed in horror as she witnessed Lindsay's face grimace while her body shuddered in pain. Sergei slowly raised his hand and quickly brought the belt down, creating another sickening slapping noise. He struck several more times. The mixture of horror and repulsion made Tracy nauseous. After a dozen or so strikes, Sergei let up and commanded his minions to return Lindsay to her former place. They dragged her over and sat her up. Tracy watched as Lindsay winced in pain and immediately rolled onto her side. Her still exposed rear end already showing several red horizontal stripes. Out of compassion, Tracy gently pulled Lindsay's skirt back up.

"DON"T TOUCH HER!" Igor snarled, as he delivered a back hand to Tracy's face.

Tracy recoiled in shock, the fresh wound stinging her cheek. Igor and Vitaly grabbed her and dragged her beside Sergei. They pinned her face-down to the floor, similar as they had done with Lindsay. Tears freely rolled down Tracy's face as she whimpered in anticipation of what was about to come.

"I have a special purpose for you *malyshka*," Sergei spoke gently to Tracy. "I have treated you special. More special than the other *shlyukhas*, but you have not been respectful to me. Now you too must learn."

Sergei raised his right arm and, with an audible swish, brought the belt down hard on Tracy's backside.

Chapter 17

Cornelius, North Carolina

C lay Whitmore drove his Range Rover up the winding driveway to the stately Courtnall house. He backed into a parking spot opposite the portico and hopped out. Wanting to maintain the confidence of his high-end clients, Clay always dressed professionally. Tonight, he wore khaki pants with a white button-down shirt and blue blazer. He carried an iPad as he spryly walked up to the front door and rang the bell. After a short wait, the large double doors opened. Clay expected to see a well-dressed butler at the door but was surprised when the opening doors revealed Charles Courtnall.

"Ah, good evening, Clay," Courtnall said with a somber voice. "Thank you for coming all the way out here in person."

"No problem, Mr. Courtnall. Like I said over the phone, we have some developments and I thought it best to discuss them with you in person."

"Very good," Courtnall said as he let Whitmore in and closed the door. "Let's take this in my study. Shall we?"

Courtnall led them through a lavish parlor, followed by a large library complete with leather furniture, a billiards table, and approximately two dozen mounted heads of game, many of them exotic. They walked through a large set of double doors into a well-appointed study that had a commanding view of Lake Norman. It was nighttime, making it too dark to see outside. Whitmore would have loved to have seen what type of floating stock Courtnall had out at the dock.

"Can I offer you a drink?" Courtnall said, as he walked over to a small bar in the corner.

Whitmore quickly assessed the assortment of crystal decanters while watching what Courtnall reached for. "Scotch would be great, sir. Thank you."

"Good man," Courtnall said.

He used tongs to place two ice cubes each in a pair of crystal glasses followed by a generous portion of scotch and handed one to Whitmore.

"Thank you, sir," Whitmore said accepting the drink. "This is a beautiful house, sir."

"Thank you. My wife, Jane, and I dreamed up every square inch of the place. I know it comes off as a bit ostentatious, but we enjoy having people out here and entertaining. We built it for that purpose. We hope, one day, soon, to have lots of grandchildren running around here," Courtnall let the last sentence hang as he stood looking out the window. "But, anyway, let's have a look at what you've found. Please, have a seat."

Whitmore took a seat in a plush leather chair seated across from Courtnall's large desk as Courtnall sat down behind it. Courtnall was slightly more casual, dressed in khaki pants and a green Augusta National golf shirt. Clay immediately guessed that Courtnall had not only been fortunate enough to attend The Masters in person but had likely been privileged to have actually gotten to play the hallowed course. He refrained from asking.

"So what have you found so far?" Courtnall asked.

"My IT people found a website for an escort service advertising college girls. There is a specific site titled *Girls of the ACC*. We found a girl matching Lindsay Meehan on this site."

"That's the young lady who disappeared from the N.C. State campus around the same time Tracy went missing?"

"Correct, sir. They even have her pictured as if she were posing in various places on the N.C. State campus and her online name is *Shewolf*," Whitmore said as he placed his iPad on the desk and opened it up. "May I?"

"Please, Clay. In fact, come around here," Courtnall said gesturing for Whitmore to join him on his side of the desk.

"Thank you, sir," Whitmore said, walking around the desk. "There are actually several girls listed on this site, each of them attached to a different school in the ACC."

"Is my Tracy one of them?"

"No, sir, but here's the interesting thing," Whitmore said, setting his iPad down in front of Courtnall and turning it on. "Each girl listed matches the description of girls who were reported missing the same day as Tracy. Look here, sir. Based on what we've learned, we put together a timeline of each girl reported missing and their suspected time of disappearance."

"How did you get that information so quickly?"

"We combed the police reports and news. We spoke with our contacts in those departments. We spotted the trend and went after the data. Now look how this lines up, sir," Whitmore began to work through his iPad. "The first two girls suspected missing were Lindsay Meehan and your daughter. Shortly after that, a Rebecca King went missing from U.N.C. Chapel Hill. About two hours later, a Chelsea Hammond disappeared from Wake Forest and then later that day, a girl named Darcy Kerrigan disappeared from Clemson. All four of them have been matched to the girls being advertised on this website."

"That certainly seems to show a pattern," Courtnall agreed. "Not that I want to see my daughter on this website, but the fact that she isn't doesn't seem to help us. Are you sure she's with this outfit?"

"A good question, sir. One we are asking as well. Although we are still investigating other possibilities, we have to consider that Tracy may indeed be with this group, so we are actively trying to identify who and where these people are."

"Any leads?"

"Not yet, sir. My IT people are fast at work trying to locate the origin of this website. They are also putting together fake profiles of a couple of my men who will pose as Johns."

"Johns?" Courtnall asked, looking up at Whitmore, eyebrows raised.

"Yes, sir. A *John* is a man who purchases a prostitute's service. If my guys can set up a rendezvous, we can nail down a location. We think it's going to be Atlanta, but we need better information."

"I see. Why Atlanta?"

"Several reasons, actually. It's a large metropolitan area with many ways in and out, by road and by air. It's a convention and sports town with a large prostitution presence. But also because that's where the trail is pointing. Allow me to show you."

Whitmore minimized the web browser and opened up an image showing a map of the southeastern United States. Each of the missing girls' images appeared as a thumbnail image in the vicinity of where they disappeared, along with their suspected time of disappearance. A red line was drawn connecting the locations.

"As you can see sir, when we trace the location and time of disappearance of each girl, we see it begins in the Raleigh-Durham area and moves west, ending in Clemson. Now we cannot confirm, but this certainly shows a trail leading toward Atlanta."

"Yes, I can certainly see that; however, that's still assuming Tracy is with this bunch. That hasn't been confirmed yet."

"No sir, it hasn't, but it's the best lead we have so far and we would be remiss if we didn't pursue it."

"I agree, Clay. I just don't want you to get tunnel vision and overlook another place she may be."

"I assure you, we are conducting an expansive investigation, sir; nevertheless, we are hunting down the source of this site as well as monitoring it to see if Tracy appears. Should she appear, we will heavily increase our resources on pursuing these animals and getting your daughter back."

Whitmore watched Courtnall open up the web browser and begin to flip through the posted images of the other girls. The man shuddered as he began to cry silently. Relatively fit and well groomed, Courtnall normally maintained a stately presence. Now, he appeared as a slouching shell of the man he normally was. Whitmore had married later in life. He and his wife had three elementary school age children. A boy and two girls. Despite that, Whitmore could not imagine the despair Courtnall was experiencing. Before him sat a man, who was not only missing a daughter, but his best chances of finding her were pinned on the hope that she was found on this website. A prostitution website. Although the alternative was worse, no man should have to hope his daughter was being kept alive because she was being enslaved as a prostitute.

"I'm sorry, sir. We are doing everything in our power to find your daughter," Whitmore said, placing a comforting hand on his client's shoulder.

"But that's just it, Clay. She's not even on this site. These are all other girls."

"I know, sir. That's why we are looking in many places and not limited to this site."

"I'm sorry, Clay. That's not what I meant. Yes, I want you to find our Tracy. With every fiber of my being, I want her found safe and sound. Even if she isn't safe, I want her found," Courtnall said looking up through tear-filled eyes. "But I just realized that I was, at first, only concerned about Tracy. I was oblivious to the fact that these girls have all been taken and enslaved as prostitutes. Their families are probably just as broken as I am. Those girls were plucked out of their young promising lives and thrown into *this!*" Courtnall said, pointing at the screen.

"We have to get them all back," Courtnall pleaded. "Their families probably don't have the resources I have to hire a team like yours. I want you to find our Tracy, but I want you to promise me you will get these other girls back to their families as well."

Chapter 18

Cornelius, Georgia

*S*leep was evasive. Courtnall stared through the darkness toward the ceiling. Jane had finally drifted off after an hour or so of tossing and turning, but Courtnall remained wide awake. The images of the other four abducted girls in skimpy lingerie haunted him. The thought of his little girl being sexually molested and beaten by strangers absolutely horrified him. He was supposed to be Tracy's protector. He was supposed to provide a safe environment for her. He hadn't. Charles Courtnall III was an expert at protecting the wealth and assets of his clients, but he couldn't even protect his own family.

Courtnall gently slipped the covers off and slid out of bed. Jane stirred slightly but didn't wake up. That was a relief. She was emotionally spent and needed whatever rest she could get. Providing his wife with a few hours of desperately needed sleep was the least he could do. He quietly slipped on his silk robe, removed his phone from its charger, and tiptoed out of the room. He walked through their sitting room, into the kitchen, and out the French doors. There was just a touch of chill in the late-night air. He shrugged it off as he walked out to the end of their dock and sat down. The late quarter moon was obscured by the clouds and the lake was calm but eerily dark. Much like his mood.

Courtnall's mind was a brooding intensity of what-if scenarios. It was his natural state. His entire professional career had been built on algorithms and *if, then* scenarios. During college, Courtnall had devoted considerable leisure time to reading the biographies of successful people. He learned much from the practices and philosophies of such people that had served him well throughout the years. One such pearl was attributed to *The Great One*, the National Hockey League's Wayne Gretzky. More accurately, it actually came from his father, the late Walter Gretzky, who coached his future Hall of Fame son to, "Skate to where the puck is going to be, not where it has been." Courtnall had become quite adept at implementing that philosophy into his practice. He not only could predict the financial trends, he often set them.

Why, then, can't I apply this to one of the most important person's in my life?

Courtnall ran through various scenarios. He was employing a highly regarded investigative team, many police agencies were involved, and he had personally hired a consultant to place a social media campaign to locate Tracy and the other girls.

I feel like I'm not doing enough. What am I not doing?

Courtnall sensed more than felt, the soft vibrations of footsteps walking down the dock. He cast a glance over his shoulder and saw the angelic silhouette of his wife approaching.

"I'm sorry, Jane. Did I wake you when I left?"

"Actually, no. I woke up and you were gone."

"How'd you know I was out here?"

"You always come here when you want to think," Jane said as she sat down next to her husband.

"True. You know me quite well, don't you?"

"Not many people do, Charles Courtnall, but I've got you figured out. In fact, I'm guessing you're racking your brain for ideas as to what else you can be doing to find Tracy."

"Yes, you could say that. And you'd be right."

"And have you come up with anything?"

Courtnall paused before letting out a sigh and shaking his head. "No."

"That's because you're doing everything in your power your can do," Jane offered.

"It doesn't feel like it."

"Is that because you're not getting results like you're used to?"

Courtnall turned and studied his wife. Her blond shoulder-length hair was highlighted by the yellow glow of the dock light. She wasn't smiling but her gentleness was readily seen in her soft, still youthful facial features. She and Tracy bore such a resemblance, they could pass as sisters. Courtnall was ever grateful for that.

"You really do have me dialed in, don't you?" He stated more than asked.

"Enough to know that you need to stop beating yourself up over this."

"How can you say that? I'm sitting here at the end of our dock while our daughter is...I don't even want to speak out loud where Tracy is or what she might be going through right now."

"You don't have to. We both know the possibilities."

"Well, that's just it, Jane. I know the possibilities. I can't help but blame myself for this."

"Charles Courtnall, you had nothing to do with what happened! Some sick animals preyed on our daughter...and other people's daughters. We live in a fallen world with sick, evil people. That's not your fault."

"No, but it's my job to protect my family."

"How? By keeping her locked up in our house? She's a college student, Charles. You can't protect her twenty-four hours a day."

"You're not upset over this?"

"I'm very upset over this. I'm just not going to place the blame anywhere other than where it belongs; on some sick person or persons. That's it. It's not the campus, it's not Tracy, and it's certainly not you. Having said that, worrying about who to blame won't get her back."

"And that's it as well, Jane. I'm wondering what else we could be doing. We have nearly unlimited financial resources and I feel completely helpless."

"It's not all about money, Charles."

"I'm quickly realizing that. Money can only go so far in trying to locate her. I could spend our entire fortune and it wouldn't do a thing to protect her if we don't find her."

"You're right," Jane nodded.

"And you know what else?" Courtnall asked, looking into his wife's eyes. "Our wealth is meaningless compared to our baby girl."

"You sound like Solomon," Jane, said with a half-smile.

"Hmmph," Courtnall grunted. "I don't feel very wise, right now."

"Why is that?"

"Because I don't know what else to do! I feel like a helpless idiot who is doing nothing to save his daughter."

"Well, there was a time when Solomon didn't know what to do either. He asked God for wisdom."

"I'll tell you something, Jane," Courtnall said with a heavy sigh. "Right now, I'm seriously doubting whether God really exists. And, if He does exist, I've got a bunch of questions for Him."

"Why? Because He allowed this to happen?"

"Precisely! This and all the other evil in the world! How can a supposedly good God allow such evil?"

"Well, first of all, we don't always know when He intervenes to stop evil, but, more to the point, if He was to stop all evil, He would have to kill all of us."

"What in the world are you talking about?"

"Think about it. If He was to stop all evil, He would have to stop all sin. Right?"

"Yes, I suppose."

"Well, since we all sin, the only way to do that would be to kill us."

"That seems a bit cruel and extreme, Jane," Courtnall said shrugging. "Why not just stop people before they sin?"

"Because then He would have to take away our free will."

Courtnall looked at his wife. "I didn't mean all of us. Just the bad ones."

"Well then define who He should kill and who He should show mercy to, Charles, because we are all sinners. Should it just be murderers and rapists? Or drug dealers? Or investment managers who bilk their clients? Or men who commit adultery? Watch porn? Steal gum from a drug store?" Jane finished with her eyebrows raised in question.

"Well for starters, the sick bastards that took our Tracy!" Courtnall shouted.

"I hear you, Charles, and, personally, I wish He had, but we know history is full of terrible things happening to people. And, you're right. God could stop these things. If He couldn't, He wouldn't be God. That fact that He doesn't stop all evil shows that He has a permissive will. He permits things to happen. Even bad things."

"Okay, but why?"

"Because, He is a logical God."

"You just lost me. *What*?"

"Charles, He cannot give you freedom *and* force you to obey Him. It's one or the other. He *chose* to give us free will. One cannot love without having the free will to choose to love. By giving us free will, He has to allow us to choose to disobey Him."

"Okay, I get the logical part, but the *reality* is we have a daughter who has been abducted and being subjected to God knows what kind of brutal horror. I just cannot reconcile the two,"

"You're right, Charles. It's evil, but that's the reality of living in a world where man is allowed to choose to disobey God. Evil permeates and we all suffer. But it's only temporary. We know He will, one day, put an end to all evil."

"So you're just willing to accept what happened to our daughter because of free will?"

"I didn't say that," Jane responded calmly. "I'm furious and I want those animals caught and brought to justice. God is all about justice and no sin will go unpunished. I'm just explaining *why* He allows these things to occur. But we need to also remember, that for everything He permits, He has a reason why He permits it. We know that, in Romans, He tells us that He works all things together for the good of those who are called according to His purpose. He allowed Joseph to be sold into slavery to preserve the Israelites and He allowed His Son to be crucified in our place to pay the penalty for our sins so that we could be forgiven."

"So we're just supposed to take comfort in the fact that something good will come of all this?" Courtnall asked, frustrated.

"No. He is just as grieved and angry as we are over this, likely more so. We have every right to be angry and to do everything in our power to get Tracy back. We just need to trust that He sees the big picture and will work this out in a way that ripples forward into a good effect."

"And in the meantime?" Courtnall asked.

"In the meantime, we continue doing everything we can, but we also pray for wisdom and ask for Tracy's protection and deliverance."

"Jane, you know me. I might go to church with you all but I'm not much of a praying man and I'm so angry right now that I don't think I'd have anything good to say."

"God knows what's on your heart, Charles. He'd rather you talk to Him in an angry yet honest manner as opposed to reciting some memorized prayer. Just talk to Him. Be real."

"Be real?"

"Yes, be real," Jane answered.

"You do realize, Jane, that I have very little experience with prayer. I have no idea how to pray for something like this, let alone 'be real.'"

Jane grabbed Courtnall's hand. "Then let me show you. We'll do this together."

Chapter 19

Atlanta, Georgia

A dark, late model SUV pulled up to the gate in front of the Petrenko Contracting Company. The driver punched in the code and the gate slowly slid aside. He drove around back where one of the garage bays was opening. The SUV pulled into the bay and the door shut behind them. The occupants waited for the door to shut completely before getting out. As the driver emerged from his side, a very large man in a dark blue blazer climbed out of the passenger side front seat and opened the rear door. A serious-looking man stepped out and looked around the garage area.

Victor Tupolev was of average height, stocky build, and possessed thin gray hair which he wore short and parted to the side. His pale blue eyes could pierce the sole of any individual he gazed upon. He wore a dark two-piece suit with a white button-down shirt and no tie. A platinum pinky ring on his right hand matched a platinum bracelet and Rolex watch. He purposefully strode to the garage entrance of the main part of the building as his men fell in behind.

Tupolev had cut his teeth as a Russian intelligence operative in the SVR. During his twenty-plus years of service, he had established many well-connected contacts around the world and developed many networks specializing in the trafficking of arms, narcotics, and humans. He was plucked from the SVR by a wealthy oligarch whom Tupolev had impressed. The oligarch sent Tupolev to the United States to establish a new criminal enterprise using his networks and knowledge.

Seventeen years later, Tupolev sat upon the largest and most feared criminal organization in Atlanta. Atlanta's size and strategic location as a transportation center made for a large trade in many criminal enterprises. Tupolev's organization either directly controlled the trade in each area or received a tax on all trade going through his city. His only rivals were the gangs that served a competing cartel. Tupolev had had a good working relationship with the *Los Fantasma Guerreros* cartel that, up until recently, controlled of the Northern border and Gulf Coast of Mexico. President Galan, the current president of the United States, had caused some major disruptions to this relationship with his effort to improve life in Central America. One of the main components of this effort was an all-out, gloves off military campaign against the cartels. Although seemingly an insurmountable task, President Galan's campaign had, so far, been far more successful than the political naysayers had predicted. As a result, the cartels had been severely hindered in their ability to move drugs into the United States. The once heavy influx of drugs had been significantly reduced. It was one of many reasons Victor heavily donated to a Political Action Committee that supported Galan's opponent.

Along those lines, President Galan had resumed the tough border control policies of a previous administration making it increasingly difficult for the cartels to move drugs and humans across the border. This cut into Victor's flourishing prostitution business. The demand for rented passion was as high as ever but the availability of cheap labor was way down. Many of the young women, young girls more accurately, Victor had used over the years were from Central and South America. They had either been sold directly to the cartels or tricked into buying "passage to America," where they believed they were going to be able to work toward citizenship through promised jobs. The girls were certainly put to work but in an illegal industry in which they were nothing more than enslaved commodities. Most would never reach citizenship. Many did not survive to reach the age of thirty.

Replacing cheap sex workers had proven costly. There were plenty of European and Asian women to be had, but they came at a higher price and cost of import. A cheaper and more often employed option was grabbing young women off the streets right here in the United States.

Teenage runaways were the most opportune targets and his crews had "specialists" that were skilled in wooing young woman off the streets and into the sex trade. They were just as vulnerable through social media. This took time and cultivation but proved profitable in the long run. When the need to fill the brothels was more immediate, Victor's men resorted to brutal abductions followed by enslavement through addiction and force. The problem with this was the increased police presence. The authorities had inadequate resources to investigate and find missing women. They certainly weren't going to use them looking for women from other countries, whom they knew nothing about. What little time and resources they had would be used to locate women taken domestically. It created an increased risk for Victor's operation but, in the age of legalized gambling and absent labor unions, prostitution was one of few profitable ventures left for organized crime and he had to assume the risk to keep the money flowing.

Sergei Petrenko had proven quite adept at minimizing the risk while creating new ways to boost the cash inflow. His brigade (the Russian criminal bosses preferred to call their crews "brigades") brought in three times the money of Victor's other two brigades. Something Victor angrily pointed out to the other brigadiers quite often. Sergei and his *Patsanovs* (foot soldiers) had mastered the art of abduction while turning the women and girls over for a higher price. An ambitious man, that Sergei. A valuable man with whom Victor would have to use special care in order to keep productive and loyal while quelling any delusions of claiming Victor's position as *Pakhan* (crime boss). This required occasional unscheduled visits to oversee the operation. Today was one such visit.

Victor and his men walked through the downstairs office where the legitimate phase of the contracting company was running. The two associates manning the office stood at attention as Victor strode through on his way to the stairs. At the top of the stairs, an armed associate similarly stood. He opened his mouth to greet the *Pakhan,* but Victor angrily waved him off. As he entered Sergei's main area of operations, Victor saw two of Sergei's underlings in the living room, hunched over laptops busily typing away. Sergei was seated in the small dining room, smoking a cigarette, and talking on his cell phone with his feet propped up on the table. Upon spotting Victor, Sergei immediately disconnected the call and stood up.

"Papa Tupolev! To what do I owe this honor?" Sergei stammered nervously while tamping out his cigarette in the overflowing ashtray.

"Relax Sergei," Victor said waving his brigadier back down into his seat. "I come in peace, as they say."

"Then can I offer you a drink?"

"*Da,*" Victor nodded. "Gennady and Andrey will drink too."

Sergei signaled Elena who immediately went into the kitchen. He smiled inwardly. If Victor accepted a drink, it was a friendly visit. If Victor included his bodyguards, it meant he was in a good mood. Elena returned with four glasses and a nearly full bottle of Beluga Gold Line vodka which she had just retrieved from the freezer. She set them down in front of Sergei and retreated back to the living room. Sergei poured the four glasses while Victor watched, with passive interest, two of Sergei's *shlyukhas* who were being escorted back to their room by another of Sergei's underlings.

"*Za vstrechu!*" Sergei toasted as the four *Bratva* mobsters clinked their tiny glasses and drank.

"So, Sergei Ivanovich," Victor began as he set his glass down, "let's have a look at your books."

Sergei signaled Elena, once again, who quickly appeared holding a laptop. She handed it off to Sergei and stood by his side as he opened to a particular spread sheet. With her help, Sergei spent the next several minutes reviewing his brigade's numbers for the month. Victor listened quietly with a passive face. Sergei wasn't fooled. Victor heard and understood everything he was being told. He normally waited to ask questions until Sergei was finished. However, once he did begin asking questions, it became readily apparent that he knew every detail.

"Impressive, Sergei Ivanovich. Your idea of placing the *shlyukhas* in a cheap motel wherever there is a college football game is proving quite profitable."

"Thank you, Papa Tupolev. I keep them here during the week to service the business travelers and ship them out to the college towns Friday mornings. This way, I can maximize their usefulness."

"Shrewd," Victor nodded. "And your truck stop revenues are up nearly fifty percent by my calculations. How is this so? Are you sending more girls?"

"No, sir. We created an app."

"An app?"

"Yes, sir. The app informs the truck drivers of who is available and at what location and time. The truck drivers come to us and the girls don't have to waste time wandering the parking lot knocking on cab doors looking for business. It is much more efficient. Additionally, sir, there is a menu on the app that lets the drivers order drugs which the girls bring to them. It's like killing two birds with one stone. For the right price, they get the service of a *shlyukha* and they drive away with a bag of coke, speed, or whatever they wish. With the same number of girls, our volume is up the fifty percent that you just saw," Sergei smiled proudly.

"I see," Victor said as he picked up the bottle of vodka and poured another round for himself and Sergei. "And you use same app for your football girls?"

"No. Everything is separated by venue. This way, if one operation gets busted, the others are unaffected. We simply close the app and start a new one."

"How do you get your clients onto the new app?"

"We have their information. We purge the app of anyone we suspect to be police and send an update to the rest. After a slight interruption, we are back in business online."

"What do you need to expand your operations?"

"I need places to keep the girls, vans to move them, and soldiers to handle them, but not many. Soldiers are expensive. I keep the girls in-line through their addictions and fear. Addictions mostly. Once they're hooked, they no longer care what they do as long as you keep feeding their cravings. I own them at that point."

"Do any ever try to escape?"

"It's rare, but if one does, I make her an example to the others." Sergei hid his tension as he wondered if Tupolev had heard of what had happened earlier.

"I see," Victor nodded, apparently satisfied with Sergei's answer. "And, what of this new idea? Your *Girls of the ACC.* How is that working out?"

"We've only had them a few days, but they were an instant hit. I can charge three times as much for them."

"How many do you have?"

"I have three that are in use."

"Three?" Victor asked in surprise. "I thought you told me you took five."

"We did, Papa Tupolev. We did," Sergei said in appeasement. "They're not completely addicted yet and they tried to escape. I had to kill one in front of the others. I made an example of her."

Sergei was very careful not to tell his boss about the cell phone. He didn't think the girls had given away their location, but he didn't want to ignite Tupolev's temper. Best to distract him with money.

"However, there is one girl I have not put to work. I have a better plan for her."

Tupolev silently responded with a hand gesture signaling for Sergei to continue.

"I'd rather show you," Sergei said, as he opened up the dark web site and turned the laptop toward his boss.

Tupolev spent a minute studying the web page.

"Am I reading this correctly? That's American dollars?" he said looking back up at Sergei.

"That's correct, sir. Four point one million dollars and climbing."

"Just because she's a virgin?" Tupolev asked incredibly. "Who's bidding on this?"

"We aren't supposed to know, but Petr has a back door built into the online account of every bidder that registers with us. We have had bidders from all over the world, but the auction runs another day and I expect the bidding to increase significantly."

"Who's the highest bidder so far?"

"It's a movie producer in Bollywood."

"India?"

"Yes, sir. There is a lot of money going through Bollywood, but I think the big players haven't even begun to bid yet."

"How much do you think you think she will sell for?"

"No way to tell, sir, but I'm hoping for ten million."

Tupolev quickly did the math in his head. His take would be significant. Tupolev knew Sergei checked every new girl for the opportunity to auction off a virgin to some sick man willing to pay big money. Inexperienced girls were somewhat of a rarity in today's permissive and hyper-sexual culture, which led them to seek after the very young teens and even pre-teens. They auctioned off well enough but nothing like what Sergei was showing him. This was a commodity worth looking into.

"That will be a good payday for you, Sergei." *And me*, Tupolev thought to himself. "Perhaps you should look on expanding this side of your business in addition to your *shlyukhas*. I am about to close on a motel down near the airport. There many shipping facilities and logistics centers there. It would be a good place to expand our business. I might think about having you run that for me as well."

"I would be honored, Papa Tupolev," Sergei responded as he considered the prospects.

"Although, if you can auction off a few more girls like her," Tupolev said pointing at the computer screen, "you will be able to buy your own motel."

Tupolev picked up his glass and finished off the rest of his vodka. He stood up quickly followed by Sergei and the bodyguards. This signaled the visit was over. Elena ducked into the kitchen and reappeared holding a backpack filled with cash. Tupolev accepted the pack and handed it over to his driver. He didn't need to count it. He knew how much would be in it. Sergei knew better than to shortchange him. A printout of the spreadsheets Sergei had shown him would be included. Most of his cut was electronically wired through a series of banks and shell corporations that thoroughly laundered the money and made it untraceable. Tupolev insisted that ten percent be paid in cash, which he used for expenses, making his illegitimate businesses virtually untraceable. He reached behind Sergei's head, pulled him close and kissed his forehead.

"This is excellent work, Sergei Ivanovich. You are a rising star in the family," Tupolev spoke looking into Sergei's eyes. "But don't ever forget who you work for."

"I won't, Papa."

"Good man," Tupolev said, gently patting Sergei's face with his hand.

Chapter 20

Buford, Georgia

A slight breeze generated scattered patches of ripples, known as "catspaws," on the otherwise calm Lake Lanier. Joe paddled Christy's paddleboard a few yards behind Chief Ramsey. Ramsey was on the final stretch of a two-mile swim. His efficient Combat Side-stroke kept him almost completely submerged and barely created any wake on the surface. Joe made more wake with the paddle board. One more week and Joe would be back in the water. After eight weeks of rehabilitating his left shoulder, Joe figured he would feel a little stiff at first, but his years of swimming and training, he hoped, would allow him to quickly regain his swim fitness.

Christy had still been asleep when Joe and Ramsey returned from Stubber's farm. She was resuming her usual night shifts in a few hours and prepping for the long night with a good nap. Joe was excited to tell her about the visit but it could wait. Ramsey wanted to get in a swim anyway. He and Ramsey had gone for a brisk run that morning. Christy had as well but at a slower pace and shorter distance. She was still quite stiff and sore from the Ironman and was simply trying to loosen up.

Ramsey continued to smoothly stroke through the water as Joe kept watch. Open water swimming was quite enjoyable but came with many hazards. Even the best swimmers could suffer a muscle cramp or inhale the water from a wave. An otherwise alert boater might not see the swimmer and accidentally them run over. From day one of

BUD/S, SEALs were taught to always have a "swim buddy" for the main purpose of safety. In this case, Ramsey's swim buddy was a more visible Joe standing on a paddleboard. As much as Joe wished he were swimming, he didn't mind the paddleboard. He was still getting used to it but found it rather enjoyable. The peaceful day and tranquil waters allowed Joe some quiet time to think.

Over the past hour, Joe had mentally worked over the possibilities of what he and Ramsey could do. The most attractive option was the tactical course. If properly arranged and operated, there was a decent economic prospect. He and Ramsey had talked to former colleagues and conducted some online research to get a ballpark idea of what courses were offering and what they were charging. The startup costs would be the biggest obstacle; insurance, capital purchases, construction, website, advertising, leasing, and basic supplies, let alone salary and benefits. It seemed quite overwhelming. It would be a risk. He and Rammer would have to live on the cheap for a while, but wasn't starting a new business always that way? Stubber, God bless him, wasn't asking much to lease the land and he said he would be willing to defer the first six months. In the meantime, they could look for other work such as personal security or even security consultants. They both had some savings built up which would help keep a business loan down, but they hadn't even looked at the numbers in detail. It was a lot to consider.

Joe smiled as they neared the dock. Christy was seated at end with her long legs dangling over the water. She wore a bright orange Tennessee Vols t-shirt and a matching ball cap.

"Hey, beautiful! How'd you sleep?" Joe asked, paddling in by the dock.

"Pretty good," she answered with a yawn. "I just woke up."

"Do you want to get in a swim? I'm starting to get the hang of this paddleboard."

"That's true, Christy," Ramsey commented while treading water next to Joe. "He only ran me over once on the way back!"

Ramsey's comment drew a smile from Christy.

"Actually, yes. I will take you up on that offer. I was hoping to get in a swim to loosen up," Christy said holding up her goggles.

"I need to wake up first, though. *And* I want to hear how it went up at Stubber's farm!"

"It actually went quite well!" Ramsey commented enthusiastically.

"Really?" Christy asked excitedly looking at both men.

"Yeah, it actually looks quite promising," Joe beamed. "We still need to figure out the numbers, but the place has a lot of potential."

"Like what?" Christy asked.

"We spent hours hiking around the area. We could easily install several different shooting ranges and there is a lot of hilly woodland with creeks. We could run woodcraft courses, small units' tactics, and even mock battle scenarios. We could have a large menu of different courses from basic pistol, rifle, tactical shooting, navigation courses, and even survival courses."

"So are you actually thinking about doing this?" She asked hopefully.

Joe looked at Ramsey and then they both looked at Christy and nodded. "We need to put together a business model with some real numbers but, yes, we'd like to give it a go."

Christy squealed with delight. "This is great! How soon do you think you could get started?"

"That's up to the Navy, but I would think within a month or two. We both have to process out and then get set up out here. We both live in furnished apartments so there isn't much to move. It's just a matter of getting out here and getting things up and running."

"Which can't happen soon enough, as far as I'm concerned," Christy said, pulling off her shirt, revealing a one-piece swimsuit underneath.

"So are you thinking of living up in Dawsonville or driving up there," she asked as she fitted her swim cap and tucked her long ponytail inside.

"We were thinking of splitting the distance," Joe said as he gently worked the paddle board to stay in place. "Cumming, Georgia is twenty minutes from Critter's farm and twenty minutes from here."

"I like that idea," Christy nodded.

"Well, here's the crazy part..."

"What?" Christy said, as she stopped prepping her goggles and looked back and forth between Joe and Ramsey who were both smiling.

"There's a nice Pearson 32 sailboat for sail at the Marina. It's in great shape and a good price. I was thinking of buying that. Rammer and I could live on that for a while to save costs. The slip fees are only three hundred dollars a month. That's way cheaper than renting a house or an apartment."

"You've got to be kidding me!" Christy laughed. "You two are actually thinking of living on a sailboat?"

"Shoot, yeah!" Ramsey said. "It'll be fun!"

"What about the winter? We might be in Georgia, but it can still get cold here."

"We're SEALs," Ramsey answered. "We're used to being cold."

"You're also crazy, Rammer," Christy teased. "Did you know that?"

"I've been told that from time to time."

"He's just kidding, Christy. The boat is hooked up to shore power. We can use an electric heater when we need to."

"You guys are really serious, aren't you?"

"Yeah, why not?" Joe shrugged with a smile.

Christy shook her head laughing. "I guess they can take the boys out of the Navy, but they can't take the Navy out of the boys."

Joe and Ramsey looked at each other and shrugged. "True," they both said.

"Alright, you ready, Joe?"

"Yep. Lead the way."

"Rammer, feel free to make yourself at home inside while we're gone."

"Thank you, Christy. I'm grabbing a shower at Critter's. Stubber's coming down and the four of us are getting a late dinner after you leave for work."

"Four vets out on the town," Christy commented. "Just don't end up in my ER. You'll get tubes where you don't want them!"

Christy fixed her goggles, dove in, and began her swim. The lake was calm and warm. It was a beautiful day. Christy was grinning under the water, but it had nothing to do with the lake.

Chapter 21

Charlotte, North Carolina

"Clay? We've found something you should see."

Whitmore looked up from his desk. Chuck Springer, one of his top assistants stood in the doorway. Chuck was above average height and slightly overweight with a shock of short brown curly hair. His wrinkled khaki pants and white oxford shirt reflected the fatigue on his face. Whitmore could relate. They had all been putting in long hours trying to find a needle in a haystack.

"Whatcha got, Chuck?"

"We think we found Tracy Courtnall on the dark web."

Whitmore was suddenly wide awake. "Really?!" He exclaimed, quickly standing up.

"Yeah, I think it's her. Roderick has it on his computer," Springer said, as he led his boss through the reception room and into a large room containing many cubicles.

"Hey, Roderick! What do you have?" A now energized Whitmore said, upon entering his computer specialist's cubicle.

"I think we may have our girl, Clay." Roderick Boulware said, with his baritone voice as he looked up at his boss.

A rising star in the firm, Roderick attended Georgia Tech on a Navy ROTC scholarship and graduated with a degree in Computer Science. He served his four years in the Navy working in cryptology before returning to Georgia Tech to earn his doctorate. He had been with Whitmore Investigative Services for a little over two years now and had proven quite valuable. Always impeccably dressed, Boulware's starched white shirt and dark suit were perfectly tailored to his runner's build. The dark mahogany skin atop his shaved head shined under the fluorescent lights, while a small pair of round reading glasses perched on his nose accentuated his intelligence.

"I have my programs chasing down the origin of the website with those other missing girls while searching the web for Miss Courtnall, but they came up empty. A lot of the heavy hitters run their trade through the dark web, so I've had my programs searching there as well. A lot of the sites are encrypted but I was able to get into most of them fairly easily. I came across one egg that took the better part of the day to crack, but here it is," he said as he turned the monitor allowing Whitmore and Springer to see.

A large image of a scantily clad young blond woman appeared. Her expression was blank, and she wasn't looking directly into the camera, but Whitmore had no doubt who he was looking at. Boulware had indeed found Tracy Courtnall.

"That's her alright, Roderick. Good work! What do we know about this site?"

"It's an auction site, sir. Whoever has her is auctioning off her virginity."

"Good grief! Are you serious?"

"Yes, sir, I'm afraid I am. The bidding is up to nearly five million dollars as we speak. Bids are coming in from all over the world."

"When does this auction end?"

"Tomorrow at noon."

"Then we have roughly sixteen hours to find her before she gets shipped out to God knows where. Any idea where she might be located?"

"Possibly, sir. I was able to trace the website to a dummy server, but I ran one of my software probes and was able to trace back to another server..."

"Roderick, I respect your skills, but I don't have the first clue what you're taking about. Just give me the bottom line, please."

"Yes, sir, I'm sorry. I've got the host server located in Atlanta. It also happens to be the same server those other girls are listed on. That pretty much links all the abductions and suggests were by the same person or persons. With a little more time, I can probably pinpoint a more precise location, but I can't guarantee our girl is where the server of question will be nor the computer operator for that matter."

"Stay on it. Chuck and I are heading to Atlanta. Keep us informed of any location updates."

"Will do, sir. I'm also placing a tracker on each bidder to try to determine their locations. They tend to be less meticulous about their security compared to whoever is working the boards for your target. I have every confidence we will bag these dirtbags but, if we don't, I will try to have a location of whoever wins the auction."

"Good thinking, Roderick. Keep us informed," Whitmore said as he and Springer left the cubicle.

"Chuck, call ahead to Gary Lee in Atlanta and give him an update. Tell him we will be there in three or four hours. Grab O'Malley and tell him to bring his go-bag. I want him to drive. I'm grabbing my bag and I'll meet you both in the lobby. We'll try to grab some sleep on the way down. Once we are there, we'll be busy. At least I hope so."

Whitmore hustled back to his office. He retrieved his cell phone, opened up to recent calls and punched the number he wanted. The phone picked up on the second ring.

"Charles, it's Clay Whitmore. I think we may have found your daughter..."

Chapter 22

Duluth, Georgia

*C*hristy heard the loud chirp of the EMS radio, signaling an in-coming call. She was just stepping into the emergency room and could already sense it was busy. She looked left to the critical care rooms. They were full. *Not good.* She turned toward the main work area where the nurse's station was; the charge nurse and physicians sat in front of computers to place orders, review labs, and dictate patient charts. The rooms surrounding the arena-like work area were all full. *Also not good.* The hallway beds were almost all occupied and there were two EMS crews with patients on stretchers. *Definitely not good,* Christy sighed. *It never ends.*

As Christy walked toward the physician work area, she heard the voice of Joe Rocque, aka "Joe Rockhead," over the PA system.

"Now hear this! Now hear this! Entering the emergency department is Georgia's newest Ironman, Doctor Christy Tabrizi!"

Christy abruptly stopped and stared at Rockhead, who was grinning from ear to ear, mischievously. Christy looked at him and mouthed the word "Really?" as a round of applause went up from the nurses and staff. She had no choice but to smile sheepishly and wave as she walked to the open chair in their work area.

"I'm going to kill you, Rockhead!"

"Ha ha ha ha! Come on now, C-breeze! You know we're just showin' some love to the queen of the nighttime ER! Besides, if you kill me now, you won't have me to help carry you through the night!"

Joe Rocque was a PA (physician's assistant) who worked a large number of the night shifts. His nickname derived, naturally, from his last name but also from the fact that he resembled a boxer from TV's *The Flintstones*, with his stocky build, mostly bald bead and perpetual five o'clock shadow. A former Navy Corpsman, who served several combat tours with the Marine Corps, Rockhead could perform many procedures and was efficient with the patients, making him an asset to whichever physician he shared the shift with. Christy referred to him as "The Clown Prince of the ER" due to his wacky sense of humor and practical jokes that never let up during a shift. Christy was always glad to have him on the shift, antics and all.

"Hey, Christie!" Dr. Jerome "Boomer" Marshall said as he hung up the phone. "Congratulations on your race. How do you feel?"

"I'm still a bit sore but working it out. Thanks, Boomer."

"Well, I followed your progress on the website tracker. It looks like you were bringing it all day. Proud of you, girl!" Marshall said extending his hand in a fist bump.

Marshall, a tall muscular African American, was a former inside linebacker for the University of Georgia. An academic All-American, he went on to medical school and emergency medicine residency at The Medical College of Georgia before coming to work in the ER. Despite his intimidating presence, he had a disarming smile and a very pleasant demeanor. Everyone assumed his nickname was attributable to his football days, but he insisted his mother had been calling him "Boomer" ever since he was a toddler in rural Georgia. He had no idea why.

"Looks like you guys have gotten it handed to you today," Christy commented, as she sat down at the vacant computer to log in.

"EMS smack down," Marshall nodded.

"Ain't gonna get nothin' less when ol' Tricky Ricky's on. Ain't that right, Tricky Ricky?" Rockhead spoke as the afternoon shift physician, Dr. Ricky LaPointe, returned from a patient room and sat down.

"What are you talking about?" Dr. LaPointe said as he sat down. "Hey, Christy. Congratulations."

"Thanks, Ricky. I think Rockhead's talking about your black cloud."

"It's not just me," LaPointe said defensively, with his omnipresent smile. "This place is always busy."

"Aw, come on now, Tricky Ricky!" Rockhead ribbed. "When you show up, the ambulances start pouring in here. Within an hour, this place looks like a mass casualty unit."

"Shoot, I don't ask for it."

"No, but you bring it, big boy! You sure as shootin' do, and you know it!"

LaPointe shrugged off Rockhead's barbs with a grin and turned back to his computer as Lily, one of the night Certified Nurse Assistants (CNA), walked over from the EMS radio.

"Doctor Tabrizi, EMS is bringing in a sixty-two-year-old male in respiratory distress with facial burns after his beard and mustache caught on fire while lighting a cigarette."

Christy sat up straight. "How far out, Lily?"

"Two minutes," Lily said apologetically.

"Alright, I'm heading there now," Christy said, as she stood to her feet and began walking toward the critical care rooms. "Please call respiratory therapy and have them come down ready for an intubation."

"You want an extra set of hands, Christy?" Marshall asked.

"Thanks, Boomer. I'll see what we've got and call you if I need you."

They had a good team of physicians. Everyone was willing to help each other out. There were many times where it was reassuring, if not beneficial, to have a partner in the room to assist with a difficult patient. Boomer and Ricky had enough to do but, if she needed one of them, it was nice to know she could call and they would come running. She would do the same for them.

Christy entered the critical care area and saw a tech pushing a patient's bed into the hallway to make room for the incoming patient. Several nurses and techs prepping the suddenly vacant room for the arriving patient. Among them were Emily Serrano and Alexis DiMartile, two of her most trusted nurses and plank owners of what, Christy called "The Night-force Elite," a solid core of nocturnal seasoned nurses and techs whom Christy trusted implicitly. As if by illustration,

Alexis already had the airway box on the counter ready, anticipating that Christy might soon need it.

"Hello!" Christy greeted her team with her smooth calm voice. "Sounds like we're going to be tubing this guy as soon as he hits the door, so if EMS doesn't have a line, we'll need one right away. We also need the emergency airway cart in the room please."

A facial burn often causes inhalation burns to the nose and throat which can lead to a rapid development of swelling that could occlude the airway. Based on the EMS report, which stated the patient was already having difficulty breathing, Christy wanted to be ready to secure the airway before it was so swollen that she wouldn't be able to. Securing the airway entailed inserting a plastic breathing tube known as an endotracheal tube through the vocal cords and into the trachea thus providing a secure conduit for vital air to pass. The process of inserting the tube was called intubation and often familiarly shortened to "tubing." Occasionally, the patient's personal anatomy or circumstances such as injury or swelling made it extremely difficult or impossible to successfully insert the endotracheal tube. In those instances, an alternative approach was necessary. The emergency airway cart was stocked full of equipment for handling the difficult airway.

"They're here!" Emily announced.

Christy saw the EMS crew rolling a stretcher into the room with an obese, white male who was struggling to breath. His stridorous breath sounds were muffled by the non-rebreather oxygen mask EMS had placed on him as well as the loud hiss of high flow oxygen. The paramedic was a seasoned and well-skilled paramedic, gave a brief report as they transferred the man onto the bed. Christy immediately assessed the patient with a focused physical exam, concentrating on airway and breathing. She instantly realized they were in trouble. Obesity alone complicates the anatomy of the airway, often making intubation more difficult as well as limiting the area for the lungs to expand leaving less room for an oxygen reservoir. The man's face was badly burned. His facial hair was long and disheveled at the edges where it had not been burnt but the burned areas were reduced to stubbly remains, covering a soot-laden face. Christy pulled the mask down and had the patient open his mouth. His tongue was swollen and tinged black with soot. Christy could not see his throat. *Not good,* she thought to herself as she remained calm on the exterior. Christy replaced the mask and addressed the patient.

"Sir, I'm Doctor Tabrizi. I understand your beard lit on fire when you were lighting a cigarette. Were you wearing oxygen at the time?"

The patient nodded as he gasped for breath. Oxygen-rich facial hair was a virtual tinder box waiting to erupt in flames when people lit a cigarette.

"Okay, just checking. I know you're struggling to breathe. The burn injury is causing the tissues on your mouth and throat to swell which are severely constricting your airway. I think we will need to sedate you and place a breathing tube in your throat to help you breathe. Do I have your permission to do that?"

The patient, Mr. Knapp was his name, nodded his agreement.

"Very good, sir. We're going to get started right now," Christy patted him reassuringly on the shoulder.

She looked over and saw Alexis had already obtained an IV and was quickly securing it in place. Michael, the pharmacist, was opening up a small box of medications to assist with the intubation.

"Michael, let's go with forty milligrams of Etomidate and 180 of Succinylcholine, please," Christy said as she stepped over to the counter and opened the tackle box full of intubation supplies.

She readied an endotracheal tube and inserted a curved metal rod known as a stylet which would make the flexible soft plastic tube more rigid, allowing for better manipulation of the tube through the vocal cords. She opted for a video laryngoscope, a curved blade that was used to lift the tongue out of the way while a small camera allowed her to see the vocal cords on a computer screen. The degree of swelling warned her that she would not be able to see the cords without the video assistance. That gave Christy an idea.

"Lily, can you grab a bottle of topical Cetacaine spray for me? There's a bottle in the med room."

"On it!" The dutiful Lily said, as she dashed out of the room.

"Line's ready!" Alexis announced.

"Meds are ready," Michael followed.

"Very well, give the Etomidate but hold the Succinylcholine, please."

Being intubated would not be a pleasant experience. Etomidate was used to sedate patients, while Succinylcholine was used to paralyze them allowing for a relaxed airway that was more compliant to intubation. The downside was paralyzing the patient meant they could no longer breathe on their own. If Christy couldn't secure the airway quickly, the lack of oxygen would soon lead to cardiac arrest. Considering the likely difficulty she would have with this intubation, Christy decided to see if she could intubate without paralyzing Mr. Knapp. If she couldn't get the airway immediately, he would still be breathing, somewhat, on his own. This would buy her some time to find an alternative airway. Christy stood at the head of the bed and noticed Kristen Crosby was the respiratory therapist.

"Kristen, can you do me a favor and ready the fiberoptic scope with a 6.0 endotracheal tube? We may need it as a backup."

Kristen nodded and turned to set up the fiberoptic scope. Christy's new plan was to, hopefully, intubate Mr. Knapp without paralyzing him. The Cetacaine spray would temporarily numb his throat and suppress his gag reflex. In this case, it seemed the safer approach. Christy looked down and saw Mr. Knapp was as sedated as he was going to be. She lowered the head of the bed so that he was flat and placed a folded towel under his head to achieve optimal position. He was still breathing with his mouth partially open. Christy crossed her thumb and forefinger and inserted them between his upper and lower to teeth in attempt to pry his mouth open further. It wouldn't budge. *So much for that plan,* she thought to herself. It was a nice thought, anyway.

"Okay, give the Succinylcholine, please," Christy calmly ordered.

She nodded to Kristen to begin breathing for Mr. Knapp with the ambu-bag while they waited for him to be fully paralyzed. There was no going back now. This man's life depended on Christy successfully negotiating a very difficult airway. She silently prayed, asking God for help and then went to work.

Christy reinserted her right thumb and forefinger and pried Mr. Knapp's, now paralyzed, jaw open. The tongue was even more swollen. She inserted the video laryngoscope and swept the tongue as best she could and advanced the scope's blade into the throat. She looked up at the screen and watched for the vocal cords to appear. The camera was immediately blurred by a pool of secretions in the back of his throat. Christy immediately grabbed the suction catheter and inserted it into the throat. She suctioned the fluids, but the screen did not clear.

"Gauze, please," Christy called out as she removed the laryngoscope.

Kristen handed her a small square of gauze. Christy quickly cleaned the lens and reinserted the laryngoscope. The picture was improved, and she could now see the vocal cords. Christy took the endotracheal tube and inserted it into the airway. It wouldn't move past the tongue. Christy tried to reposition the laryngoscope and tongue as precious seconds ticked by. The airway and tongue were too swollen. There wasn't enough room for the tube to pass.

"Kristen, get the fiberoptic scope ready," Christy said, managing to keep her demeanor calm, despite the near panic welling up within her.

Christy grabbed a different laryngoscope. This one, a Miller blade, didn't have a camera but it was flat and thin, which she hoped would give her some space to work with. She inserted the blade, swept the tongue, and advanced down into the throat. Christy peered through the small opening, hoping to catch a glimpse of the vocal cords with her eyes but only saw swollen tissue. The seconds continued to tick by.

"Sats are dropping!" Emily warned. "Ninety-two percent."

"Alexis, take the laryngoscope from me and keep it in this position," Christy spoke as she demonstrated how she wanted it done.

Alexis moved next to Christy and assumed control of the laryngoscope. Her hands free, Christy took the fiberoptic scope and began to feed it into the airway. She toggled the manipulator switch and maneuvered the tip until the vocal cords appeared on the monitor screen.

"Ninety percent!" Emily called out.

Once the patient's oxygen saturation dropped below ninety percent, they decompensated quickly. Patients, like Mr. Knapp, with long-standing lung disease were a little more compensated at lower sats but this was getting too close. Christy maneuvered to tip of the scope through the vocal cords and into the trachea.

"Advance the tube, please, Kristen," Christy commanded, and she held the scope steady in effort to prevent it from slipping back out of the trachea.

"Eighty-eight percent! Eighty-six percent!"

Kristen began to slide the endotracheal tube down the length of the fiberoptic scope. Christy prayed it would have room to move past the tongue. It didn't.

"It's hung up, Doctor Tabrizi."

"Alexis, lift up on the tongue a little more, please," Christy spoke. "Try it now, Kristen."

"Eighty-three percent!"

"It's moving!" Kristen proclaimed.

Christy watched the screen. After what seemed like an eternity, the endotracheal tube appeared on the screen as it advanced past the camera at the tip of the scope.

"Thank you, Lord," Christy spoke out loud. "Okay, Kristen, hold the tube in place as I back out the scope."

Christy quickly removed the fiberoptic scope and set it aside. She then took hold of the endotracheal tube while Kristen attached an ambu-bag and began to squeeze it, pumping vital oxygen back into the lungs. Emily listened to the lungs with her stethoscope and gave a thumbs up, confirming good tube position as evidenced by good breath sounds on both sides.

"Sats are coming up! Eighty-eight percent...Ninety percent... ninety-two."

Christy and the entire room breathed a collective sigh of relief. She took over bagging Mr. Knapp while Kristen placed a harness around his face and secured the endotracheal tube. Kristen then attached a ventilator to the tube and relieved Christy. Christy placed her stethoscope on the patient's lungs and listened for herself. Satisfied, with the tube's position, she completed the rest of the exam, reviewed the current vital signs, and discussed vent settings with Kristen.

"If you guys could start him on a Propofol drip, Normal Saline at 150 cc's per hour and give him fifty micrograms of Fentanyl, I'll call the burn center and arrange a transfer. Thanks everyone. Good work!"

Christy started walking back to the work area. In the hallway stood two more EMS crews standing by their stretchers waiting for a place to drop their patients off. Both stretchers carried little old ladies. One black, one white. Neither looked very functional. Both looked quite old. *That won't be easy.* Christy almost made it to her desk when another nurse, Sharon Kisner, popped out of room 8 and waved in Christy's direction.

"C-Breeze! I need you in here!"

Christy changed course and headed for room 8. She hadn't even logged into her computer yet and she already had two critical patients. It was setting up to be another long and difficult night. *It never ends.*

Chapter 23

Atlanta, Georgia

Lindsay was nauseated. She feared it may be, in part, due to withdrawal from the heroin her captors had been forcing on her. She hoped it wasn't. She had never used drugs in her life. Ever since middle school, she had been a driven athlete, especially once she began training in Mixed Martial Arts. Over many years, Lindsay had developed and maintained a strict discipline of diet and exercise. Never once did she ever entertain drugs or even tobacco. Now she was having heroin forced into her system against her will. She would rather die than go down the dark path of addiction. Her brother, Joel, was an addict. She loved him beyond measure, but she couldn't stand seeing the destruction his addiction was doing to him. He chose to experiment with drugs. Lindsay still loved him and tried, many times, to convince him to get help, but he wasn't interested. Her parents didn't help. They enabled his lifestyle by getting him out of trouble and letting him live at home with little to no responsibilities. They meant well but couldn't see that what they were doing wasn't helping Joel. She vowed to escape her thug captors before she was fully addicted. Once addicted, there would be little to no chance for escape.

She hoped the nausea was due to the spoiled college guy who had bought her services again. A few nights ago it was him and his friends all making sport of her while one of her captor/pimps nonchalantly supervised. Tonight, however, he sat across a small table from her, wearing a navy blue blazer and striped tie. The coat had some type of crest over the heart. Before leaving the apartment, where Lindsay and the others were being held captive, the woman, Elena, had given her a matching blazer to change into along with a light blue oxford shirt and a short blue plaid skirt. According to Elena, the college boy, Clinton was his name, had requested Lindsay personally and sent the school uniform over, insisting she wear it to his house.

Lindsay looked around. College boy's friends were nowhere to be seen. Elena sat in the adjoining room playing with her cell phone. Vitaly had driven them over and originally stood watch in the room but college boy Clinton had requested Vitaly sit outside. Elena was allowed to remain. Apparently, this satisfied Elena and Vitaly stepped out.

Clinton had actually ordered in dinner from a fancy seafood restaurant and even set the table with candles. Not that she cared, but he insisted on Lindsay going by a different name; Bethany. By the way he was talking, Lindsay was under the impression that he was acting out a fantasy with this role playing. Maybe a high school crush? It was creepy, but, then again, any guy that was willing to spend money for a prostitute was creepy in her book.

"Bethany, my love, what troubles you? I've gone to great lengths to provide your favorite dinner and you've barely touched it."

Lindsay just shrugged her shoulders. What was she supposed to say? *This is so bizarre!*

"Are you troubled over breaking Kip's heart when you broke up with him for me?"

Lindsay looked up and quietly nodded. *Just go along with it. Maybe he'll use up his rented time talking.*

Clinton reached across the table and took her hand. His attempt at a reassuring smile came across as a patronizing smirk. Some women probably found him attractive, but Lindsay found his pompous demeanor and lascivious stare utterly repulsive. He reminded her of a softer version of Gaston, Belle's arrogant and brutish admirer from *Beauty and the Beast*. *Repulsive*, she repeated to herself.

"You did the right thing," he said, continuing with his smirk. "You're much better off with me. Once I complete law school, I'll follow my father's footsteps into public office. First Congress, then, one day, I will assume my father's seat in the Senate when he retires.

We will be treated like royalty. Wherever we go people will welcome us with a red carpet. They'll clamor for my favor, but it will be you they fawn over, my queen."

He gently kissed the back of her hand. Lindsay fought the urge to pull her hand away. As repulsive as this was, it was far better than what they could be doing. *Just play along, Lindsay.*

"We were always meant to be together, you and I," he spoke dramatically.

Whatever, Senator. Lindsay thought to herself.

"I've known it ever since high school. I knew, when you foolishly chose Kip over me, that you would eventually see I was the better choice. Kip may have been a football star, but his day is over. It was only a matter of time before you saw his shooting star fade over the horizon, while mine was just beginning to rise. And here I've been, Bethany, waiting for you. Waiting to rescue you," Clinton said as he began to stroke her hand with his thumb.

Oh this dude is whacked! Lindsay thought, as she struggled to keep a straight face. *What is he, living out some power-trip fantasy about some girl that blew him off in high school? Whacked.*

Lindsay decided to play along. She squeezed Clinton's hand and gave him a subtle smile.

"You are so right, Clinton," she started. "I was an immature schoolgirl, but I know better now." *Play to his ego,* Lindsay thought as a plan began to form in her mind.

Clinton's smirk intensified into a knowing smile. He nodded.

Does that mean he approves of my role playing or is he really that delusional?

"I know, my love. I know. I've always known, but that's okay. We're together now. I forgive you."

Delusional or textbook narcissist, Lindsay concluded. *Does he even remember what he and his pervert friends did to me the other night?*

Clinton stared at her with that annoying smirk. Lindsay gazed back with feigned interest.

Narcissist. A spoiled, entitled narcissist. Perfect, now I'm really nauseated.

Clinton stood and, still holding Lindsay's hand, led her up from her chair. He gave another sickening smirk and led her out of the dining room. Elena stood, but Clinton waved her back into her seat. He led her down the hall to his bedroom and shut the door. Lindsay's disgust ratcheted up a notch when she saw the room was lit up with candles and the bed was covered with rose petals. *Just who does he think he is trying to fool? Shoot, maybe he actually is delusional. Use it to your advantage, girl,* Lindsay thought to herself as her years of martial arts training instinctively kicked in.

Clinton turned and faced her. He brought his hands up and cradled her face. The pompous smirk reappeared.

"I've waited many years for this night, Bethany. I wanted to make it special, just for you. I hope you know just how much I care for you," Clinton spoke.

He closed his eyes and gently kissed Lindsay on her forehead. Then her eyelids. His breath reeked of stale cigarettes, wine, and garlic. It was bad, but she had suffered far worse the past few days with older men who were overweight, scruffy, and who didn't care an iota about personal hygiene. Lindsay pretended to enjoy Clinton's advances, patiently allowing him to kiss her as he removed her blazer. He set the blazer down and began to unfasten the top button of her shirt. Lindsay gently placed her hands on his chest, stared up into his eyes, and feigned a sultry smile. She slowly moved her hands up under his academy blazer and began to slip it off his shoulders. Clinton smiled and nodded encouragingly. Lindsay reached up, removed his tie, and draped it around her neck in a teasing manner. She then slowly began to unbutton his shirt, staring into his eyes as she poured it on thick with the smile. Clinton ate it up, smiling with delight. She unfastened the last button, slid her hands across his chest and under his shirt. She then slowly pulled the shirt off his shoulders and down his arms. She stopped as his shirt was halfway down his arms and pretended to claw his upper back before reaching up and cradling the back of his head. Lindsay looked up at Clinton, opened her mouth slightly and pulled him in for a kiss. Clinton slowly leaned in and closed his eyes.

With a blur of motion, Lindsay reared her head back, jerked Clinton's head down and delivered a bone crunching head butt to his nose.

She immediately followed this with a sharp knee to his groin followed by a hard jab to his soft solar plexus. Unable to breathe, Clinton doubled over in silence as blood freely flowed from his flattened nose. Lindsay delivered a hard elbow to the back of his neck, using his momentum to knock him forward onto his bed. She pounced on his back and applied a rear choke hold. Weakened by her attack, he was unable to resist and quickly passed out.

Lindsay wasted no time. She eased him face down on the floor and used his tie to bind his wrists behind his back, followed by his ankles with a lamp cord. She looped the excess lamp cord around the tie and secured the loop tightly, rendering him awkwardly hogtied. She opened his dresser and pulled out a pair of socks, one of which she stuffed in his mouth. Noticing that Clinton was starting to wake up, she applied another choke hold until he went back into unconsciousness.

Lindsay quickly searched his pockets and pulled out his wallet and cell phone. She removed the cash and tossed his wallet aside. She opened the cellphone, but it required a facial ID to unlock it. She pulled Clinton's head up by his hair and held the phone up to his face, praying his face wasn't too deformed for his phone to recognize. It worked. Lindsay quickly disabled the security feature and then disabled the phone location feature as well. She quietly rummaged through his dresser until she found a dark t-shirt and sweatpants. They were several sizes too big, but they would have to do. Lindsay quickly stripped out of her schoolgirl outfit and donned the t-shirt and sweatpants. She tied the sweatpants tight around her waist and pocketed the phone and cash.

Lindsay quietly unlocked the bedroom window and opened it. There was a screen in place, stretching the height of the sill. *Shoot!* She tried to quietly remove the screen, but it wouldn't budge. There were two small knobs on the bottom of the frame, which she assumed were the pins that secured the screen in place. She tried to pull them out, but they were corroded from years of non-use and would not budge. Clinton began to stir as Lindsay frantically looked around his room. On the corner of his desk was a letter opener.

Prissy boy doesn't have a pocketknife, but he has a letter opener. Go figure, she thought to herself as she used the letter opener to cut open the screen.

Clinton began to grunt, but, thankfully, his mouth was muffled by the sock. Lindsay thought about subduing him one last time but decided against it. It was time to escape. She finished cutting open the screen and looked out. Vitaly's black BMW was backed in the driveway but there was no sign of Vitaly. Lindsay couldn't tell if he was in the car or walking around. She would have to chance it. She swung a leg up onto the windowsill and readied herself for the six-foot drop. Suddenly, the bedroom door burst open. Elena stood in the doorway with a Glock handgun pointed toward Lindsay.

"You move and you're dead, *shlyukha!*"

Chapter 24

Atlanta, Georgia

"*G*et your leg out of the window or I'll shoot the other one," Elena spoke forcefully, with her thick Russian accent.

Lindsay froze as she weighed her options. *Do I call her bluff and jump?*

As if reading Lindsay's mind, Elena fired a shot into the wall, just missing Lindsay's leg. The loud report brought Clinton back to full alertness. He stared in a wide-eyed panic at Elena as he struggled against his bindings. Lindsay slowly removed her leg from the window and stood with her hands raised.

"That's better, *shlyukha*. Now, walk slowly past me and out the door."

"Are you sure you want to do that?" Lindsay asked. "I called the police a few minutes ago. They will be here any minute. You've got just enough time to get away."

"You don't scare me," Elena sneered. "We own the police. They will do nothing to us. We pay them much more than the city does. They look out for us. It's good business."

"There is no way you own all of the police in this city!" Lindsay shot back.

"No?" Elena calmly asked, her dark eyebrows arched. "Okay. We wait. You'll see."

Elena shrugged her shoulders, pulled out Clinton's leather swivel desk chair, and sat down.

"You're right," she said nonchalantly. "We don't own all the police, but we own enough. Especially some important ones. They're all smart enough to know not to arrest the senator's son. Many are customers of our bordello. We give them girl, *on the house,* as you Americans say. They know right where we work but they never bother us. Why do you think that is, *shlyukha?*"

Lindsay was caught off guard. All she could do was shrug her shoulders.

"Aha, not so smart now, are you?"

Vitaly appeared in the doorway, breathless from having run in when he heard the gunshot.

"It's okay, Vitaly," Elena said reassuringly. "The *shlyukha* thought she could outsmart us and tried to escape. Take her out to the car while I fix things with the senator's son."

"*Da,*" Vitaly relied dutifully, as he walked into the room and grabbed Lindsay by her right arm.

In his right arm, he casually held a Glock pistol trained at Lindsay's torso. He marched Lindsay out of the room as Elena stooped down to untie Clinton. As they walked toward the front door, Lindsay could hear Clinton screaming at Elena. He went on about getting his money back and referring to Lindsay as "a psycho whore." Lindsay smiled inwardly.

The inward smile was quickly erased as she realized just how close she had come to escaping this nightmare. She should have taken her chances and jumped out the window. Elena might not have shot. No that wasn't true. They had no problem killing Chelsea yesterday. They weren't about to take a chance on someone escaping and pulling down their organization. Lindsay knew she and the other girls could all be replaced. They would have no problem putting a bullet in her. *I still should have jumped,* Lindsay scolded herself. *I'd rather die trying to escape than endure this hell any longer.*

They reached the car and Vitaly instructed her to get in the back. Lindsay turned and faced him.

"No! I'm not going back. I can't go back," Lindsay snarled. "Do you have even a shred of humanity? How can you do this?"

"As you Americans say, *it's a living,*" Vitaly said nonchalantly.

"Well, it's a dark, miserable existence for me! I'm done! You may as well shoot me right here because I am *not* getting in that car!"

Vitaly leveled his gun and placed it on Lindsay's forehead.

"That can be arranged," he sneered through crooked yellow teeth.

In a blur of motion, Lindsay's right arm circled across her left side and up into Vitaly's forearm as she sidestepped and pivoted out of the gun's line of fire. She grasped his forearm with her left hand while grasping the top of the gun with her right and pulled him down and into her. Using her body weight, she wrenched his wrist and arm inward until his muscles lost their mechanical advantage and his grip loosened. Lindsay yanked the gun away while delivering a swift kick to Vitaly's chest, allowing her to gain some separation. She quickly racked the gun's slide and turned toward him.

"Get down on the ground!" She commanded, pointing Vitaly's gun at him. "Now!"

Vitaly snarled and charged. Lindsay fired three quick rounds and Vitaly fell at her feet. She shot another round into his head, just to be sure. She knelt beside him and quickly searched his pockets. She removed his wallet, cell phone, a spare magazine for the gun and the car keys.

"Hey! Stop!" Elena yelled as she ran in Lindsay's direction.

Lindsay fired two shots toward Elena who fell forward. Lindsay wasn't sure whether she hit Elena or made her dive for cover, but she wasn't waiting around to find out. She jumped into the car, found the start button, and fired it up. She shifted the car into gear and floored the gas. Gunshots rang out behind her as she raced out of the drive-way and, not knowing which direction to turn, opted to turn right. She was instinctively keeping as much car between her and Elena's gun as possible. The rear passenger window shattered and something struck Lindsay in the right chest. She kept driving. The gunshots sounded louder through the back window, but they suddenly stopped. Lindsay figured Elena was out of ammunition. It was of no consequence; she was rapidly gaining speed and out of range.

Lindsay purposefully ignored the sharp pain in her right side as she pulled out Clinton's phone and powered it on. Her original plan was to call the police but, after Elena's revelation, Lindsay wasn't sure she could trust the police. Perhaps Elena was bluffing, but Lindsay decided it wasn't worth the risk. She would put Atlanta in the rear-view mirror and head out of state as quickly as possible. If she was pulled over, she would tell the police the truth. The truth was on her side. She thumbed a driving app and glanced at it trying to figure out where she was. She looked up and realized too late that she had just driven through a stop sign. There were no cars on the residential street, but she hoped there wasn't a police officer parked while watching the intersection. No flashing lights appeared. Lindsay breathed a sigh of relief.

At the next intersection, she turned right and drove two blocks before turning left to resume a parallel course. She then felt safe enough to pull over and work the app. She decided the first priority was to get out of Georgia. She entered in Greenville, South Carolina and resumed driving. Once in Greenville, she would call the police and tell them about the other girls in the apartment. She had memorized the location Tracy had shared with her after pulling it up on Erik's phone during last night's catastrophe. She would ditch the car in Greenville and call her parents. Only when she was back in her father's house, with a lawyer present, would she call the police and tell them about the incident back at the delusional college boy's house. Lindsay wondered whether or not the press would bury the story or have a feeding frenzy. A senator's son, prostitution ring, murdered pimp. She guessed it would depend on the senator's political party.

Lindsay breathed a slight sigh of relief as she turned down the on-ramp for Interstate 85 North. Greenville was only two hours away. Traffic was light. She could have gone faster but didn't want to risk being pulled over. Lindsay felt her adrenaline ebb with every passing mile, and the sharp pain in her right side became more noticeable. Breathing seemed to make it worse. Had she been hit? Using the back of her right hand, she felt the side of her ribs. It felt wet. *No!* Lindsay held her hand up under the dashboard lights and her concern was confirmed; blood.

It can't be that bad. I feel okay. Maybe it just nicked me?

Her thoughts began to race as she drove up the interstate. Was she well enough to continue on to Greenville? Rural Georgia stretched most of the way between Atlanta and Greenville. Should she get off and go to a hospital before she got too far into the country? What Elena said about the police weighed heavily in her mind. Lindsay absolutely did not want to risk being caught by an officer on the take and returned to Sergei's outfit. She would rather die out here on the road. Not one more beating, not one more shot of heroin, and not one more night of strange men raping her. That's what it was. Rape. Forcing themselves on a woman against her will. It didn't matter that they paid for it. Sergei was the one being paid. Lindsay and the others were simply sexual slaves. The only way she was going back was with a gun so she could shoot every last one of Sergei's outfit.

The loud vibrating noise of the rumble strip on the side of the interstate snapped Lindsay back to attention. *Was I falling asleep?* Admittedly, she was feeling drowsy. The adrenaline was mostly worn off and she hadn't been allowed to sleep much over the past several days. Too busy servicing Sergei's never-ending parade of clients. Lindsay felt herself starting to drift off again. She noticed that she was beginning to have a hard time catching her breath. She felt her right side again. The entire lower half of the shirt was wet, as was the car seat. *Am I bleeding out? Is that what's going on? And why am I having a hard time breathing?*

The rumble strip sounded again. Lindsay over corrected the steering wheel and nearly sideswiped the car passing on her left. The driver blared his horn as he sped by. Lindsay could barely make out the car as she realized her vision was blurry. Something was definitely wrong. She must be bleeding out and going into shock. She fought off the panic and decided she was going to have to find a hospital, and fast. She tried to operate the phone app to search for a hospital but her right arm was too weak to pull it off. Her left arm wasn't doing that much better with the steering wheel. She noticed a lot of colorful lights and restaurant signs lining each side of the interstate and assumed she was in a populated area. She watched the exit signs praying she would see a blue sign with a white letter H. *There!* Up ahead was an exit sign with a small hospital marker attached. Due to the blurriness, Lindsay had trouble making out the name of the exit. *Pleasant Hill Road?* Something like that. She veered onto the off-ramp, desperately trying to stay in the lane. The light was green allowing her to turn left as she followed the signs for the hospital. She barely had enough strength to turn the wheel. She followed the road, hoping the hospital was close as she felt she was on the verge of passing out. The road began to meander, making it increasingly difficult for Lindsay to stay in her lane. A loud horn blared as headlights filled her vision and caused Lindsay to veer right, barely avoiding a collision.

Finally, the sign for the hospital appeared up ahead. Lindsay was grateful she even saw it. She carefully turned left and followed the signs leading her to the emergency department which took her around the left side of the hospital toward the back. She drove up to the entrance, put the car in park, and shut off the engine. She opened the door and mustered the strength to stand to her feet. She felt wobbly and had to steady herself with the door. She stumbled through the sliding doors and found her way to a seat in front of a registration desk. The waiting room was filled with a hodgepodge of people, most of whom appeared angry or impatient, while others talked or played on their cellphones.

"May I help you, ma'am?" The registration clerk looked at Lindsay from the other side of the desk.

"Yes. I need to see a doctor," Lindsay said, surprised at how difficult it was to summon the breath to speak.

"Of course. What is your chief complaint today?"

"I think I've been shot."

Chapter 25

Duluth, Georgia

*C*hristy clicked the button to send a prescription to a local pharmacy. She slowly shook her head in disbelief. The patient had bumped her elbow on a doorframe, insisted on X-rays when there was no sign of fracture and now, with no fracture seen on X-ray, was demanding oxycodone by name. Christy tried to explain that a bruised elbow did not warrant a prescription for opiate pain medicine, but the patient was not willing to accept that. In the back of her mind, Christy was cognizant of the future patient satisfaction survey this patient would be filling out. Hospital administrators placed great importance on these surveys and wanted the doctors to create happy patients who would, theoretically, fill out highly satisfied surveys. At many hospitals, these surveys directly factored into a doctor's performance driven compensation and even their future retention as an employee. Christy, ever the idealist, was more concerned about practicing sound medicine and doing what was in the patient's best interest. She was able to negotiate this patient into a prescription for a strong anti-inflammatory. It was the right thing to do and, who knows, maybe she wouldn't receive a terrible survey. *Fat chance.*

Christy closed out the chart and looked on the main board to see who was next to be seen. Even at this late hour, there were still many patients in the waiting room. There were five in rooms that were still waiting to be seen. All were level three priority. Christy clicked on the one with the longest wait time. It was a fifty-three-year-old female with "multiple complaints." Christy winced as she read the triage nurse's synopsis; abdominal pain radiating into the legs, nausea, headache, chest pain, and sore throat. The patient had a long list of medical problems and an equally long list of medicine allergies. Christy leaned back in her chair, closed her eyes, and groaned. Patient's bringing in a list of complaints were seldom easy to work up and, quite often, there were no serious problems found. This usually perplexed and upset the patient leading to many more questions and complaints. They often took up a lot of time and resources which made a very busy ER shift even more difficult.

Christy savored leaning back with her eyes closed. The first night back was always an adjustment. A ten-minute rest would feel so good right now. Christy would have settled for five minutes. As it was, there wasn't time even for one minute. She opened her eyes, stood up and began to head to the patient's room.

"TRAUMA LEVEL ONE, NOW! TRAUMA LEVEL ONE, NOW!" Came a female voice over the PA system.

"Mittelschmerz!" Christy uttered her substitution for a curse word and quickened her pace as she diverted toward the trauma/critical care pod.

Things were busy enough as it is. Of the three levels of trauma, a Level One was the most serious. Examples included penetrating injuries to the chest or abdomen from such things as a gunshot or a knife stabbing. It could also be a person involved in a bad car wreck with unstable vital signs. The fact that this one was announced overhead meant the person came through the front door as opposed to an ambulance. An ambulance usually radioed ahead what they were bringing in and how far they were out, allowing the Emergency Personnel a few minutes to prep. Not this one. All Christy could do was beat feet to the trauma bay and deal with whatever was being wheeled back.

"Anybody know what's coming in?" Christy asked as she entered the room.

"No clue, C-breeze," Emily said as she readied a mayo tray with IV supplies.

Christy glanced down the long hall as she threw on a pair of gloves. She saw the triage nurse, Bobbi Brock, and the fast track nurse,

Suzanne Matthews, pushing a stretcher along with Grant Bosheers, one of the security guards.

"Gunshot to the chest!" Bobbi yelled ahead as they approached the room.

"Any vitals?" Christy asked.

"No, she drove up and nearly collapsed in triage," Bobbi said breathlessly. "We brought her right back."

Christy looked down and saw a young brunette, struggling to breathe, wearing a blood-soaked baggy t-shirt and sweatpants. "Ma'am, I'm Christy Tabrizi. I'm one of the ER doctors here. Can you tell me your name?"

"Lindsay Meehan," she spoke weakly.

"Okay, Lindsay, we're going to take good care of you," Christy said reassuringly.

Like a well-choreographed ballet, the team of nurses and techs went to work. Lily used a set of trauma sheers to quickly cut off all of Lindsay's clothes, while Emily began to prep Lindsay's left arm for an IV. Alexis hung two liter bags of Normal Saline to rapidly run through the IV's. Sharon began asking Lindsay for her birthdate, social security number, and basic medical information and entered it into the computer. Another CNA, Ronika, appeared with a cooler containing Type O negative blood.

"Take some deep breaths, please," Christy requested as she placed her stethoscope on Lindsay's chest.

Christy immediately noticed that Lindsay's right chest was absent of breath sounds. The lung was normally inflated and in direct contact with the chest wall. The lack of breath sounds suggested that there was either air between the collapsed lung and chest wall, what is known as a *pneumothorax,* or there was blood in that space, known as a *hemothorax.* The left lung sounded good as did Lindsay's heart sounds.

"Breath sounds absent on the right, normal on the left," Christy called out to Sharon who dutifully wrote down the findings.

Christy then assessed Lindsay's pulses; first the radial pulse on both wrists, then the dorsal pedal pulses on the feet.

"Peripheral pulses are weak but palpable, one plus times four. Blood pressure is 84/40. Give both units of Type O negative, please and send for more," she called out. "Lindsay, can you wiggle your toes for me?"

Lindsay immediately moved her toes around.

"Good," Christy said, as she moved to the head of the bed and shined a light in Lindsay's eyes. "Tell me what city we are in and what month this is?"

"We're near Atlanta and it's September."

"Good. Thank you," Christy gently patted her patient on the shoulder. "Pupils are six millimeters and reactive bilaterally. Glasgow Coma Scale is fifteen. Let's get a chest X-ray, please."

"Fifteen? Is that bad?" Lindsay asked.

"No. Quite the opposite," Christy answered. "It means you're perfectly normal and not showing any signs of head injury."

"That's good but I don't feel normal. I feel so weak and I can't catch my breath."

"Well, we're about to address that," Christy said as she pulled the portable ultrasound machine over. "I think your lung is injured from the gunshot wound. You've also lost a lot of blood. We're getting a chest X-ray to look at your lungs, while I use ultrasound to look for any bleeding around your heart or in your abdomen."

Christy deftly maneuvered the ultrasound probe around Lindsay's chest. The heart was pumping well but the left ventricle was collapsing, indicating Lindsay's blood volume was low. There was no blood around the heart. Christy moved the probe down to Lindsay's abdomen and checked the three most likely areas for blood to collect; between the liver and right kidney, between the spleen and left kidney, and deep in the pelvis. Christy was relieved to see that all three were clear.

"FAST exam is negative," she called out using the common acronym for *Focused Assessment with Sonography for Trauma* ultrasound test.

"Clear for X-ray!" Nina, the nighttime radiology technologist called out.

Christy and all the staff, who weren't wearing lead aprons stepped out into the hall to avoid unnecessary exposure to the radiation. Nina recently returned from a prolonged personal leave. Christy was glad to have her back. A veteran of the ER and a fellow nocturnal creature, Nina was the consummate professional when she wasn't laughing and smiling. She fit right in with the Night-force Elite.

"What do we have, Christy?" Came a familiar voice from behind her.

Christy turned and saw the tall, forty-ish Dr. Jeffrey Wilcox. Wilcox was the current Chief of Surgery and a favorite of many due to his pleasant demeanor and solid surgical acumen. Christy was very pleased to see him standing there.

"Hey, Jeff. Thank you for coming in so fast."

"I was here. Just finished up an appendectomy in the OR. So what do we have?"

"Twenty-year-old, white female with a gunshot wound to the right chest. We're getting a chest X-ray right now, but my guess is a hemothorax. BP was 84/40 with weak pulses but we're infusing IV fluids, and I just ordered blood. FAST is negative, including the heart."

"Well, if that's what it is, I'll put a chest tube in her down here. If we can stabilize her, I'll take her to CT scan, if not, then I may have to crack her chest, but I'd prefer to do that in the OR."

"X-ray's up!" Nina called over to Christy and Wilcox.

Both stepped up to look at the image on the portable X-ray unit's screen. The left lung appeared normal, but the right lung was pure white confirming a large hemothorax.

"There you have it," Wilcox commented. "I'll set up for a chest tube if you don't mind finishing the secondary."

"Works for me, Jeff. Thank you."

Christy was trained to place chest tubes and did so often enough but was always happy to share duties. Many hands make light work. She efficiently conducted a secondary survey; a head to toe physical exam looking for any other injuries. They rolled Lindsay onto her left side. Christy, Wilcox, and Alexis gasped when they saw the red stripes. Christy looked for and located the gunshot wound; a small one-centimeter hole just lateral to her right shoulder blade. No other wounds were seen, suggesting the bullet was still in her chest. Dr. Wilcox began prepping Lindsay's right side with Betadine. Christy looked up at the monitor at saw the blood pressure was slightly improved to 91/54. She decided to stay with Lindsay and make sure she didn't crash while Dr. Wilcox was placing the chest tube. If she was still actively bleeding, they would know relatively soon.

"You've been shot, and you have a bunch of horizontal stripes across your back and buttocks. Do you mind if I ask what happened?" Christy asked, leaning in close.

"Long story," Lindsay said looking up at the ceiling. "The Cliff's Notes version is; I was kidnapped while going for a run five days ago and was forced into prostitution. One of my pimps shot me while I was trying to escape."

Christy raged on the inside but maintained a level of calm.

"What did they do to you?"

"They beat me, raped me, whipped me with a fan belt, injected me with heroin, and pimped me out about ten to twenty times a day. And then they shot me."

"Animals," Christy said quietly.

"You're right," Lindsay responded icily.

She winced, slightly, as Dr. Wilcox gave a brief warning and then began to inject Lidocaine into the nerve under her fifth rib.

"Do the police know?" Christy asked.

"No!" Alarm flashed across Lindsay's face. "You can't tell them! They're in on it. I think the gang that was pimping us is Russian mafia. They said they own the police and I believe them!"

"Whoa, whoa, Lindsay," Christy said in a calming manner. "You're our patient now. We aren't going to let anything happen to you. Trust me."

"I trust you. I just don't know if we can trust the police. There are others. We have to get them out of there before we tell the police. The police will tell the mafia and then they'll just move the other girls. We can't let that happen. They'll keep abusing the others until they have no more use for them and then they'll kill them. We *have* to help them! Someone has to rescue them!"

"How are we supposed to rescue them if we don't tell the police?"

"I don't know, but there has to be somebody who can go down there and rescue them. I know exactly where they are. There are at least eight more being kept upstairs in a building across from a Walmart on Clairmont Road near 141. I have their names. Write them down. Tracy Courtnall…"

"Wait, let me get out my pen," Sharon requested from the computer. "Okay, go ahead."

"Tracy Courtnall," Lindsay continued. "Darcy Kerrigan, Rebecca King, and Chelsea Hammond. The leader, Sergei, shot her to death yesterday. Somebody *has* to go rescue them!" She pleaded.

Christy saw Dr. Wilcox make his initial incision. Lindsay didn't seem to notice. Her eyes remained locked on Christy's as she pled the case for the other girls. Wilcox worked fast. He penetrated the muscle between the ribs with a large curved hemostat. Blood began to ooze out. He opened the hemostat to enlarge the hole which caused the blood to rapidly flow out. He then inserted a clear plastic tube and hooked it up to a suction device. Blood flowed out in a rapid state. The *Pleurovac*, a collection device that measures the output, could take a liter of fluid. It was filled up with blood and overflowing within a minute. Blood continued to flow out through the tube. Wilcox muttered an expletive and clamped the chest tube.

"Call the OR," Wilcox spoke urgently. "Tell them we're on our way!"

"Pressure's dropping!" Alexis called out. "76/32!"

"Would you like me to intubate her, Jeff?" Christy asked.

"No time for that, Christy. I'll have anesthesia take care of it. Let's roll, people!"

Lindsay looked up at Christy and squeezed her arm. "Promise me, you'll send help! Promise me!"

"I will, I promise." Christy said as the nurses began to wheel Lindsay out the door.

Christy was suddenly all alone in the trauma bay. The floor was littered with discarded gloves, gauze, syringes, and all of usual supplies rapidly used during a trauma resuscitation. There was a pool of fresh blood six feet in diameter with bloody footprints leading out the door.

Christy took a minute to collect herself. She could still hear Lindsay's desperate plea to help the other girls. She knew most police officers were, by and large, honorable, honest, and decent men and women who put their lives on the line to protect others. Conversely, a few months ago, Joe had nearly been killed by the mafia in Niagara Falls. Several dirty cops, owned by the mafia, played a role in that incident making Christy inclined to believe Lindsay's assertion. If they couldn't trust the police to rescue those other girls, who could they trust? Christy could only think of two. Joe and Chief Ramsey. *But how can I ask them? I can't do that! It's not fair to them. There has to be another way,* Christy thought to herself.

She searched her brain but couldn't think of another option. They would have to risk the police. The odds had to be in their favor. There couldn't be that many crooked cops. She quickly remembered that it only took three in Joe's case. She also promised Lindsay that she wouldn't involve the police until *after* the other girls were safe. Her thoughts returned to Joe and Ramsey. Once again, she dismissed that thought. How could she ask them to risk their lives for someone they didn't know? *Isn't that what they do for a living?* Yes, but this was different. Way different. The debate inside Christy's head became overwhelming. She decided to do what always worked best for her when she couldn't make a decision. Christy folded her hands and bowed her head.

Lord, please heal Lindsay physically and emotionally. Guide the hands of Jeffrey Wilcox and all those providing care for her. Please protect the other girls and send someone to rescue them. I don't want to ask Joe, but I don't know who else to ask. Please give me the wisdom to know what to do or just send someone right now to deliver them. In Jesus' name I pray, Amen.

Christy stood up and walked back to her desk. The ER was still buzzing. An emotional trauma didn't change that. She needed to get back into the saddle and knock out some charts. She stopped in her tracks as she neared her desk. Standing before her, grinning widely were Joe and Chief Ramsey.

"What are you guys doing here?" Christy asked pleasantly surprised.

"We figured you might be dragging a little your first night back after the Ironman, so we brought you a thermos of genuine Navy Chief Petty Officer's Top Secret Salty Brew." Joe said, holding up a stainless-steel thermos.

"You mean like what you made us on the sailboat?"

Ramsey began to guffaw. "Whatever bilge water this cake eater brewed cannot compare to what's in that thermos. We Chiefs have to take a vow of silence when we learn that special coffee."

"Well thank you, Matt. I'm sure this will be just the ticket to get me through this shift."

"Yeah," Joe said taking on a serious tone. "Doctor LaPointe said that you guys are getting killed and that you were in with a bad trauma. Everything go alright?"

"Uh..." Christy said looking around as the previous debate resumed in her head.

She was quickly reminded that she had just prayed for help with the issue. Standing before her were the two people most capable of handling the situation. She had dismissed the thought earlier but could not ignore the fact that, as unlikely as it was, here they were.

"Come with me," she said as she turned and led them into a supply room.

"Christy, what's going on? Is our being here going to cause trouble?" Joe asked.

"No," Christy shook her head with her eyes closed in thought. "It's nothing like that. I love that you guys came in. It made my night! It's just that, well, the trauma I just took care of has me a bit shaken up."

"Why? What happened, Joe asked as he hopped up onto a counter for a seat.

Christy spent the next several minutes explaining what Lindsay had revealed.

"What's that address again?" Ramsey said as he opened up his phone.

"No. You guys! I'm not asking you to act on this," Christy protested. "I'm wondering if you have any ideas how to help them."

"Besides us or the police? None, Christy. There isn't time to figure out another option," Joe said. "Rammer and I will handle it."

"I don't want you to handle it! It's too dangerous. She said these guys are hardcore. They're not going to let you just waltz in and walk out with those girls. They may try to shoot you."

"We're used to that," Ramsey shrugged dismissively.

"Christy," Joe said taking her hands in his. "We swore an oath to protect and defend. It wasn't so we could wear a uniform. It's because that's who we are. It's what we do. Chief and I know how to handle this. We'll go down and recon the place first. If it looks actionable, then we'll exercise every precaution and we'll get those girls back. Those are people's daughters. What's being done to them is not right. If we can handle it, we will."

"Promise me you'll be careful, Joe O'Shanick?"

"I promise."

"I'll make sure he does. Just like always, ma'am," Ramsey said, now in full Chief Petty Officer mode.

Christy cracked a smile at Ramsey.

"Okay, you two. I do appreciate this. Keep me posted."

"Will do," Ramsey said as he started for the door. "I'll wait for you outside, Joe."

Joe hopped off the counter and gave Christy a long hug. After a minute, Christy leaned back and looked up into Joe's eyes.

"I'm really looking forward to you guys moving here. I think this will be really good for us. Please be careful tonight. I'm praying for you."

"I will, hon, I promise."

Joe gave Christy a quick kiss and held her hand as they walked out into the ER. They separated, their hands lingering until the distance pulled them apart. Joe turned for a final wave and disappeared out the door with Ramsey. Christy's gaze lingered at the door as it closed. The sound of the EMS radio chirping an incoming call jarred her back to reality. Christy sighed and returned to her work.

Chapter 26

Atlanta, Georgia

" *M*an, what I wouldn't give for some ISR coverage, right now," Ramsey commented as he and Joe studied the building in question.

ISR stands for Intelligence, Surveillance and Reconnaissance, often provided by military drones flying over an area of interest or conflict. It provided military personnel with real time information using video feed, infra-red, and other means of eavesdropping and reconnaissance. After leaving the hospital, Joe and Ramsey hastily returned to Critter's home to properly outfit themselves for this impromptu mission. Upon learning what they were planning, Critter took them into his basement where he had a gun-smithing shop along with a wide array of weapons and equipment. Joe and Ramsey refused to take any of Critter's weapons. They had their personal handguns and didn't want to use anything that could blow back on Critter, should this op go south. Critter understood but insisted on outfitting them with a rudimentary form of communications. He provided each with a set of Razor shooter's earmuffs that had electronic hearing enhancement but reacted instantly to loud sounds, such as gunfire, by briefly shutting off the sound to protect one's hearing. They had an audio jack to which Critter attached small mounted two-way radios with boom mikes made by the same company for the earmuffs. This provided Joe and Ramsey a way to communicate with a range of up to three miles. Critter gave them several other useful items as well. He also offered to come along but Joe wouldn't think of placing their host at risk.

Joe and Ramsey had taken up position on opposite sides of the building where the girls were being held. Joe was across the street, on the sidewalk of Clairmont Road, an elevated street above the building, watching the front of the building. Ramsey watched the back entrance, where the garage doors were.

"I hear you, Rammer. I know the upstairs windows are boarded up, but I'm getting the feeling that there is nobody home. If they really are pimping a dozen or so girls out of there, we should at least be seeing some foot traffic. So far nothing."

"You want to go take a closer look?" Ramsey suggested.

"Not yet. No sooner did I say that and then I've got two males walking in that direction. Let's see if they drop in for a visit."

"Roger that," Ramsey answered. "Keep me posted. I'm blind back here."

"Nag, nag, nag," Joe teased, as he studied the two individuals.

Two forty-ish appearing males walked at a rapid pace with their heads down. They approached the main entrance, a glass door with the contracting business' name and number stenciled on the upper half. One of the males tried the door but it was locked. They looked at their watches and shrugged. One of the men walked out a few feet and looked up at the second floor. Apparently, he didn't see what he was looking for. After about a minute, they turned and walked back in the direction from which they came.

"Shoot, Rammer, I think they've bugged out. Our two John's just left disappointed. The door was locked. I say we go in and take a look. Rally point in five."

"Roger that, Joe."

The rally point was a designated spot under a large tree just below Clairmont Road. Ramsey was melted into the tree when Joe arrived.

"There's a back entrance that isn't lit up, Joe. We can pick the lock and sneak in through there unless you think the front is better."

"That works. No telling when another John may come walking up," Joe said gesturing for Ramsey to lead the way.

They quietly scaled a fence in the least observable spot and stayed close to the back wall of the building as they crept around to the door. Ramsey removed a lock pick set and went to work on the dead bolt and knob. He had both unlocked in under two minutes. He replaced the pick set and readied his handgun. Both were carrying a Smith and Wesson M&P Shield 9mm. Ramsey slowly opened the door. He stopped it immediately when he detected the first hint of a squeak. Joe turned his back and Ramsey removed a small can of WD-40 from his pack. He applied a liberal amount to each hinge and slowly worked the door open. They were in.

The inside of the garage was dimly lit by an outdoor light shining through a grimy window. They quietly picked their way through until they found the door to the entrance area. Ramsey tried the knob and found it unlocked. He slowly opened the door into a similarly dark room. A quick search of the room found it empty other than some office furniture. They made their way down the hall to a stairwell tucked into the back wall. Joe peaked around and looked upstairs. It was completely dark. He listened for any sign of activity and heard none. Shaking his head, he gestured toward Ramsey, indicating he couldn't detect anything. They both donned a set a of night vision goggles and started up the stairs.

Joe kept to the edges to minimize any chance at a loose step groaning under his weight. They reached the top of the stairs and found a landing with four open doors, two to a side. A quick look in each room showed no sign of any person. They entered the first door and realized they were in an apartment. A couple of folding tables were set up along with a longer folding table and some folding chairs. They cleared both bedrooms and found a single mat and a folding chair in one. No people and, thankfully, no dead women. One by one, they cleared the other three apartments. The place was deserted.

"It's as empty as a ship's chapel during shore leave," Ramsey said as he disengaged his night vision goggles.

"Yeah, no kidding," Joe agreed as he raised his goggles and switched on a helmet mounted flashlight. "We probably missed them by at least an hour. Let's have a look around."

Ramsey switched on his light and followed Joe into the first apartment. Aside from the abandoned tables and chairs, there wasn't much else in the living room. The kitchen had a trash can overflowing with fast food wrappers and empty water bottle and energy drink cans. The countertop had more cans and refuse. The freezer held two bottles of high-end Russian vodka and an assortment of candy bars.

"If they left their vodka, they bugged out in a hurry," Ramsey said as he pulled out a frozen Kit Kat and tore into it. "I love these things."

"Me too," Joe said. "But we probably shouldn't touch anything else. This place is likely a crime scene."

"Roger that," Ramsey said taking a bite of his candy bar.

The refrigerator was loaded with energy drinks and bottled water. In the corner were several more cases of bottle water. The bedrooms were mostly empty with the exception of a solitary mat left in one room along with a folding chair in each room. Joe caught something as his flashlight swept over the far corner. He leaned in close to get a better look.

"Hey, Rammer, take a look at this,"

"What do you have, Joe?'

"That girl's name was Lindsay Meehan. Look. Her name is scratched into the paint along with the names of four other girls. That confirms we've got the right place. We just missed them. Let's see if they left anything else for us."

Joe used his cellphone to take a picture of what he found. He then stood up and gave the room a thorough once over before checking the other room again. They found nothing else of use. They moved on to the next apartment. There were inflatable mattresses on the floors of each room including the dining room and living room. Trash cans full of used condoms were also found in each room. The other two apartments yielded the same findings.

"Looks like the first apartment was the operations center and the other three were the entertainment rooms," Ramsey said as they stepped out into the landing. "They must have kept..."

Ramsey stopped talking in mid-sentence when he saw Joe freeze and incline his head toward the stairwell. Joe shut off his flashlight, slowly backed away from the stairs, and took up position from the side with his handgun pointed at the stairwell. Using hand signals, he communicated to Ramsey that he heard people downstairs. Ramsey shut off his flashlight as he took up position behind the doorframe of the nearest apartment and trained his gun on the stairwell.

Joe saw what looked like several flashlight beams begin to dance around in the stairwell. They grew brighter and were accompanied by the faint sound of several feet working their way up the stairs. He waited, patiently as the first man reached the top of the stairs. The flashlight beam was pointed away from Joe, but he could see enough to determine the man was wearing a headlight. A second man appeared behind the first one. Both appeared to be armed with handguns held at the low ready position.

"DON"T MOVE!" Joe yelled.

Chapter 27

Atlanta, Georgia

"Slowly place your guns to the ground. You try anything and I'll put a round through your ear," Joe commanded.

Both men complied, slowly placing their guns on the floor as ordered. They stood back up, with hands raised.

"Good. Now kick your guns to your left and then lay face down with your hands over your heads."

Both men did as instructed. Joe saw a glow in the stair well. He raised his voice.

"The two gentlemen in the stairwell are to slowly walk upstairs holding their guns by the barrel with the hand grip facing us."

The men complied and Joe had them place their guns on the ground and kick them aside when they reached the top of the stairs. He then had them join their two friends on the ground.

"Good. I don't want any more surprises. If there's anyone else downstairs, I want them up here now in a similar fashion."

"It's just the four of us, the lead man said with an American accent."

"Are you sure?" Joe asked. "Because if there is even one more person down there, the first round goes in your ear."

"It's just us," he said with resignation. "Can we talk?"

"In a minute," Joe responded. "One of my teammates as going to search you. Turn off your headlamps and then keep your hands clasped behind your heads."

Joe turned on the mini-flashlight mounted to his helmet. Ramsey quickly and methodically searched each of the four men. His search found no further guns but did produce wallets, cellphones, two multi-tools, a lock pick set, and several pocketknives. Joe looked through the wallets and sighed.

"Alright, you guys can stand up. Which one of you is Clay Whitmore?"

"That'd be me," said the lead man as he turned over and stood up.

"You guys are all investigators?" Joe asked.

"That's right," Whitmore answered. "My firm was hired to find a missing girl. We tracked her to this location. Who are you?"

"I'm Joe and this is Matt," Joe said pointing over at Ramsey who covered the group with his gun. "I think we're looking for the same girls."

"You guys are investigators too?" Whitmore asked.

"Not exactly," Joe answered.

"Not exactly?" Whitmore countered suspiciously. "Then just who are you and what are you doing here?"

Joe took a few minutes to explain as he and Ramsey handed Whitmore and his team their guns and belongings.

"So you just expect me to believe that you two are a couple of good Samaritan's who are acting on your own goodwill?"

"I know it sounds a little far-fetched, but that's the truth. If we were anything else, would we have handed back your weapons?"

"No, but I'm a thorough man. I don't believe two guys just happened to be looking for the same girls as us just because some ER physician asked you to. I need something more to know that I can trust you. So who do you work for?"

"Our employer is the Navy, but we really are here on our own, Mr. Whitmore."

"Navy? You got your military ID's on you?"

Joe and Ramsey pulled out their wallets and handed over their identification cards. Whitmore looked them over, comparing the photographs with the men who stood before him.

"O'Shanick? You're the guy who went over Niagara Falls!" Whitmore said in recognition.

"Yeah, that was me," Joe said, with an embarrassed shrug.

"You were all over the news a few months ago between that and your run-ins with the mafia and the cartels."

"My reputation precedes me," Joe said hoping to move on to the subject at hand.

"Okay, if I recall, you're a Navy SEAL. May I assume he is too?" Whitmore asked, pointing toward Ramsey.

"That's affirmative. He's our Master Chief."

"Alright then," Whitmore nodded. "That makes more sense."

"We'd prefer you keep that just between us," Joe said.

"I hear you, and we will," Whitmore said as his other three men nodded along. "I was a Marine myself, once upon a time. I know you guys like to keep quiet about what you do. Especially something like this. I get it. So how long have you been here?"

"Not long," Joe answered. "Maybe about ten minutes before you showed up. The place is deserted. It looks like there was definitely a brothel in operation here, but they must have packed up and moved when they found out one of their girls ran off."

"Mind if we have a look around?" Whitmore asked.

"Not at all. Ramsey and I found a few things that may interest you."

"Good, why don't you show me," Whitmore said before looking back at his men. "Gary, would you and O'Malley keep an eye on things out here?"

"You got it, Clay," the one named Gary answered.

Joe, Ramsey, Whitmore, and Chuck Springer spent the next ten minutes combing through the rooms. Joe showed them the wall where the girls had scratched their names. The names lined up with those Whitmore had been investigating.

"Well, we've got the right place but we're about an hour or two late," Whitmore said, punctuating his conclusion with an expletive of frustration.

"Mr. Whitmore?" Joe asked. "We were told about this place by the girl that escaped. How did you find it?"

"My team tracked it down online. They traced the website posts to a computer here. Or at least it was here."

"Do they still have it? Maybe they can find the new location."

"You're right," Whitmore said, as he pulled out his phone and opened up his list of contacts. Looking up at Joe and Ramsey, Whitmore smiled sheepishly, "I would have thought of that within a minute. I swear."

Joe and Ramsey chuckled in response. Whitmore spoke into his phone. The conversation went on for several minutes before he hung up.

"My main tech guru says they're likely using a laptop, because he can only trace them when they are online. Next time they log on from that computer, he should be able to locate them within five minutes. That's if they use the same computer. If not, then he can also backtrack from their websites. Roderick said he placed a virus into their code that will alert him the second they log into the admin site. From there, he will try to locate them."

"So what do we do now?" Chuck Springer asked.

"We stay on the trail, but I think we have to get the police involved now," Whitmore answered.

"I agree," Joe started, "but just so you're aware, the girl at the hospital said the Russians own a significant amount of the local police."

"Yeah, that doesn't surprise me," Whitmore answered. "This is Victor Tupolev's territory. He's former Russian SVR. He has a huge network of influence with the locals as well as politically. That being said, I've got guys down here I can trust, but this is now a confirmed kidnapping across state lines so we can now get the FBI involved."

"Won't that push us out?" Springer asked.

"Maybe, but not right away, Chuck. We'll give them what we know while we keep up the hunt ourselves. I've still got enough contacts down here that we can remain abreast of what each other is doing and stay out of their way. If we get pushed out, I'm alright with that. Finding those girls is the mission. The FBI has way more manpower and resources than we do. It's the right thing to do. But you know as well as I do, nothing happens fast with the feds. We are just as likely to get back on the trail and locate this ring ourselves. If and when we do, we will move in fast."

Joe nodded along. He liked Whitmore's attitude. Mission oriented and resourceful.

"You guys need a couple of door-kickers?" Joe offered as Ramsey nodded his agreement.

Whitmore nodded appreciatively. "Now that you mention it, we just might. Door-kicking really isn't our thing. This might go down so fast that your skills might just make the difference between success and failure. I'm not good with failure. You guys would really do that?"

"Yeah," Ramsey answered. "We're not good with failure either."

Chapter 28

Buford, Georgia

The Nothing Box. There was a popular video on the internet titled "A Tale of Two Brains." In it, the speaker, Mark Gungor, humorously compares the mindsets of men and women. The speaker claims that women's brains are complexly wired and constantly in motion thinking of everything whereas men's brains are made up of many boxes; a box for the wife, a box for the kids, a box for the job, a box for the car, and so on. For nearly all men, each box was to be dealt with separately and no interaction was allowed to occur between the boxes. Gungor claims that a man's favorite box is a box where absolutely no thought or emotions occur. The man thinks of nothing and the box is aptly called *The Nothing Box.* Joe was in his nothing box.

He and Ramsey had exchanged contact information with Whitmore before parting ways last night. Frustrated over their mission fail, Joe and Ramsey discussed the issue at length during the drive back and concluded they did what they could and would be ready to respond should Whitmore call. Joe could hear the disappointment in Christy's voice when he called her and updated her on the failed mission. He knew she wasn't upset with him, but it pained him, nonetheless, to hear her sorrowful tone. The Meehan girl was clinging to life in the ICU after a close call in the operating room and the ER had still been packed at the time. He hoped her shift had finished easier.

He and Ramsey had gotten in a lunge-run after waking up this morning. They performed walking lunges the first two miles followed by a brisk four-mile run. It had helped to clear the mind. Joe followed it up with a relaxing shower and now sat out on Crittendon's deck overlooking Lake Lanier while the sun rose higher and the birds broke the silence with their musical interlude. He and Ramsey were going to stand by here, ready should Whitmore call, while they put pen to paper and begin to plan out their new business idea. It would be a busy, thought-filled, and potentially action-filled, day which made this peaceful outdoor visit to Joe's *nothing box* all the more relaxing.

An anticipated sound broke through the stillness of Joe's mind. The barely audible sound of Christy's SUV turning into her driveway spurred his mind enough to stand up and start heading in her direction. Joe walked across the yard in his bare feet toward her house. A sliding glass door opened, and Christy stepped out onto the lanai. She wore navy blue scrub pants and a plain gray t-shirt. She stretched her arms high overhead as she yawned.

"You look beat," Joe commented as he stepped up onto the lanai and the shared a prolonged hug.

"I am beat," she replied quietly, while resting her chin on his shoulder.

"Well, don't let me keep you up. Hit the rack and I'll see you when you get up."

"I will, soon," Christy replied as she stepped back, grabbed Joe's hand, and led him to her porch swing. "But, first, I just need a little love and a friendly ear."

Joe took a seat and stretched his arm across the back. Rather than sit down, Christy curled up on her side and rested her head in Joe's lap. She let out a deep breath.

"Sounds rough," Joe said as he began to gently massage her shoulder. "I'm all yours."

"I hope you don't mind," she began, "I just need to download and vent a little after my shifts. I usually meet with Stacy or another colleague in the lounge. We all do that to some extent. It helps relieve the burden we keep bottled up throughout the shift."

"I get it," Joe offered. "We usually do that to after a mission, or even a hard day of training."

"Except, with you guys, it's probably in some dive called *The Crow's Nest* or something like that," Christy joked.

"True, except ours is called an *After-Action Report*," Joe joked back. "But after that we meet up at *Annie O'Malley's*. I'm sure it's quite similar to your doctor's lounge."

"Minus a few beer bottles being broken over people's heads, you're probably right," Christy quipped.

She didn't speak for several minutes. Joe continued to rub her shoulder and neck as the swing gently swayed back and forth. He began to think she had fallen asleep when he heard her sniffling.

"Christy, what's wrong?"

"I can't stop thinking about Lindsay and those other girls. It's like San Pedro all over again. Did I tell you she was Navy ROTC at NC State?"

"No, you didn't."

"And a Mixed Martial Arts competitor too. That's how she got away. One tough girl, yet they still abducted her, beat her, raped her, and now she's in critical condition from her gunshot wounds."

"That's terrible," Joe offered.

"It's *not* right!" Christy answered. "And what about the other girls? What's going to happen to them? I treat similar victims every week in the Samaritan's Shelter. I see the damage and the monumental task it is to help these women overcome their addictions and wounds, while trying to piece their lives back together. You know what?"

"What?"

"They're the lucky ones. They escaped with their lives. They at least are free from being slaves and have a chance at a normal life. What about all those who don't make it out?"

"I can't imagine."

"Did you know there are an estimated one to two million prostitutes in the United States?"

"No."

"Forty-two million worldwide. Most between the ages of thirteen and twenty-five. Some even younger. In the United States, most are forced into it. Is there anything really being done about it?"

"To some degree, I think there is," Joe answered. "I read about prostitution rings being broken up at state and federal levels."

"Yes, but less than one percent of the women involved in prostitution are rescued. There are approximately 100,000 arrests a year but most of those women are released right back into the hands of the gangs that control them. The others return to their controllers because they are either addicted or have nowhere to go. But that still leaves over ninety percent who have no chance of escape. There has to be something that can be done."

"Well you're doing something, Christy. You and Stacy help out in that recovery shelter. You're giving those women a place to go and a path to recovery."

"Yes, but we are barely scratching the surface. I'm talking about finding and rescuing these girls from their controllers. So few ever get the chance. You and Rammer might have rescued a dozen or so last night had you known earlier. That would have been something. And thank you, by the way. I had no right to ask that of you. I let my emotions get the best of me."

"Are you kidding me? That's what we do. I'm as upset as you are that we missed them. We gave our information to the investigators and offered our services to help retrieve the girls should they find them. Don't feel bad about asking us. I'm glad you did. I've been out of the fight for weeks and it was good to get froggy. I just wish we had pulled it off."

Christy rolled onto her back, looked up at Joe and smiled. "I know. I'm here today because you came for me last year when the cartel grabbed me. And again a few months ago when the mafia grabbed me and your sister."

"Yeah, but that was different. Of course I was going to..."

"Shush," Christy said, as she reached up and playfully pinched Joe's lips closed. "You didn't know me when those cartel guys drove off with me, but you came after me anyway. It's who you are, Joe O'Shanick. It's one of the many reasons why I love you."

Joe tried to speak but Christy clamped down further and made a face of mock warning.

"I'm not done yet."

Joe smiled and nodded his accession.

"Like I said, that's who you are. I want to make sure you know that I am one hundred percent behind you if you want to stay in the SEAL teams. As much as I love the thought of you moving here, I want to be sure you won't regret leaving the teams. I can get a job anywhere and I'm willing to move if staying in the teams is what you want."

"What I want is right here," Joe spoke after Christy removed her hand. "Do I love being a SEAL? Yes, but the things I love most about the teams are quickly coming to a close. Everything is changing. I've changed. I'm a much different man than the one you met a year ago. You've had a lot to do with that. I'm ready for something knew. I'm ready for this."

"Yes, but you can have this and still be in the teams," Christy countered.

"Not the way I want it. I'd be gone a lot; spin ups, long training hours, training out of town, lengthy deployments. That's no life for a family. I'm either all in with the teams or I'm all in with you. It's darn near impossible to do both. I've seen too many guys try, and it rarely works out. Even if I stayed in for now, my future with the teams is limited. I'd eventually have to step down. I don't want to look back and regret losing what I could have had with you."

"I think we could make it work, but, wait..." Christy looked up with her eyebrows furled. "Did you say family?"

"Well, um, yeah," Joe stammered. "I mean, not right away, but, well, yeah. I'm thinking long term, big picture here. Am I catching you off guard? Am I jumping the gun, here?"

Christy's mind raced back to June. A mafia soldier held a gun in her face and was pulling the trigger when Christy had a vision of her and Joe with young children. Within a nanosecond, she had vividly seen their future young family playing in the snow and swimming in the river where Joe's parents lived. She kept that vision to herself but knew, from then on, that she and Joe would have a future together.

"No," Christy said as she pulled him close for a long kiss. "I'm thinking long term as well, Joe. I just didn't know where you stood. Hearing you talk about us as a family just made my day."

"Oh. Whew!" Joe said with a sigh of relief. "I thought I just spooked you there."

"Nope. You'll have to try harder if you want to spook this gal, Joe O'Shanick."

"Well that makes me all the more convinced that resigning from the Navy and moving nearby is the right thing to do."

"Well, it certainly resonates well with me, but you still have a couple of weeks before you have to inform the Navy of your decision. I want you to think and pray about it so that you're absolutely sure."

"How about we pray about it together?" Joe asked.

Christy grasped Joe's right hand with hers. "Yes, let's do that."

Christy's Garmin watch vibrated an incoming text. She glanced at the screen and her face turned white.

Christy's reaction sent alarms off in Joe's head.

"Christy? What's wrong?"

"It's Jeff Wilcox, the surgeon who took Lindsay to the operating room," Christy spoke as tears began to form. "She just died."

Chapter 29

Atlanta, Georgia

*A*t least there was natural light. That was the only positive thought Tracy Courtnall could muster. Sometime last night, Sergei and his minions had hastily moved them to this new location. Each girl had been bound with zip ties and placed in the back of a windowless moving van. They arrived at this new location a short while later. The room had a bed and a window. The window had thick steel bars and the view was a brick alley but at least there was natural light. Tracy hadn't seen real light since she was abducted from campus nearly a week ago.

She still had no idea what was happening. Lindsay had not returned before they were moved. Had she managed to escape? Tracy could only hope so. Maybe that's why they were moved so urgently. The other two girls, Rebecca and Darcy, were also moved with her but placed in another room. Tracy was now all alone. What did that mean? Her mind ran through a flurry of scenarios, none of them good. Tracy flopped back on the bed and fought off another wave of tears. If there weren't bars on the windows, she would take her chances and jump. They looked to be one floor up. She didn't care. Anything was better than the hell she was in.

The door opened and Elena walked in carrying a fast food bag, along with a beverage of some sort. She set it down on the small nightstand next to the bed and walked out without a word. The door shut and Tracy heard the lock click. The smell of the food captured her attention. Her last meal had been a stale hamburger and a bottle of water sometime yesterday. The aroma reaching her nostrils reminded her how hungry she was. She opened the bag and found two cheeseburgers, a container of French Fries, and a few packets of ketchup. A week ago, she wouldn't even consider fast food. Ever the fitness enthusiast, Tracy was very health conscious with her diet. She could not have cared less today. Having been nearly starved for a week, this was like a gourmet dinner at a five-star restaurant. Tracy tore into the first cheeseburger, finishing it in four bites. Afraid, she might make herself sick, she forced herself to slow down. She reached for the large Styrofoam cup and took a sip. *A chocolate milkshake!* Tracy couldn't even remember the last time she had allowed herself such a treat. It was heavenly. She took two more big sips and quickly regretted it when the frozen brain kicked in. She sampled some fries to warm things up. *Slow down, girl. This is the only thing close to pleasure you will have all day.*

Twenty minutes later, Tracy reclined on the bed. Satisfied by her first real meal in nearly a week, she found herself able to daydream. She envisioned herself on her daddy's boat. She was a little girl, sitting on his lap steering the big boat as they cruised around Lake Norman. Daddy's left arm was wrapped around her waist, holding her tightly as she steered. The sun reflected off the water while the wind blew through her hair. Her brothers sat on the bow laughing as their boat cruised across the waves. Her mother grinned contentedly, while soaking up the sun as she reclined in the large seat next to them. Tracy lost herself in the memory. It was the only pleasure she had felt since this ordeal began.

The door opened and Elena walked back in, accompanied by Pockmark man. Tracy was repulsed by the sight of his crooked yellow teeth as he sneered at her while Elena held out a black lace thong with a matching see-through brassiere.

"Put these on, *shlyukha*," Elena ordered.

Tracy looked at the skimpy outfit with dread. She knew this day was coming. Having been skipped over in favor of the other girls, the past few days had not done anything to give her a false sense of hope that she would, somehow, be spared the horrible realities the other girls were experiencing. Tracy looked up at Elena with watering eyes. Elena scowled and thrust the lingerie at Tracy.

"Now."

Tracy reluctantly took the lingerie and looked over at Pockmark. Apparently, he wasn't going anywhere. Tracy quickly removed the plain t-shirt and shorts she had been given. It was the first day she had been clothed. She loathed the thought of changing in front of Pockmark but didn't seem to have a choice. She slipped into the lingerie and sat back down on the bed, wishing she could pull the blanket around her.

Elena looked Tracy over and nodded slightly. She removed a backpack from her shoulders and took out a hairbrush and a small cosmetics bag. Over the next several minutes, she went to work applying blush, eyeliner, mascara, and a bright red lipstick to Tracy's face. She then worked Tracy's long blond hair with the brush. Finished, she stood back and looked Tracy over. Apparently satisfied with her work, Elena nodded and tipped her head toward the door. Tracy slowly rose and padded her way to the door in her bare feet.

"Move it, little girl!" Pockmark said with a brisk slap to Tracy's mostly exposed rear end.

Tracy reflexively moved her hands to cover her backside as she hot-footed out of the room to Pockmark's sinister laugh. The slap stung, but she tried to remain stoic. She didn't want to give Pockmark the satisfaction. Elena led her into another room. There was a bed with dark red satin sheets. Tracy looked around. The rest of the room was bare.

"Wait here," Elena commanded.

This is it, Tracy thought as she shrunk into a corner and tried to fight off the tears. She had been dreading this moment since her capture. She looked down at her hands. A platinum ring adorned her left ring finger. The band bridged into the outline of a heart which contained a cross made up of diamonds. Engraved in the band were the words "True Love Waits." Her father had given it to her when she was fourteen at a church-led purity ceremony. Tracy had promised to remain pure, keeping her virginity until her wedding day. The church youth pastor, Pastor Steven, a young but dedicated minister, had steadfastly tackled many socially relevant but difficult topics; drugs, peer pressure, bullying, social media, and, chief among them, sexual morality. Whereas many pastors were reluctant and often avoided this topic, Pastor Steven unapologetically faced it head on with his youth group. He was well aware of and willing to address the sexual temptations and cultural expectations the youth were facing in today's hyper-sexualized society. He helped them learn that sex was God's gift to married couples. A wonderful gift that was not only meant to create children but meant to be enjoyed between a husband and wife as often as desired. Conversely, he showed how it could be harmful for those not married. Sexually transmitted diseases and unwanted pregnancies were only part of it. There were also the spiritual and emotional connections that were carelessly made and ripped apart. This led to extensive emotional trauma that could severely hinder one's commitment and relationship with a future spouse when one day married. He compared sex to fire. If used in a fireplace, it's proper place, it will warm one's house. Allow that fire anywhere else and it will burn the house down. Tracy's small group leader, Miss Valerie, expanded on this many times with Tracy and her friends.

Tracy understood and willingly made a purity commitment at a crucial time. The next four years of high school had not been without temptations. Her natural beauty had certainly attracted the attention of many boys. She suddenly realized that it wasn't so much the ring that helped her remain true to her promise. It wasn't even solely due to the teaching and guidance of Pastor Steven and Miss Valerie. All of that definitely played a role, but it was the man behind the ring. Tracy's father had always been there for her. He had always been a devoted father and a loving mentor. She *knew* she was loved by a good man. There was a sense of completeness and security in that. Likewise, her older brothers learned from their father's example and also made her feel loved and respected. As such, she never felt the need for another boy's attention to the point that she was willing to sacrifice her virginity to get it.

Tracy nervously twisted the ring around her finger, dreading that it was about to be figuratively torn off by some strange man, who would force himself upon her and ruthlessly steal what she had meticulously tried to protect. The tears began to form. She squeezed her eyes shut as she began to tremble in fear. Like many young women, Tracy had dreamed of her wedding day. She envisioned being escorted down the aisle by her father. Just before he was to hand her off to her soon-to-be husband, Tracy would ceremoniously remove the ring and hand it to her father signifying that the promise had been kept. It would also signify to her husband that she had waited for him. That priceless moment was about to be ripped away from her in an act of brutal perversion.

"Oh, God, please don't let it end this way," Tracy cried out in prayer.

Elena walked back in with Pockmark and another man. He was tall and thin with a trimmed beard and long dark hair pulled into a ponytail. Tracy recognized him. He was usually hunched over a computer in the main room. A sharp tingle ran up her spine when she realized there was an expensive digital camera slung around his neck.

Oh, God, no! They're going to film this and plaster it all over the internet!

Chapter 30

Atlanta, Georgia

The governor's office was a large, plush room with rich green carpeting. The walls were exquisitely paneled in dark wood and adorned with oil paintings depicting Georgia's history and landscape. One exception to this was a large painting displayed in a prominent place opposite the main entrance to the office. A location where it was sure to be seen by all who enter. It consisted of a black backdrop behind the white lace neckpiece frequently worn by the late Supreme Court Justice Ruth Bader Ginsburg. A simple painting that the current Governor believed spoke volumes. So much so that on her Inauguration Day she ceremoniously replaced a colorful painting of Augusta National's *Amen Corner* with this painting. Her words in front of the camera were, "The resistance has replaced the patriarchy!"

Governor Judith Maynard-Worthington stood behind her massive desk as she awaited her personal assistant to show her next appointment in. She was of medium height with a stocky, overweight build that was unsuccessfully downplayed by a tailored, gray business suit. A light blue blouse served to accentuate the plainness of her medium brown hair. She wished she could greet her next guest while seated behind her desk in a show of power, but he could serve useful in the future and she knew how to appeal to his vanity.

"Why Senator Williams! To what do I owe this honor?" She greeted him cheerfully, as the senior senator of her state was shown into her office.

"Well, Governor, I wanted to drop by in person to let you know that I have some good news. I was able to secure that four billion dollars of federal money to fund your interstate expansion budget shortfall," the senator said as he approached her desk with a smile.

"Well that's very good news!" Maynard-Worthington said with a practiced smile.

Senator Williams was, in her opinion, a self-serving political hack. They were members of the same party but that was about all they had in common. He was the embodiment of the patriarchy. A champion of women's causes publicly, while a known philanderer and abuser of women privately. Were it not for a media willing to look the other way, he would never have made it to any office other than dog-catcher. He was overweight, medium height, with a bulbous red nose and thick gray hair parted to the side. The perfect caricature of the career fat-cat politician. The senator's only qualities Maynard-Worthington found endearing were his money and power, which he used to further his state. Their state. Judith knew she could go farther with him as an ally rather than an enemy. His mention of her budget shortfall was an intentional barb, but she kept her smile and ignored it.

"Please, have a seat, Senator," she said extending her hand towards one of two plush sitting chairs.

"Thank you, Governor," he said as he set his bulk down.

"May I offer you some coffee?" She asked, realizing that his taking a seat meant he was going to stay awhile despite being worked into her busy schedule.

"Yes, please," he answered absently as he unbuttoned his suit coat and fumbled around for a handkerchief to mop his already sweating brow.

Governor Maynard-Worthington nodded to her assistant who poured from a sterling silver coffee pot into a china cup. He consulted a cheat sheet on his cellphone and mixed in cream and sugar to the senator's known liking. He set the cup and saucer down beside the senator and stood off to the side.

"Not that I ever had any doubt, but how did you manage to secure the funding?" Maynard-Worthington asked.

"Oh, it was nothing special," he answered with a dismissive wave. "I just did a little horse trading with a colleague in the House and he added it into the new stimulus bill they just passed."

"You mean the one that might not pass the Senate?" She asked with concern.

"Oh, it'll pass, Governor," he said with a serious nod. "We've had to reach across the aisle and twist a few arms, but it will pass. I can assure you of that."

"Although I have no doubt in your abilities to persuade certain members, President Galan is already on record stating that bill is nothing but a cleverly named pork bill that will add another 1.9 trillion to the debt and that he will veto it. Will you be able to secure a veto-proof majority?"

"We're working on that. Senator Fowler is taking this matter to the campaign trail and will convince his followers that it's the right thing for America. The press will do their part. We may have to rewrite a few things, but we'll get it passed, or we may have to delay the vote until after the election. Once Fowler is in the White House, we won't need a veto-proof majority."

"You mean *if* Fowler is elected," Maynard-Worthington corrected.

"Oh, he'll win," Williams said confidently. "The press has done an excellent job running on the narrative that Galan is using his war on the cartels to prop up the Gulf Cartel by targeting all the opposing cartels. The polls are showing that enough people are buying it."

"Yet the evidence proves otherwise. Aren't you worried that could come back to bite you?"

"Bite who?"

"The party."

"Nah," Williams waved dismissively, "Most people don't read past the headlines. Those who do will see the anonymous high-ranking sources and that will be all they need to believe it. Most people will believe what they want to believe. Give them a few sound bites and slogans and that's enough for them. I don't have to tell you that, Madame Governor."

"No, you don't, Senator," Maynard-Worthington said, subtly returning the accusation. "So, you're saying we just need to wait out the election and this funding will come in?"

"Yes, ma'am," Williams nodded.

"And what will be expected of me in return?"

"Nothing other than your continued support for Senator Fowler's campaign. Georgia is a crucial state in the electoral college as we all saw in the last election. Your state could be the difference. Help us get the good senator over the finish line and we will all reap the benefits."

"So that's it?" Maynard-Worthington asked with a hint of suspicion. "Nothing for you personally?"

"Well, I'm not up for re-election for another four years. Although I would cherish your support at that time, I'm sitting fat and happy where I'm at right now. It serves me to serve you and our state, ma'am."

"Your commitment to the people of our fair state is certainly noted and appreciated, Senator," she answered graciously while beginning to stand to conclude the meeting. "If I can ever be of service to you, you have only to ask."

"Now that you mention it," Senator Williams said as he remained seated, "I do have a small personal matter I could use your help with."

"Oh? And what might that be?"

Williams subtly motioned toward Maynard-Worthington's personal assistant.

"Paul, would you mind excusing us for a moment?" she asked.

She waited for her assistant to shut the door before sitting back down.

"Okay, Senator, what personal matter do you need my help with?"

"Ma'am, I'm coming to you as a friend. This is a rather sensitive matter and it has the potential to cause great embarrassment to our state should this get out. I'm hesitant to even bring it up and I know you'll be discreet but..."

"Just tell me what it is, Senator," she said with exasperation.

"Well," he winced, "there was an incident last night involving my son."

"You're referring to your son, Clinton? The one attending law school here in Atlanta?"

"Yes, ma'am."

"Did he get caught with his pants down again?"

"Not exactly."

"Then just what *is* the problem here, Senator?"

Senator Williams spent the next several minutes explaining the situation to Governor Maynard-Worthington.

"Well, this goes way beyond that high school junior he was caught with at his fraternity house a couple of years ago. One would think he would have learned his lesson, Senator."

"What do you want me to do, Governor? He's a twenty-three-year-old male in his oat-sowing years," Williams said with a shrug.

"What you and your son do doesn't concern me until it either puts a black mark on our state or I have to bail your fat rear-end out, Senator. I would hope you would have taught your son to be more careful, but then I have to remind myself of who I'm talking to and remember the apple doesn't fall far from the tree."

"Now, just a minute, there, Governor! I resent what you're insinuating! Is this any way to treat your senior senator who just secured a tidy sum of federal dollars to bail out your failing project?"

"Oh this is rich!" Governor Maynard-Worthington replied with an eye roll. "You come to me, hat in hand, to help your son out of a sticky wicket, and to keep the press from printing the biggest scandal since you and Senator Fowler were found with those two underage Guatemalan girls, and you get offended when I call you out on your indiscretions? Do you really think I'm going to be able to keep the press off of this one?"

"Look, all I'm asking is that you lean on your attorney general to convince the DA to keep Clinton's name out of the press. He's done nothing wrong."

"Senator! Your son hired a prostitute who shot the pimp at your son's house!"

"But he never actually slept with her. No crime was committed. I just want his name kept out of this. He's a good kid. He made a mistake. I don't want this to hurt his future career."

"Oh for Pete's sake, Senator! You mean you don't want this to blow back on your career."

"I really am just looking out for my son, Governor, but keeping my name out of this would be good for all of us. You know that," he pleaded.

Maynard-Worthington sighed, shaking her head. "I think I can get the DA to sweep this one under the rug before word gets out. Nobody's going to care about some hooker shooting a pimp. I'll see to it your son's name stays out of it."

"Thank you, madame Governor," Williams said, as he began to heft his bulk in preparation to stand.

"But I'll need something from you, Senator," she spoke in a deliberate tone.

Senator Williams froze in his seat. "What would that be, ma'am?"

"I want a position in Fowler's administration. Something that begins with Secretary."

Maynard-Worthington watched as Williams squirmed under her glare. Earlier that year, he had dangled the possibility of her being picked as Fowler's running mate if she would endorse him during the primaries. Having presidential aspirations of her own, she jumped at the opportunity only to be passed over when Fowler named a popular Hispanic congresswoman from California. Deep down, Maynard-Worthington knew Congresswoman Fuentes was a smart choice for Senator Fowler. She was attractive, sassy, and well-portrayed by the media. She had already proven be a good weapon in his viscous campaign against President Galan; nevertheless, Judith Maynard-Worthington considered herself well-suited for the presidency and would take a cabinet-level position in Fowler's administration to enhance her resume. Senator Williams was tight with Senator Fowler. Two peas in a pod, as the old expression goes. Williams was vulnerable, and she intended to exploit it.

"Excuse me, ma'am?" Williams sounded flabbergasted. "Did you just ask me to seek out a cabinet position for you?"

"No."

"Oh, whew! I was gonna say..."

"I didn't ask," Judith said sternly, "I demanded. And not some low-level position either. You dangled the vice presidency before me a while back. I expect no less than Secretary of Education, but I think Secretary of State would be more appropriate. Unless you would rather take your chances with another scandal?"

"Now, you *know* I can't promise anything like that!"

"No?" The governor asked sarcastically. "Just like I can't promise I'll be able to keep your son out of the press either."

"Okay, okay, but you're going to have to give me some time to work on this. There's less than five weeks to the election. He won't publicly name anyone until after the election is over, so you'll have to be patient with me."

"That's okay, Jeffrey. It will be weeks, if not months, before this goes to trial. A lot can happen between now and then."

The two stared at each other in a moment of contemplative silence.

"Now, if there's nothing further, Senator," Governor Maynard-Worthington said as she stood up, "I have a photo-op with the state spelling bee champions."

Chapter 31

Atlanta, Georgia

S ergei blew a large cloud of smoke up in the air as he lounged at a long folding table. His right leg was propped on the table as he listened to Victor Tupolev scold him over the phone. Allowing the *shlyukha* to escape was a costly mistake. Sergei was well aware of that, but still had to endure an earful from his boss. Victor was ruthless but he was also shrewd. Sergei's crew earned more money than any other crew in Victor's syndicate. They were increasing their revenues every month and Victor knew it. He was not about to come down on Sergei too hard. He was simply flexing his muscles. Sergei knew to simply take his tongue lashing and express the proper amount of remorse and deference. The Courtnall girl's auction was up in an hour and that payoff would be at least fifty times what he was currently bringing in a month. Victor would be more than pleased with his cut.

"*Da, Mr. Tupolev.*"

Sergei clicked off his phone and dropped it onto the table. He sat in contemplative silence while he finished his cigarette. Their new location was adequate. It was a small apartment building in Atlanta's International Village, one of several Tupolev owned through a subsidiary corporation. He used it to house illegal immigrants temporarily when he smuggled them into the country. Many were young women. Most were part of his flourishing *Mail Order Bride* business. Others were imports for his pornography business and some were handed off to Sergei or the others to work in the prostitution rings. Due to the high rate of turnover, Victor kept these apartments furnished. The *shlyukhas* still had to cram several to a room, sleeping two to a twin bed, but they would consider that a luxury compared to the mats they had been sleeping on.

It was only temporary. As soon as Elena called in and reported what happened, Sergei contacted Victor who quickly vacated the second-floor apartments to make room for Sergei's crew. Since this was a more permanent establishment of Victor's holdings, there would be no business on these grounds. He didn't want to risk the exposure. Sergei would only operate the truck stops and house calls while arranging for some motel rooms as well. As soon as they found a more suitable and disposable location, they would move. For Tupolev, that couldn't be soon enough. Before hanging up, he implored Sergei to find a solution before the day was over or he would find one for him. It was nothing personal. It was simply business.

Business. Sergei had a few ideas of his own when it came to business. The auction angle paid well but was contingent on finding women who would fetch a fair price. An eighteen-year-old virgin with supermodel looks was extremely rare. Higher-priced call girls, like his *Girls of the ACC,* was promising but he couldn't price himself out of the market. His immediate need was having a more stable place to conduct his business. A place easily accessible to those who were willing to pay for their carnal pleasures but not easily found by the police. There was a delicate balance to be struck. *Shlyukha's* were easy enough to obtain, and discard. Sergei's only major concerns were making money and keeping his organization below law enforcement's radar.

Sergei stubbed out his cigarette and swung his leg off the table. He stood and stretched with a yawn, before walking into the living room where Elena and Petr were hard at work.

"How are we doing?"

"It's picking up, boss," Elena said looking up at Sergei.

"She's right," Petr said while working his laptop. "The bidding picked up earlier after we posted the photos Elena and Igor took of the girl. She's very photogenic and the bidders seem to agree."

"Where are we at with the bidding?" Sergei asked, always concerned about the bottom line.

"Six point two million dollars and climbing, boss," Elena answered.

"That's all? I was hoping for ten million."

"We're not done yet, Mr. Petrenko," Petr said encouragingly. "Bidding usually accelerates about this time, but especially the final minutes. There are some heavy hitters on here. I don't think we're done by any means."

"Heavy hitters? Like who?"

"Two appear to be members of the Saudi family. The Bollywood producer is still here. Another appears to be from China although I can't get a good hit on him. There's a Japanese tycoon and what looks like one of our oligarchs from the Rodina," Petr said using the old Soviet term for the motherland.

"Do we know which one?" Sergei asked hiding his alarm.

If it was Tupolev's benefactor, this could get ugly real fast. If he were to discover he was being charged a hefty sum from his own organization, he might blow a fuse. Sergei would likely have to hand the girl over for free in order to spare his own life.

"Not at this time, Mr. Petrenko. Those guys never conduct their business without a few intermediaries as cutouts. I'll work on it, but it won't be easy."

"Can you do that without exposing yourself?"

"I'll be honest, sir, it's a fifty-fifty chance at best. They have much deeper pockets than we do. Some of the best hackers are in their employ."

"Very well. Hold off unless he wins the bidding. Proceed with caution, Petr."

The only thing worse than being caught selling a *shlyukha* to their oligarch benefactor would be getting caught trying to sniff one out. Hopefully somebody else would be top bidder and they could collect their windfall without incident.

"New bid, six point three million," Petr announced. "Those pictures of yours really helped, Elena!"

Sergei grunted in acknowledgment. He knew Petr had an eye for Elena. It was probably more for job security. She was a cold-hearted woman. A former ballerina, she was excessively thin, and her face retained the waif-like sunken cheeks of a past eating disorder. After a career disappointment in the ballet, she turned her ambition elsewhere. She quickly found a place with a criminal enterprise in Moscow. She was ruthlessly pragmatic and devoid of a conscience. What little attractiveness she may have had was nullified by her coldness. Sergei found her quite useful and was glad Tupolev placed her in his crew. Tupolev had learned of her through a paid contact in the RVU and eventually recruited her to come work for him. Even though she technically worked under Sergei, she was a rising star in Tupolev's organization who may one day run her own crew. Petr appeared to know this and seemed keen on worming his way into her very small circle of trust. Sergei didn't care. As long as Petr performed usefully, he could pursue Elena in whatever way he chose.

Back to the matter at hand. They were also down two girls. More actually. Sergei wanted to rapidly expand this operation. Once they settled into their new place, he would send Elena and Igor out to find more. The *Girls of the ACC* unit needed more *shlyukhas* and he wanted to get a *Girls of the SEC* unit up and running as soon as possible. The Courtnall girl would bring a nice price. If only there was a way to find more like her?

Sergei's thoughts were interrupted by the sound of his phone ringing. The ring tone was specific for Tupolev. *Now what?* Sergei quickly walked back to the table and answered his phone.

"*Da,* Mr. Tupolev?"

"Shut your auction down," Tupolev spoke with perceivable urgency.

"What? Why?"

"Now, Sergei!"

"Are you saying you want it canceled before a winner is named? Before we receive a large payment?"

"That's exactly what I'm saying, Sergei. Shut it down and have your tech geek scrub all traces of it from the internet. Now!"

"Petr! Elena! Shut it down and remove it from the internet," Sergei spoke, loudly so as to be heard by his crew as well as Tupolev.

His order was met by the befuddled looks of Petr and Elena.

"Shut it down! All of it!" He repeated as he pointed to his phone and silently mouthed Tupolev's name.

Understanding registered with Petr first. He quickly nodded and went to work on his laptop.

"It's being taken care of as we speak, Mr. Tupolev," Sergei spoke as he stepped out into the hall. "May I ask why? We stand to lose a lot of money."

"Because, apparently, your Petr is no match for the hacker our benefactor has working for him."

"What?"

"I just received a call from Russia. Our superior knows of your auction. He said that, if he can trace you, the government can trace you. He does not want to draw the attention of the FBI."

"Mr. Tupolev, does he have any idea how much money this girl will bring us?"

"His men are inside your computers. They know exactly what the little *shlyukha* is going for. He doesn't care. We exist at his pleasure, Sergei. We have no choice but to do what he says. Do it now."

Sergei could hear the seriousness in Tupolev's voice. He rarely mentioned their nameless oligarch. It seemed to Sergei, that Tupolev was given free reign over his American enterprises as long as he ensured the oligarch received his tribute. This was the first time Sergei could recall Tupolev acting on an order from above. For a brief moment, Sergei forgot about the large sum of money that had just slipped out of his hands. A brief moment.

"It's being done, Mr. Tupolev. It is a shame, sir. That would have been a very nice payday for you and me."

"I'm aware of that, Sergei, but keeping the FBI off our backs is of greater importance. You will need to find a more skilled man for your computers."

"*Da,* Mr. Tupolev."

Sergei understood what was really being communicated. He was to dispose of Petr. Permanently. That would be easy in and of itself. The harder part would be recruiting a more skilled and reliable replacement.

"I may have a consolation for us, however," Tupolev spoke, in a more clam manner.

"What would that be, Papa Tupolev?"

"I know someone who would be interested in your girl. We may not get the money you were hoping for, but he would still pay a good price. I'm going to make a few calls, Sergei. I will get back to you."

The phone clicked dead. Sergei stared at it for a few seconds. He noted the total time on the screen. The call had not lasted two minutes, and everything had suddenly changed.

Chapter 32

Atlanta, Georgia

That was easy. Tupolev had a brief moment of mixed emotions. For a second, he was disappointed that Sergei fell for that ruse. Sergei was cunning and clever, a productive brigadier who brought in good money. Victor would choose Sergei to succeed him in the organization should anything ever happen to him. Based on this, Victor congratulated himself for his own skill in fooling Sergei.

It was just business. Sergei would have likely sold the girl for a large sum, of which, Victor would have received a nice tribute. Ever the opportunist, Victor saw a way to improve his payout.

Los Fantasma Guerreros, the paramilitary cartel of Mexico was regrouping after President Galan's war on the cartels had nearly decimated them over the past year. Prior to that, the cartel had virtually out-hustled and nearly killed off the competing cartels in their territory. The Gulf Cartel was the only rival that remained, but even they were quick to stay out of the way of *Los Fantasma Guerreros,* who were more commonly known as LFG.

LFG's new leader, Pedro Cardenas, was rebuilding their organization while simultaneously fighting the American and Mexican forces. His main source of income came from drug and human trafficking to the United States. It had always been that way; however, President Galan was fighting the drug trade on many fronts and had succeeded in securing the border while hunting down and prosecuting the cartels. Despite this, there remained a large demand for the cartels' product. Cardenas was developing new methods of transporting their product into the United States. It was moderately successful at best and the result was an increase in cost to purchasers like Tupolev. Both men were desperate for Galan's demise and were secretly funneling money into Senator Fowler's campaign. Fowler was a vocal proponent of open borders and never shied away from any opportunity to publicly criticize President Galan's war on the cartels. A Fowler White House would be much better for business. His open border and immigration policies would lead to mass surges at the borders. This would overwhelm border agents which would allow LFG and other cartels to move drugs and humans across the border at lesser patrolled locations. Prices would go down for Tupolev, and Cardenas would be able to move more product. It was a win-win for both of them. One that drew them closer as allies.

It wasn't Tupolev's oligarch who called him earlier. It wasn't any oligarch. It was Cardenas. They had spent nearly an hour strategizing and discussing business. Tupolev, particularly, was after Cardenas to sell exclusively to Tupolev in his territories. Cardenas told him it would be much easier to do when Fowler was president and steered the conversation in that direction. Tupolev was eager to reveal his efforts toward that end. In addition to funneling money into the Fowler campaign, Tupolev had convinced his oligarch that an "October Surprise" incriminating President Galan would be good for their organization. Considering the tough stance and sanctions President Galan had placed on Russia, a disinformation campaign hatched from Russian intelligence sources would not be difficult to engineer and was already in the works. Cardenas had stressed the importance of ensuring Fowler would be securely in their camp. Both men knew that politicians, like Fowler, would pander and promise the world for money and votes but would ultimately do what served them best. Cardenas was vehement that they keep a firm handle on Fowler. Tupolev assured his counterpart that he had enough government and media sources to obtain sufficient leverage over Fowler, should he be elected. Cardenas wasn't convinced. Despite Fowler's and the media's support for mass immigration and open borders, Cardenas' sources informed him the majority of the American public, including many of the Latino citizens, supported President Galan's anti-cartel efforts and tough border stance. He was concerned Fowler would stick his finger up in the air, test the wind, and possibly follow public opinion. In an effort to pacify Cardenas, Tupolev revealed, more than he cared to, some of his government influence. This effort seemed to have its desired effect and Tupolev quickly moved the conversation in a different direction.

It was no small secret that Cardenas, and his inner circle within the cartel, had an insatiable appetite for pretty young woman, particularly blonds, which were a rarity in their part of the world. Knowing this, Tupolev dangled the Courtnall girl before Cardenas by vividly describing her physical attributes. *Oh, and did I mention she is a virgin?* He had Cardenas look her up on the auction site while on the phone. Cardenas was instantly hooked. In order to increase his bargaining power, Tupolev pointed out the current and prospective price she would fetch. Cardenas offered to reduce his drug prices by five percent in exchange for the girl. Tupolev countered with exclusive purchasing rights of all product, effective immediately and would give the girl up for the current highest bid. They had haggled for several minutes and reached an agreement of exclusive purchasing rights and three million for the girl. Tupolev would keep two million for himself and pass one million down to Sergei. Sergei would be disappointed but would have no choice and would take the money. Tupolev would get what his tribute would have been had the girl sold for ten million but would reap much more by putting his local competitors out of business, when their source of product was no longer selling to them. Sergei would make the money up in the long run with the discounted product. Tupolev would make sure he understood this.

Tupolev smiled as he sat on the terrace of his large penthouse overlooking the surrounding upscale Buckhead area. With one phone call, he had just made two million dollars and increased his market share tremendously. All over a spoiled American princess. After tiring of her, Cardenas and his men would eventually cast her off into a prostitution ring. Her fate was what it was. Tupolev would not give it a second thought. He was more concerned with his own wealth and security. There would be a number of gangs and organizations out for revenge after being pushed out of the market. Tupolev looked at the bulletproof glass shielding his terrace and laughed. *Come and get me, you little peasants!* He pressed a button on the glass table, signaling his staff that he was ready for lunch. He looked at his watch. Enough time had passed. It was time to call Sergei back.

Chapter 33

Cumming, Georgia

A peaceful chorus of bird chirping was accompanied by the rhythmic, hollow, metallic pings of halyard lines on sailboat masts. The pleasant sounds of the marina were matched by an equally pleasant light breeze floating in from the water, which provided a little relief from the noonday heat. The marina was relatively devoid of activity on this early fall weekday.

"Peaceful," Joe commented, as he breathed in the mixed aromas of boat wax, motor oil, epoxy resin, and teak oil.

"Yeah, I could live here," Ramsey agreed. "Is that the boat up there?"

"Yep. A white Hunter 33."

"What happened to the Pearson you saw the other day?"

"It's still for sale. This one just came up this morning and it's a better price. I figured I'd take a look."

As they neared the boat, Joe noticed the name, *Boys n Ivy,* artfully painted along the side. The head of a man with thinning gray hair and a well-trimmed beard appeared from below. Spotting Joe and Ramsey, he smiled and climbed the rest of the way into the cockpit. He was shirtless and well-tanned with wiry arms and just a hint of bulge at the waistline.

"Would you be Mr. Wilhelm?" Joe asked.

"That's me!" He replied cheerfully. "You must be the gentleman I talked to earlier this morning. Joe, if I heard you right. C'mon aboard!"

"Thank you, sir," Joe said, as he and Ramsey stepped up onto the boat.

"Dennis Wilhelm," the man said, offering his hand in greeting.

He had a pleasant smile and blue eyes that were rimmed with the wrinkled crow's feet of a man who had spent many years in the sun.

"I'm Joe O'Shanick and this is Matt Ramsey," Joe said as he shook the man's hand. "Thank you for being willing to meet us on such short notice."

"Oh it's no problem. I was coming down to clean her up anyway. Have a look around," Wilhelm said. "She's a great boat. My wife and I have had her for nearly thirty years. She races well, but, unlike many racing sailboats, she has all the creature comforts one would want for a boat this size."

Joe and Ramsey spent the next twenty minutes giving her a thorough top down inspection. It became readily apparent that this man took very good care of his boat. All the rigging was in great shape, the hull was well maintained and there was no evidence of leaking or mustiness below. The diesel engine was clean, fired up right away, and ran well.

"Looks like you've kept her in great shape, sir," Joe commented as he climbed back up into the cockpit.

"You can call me Dennis, son, and, yes, I have treated her like a baby all these years. Something my chiefs drilled into me years ago when I was in the Navy."

Joe and Ramsey exchanged a grin. Wilhelm picked up on it and smiled.

"Are you boys Navy too?" He asked.

"Affirmative, sir," Ramsey answered. "When did you serve?"

"I went in right after high school in seventy-six. Did my four years as a Boatswains Mate on a destroyer and got out. Those were the post-Vietnam Carter years. Not exactly the best time to be in the Navy. If I'd have known Reagan was gonna be elected, I may have stayed in, but I got out and went back to school on the G.I. Bill. Became a science teacher and just retired this past year. Overall, I can't complain. How about you boys? You look like frogmen."

"What makes you say that?" Joe asked.

"Because nobody in the Navy is built like you two unless they're SEALs. Life at sea on a tin can won't make anyone fit and lean. It's even worse for the submariners."

"You're very observant," Joe commented. "I hope our status as knuckle-draggers won't be a deal breaker for you."

"Not at all. Does that mean you're interested?"

"I sure am. I'd like to talk it over with my dad first. He served as Boatswains Mate around the same time you did. He's my sailboat guru. Can I ask why you're selling her?"

"Sure," he said happily. "Our youngest son and his wife live down in Florida. They're expecting their first child and, now that I'm retired, we're moving down to be near them."

"Won't you miss sailing?" Joe asked.

"Oh, we'll still be sailing. We're moving to Destin," he said, his blue eyes twinkling. "I'm just looking for something bigger we can cruise to the Keys in. This could probably handle it, but I'd like something a little bigger and, besides, I don't have a trailer for her. It would cost too much to have her shipped down there anyway. Which raises a question; if you were to buy this boat, would you be moving her to wherever you're stationed?"

"No. Actually, we're both about to get out. Chief Ramsey and I are going to start up a business up in Dawsonville, and we'll live on board here for a while to save costs."

Wilhelm eyed both men with curiosity. Joe and Ramsey quickly picked up on it.

"It's not what you're thinking," Joe quickly spoke. "I have a girlfriend who lives nearby in Buford."

"And you'd rather bunk with a Chief Petty Officer than her?" Wilhelm asked incredulously.

"Well, no, but she and I are waiting until we get married."

"Wait! What?" Ramsey interjected. "You and Christy are getting married? When did this happen?"

"Easy there, Chief. No plans yet. That's just our rule. No shacking up until we're married."

"That's a good rule, son," Wilhelm said. "Ivy and I waited as well. Of course that was back in the early 80's and things were a lot different back then. Kinda miss those days when family meant something. You know what I mean?"

"I sure do," Joe said, thinking of his own family.

He was the middle of five children. His parents were hard-working, devoted parents with a rock-solid marriage. If he and Christy were to one day marry, he prayed they could build on the example his parents set.

"Does this girl of yours enjoy sailing too?"

"She sure does," Joe answered proudly.

"Then you make sure you do marry her, son. A traditional woman who likes to sail is a rare find these days."

"Aye, sir," Joe said with a grin.

"So are you both chiefs?"

"No, sir," Ramsey answered. "Joe here's an officer, but one of the good ones, so we don't hold that against him."

"And are you a Senior Chief?"

"Actually, I just made Master Chief last year."

Joe felt his phone begin to vibrate while the two others continued to talk about all things working man's Navy. Looking down, Joe saw the caller's identity and did a double take. He politely excused himself from the conversation and hopped down onto the dock as he answered the call.

"Joe O'Shanick," he said by way of greeting.

Joe talked quietly out of earshot for a minute and then hung up his phone. He hurried back to the boat.

"Mr. Wilhelm, I'll get in touch with you this afternoon. I'm very interested, but Chief and I have an urgent matter to attend to. Chief, we gotta roll!" Joe said as he turned and ran up the dock.

Ramsey hurried after him. He caught up as Joe was quickly climbing into his truck.

"What is it, Joe?" Chief asked, as Joe sped out of the marina.

"That was Whitmore! They've located the girls!

Chapter 34

Chamblee, Georgia

The mid-day traffic was moderately congested on I-285. That was life in the greater Atlanta area. Joe did his best to avoid drawing attention as he weaved his truck in and out of traffic. They were currently boxed into the left lane, stuck behind a car driving at the same speed as the cars in the adjacent lane. It was clear in front the car. There were six lanes to choose from and the driver was content to drive below the speed limit in the far-left lane.

"C'mon, fella! If you're not going to dance, get off the dance floor!" Joe spoke through his windshield. "Honestly, Rammer, it blows my mind how many people are seemingly unaware that the left lane is for passing."

"Nothing you can do about it now, Joe. We need to get over to the right. Our exit is just a mile ahead."

Joe signaled right, slowed down, and picked a space between cars. He merged right and kept working around traffic until he was one lane over from the exit lane. The exit had already begun to veer away from the interstate, but another car blocked the way. Ramsey looked over and quickly did the math in his head. *No freaking way!*

"Don't do it Joe! Just take the next exit."

Without warning, Joe hit the brakes, veered right, and stomped the gas, passing in front of an SUV by mere inches.

"WHOA! WHOA!" Ramsey shouted, as he gripped the overhead handrail and stomped on the floor as if there were a brake pedal.

The truck shot across the lane and then bounced across the grassy strip separating the interstate from the exit lane. They regained pavement and weaved between two cars into the right lane. The traffic light at the end of the exit turned yellow, prompting Joe to punch the gas. Ramsey gripped the rail tight in preparation for a hard right turn. The light turned red just as Joe reached the intersection. He cranked the wheel and the truck leaned left as they turned a hard right onto Chamblee Dunwoody Road.

"I think you had us up on two wheels there, Fireball," Ramsey said as he released his death grip.

"We made it, didn't we? And that's Richard Petty to you!"

"Richard dipstick. For someone not wanting to draw attention, you sure have a funny way of driving. We skidded through a red light back there."

"It was orange," Joe countered. "Alright, look sharp. Whitmore gave us a spot to park a block away from the apartments. He's meeting us there for a sit-rep."

They drove on for a couple of miles, before veering off onto a quieter road. As promised, Whitmore's Suburban was parked on the side with an orange traffic cone reserving a spot behind it. Joe pulled up and killed the engine. He and Ramsey got out and walked up to the Suburban. Whitmore's head peaked out of the passenger side window.

"Hey guys! Hop in the back."

Joe and Ramsey opened the door and slid into the back seat.

"Thanks for getting here so quickly," Whitmore said, as he extended his hand back and shook their hands. "You guys remember Pete O'Malley."

Joe and Ramsey shook hands with O'Malley, who was seated behind the wheel.

"So what do we have, Clay?" Joe asked.

"There's an apartment complex one block up from here. My guys pinged their location right before I called you. They narrowed down to the exact building, but there are four apartments in there and they couldn't tell us which one. I had one of my men disguise himself as a UPS driver with a shoebox-sized package. He went door to door and then pretended to have the wrong address. Three of the apartments answered and don't fit the bill. One was an older Indian couple, one was an elderly Asian man, and one was a young Asian family."

"And the fourth?" Joe asked.

"Drapes closed and no one came to the door," Whitmore answered. "We have guys watching the building front and back. A twenty-ish appearing white male drove up just a few minutes ago with a large bag of McDonald's. We got his picture before he entered the apartment in question. I sent Gary Lee back up there in his UPS disguise and they didn't answer, so that raises my suspicion even more. We put a tracer on the guy's car, and he looks like he could be Russian. I have my tech guys running a facial recognition search and a license plate search as we speak."

"Any sign of the girls?" Ramsey asked.

"Not yet," Whitmore shook his head. "That's my concern. Even if we have the right place, we have no way of knowing this is where they are keeping them."

"Except a young, possibly Russian male just showed up with a large bag of hamburgers and we know they at least *did* run their computer ops where they kept the girls," Joe remarked.

"*And* there were fast food wrappers all over their last place," Ramsey added.

"Yes, all true, but not enough for me to ask you guys to go up there and kick down their doors," Whitmore commented.

"Where is the FBI with all this?" Joe asked.

"That's a good question," Whitmore said, shaking his head. "They were still processing the paperwork when a stand down order came from higher up the chain of command."

"Repeat your last?" Ramsey interjected.

"I'm not kidding. My contact told me the Atlanta field office was given a stand down order on this one from above."

"How did they even get wind of this and who gave the order to stand down?" Joe asked.

"I'm not certain, Joe, but that tells me one of two things; either there's a bigger operation going on against the Tupolev organization and they don't want a new investigation fouling it up, or Tupolev has someone looking out for him that is well placed."

"Both options suck for those girls but the second option really sucks," O'Malley commented from the front seat.

"True enough and it's high enough that my contact can't decipher who's involved," Whitmore added.

His phone rang and he touched his earbud to take the call.

"Rod. What do you have for us?"

Whitmore grabbed a pen and scribbled on a small pad of paper as he listened.

"Yeah? ... Okay, great! ... Yes, stay on this and keep me updated! Thanks, Rod." Whitmore said as he clicked off.

"Alright! We've got something," He said excitedly. "My computer guy matched the plates on the guys car to an Aleksey Androv."

"That sounds Russian to me," Joe remarked.

"Yep," Whitmore nodded, "but there's more. His photo matches his driver's license. He's here on a work visa *and* he is a suspected associate of Tupolev's organization."

"How do they know that?" Joe asked.

"He was rolled up in a drug raid six months ago with several known members of Tupolev's organization. His charges were dismissed, and he was let go, but somebody was taking notes," Whitmore smiled. "*Now* I'm ready to nail these scumbags. You guys don't have to do this if you're not comfortable with it, but if your still in, tell me how you want it to play out."

"We're gonna gear up and then let's drive around the area for a quick recon," Joe answered as he and Ramsey exited Suburban.

They walked back to Joe's truck, grabbed two bags out of the bed toolbox and returned to Whitmore's Suburban. Back inside the vehicle, both donned their tactical vests and headgear with the communicating headphones Critter loaned them. They linked frequencies with Whitmore's team and assigned call signs.

O'Malley drove them around and through the apartment complex. The apartment in question was closest to the road. Each upper unit had both a front and a rear entrance, the front with a set of stairs, the back with a fire escape. It was a relatively hot early afternoon. Kids were in school and adults were either working or staying indoors with their air conditioning. There was essentially no one lingering outside. The only way this could be better would be if it were dark outside. But they didn't have the luxury of time.

"What do you think, Rammer?" Joe asked. "I'm thinking a standard front door breach followed by a two man take down, secure the hostiles, grab any girls and intel then make our way out. We have Whitmore wait for us out front and place two of his men by the fire escape to stop anyone trying to squirt out the back."

"I'd prefer, four men, a couple of flash-bangs and live fire, but I guess we gotta race the car we brought to the track," Ramsey answered.

"I can't do anything about the live fire, but I think I can help you with the flash bangs, fellas," Whitmore answered, holding up a box of six flash bangs. "These are civilian grade, but they should still do the job."

"We'll take them," Joe said, as he and Ramsey each took three and stuffed them into their vests.

"This will draw attention," Ramsey warned.

"I realize that," Joe answered, "But so will kicking down a door and I'd rather stun them than catch a bullet on the way in. We need to move fast, sweep up what we came for, and get out."

"Clay? They may try to squirt out the back. Can you put two men out back to monitor the fire escape?"

"You've got it," Whitmore said as he spoke into a small handheld radio.

"What do we know about the door?" Joe asked.

"What do you mean?"

"Is it steel or wood? Is there a deadbolt? Doorbell camera? Those kinds of things," Joe said. "We need to plan how to breech that door if they aren't answering.

"Ah, I got you," Whitmore answered as he relayed the questions into his radio.

"Steel door with a deadbolt. No cameras that I saw," came Gary Lee's voice through the radio.

"What do you think, Rammer?"

"My guess is both the deadbolt and the knob are locked but using the same key. The stealth approach would be to pick them both at the same time, but we only have one set of lock picks."

"It just so happens, I have a set right here," Whitmore answered to the startled looks of Joe and Ramsey. "Well, I *am* an investigator."

"Works for me," Joe said accepting the small tool set from Whitmore. "Let's roll."

Whitmore spoke into his radio as O'Malley put the Suburban in drive. They parked in the street, just around the corner and out of sight of the apartment. Joe and Ramsey pulled up their balaclava face masks and exited the vehicle. They quickly covered the short distance and were met by Gary Lee in his UPS uniform. He marched up the stairs while Joe and Ramsey crept up to the front entrance, staying low and out of sight. Lee began to knock on the door. No one answered. Joe and Ramsey both pulled out a set of lock picks and quietly went to work on the locks, while Lee knocked. Once they had the door unlocked, Lee stepped down the stairs and joined Whitmore. Ramsey prepared two flash-bang grenades while Joe slowly turned the knob. Ramsey nodded and Joe flung the door open wide. Ramsey tossed in both of the flash-bangs and the two men turned and shut their eyes. Their hearing protection had an automatic sound shut off for any loud noises. What was a deafening crash to those inside, was a mildly audible report through their earmuffs. Joe entered the apartment first. He held an FN High Power 9mm handgun up as he scanned his sector while button-hooking left. Ramsey followed closely behind, carrying a Glock Model 19. A man with a ponytail was writhing on a couch, clutching his ears with his eyes shut. The room was otherwise clear. The fast food guy suddenly appeared from one of the bedrooms, reaching for something behind his back.

"Stop!" Ramsey yelled. "Slowly put your hands up and turn against the wall!"

With a look of shock, the man complied. Ramsey quickly removed a small Taurus .40 caliber handgun from the man's waistline and forced him to the ground. Joe covered while Ramsey quickly applied zip-ties to the man's hands and feet. Ramsey then covered the hall while Joe secured the man on the couch. In an ideal situation, they would have had several more teammates to continue room clearing while a few hung behind to secure the hostiles. This was far from ideal. As if to prove the point, two loud gunshots struck the wall by Ramsey while he and Joe were forming back up to continue their sweep. Ramsey ducked to the opposite wall, taking himself out of the line of fire. The shots had come from a room on his side. He readied a flash-bang, held it up for Joe to see and hooked it around the corner toward the door. The grenade detonated with a loud report and Joe followed it into the room. Ramsey followed closely behind.

"Clear!"

"Clear!" Each man reported, informing the other that his sector was clear of hostiles. A door leading out back was open.

Ramsey gave it a quick check and saw muscular male standing on the fire escape with his hands in the air. Two of Whitmore's men had their guns trained on him. Ramsey was relieved to see it didn't turn into a shooting match.

"They got him," Ramsey said turning back to Joe. "Let's clear the last room."

Joe readied another flash-bang and tossed it into the open door. They turned and covered their eyes until it detonated and then followed it in. Ramsey entered first followed by Joe. Four women were sprawled on two beds as they rocked back and forth holding their ears. No hostiles.

"Clear!" Ramsey called out.

"Clear!" Joe answered.

"Jackpot." Ramsey commented as he took in the scene.

"I sure hope so," Joe answered. "Let's get Whitmore and his men in here. We'll clear it out and get these girls somewhere safe."

"What about the three stooges?"

"They can handle that too. This is his mission. We're just the knuckle draggers. We can help, but it's his call."

Joe toggled his radio. "We're all clear in here, Clay. Four ladies and three hostiles, all contained."

"Roger that. Coming in."

Whitmore and his men quickly filed in along with the one male who tried to escape out the back. Joe met them out front while Ramsey stayed with the girls who were still disoriented from the grenade. The men immediately began to comb the room and found two laptops; one was on the coffee table in front of the guy with the ponytail.

"Chuck, get Roderick on the line and help him get into those computers. Gary, you Marco and Stevie get these three dirtbags ready to roll," Whitmore said as he took charge of the situation.

"O'Malley, Isaiah," he said speaking into his radio, "get the van and Suburban up here now."

"Okay, Joe, show me what you found."

"Coming in, Chief," Joe spoke ahead as he and Whitmore walked back to the room.

They entered the bedroom where Ramsey had the four girls seated on one bed. Of the four, there were two blonds, one with sandy brown hair and one brunette. All appeared drowsy, disheveled and on the thin side.

"This is strong work guys!" Whitmore joyfully exclaimed. "I can't thank you enough!"

He turned to the girls. "Would one of you happen to be Tracy Courtnall?"

He was met with blank stares.

"Do any of you know who I'm talking about?"

"I do," one of the girls spoke up. "But she's gone. They left with her and the two other girls a little while ago."

Chapter 35

Atlanta, Georgia

"Any idea where they were going?" Whitmore asked with concern.

"No," the blond answered. "They were in the other room. The pockmarked guy and the skinny gothic lady grabbed them and left. Probably just another business call. They're working us out in the truck stops and motels round the clock."

"Alright," Whitmore said, his disappointment evident. "We're gonna get you ladies out of here. Is everyone alright?"

His question was met with hesitant nods. Whitmore realized these girls had likely been shuffled from place to place many times by different people. Their fear and distrust must be off the charts. He squatted down before them.

"Hey, listen. I know you must be frightened. My name is Clay, and this is my team. We need to move now before they come back. I need you to stand up and come with us right now!" He said as he pulled one girl to her feet.

Joe and Ramsey helped the other girls up. The three men quickly led the girls out of the apartment.

"I know your probably scared and confused, but we came to rescue you from this hell you've been enduring," Whitmore said as he quickly led the procession down the stair and out to the waiting van. 'We're going to get you someplace safe, get you medical care, and help you find your families or a safe place to go if you prefer. I know what these people have been doing to you and I want to assure you that this nightmare is over."

Whitmore, Ramsey, and Joe helped secure the girls into the van. The rest of his team filed out with the three Russian thugs and a bag of items they collected. Chuck Springer was speaking to Roderick on his earbuds and carrying two laptops. He hopped in the front passenger seat of the van. They placed the ponytail guy and the other two face down in the back of the van along with two members of Gary Lee's team. Joe and Ramsey jumped into the Suburban with Whitmore. O'Malley gunned the engine and they shot out of the parking lot and down the road followed by the van. They turned back onto Chamblee Dunwoody Road and were soon passed by several police cars racing the opposite way.

"Whew! That was close!" Whitmore exclaimed. "In a perfect world I would have just led the police to the place and let them handle it, but I couldn't take the chance based on what we've heard. I have several FBI agents I trust. Even though the investigation was called off, these guys will help us out. I just want to sort everything out first."

"Roger that," Joe answered. "However, it sounds like we're still short of your primary objective."

"You're right," Whitmore said muttering an expletive. "We'll keep at it. We've got their laptops and cellphones and we are on their trail. That's more than we had an hour ago. We'll bag em'."

"We've also got three members of their crew," Ramsey spoke up. "I say we ask them."

"I doubt they'll talk," Whitmore said.

"Convince them to talk," Ramsey countered.

"Guys, I can't do that."

"Then we'll do it," Joe responded.

"Much as I appreciate the offer, I can't ask you to do that," Whitmore pleaded. "We can't do those things here."

"Did you see the condition those girls are in? Do you know what's being done to them? What they're being forced to do? I don't give a flying leap what somebody says we can and can't do," Ramsey countered. "If one of those missing girls was your daughter, what would you do?"

"I'd dip them in hot burning acid until they talked," Whitmore conceded.

"And if it was your daughter, but you were unable to do it and someone else could...?" Joe prompted.

"I hear you, Joe, and you're right. I just have to watch my step. One wrong move and my license gets yanked, just like that," Whitmore said with a snap of his fingers.

"Well, let us do this then," Joe offered, "You see after the girls and work your computer guys while, Rammer and I see what the three stooges know. You can remain completely in the dark."

"I'm not sure, Joe."

"Clay, those girls are out there, somewhere. Every minute we burn increases their chance of remaining missing, let alone what may be done to them. As Edmund Burke once said, *"The only thing necessary for the triumph of evil is that good men should do nothing."* We need to gather intel and move on it, most ricky tick!"

"You're right," Clay nodded solemnly. "Alright, we're heading to Gary's house near Lawrenceville. It's a secluded old farmhouse. He lives alone and has a detached garage out back. When we get there, the garage and the dirtbags are yours. Don't tell me anything other than useful information. I need plausible deniability."

"Deal, Clay," Joe answered. "You sound like a politician but you're doing the right thing."

"I feel like a politician," he commented wearily.

"Well, get in touch with your inner Marine because those girls and their families are depending on us," Joe said clapping Whitmore on the shoulder. "As well-funded and connected as these Russians are, we're going to have to cowboy up."

A short while later, they turned down Gary Lee's shaded driveway. The wooded lot was decently secluded and separated from nearby houses. Rare for the greater Atlanta area which seemed to be one subdivision after another.

"Chief, let's grab the guy with the ponytail first. He had a laptop near him and may know something. The other two look like hired muscle."

"Copy that, Joe."

They exited the Suburban and walked up to the van. Whitmore opened up the rear doors where two of his associates were seated on the floor as they kept watch over the three bound, gagged, and hooded Russians.

"You guys can take Tweedle Dee and Tweedle Dum inside. We want to have a word with Woodstock," Joe said as he dragged the ponytail guy out of the van.

Lee's garage was a gear-head's dream. It was extra wide with two garage bays and nearly two cars long allowing for a deep work area and an overhead loft. Ramsey grabbed the man's wallet and forcibly sat him in a chair. He took out the license and compared it to the sweating man seated before him.

"Petr Orlov?" Ramsey said as he looked back at Orlov. "I doubt Tupolev would have you working over here if you didn't speak English so I'm going to get right to it. You're done. You will likely be deported back to Russia where you will serve time in a Russian prison. You and I both know that a guy like you won't last long in one of those gulags. I know we're not supposed to refer to them like that but we both know that's what they are. On the other hand, if you cooperate and give is the information we want, you just may have your charges reduced to something light enough that you aren't deported. So what do you say? Ready to talk?"

Ramsey pulled down Orlov's gag. Orlov immediately began to speak in rapid Russian. Ramsey was having none of it. He thrust his hand out and clamped down on Orlov's trachea, immediately choking off his ability to breathe.

"Change your channel there, Ivan! I asked you to answer me in English! You want to try again?" Ramsey asked with a hard shake for emphasis.

Choked of his air supply, Petr was in a silent state of panic. His eyes bulged as he vigorously nodded his head. Ramsey released his grip with a shove.

"Okay, Petr, let's try this again. I already know a lot about you and what you guys have been doing. I'm going to ask you some questions. If I catch you in a lie, you will instantly regret it. Do you understand?"

Petr responded with a nervous nod. Joe looked on dispassionately. Enhanced interrogation techniques were taboo in today's political culture. He understood why, but he didn't necessarily agree. The girls they were looking for had been subjected to extensive horror and torture. If they weren't located and rescued, their nightmare would continue. Those innocent girls were receiving merciless torture at the hands of the guilty. Joe had no trouble giving the guilty a dose of their own medicine if it meant the girls would soon be rescued from their horror.

A few months ago, he had personally used these techniques on some key mafia members. Had he not, Christy and his sister, Marina, may not be alive today. Joe never wanted to torture let alone kill anyone, but, if it saved lives, he would do so when necessary. And he would not lose any sleep over it. He listened in and jotted down key information as Petr began to sing.

*****

A short while later, Joe and Ramsey marched Petr into the house. They found Whitmore, Springer, and O'Malley hunched over a kitchen table that was covered with laptops and tablets. They appeared to be heavily involved in an online meeting with a sharp-dressed black man. Whitmore noticed them and looked at Joe with hopeful eyes.

"You got something?" He asked.

"This one's name is Petr Orlov," Joe said as he held firmly onto Petr's still bound arm. "He's their main tech guy. He claims his boss, Sergei Petrenko, told him to shut the auction down without giving a reason. Shortly after that, Petrenko told him and the other two to mind the shop while he and two others left with Courtnall and two other girls."

"Well that explains why we can no longer find it," Whitmore replied. "I guess they got the price they were looking for."

"That's just it, Clay, he says they didn't. They shut the auction down with thirty minutes to go. Petrenko was expecting furious bidding as time ran out and was literally counting the money he thought they would get."

"That doesn't make sense. Maybe he thought they were compromised?" Whitmore offered.

"Petr doesn't think so. He says, if that were the case, Petrenko would have shot him. He thinks they either got a private buyer or Victor Tupolev ordered them to shut down."

"But he doesn't know for sure?"

"No, but he thinks it was Petrenko acting on orders. He said Petrenko seemed angry and was also in a hurry when they left with the girls."

"Okay, let's park that theory for the moment," Clay said with his eyes narrowed in thought. "Does he have any idea where they may have gone?"

"No clue," Joe said shaking his head, "but he's pretty sure Petrenko is with them. Can your tech guys ping Petrenko's cellphone?"

"That's one of the things we are trying to do right now. Roderick is working Orlov's phone but it's all in Cyrillic."

Joe grabbed Orlov's bound wrists and abruptly lifted them up behind him. Orlov grunted in pain.

"I'm sure Petr would be happy to help you guys navigate his phone. Wouldn't you Petr?"

Orlov grunted and nodded in reply.

"Well that's mighty sporting of you, Petr," Joe said as he roughly deposited Orlov in a nearby chair.

Joe came around front, placed both hands on Orlov's shoulders and got down in his face.

"Like we said; if you cooperate, things will go well for you. You will never have to face Petrenko or Tupolev. If you decide to get stupid and send us on a wild goose chase, you will deal with me and you will ultimately end up in a gulag where you and I both know Tupolev will find you."

Orlov swallowed hard and nodded his understanding.

"I think Petr's ready to play ball, Clay. What do you need from him?"

"He can start by telling us which contact is Tupolev."

"It's not in there and I do not know it," Orlov replied with a weak voice. "Only Sergei and Elena are allowed to speak to him or know such things."

"Okay, that's not surprising. I just thought I'd ask," Whitmore responded. "How about Petrenko?"

"It's not allowed in phone, but I know the number. Actually, it's the most recent number in the call log."

Whitmore tapped a few keys on the phone and held it up for Orlov's to see.

"This one?" He asked.

Orlov nodded in response. Whitmore turned to the laptop and spoke to his computer expert, Roderick Boulware.

"Rod, we've got Petrenko's number. I'm going to read it off to you."

"Great! Let's have it, Clay," Boulware spoke through the computer.

Whitmore read off the number and Boulware went to work. Joe looked down and saw a defeated Orlov. Whitmore paced the room, pecking away at his phone, while waiting on his computer team.

Joe nudged Orlov's shoulder. "What about Elena and Igor's numbers? You said they went with Sergei and the girls."

Upon hearing this, Whitmore came back over and held up Orlov's phone. Orlov read off the appropriate numbers which Whitmore relayed to Boulware.

"Okay, we've got a hit on the first number," Boulware said with his rich baritone voice.

"A GPS hit?" Whitmore asked enthusiastically.

"Indeed it is, Clay. He is pinging at the Gwinnett County Airport, not far from your position."

"Uh oh," Gary Lee commented. "That's an executive airport, Clay. Private charters, rich people with private jets and the like."

"They sold her," Whitmore spoke solemnly. "Those demonic scumbags sold her after all!"

"Clay, if we hustle, we might still be able to catch them," Joe suggested.

"You're right, Joe," he answered. "Rod, get a trace on the other two phones. I also need you to break into the airport's flight tower and find out all filed flight plans. They haven't taken off yet, so just the upcoming flights. Find out who owns each jet as well. Joe? You and Ramsey come with me. O'Malley, you drive. Let's move!"

Chapter 36

Lawrenceville, Georgia

O'Malley raced the Suburban as fast as he thought he could get away with. Even a brief stop by the police could cost them precious minutes. Beside him, Whitmore absently peered out the windshield as he listened to Boulware's updates. The team was linked in on an online meeting site. Joe and Ramsey sat behind them where they discussed different take down scenarios.

"Although we're licensed to carry in this state, the problem, Rammer, is we don't have the authority to detain anyone by deadly force. We could drive right up to their plane and they can thumb their noses at us while they taxi away."

"So our options are to draw them into pulling their weapons on us and then we have a right to defend ourselves, which is probably flimsy. We could go in with a full-on take down and take our chances in court or we get someone with arresting authority to drop what they're doing and meet us at the airport in five minutes based on limited intel. Not good, Joe."

"Tell me about it. Wait," Joe said holding up his index finger and looking up to the front seat. "Clay! We're outside of Atlanta, what if we get the county sheriffs on board. We're gonna need someone with arresting authority."

"We have the authority to detain someone of we catch them committing a felony, which this most certainly is," Whitmore answered. "We just don't have the authority to use the threat of deadly force."

"How do you propose to stop them, Clay? Rough language?" Joe countered.

"Hold on a second," Whitmore said as he tapped his ear pod. "Go, Rod!"

Joe looked at Ramsey. "He doesn't have a takedown plan."

"Not his area of expertise. He's an investigator, not an operator. Take-downs are our bailiwick, but I'm not sure what all we can do. There are too many unknowns, Joe. We don't even know if the girls are at the airport. If they *are,* we don't know which plane they're on, if any. Even if we knew, how would we stop them? We have rules of engagement that are worse than we had in Iraq. We can't use any force. Those Russian mobsters can flip us the bird while they fly off yonder."

"That's why we have to get the police involved and right now," Joe answered as he looked up at Whitmore.

"Shoot! Are you kidding me?" Whitmore shouted into his earpiece. "Okay, have Diaz and Henderson go after them. I'll reach out to my friends at the FBI. Yeah, good. Keep me posted," Whitmore said as he touched his earpiece, ending the call.

"What do you want to do, Clay?" Joe asked.

"We need some help. I've got Springer calling the county sheriffs right now, but we've got another problem. The other two people with Petrenko are driving away from the airport. Rod has a track on their phones, and they appear to be together. I'm putting one of my teams on them now, but I still want to hit the airport. Sergei's phone track still has him there. Rod's team is using GPS and contacting the flight tower to try to narrow down which plane might be theirs. I'm going to hit one of my FBI buddies up for any kind of assistance they can give us."

"I thought they were on a stand down order?" Ramsey asked.

"Yeah, but I'm going to see if I can cash in on a favor."

"Airport's just up ahead, Clay!" O'Malley said as he steered out of a right hand turn onto Hosea Road.

"Rod says to turn onto Briscoe Boulevard. It's right after the train tracks. Petrenko appears to be about a quarter mile down, based on his GPS location."

O'Malley turned them onto Briscoe Boulevard which ran alongside a collection of hangars and buildings that made up the airport. On the far side of the buildings, dozens of aircraft of various makes and sizes could be seen.

"Does he have an idea of which aircraft they might be boarding?" Joe asked.

"No, but he's got the location dialed in. Wait..." Whitmore habitually held his earpiece as if to hear better. "Okay, turn into the next lot between those two buildings!"

O'Malley turned left into a small parking lot. A tall chain link fence spanned between the buildings barring entrance to the tarmac. Two aircraft could be seen parked on the other side of the fence.

"Pull up to the fence, Pete, so we can have a look," Whitmore spoke to O'Malley. "Get pictures of the tail numbers. I'm gonna see if Rod can identify them."

Joe studied the two airplanes through the windshield. Both were Cessna's. One was a turboprop that had its propeller in motion and appeared about to taxi. The other was a Citation with twin jets that also appeared to be running but the entry door remained open.

"That prop plane looks like he's about to take off, Clay," Joe warned. "We need to get out on that tarmac and block him!"

"In this?" Whitmore asked, astonished.

"Yes, in this!" Joe answered. "Can you think of a better way to stop and aircraft from taxiing out to the runway? It'll buy us some time until the police get here."

Whitmore looked at Joe open mouthed.

"Now, Clay! There's a security entrance a couple of buildings over. We need to double time it, right now, if we're gonna catch them!"

"Alright!" Whitmore nodded to O'Malley.

O'Malley shifted into reverse and began to back out. At the same time, the airplane's propeller began to increase in loudness and the aircraft lurched into motion. O'Malley braked to a stop while Whitmore let out an expletive and pounded his fist on the door. The Cessna quickly moved out to the taxiway and rolled out of sight.

"Work the problem, Clay," Joe admonished from the back seat. "They could still be on the other aircraft. Ask Roderick if Petrenko's signal is moving while we head over to the entrance."

"Joe, take a look at this," Ramsey said as he pointed out to the tarmac.

All four men watched as a dark late model SUV rapidly approached the Citation Jet. It pulled to a stop and the doors opened. Two large men in ill-fitting suits emerged along with a shorter stocky man with thin graying hair wearing a sport coat and slacks.

"Tupolev!" Clay exclaimed. "Let's go!"

O'Malley finished backing out and threw the Suburban into drive. He sped out of the parking lot and back up Briscoe Boulevard until they came to the entrance point Joe spotted earlier. They pulled up to the gate where they were met by a barrel-chested, upper middle-aged man in black pants and a blue security uniform shirt. O'Malley rolled down the window.

"Only authorized vehicles are allowed beyond this point, sir," he said.

"Sir, I'm Clay Whitmore, private investigator," Whitmore said leaning over from the passenger seat while holding up his credentials. "There is a plane getting ready to take off carrying several girls who have been abducted. If we don't get in there right now, they're gone."

"I'm sorry sir, but if I let any unauthorized vehicle past this point, I'll be fired."

"If you don't help us stop that plane, at least three girls will be sexually assaulted for who knows how long and may never see their families again!" Whitmore yelled.

"Sir, I..."

"I don't have time for this!" Joe yelled as he rolled down his window and thrust out his military ID card. "Sir, my name is Lieutenant Commander Joseph O'Shanick, United States Navy. We are tasked with the rescue of those three girls and you are impeding our mission!"

Joe scowled at the man with a menacing glare. Normally, his green eyes lightened up his dark, chiseled features, a genetic combination from his Irish father and Filipino mother. Currently, his eyes took on a mood that spelled danger.

"I suggest you either open that gate or get your superior on the horn immediately Mr. Nichols!" Joe said reading off the man's identity badge.

"I'll get my boss, sir," the man said as he stepped back a few feet, unclipped a handheld radio, and spoke into it.

"Sorry, folks. Park's closed. The moose should've told you outside," Ramsey said mimicking John Candy's character in National Lampoon's Vacation.

O'Malley laughed out loud while Joe suppressed a laugh as he watched the security guard nervously speaking on his radio. After a minute, the guard returned.

"My supervisor will be here in a minute. He says to wait here."

"We may not have a minute!" Joe shot back.

"It's above my pay grade, sir. I'm sorry."

"Rod says the first plane is registered to a local orthopedic surgeon," Whitmore spoke from the front. "The jet we just saw Tupolev getting on is registered to a shell corporation in the Bahamas."

"So we don't know if it belongs to him or the auction winner," Joe surmised.

"Correct," Whitmore nodded, "but Rod's looking into it."

"Well, regardless, of who owns the plane, if we don't stop it, it's a moot point," Ramsey commented.

"I think this is our guy," Joe said.

A white Ford F-150 pickup with white flashing lights pulled up alongside them. A stocky, middle-aged man wearing the white shirt of a supervisor stepped out and walked up to Whitmore's window.

"Something I can help you with, gentlemen?"

"Yes, sir, there is," Joe said as he handed over his ID and explained the situation to the man.

"I see," the man answered. "And what is the tail number of that aircraft?"

Whitmore held up a small notebook, allowing the man to read the number. He stepped back and spoke into his radio. Joe watched the airfield, convinced he was going to see the jet in question lifting off from the runway. *Where were the sheriffs?* He was tempted to jump out of the truck and head to the plane on foot. He would have been there by now. The security supervisor came back up to the window.

"Two of y'all ride with me. The rest hang back here until I call for you," he said as he turned and headed for his truck.

"Joe, let's you and I go," Whitmore said as he unbuckled and opened his door.

Whitmore slid into the rear seat of the pickup allowing Joe to take the front. The security supervisor, Tate was his name on the badge, put the truck into gear and inched up to the security gate as it slowly rolled open. He squeezed through the opening and punched the gas.

"Your plane had just been given taxi clearance but it's still on the ground. I called the flight tower and told them to hold it for a security boarding. If your girls are on there, then we'll get the cops in here. It's the best I can do."

"Thank you, Officer Tate," Joe replied.

"I've got two daughters myself," he said sympathetically.

A metallic voice crackled through his radio. He spoke into the device and then held it up to his ear, waiting for the reply. The voice crackled in response. He muttered a few choice words and stomped on the gas.

"What's the matter?" Joe asked.

"Your plane just disregarded the flight tower and is taxiing toward the runway."

"That plane can *not* take off!" Joe yelled.

"I'm on it!" Tate responded loudly.

They rounded the corner and turned down the taxiway. The Citation jet was several hundred yards ahead and rapidly moving away from them. Tate accelerated even more, but Joe could see they wouldn't make it in time.

"He's gonna reach that runway before we can get to him," Tate spoke urgently.

"How would you have stopped him?" Joe asked as he considered several options.

"I was going to pull in front of him and block his progress. Those birds don't veer well when on the ground."

"He will have to make two left-hand turns to get on the runway," Joe said thinking out loud. "He has to slow down to do that. If you floor it, we might catch him when he does that!"

Tate floored the pedal in response. The distance began to close as the aircraft slowed to make the first turn. With a little over a hundred yards to go, the aircraft leaned over as it made a hard left. Whitmore and Tate cursed in unison. Joe peered ahead, processing the situation.

"Veer left!" He yelled to Tate.

"What?" Tate replied in confusion.

"Veer left! Cut across the field on get on the runway ahead of him!"

Tate braked and cut the vehicle hard left. The truck began to vibrate as it bounced across the grassy field. The aircraft had reached the runway and was beginning to line up for takeoff. Joe watched as the pilot maintained speed through the turn. The truck reached the runway just as the airplane began to accelerate.

"Turn towards him!" Joe yelled.

"Are you out of your mind?!" Tate yelled back.

"Just do it!" Joe responded. "Take him head on! Aim straight for his nose gear!"

"I can't do that!"

"If you don't do that, three girls may never see a normal life again!" Joe challenged. Would you do it if one of them was your daughter?"

Tate cursed again as he turned the wheel and began to head straight for the oncoming aircraft. Joe and Whitmore cinched their seatbelts tight. It was a classic game of chicken. Joe was hoping for a sane pilot who would brake the plane to a stop. Watching the distance rapidly close, Joe realized that wasn't going to happen. *Surely he's not going to keep going straight?* If the airplane veered, it would either tip or run off the runway. Either way, it would not be taking off. If it didn't veer, well, Joe wasn't sure. He hoped they would sheer the landing gear and slide beneath the fuselage, but the aircraft was fairly low to the ground. It was beginning to look like they were heading for head on collision. Over in the driver's seat, Tate was letting out a stream of expletives as the oncoming luxury jet rapidly approached. The aircraft filled the windshield causing Joe to reflexively grip the door handle. From the backseat, Whitmore screamed.

Chapter 37

Lawrenceville, Georgia

Whitmore's scream startled Tate who reflexively cranked the steering wheel to his left. The truck heeled over as it veered left, narrowly missing what Joe thought was an inevitable collision. Joe rapidly twisted in his seat to witness the luxury jet's swept wing pass over the bed of the truck, just missing the cab.

"Hold on!" Tate yelled as a drainage ditch loomed up ahead.

Tate stomped on the brakes, but they were too close. With a sharp jolt the truck struck the lip of the concrete ditch and lurched across to the other side where the front tires struck hard, causing it to lurch even higher. Joe's head hit the ceiling when the rear tires struck the opposite side, causing the front to slam onto the ground. Tate grounded them to a halt a dozen yards later. All three sat for a moment in silence while drawing a collective breath.

"You guys alright?" Tate asked while trying to catch his breath.

"Yeah," Joe replied, the disappointment evident in his response.

He looked back at Whitmore, who was using his hand to wipe the perspiration off his forehead. Through the rear window, Joe caught a glimpse of the airplane as it rose into the sky.

"We need to figure out where that plane is headed and do it fast," Joe said.

"I'm on it," Clay responded as he pressed his earbud and began to speak.

Joe looked at Tate. "Is this thing still drivable?"

Tate eased off the brake and they began to roll forward. "Seems okay,"

"Built Ford tough, I guess," Joe said, as he craned his neck and saw the aircraft conducting a banking turn to the south as it faded out of sight.

"I'm sorry about that back there," Tate began. "I chickened out last second."

"It's alright," Joe sighed. "If you hadn't, we probably wouldn't be alive and having this talk. We'll just have to find another way."

"I sure hope you do," Tate's voice trailed off as he answered.

They drove back to the security entrance in silence, save for Whitmore talking into his earbud. Upon reaching the gate, the three men were met by the sheriffs. After giving their accounts, they all went their separate ways. Joe and Whitmore joined back up with Ramsey and O'Malley in the Suburban. As Whitmore continued to talk on the phone with his team, Joe brought Ramsey and O'Malley up to speed on what had transpired.

"Take us back to the house," Whitmore instructed O'Malley, briefly diverting from an intense phone conversation with his team.

Joe and Ramsey listened on to Whitmore's side of the conversation. It was difficult to follow, only hearing what Whitmore was saying, but it didn't sound encouraging.

"Alright, let's go with that. Call me as soon as you hear anything," Whitmore said as he disconnected the call.

"What's the sit-rep, Clay?" Joe asked from the back.

Whitmore took a deep breath and collected his thoughts before responding.

"It's a goat rope," he said shaking his head. "My computer guys still don't know who owns that airplane, but they've traced it to a shell corporation in the Bahamas believed to have ties to a Mexican cartel. They were able to obtain the aircraft's flight plan which has it flying to Key West."

"That's good!" O'Malley exclaimed. "It's a small airport *and* it's in the continental United States. We just need to alert the authorities and they can nab them when they land."

"I don't know," Joe said skeptically. "This guy, Tupolev didn't get where he is by being stupid. He knows someone's after him. He has to know he's vulnerable like that. The only way he's landing in Key West is if he owns the police down there, which I highly doubt. I'll bet a dollar to a donut they change their flight plan mid-flight. If you don't have your FBI buddy onboard, I think it's high time you did. We're going to need their muscle to get Air Traffic Control to keep us informed of where this bird is headed. We'll also need their help nabbing these dirtbags wherever they land. They've got a lot more reach and can coordinate with the locals."

"I'll call him right now," Whitmore replied. "But I'm still going to have the authorities waiting on them in case they land. I'm also going to see if I can get a contact to head down there and scope things out."

"Perfect," Joe agreed. "Play both scenarios. Is there another scenario we aren't thinking of?"

"Chasing that airplane to wherever it lands and intercepting them on the ground is all we can do."

"What about the other two cellphone signals?" Joe asked. "Have your guys intercepted them yet?"

"Not yet. They're trailing them though. Caught up with them when they were stopped at gas station. They said it *is* a van, but it's a panel van so they can't see into the back. A stocky guy driving and, Diaz says, and a woman who looks like Morticia, from the Addams Family in the passenger seat. That's all they could see. I have another team heading their way, just in case the girls are with them."

"Good call," Joe said in agreement. "I doubt it'll be that easy. They didn't bring the girls out to the airport and take off in a hurry if they were sending them back with the hired help. My money says they're on that plane, but I think we should grab the two on the ground and see what intel we can get out of them."

Whitmore looked at Joe in solemn contemplation. "You don't want to let the police handle that?"

"Handle what?" Joe retorted. "They don't have anything to arrest these guys over and, even, if they did, the thugs will just clam up and demand their lawyers. The girls will be long gone by then."

"O'Malley, link up with Isaiah and Diaz," Whitmore spoke and then turned his attention back to Joe. "You're right. I'm just not used to operating this way."

"Unfortunately, we are," Ramsey stated.

"I get it," Whitmore said with a nod. "You guys have seen a lot of bad actors. Haven't you?"

"Evil. Pure evil," Ramsey commented. "But it's what we do, and we are trained to deal with it."

"You probably see a pretty dark side of life as well," Joe offered.

"Nothing like what you see," he replied. "We handle mostly white-collar crimes; embezzlement, insider trading, employee background searches, and divorce cases. Occasionally, we get asked to help locate missing children, but I've never seen anything like this bunch of reprobates."

"Clay, if these guys head back to their apartment, won't it be crawling with cops?" Joe asked.

"Probably," he answered.

"Then they're likely going to turn around and head back out the way they came. That should buy us some time to get close. Your guys could eyeball them and confirm while we wait out by the main road. We could leapfrog a tail on them and follow them to their next location."

"We do have a trace on their cellphones," Whitmore reminded.

"I know that," Joe responded, "but there's nothing more reliable than a Mark One eyeball; besides, with us, we will have three vehicles. I'm thinking we could box them in and perform a quick snatch and grab. I still think the girls are on that plane but would just as soon confirm that and find out what these goons know ASAP. Have you heard anything back from your FBI guy or your computer team on the whereabouts of that aircraft?"

"Nothing from the FBI yet. Rod says the aircraft is still heading towards Key West. I've got an associate in Miami heading that way but won't get there before they land. The Monroe County Sheriffs have been notified as well."

"About as good as we can hope for, I guess," Joe commented.

"Wait a minute!" Ramsey spoke up as he pulled out his cell phone. "I've got an old teammate who lives in Key West."

"You serious?" Joe asked. "Who?"

"A guy named Dave Zivojinovic, if I said that right. Nobody ever could pronounce his last name, so we just called him *Big Dave*. He left the teams before you got there, Joe. Demolitions expert and a good one at that. A hurricane hit the Keys a few years back and he went down to start a restoration business for water and smoke damage. Did so well, he expanded into carpentry and home rebuilding. Been there ever since," Ramsey said as he dialed his phone and held it up to his ear.

"Big Dave!" Ramsey spoke into his phone. "Matt Ramsey here. How are you doing there, you salty old..."

Ramsey conversed with his old a friend for several minutes before ending the call.

"Done. He'll head to the airport in half an hour. Plenty of time to get there before they land. He said if they do land there, he will call in a couple of his buddies to help track them."

"That's great, Matt! Thank you!" Whitmore said from the front seat. "Text me his contact information and I'll make sure he is compensated for his efforts."

"That won't be necessary, Clay. Big Dave is the kind of guy who would give you the shirt off his back. Once I explained the situation, he was all in."

"Give it to me anyway. He deserves to be compensated. I take care of everyone who helps us out. It's just the way I do things."

"Roger that," Ramsey nodded with a thumbs up.

"While you were on the phone, I talked to one of my FBI guys. I updated him on the situation and sent the photos of Tupolev getting on the plane. He's taking it up the chain of command. Who knows? Maybe the new circumstances will change things and get them onboard."

"Forgive me if I don't hold my breath on that one, Clay," Joe muttered. "If by some miracle they do, by the time that decision filters back down to an actionable command, Tupolev and those girls will be long gone. I think we're on our own with this one."

"Alright, here we go!" Whitmore announced with his left hand touching his earbud. "They just turned back down Chamblee Dunwoody Way, heading toward that apartment."

Whitmore paused as he listened in. He squinted his eyes in concentration.

"They're slowing down. Diaz says there are multiple police cars there. Where are we, O'Malley?"

"We're on 141. A few minutes away."

"They're moving on!" Clay announced as he looked at the GPS map on his iPad. "They drove right past the place. Diaz says they're about to turn right onto Peachtree. Stay on this road. It runs parallel to Peachtree before curving right and running into it. If we beat them to the intersection, we can pick up their tail."

"You got it, boss," O'Malley answered.

"Cameron?" Whitmore spoke into his earbud. "How far out are you?"

Whitmore looked back at Joe, "The other team is ten minutes away."

Whitmore shut his eyes as he fingered his earbud as if listening in. His eyes snapped open and he swiveled his head back to the road ahead.

"Diaz says they took the first right onto Pierce," Whitmore spoke excitedly as he looked up from his tablet. "That's it coming up on the left! Turn left here!"

The SUV heeled right as O'Malley cut the wheel left turning onto a two-lane side street. A large stand of trees lined the corner, giving Joe an idea.

"O'Malley, turn left into that parking lot!" Joe spoke loudly.

O'Malley dutifully followed Joe's command. Joe quickly ditched his tactical vest and concealed his handgun. Ramsey followed his lead.

"Alright," Joe started, "turn and get us into position as if we are about to pull out of the parking lot. Clay, are you okay with a little fender bender?"

"I guess. What do you have in mind?"

"We'll pull out in front of the Russians and hold them up at the stop sign. Have Diaz hit them from behind and run them into us. We'll all get out like we're inspecting the accident. Rammer and I will grab the Russians. Have Diaz and Isaiah check for the girls."

"Do what he says, O'Malley," Whitmore nodded to his driver, as he gave Diaz instructions over the phone.

"Be sure to stop a little short of the intersection," Joe coached. "Let's let these trees give us as much cover as we can get from the main road."

"Gotcha," O'Malley nodded.

"Diaz, says it's a white panel van," Whitmore announced. "We should see it any second."

"There it is." Joe spoke. "Slowly pull out and head to the intersection, O'Malley."

O'Malley pulled out and cruised to a stop just short of the stop sign.

"Lure him in, O'Malley," Joe coached. "Take your foot off the brake but don't hit the gas. Wait for him to get closer and then stomp on the brake. Now!"

The SUV lurched to a stop. A split second later, the white van did the same just short of rear-ending Whitmore's SUV. Joe and Ramsey faced each other, as if in discussion, while using their peripheral vision to watch behind them. A few seconds later, Diaz struck the van from behind, forcing it to run into the back of the SUV. Joe and Ramsey opened their doors along with Whitmore and O'Malley. They stepped out, throwing their hands in the air, and acting furious. Joe shuffled toward the driver's side door of the van which was just starting to open. A stocky man with short, dark, curly hair and a pockmarked face began to step out. Joe suddenly lunged his full body weight into the door, violently slamming the man into the door frame and pinning him. Joe struck the man in the nose with the butt of his FN High Power handgun. He then grabbed the momentarily stunned man by the back of his hair and shoved him to the ground. Joe had his handgun trained at the man's head while O'Malley placed his knee on the man's spine and quickly zip tied the man's hands together. On the other side of the van, Ramsey smashed the passenger window and dragged a gothic looking, raven-haired female out the window. He and Whitmore, similarly tied up the woman and forced her to walk to the SUV. Diaz made a quick search of the van's interior.

"It's empty boss," he yelled up to Whitmore who was helping Ramsey put the female into the SUV.

"I'm not surprised," Whitmore yelled back. "Move the van into the parking lot and then follow us back to Gary Lee's house."

Ramsey manhandled the rail thin woman into the backseat and deposited her on the floor. He jumped in after her and sat in the seat using his legs to keep her pinned to the floor. Joe shoved the pockmarked man into the middle row and climbed in beside him. Whitmore climbed in on the other side. They closed the doors and O'Malley turned right, putting them back onto 141, and sped off.

Chapter 38

Dallas, Texas

"...because better security and a better economy means better jobs and a better life, especially for Texans!"

An enthusiastic response of applause rose up from the near-capacity convention center crowd. The speaker was a confident-appearing man with a slight build enhanced by a tailored suit with padded shoulders. His graying blond hair was well-coifed, and his skin had a golden tan, the result of a spray-on tan from an expensive spa he frequented. He stepped back from the podium and smiled as he gestured with his arms urging the crowd on. The noise soon died down and he stepped back up to the podium.

"Which means?" He asked excitedly as he prompted the crowd for his traditional rally cry.

"Which means?" A little louder. "C'mon folks, say it with me!"

"Better days are just ahead!" The crowd shouted in unison as they shouted the slogan of Senator Robert Fowler's presidential campaign.

On cue, the song "Better Days" by The Goo Goo Dolls began to play loudly over the PA system. The crowd roared their approval. Senator Robert Fowler surveyed the crowd approvingly. His adrenaline surged as he absorbed the adoring crowd's energy. There were many reasons he sought public office years ago, but *this* was what kept him coming back. Now he was on the grand stage. A little over a month away from the highest office in the land and the polls had him a five-point favorite. It was so close, he could feel it, just like he felt the adulation of the crowd. It was addicting. Wealth he had. His family was worth a small fortune and Fowler had amassed his own over the years; first as a commercial real estate attorney, then even more as the senior Senator of his home state of Arizona. As much as he enjoyed his wealth and all its trappings, it couldn't match the emotional high he experienced in moments like this. It was powerful. In fact, power was the key. He had just fired up a crowd through the simple words of a speech prepared by a staffer. The speech was artfully manipulative through key slogans and hot topic issues yet devoid of substance. It didn't matter. The crowd responded to his words. No, not his words, how he delivered the words. Fowler used the words to reach the people on an emotional level and their near worship-like response was intoxicating. Yes. He was ready. Bring on the world stage. Bring on the heads of state. His opponent, the incumbent president, Jorge Galan, was critical of Fowler's lack of experience with foreign policy and leadership. Screw him. Fowler would use his charm and persuasion to win the world's approval. He would have the keys to America and all of her vast wealth and resources. Foreign heads of state would be putty in his hands, just like this crowd.

His anticipation was jarred back to the present when his wife, Cassandra, stepped up next to him and grabbed his hand. Together, they sauntered about the stage, hand in hand, waving to the crowd and occasionally pointing to individuals as if they knew them. The cheering continued.

"If only they knew you like I do," Cassandra whispered in his ear while looking at the television camera with a smile.

Fowler kissed his wife on the cheek in response, which made the crowd cheer louder.

"All the world's a stage, my dear," he whispered back.

Cassandra, nearly twenty years his junior, was his second wife. His first wife, a blue-blood socialite had died of cancer before their marriage, which had been rocked with infidelity and bitterness, had ended in a costly divorce. Fowler had wisely parlayed her death into a sympathy vote helping him win his first bid at office. Cassandra, a former professional football cheerleader and personal trainer, had assumed the duties of a prominent senator's wife amazingly well. Beneath her seemingly innocent beauty, lurked a deceptively cunning and perceptive woman. *A she-devil,* Fowler thought. She had figured him out early into their marriage. Perhaps even before they were married, if Fowler was honest. It was more than just gold digging. Cassandra could have left him years ago with a hefty divorce settlement. No, she was ambitious in her own way and was willing to play the long con, so long as Fowler took her where she wanted to go. First Lady would suit her just fine. It was the biggest carrot he could dangle before her to keep her from derailing his career with a costly divorce. Fowler sighed through a practiced smile. Cassandra knew his weaknesses. Her whispered comment was a purposeful jab to keep his ego in check and remind him of just how much she was in control. Their marriage was a sham, but both were ambitious enough to perpetuate a blissful facade for the benefit of the public's perception. No problem there, they were both practiced experts in that.

They retreated to the back of the stage. With a farewell wave and smile, Robert and Cassandra Fowler disappeared behind the curtain. They immediately let go of each other's hand and hastily made their way toward the Secret Service motorcade. Fowler's chief of staff, Theron Belknap, leather folder in hand, joined them in the back hallway.

"Cassie," Fowler began, "I've had some rather urgent matters to attend to. I'll see you on the plane."

"Knock yourself out, superstar," she muttered out of the side of her mouth before increasing her pace and distancing herself from her husband.

Belknap ignored her. He was one of the few people who knew the real workings of the Fowler household. His boss was a nearly uncontrollable philanderer but, fortunately, Mrs. Fowler was quite active herself, only rarely with her husband. Belknap had amassed plenty of evidence for contingencies. She would likely toe the line for her own interests, but he had a hard-drive full of photos and recordings to persuade her, just in case.

"What do you have for me, Theron?" Fowler asked.

"I have the final draft of the defense appropriations bill for you to look over, sir. We increased the funding by an additional thirty billion over President Galan's proposal..."

"Call him Jorge or Galan, Theron, but for Pete's sake, stop using the title president with that name! Did you see that crowd tonight? We're peaking at the right time, so let's think positively," Fowler finished adding a patronizing clap on his chief of staff's back.

"Yes, sir. Anyway, I drafted a press release, but I really think we should fly back to Washington and take it to the press. Let them rave about your rally for the next few hours and then hit them with some policy. I'm thinking a live press interview from the Rotunda on Chelsea McMann's show, stress the point that you don't think Galan is doing enough for our brave men and women in the armed forces, yada yada yada."

"That's good, Theron, let's do that. Only we are still flying back to Phoenix. I have plans and I'm not breaking them. I'll do the press appearance," Fowler said by way of appeasement, "it will just be with a different background. Now, back to the defense appropriations bill? Are we sure it will pass?"

"Who cares, sir? So long as you show the voters you care about the military and are willing to outspend Pres...I mean, Galan, then it's a win. If it doesn't pass, we'll spin it to our advantage. Blame the opposition for cutting the military's budget. That always plays well."

The truth was, Fowler, despite being a member of the Senate Armed Forces Committee, didn't care a wit about the military. His interest was in controlling how the massive defense budget dollars were spent as well as having access to vital information. Information was power. Power was everything; nevertheless, there remained a large contingent of swing voters that favored the armed forces and he was not opposed to political posturing, let alone increasing the federal debt to gain their votes.

"Good. Senator Cohen and I will take it to Speaker Hobson first thing on Monday. What else?"

"Senator Williams wants to collect that favor you owe him," Belknap said with a wince as Fowler climbed into the armored SUV.

"Now?" Fowler said as Belknap ran around to the other side and climbed in next to his boss. "I thought he'd hold that one until I was president. What's he want?"

"A high-ranking cabinet post."

"You're kidding me, right?"

"No, sir. He's serious."

"What's his angle? I thought he was happy right where he is? He told me so himself. He'll never run for president, but he could likely hold on to his senate seat for as long as he wants. If he joins my cabinet, he'll be out as soon as my two terms are done. Or sooner. I don't get it, Theron."

"It's not for him, sir."

"Oh, dear God, who?" Fowler asked with a wince.

It was Belknap's turn to wince.

"Governor..."

"No! Don't say it!" Fowler held up his hand in protest with a painful expression on his face.

"...Maynard-Worthington."

"NO! Oh, God, no! Not her! Oh, man! We were having such a good day and now this?"

"I know, sir. She's not my favorite person either, sir. I'm sorry."

"I can't stand to even see her smug face on the news and now Williams wants me to appoint her to my cabinet? Please tell me he's not serious?"

"I wish he wasn't, sir." Belknap said contritely.

"*He* can't stand her either!" Fowler said shaking his head in frustration. "He must have really stepped in it this time to have to cash in a favor for that pushy lesbian."

"Be careful, sir. You don't want people hearing you talk like that."

"Ah," Fowler waved his chief of staff off dismissively. "We're safe in here and, besides, it's true."

"It doesn't matter, sir. One wrong word can sink your entire campaign. You need to watch what you say...and do," Belknap added.

"What are you getting at, Theron?"

"I'm saying, I think you should reconsider your plans for this weekend. Sir."

"No, Theron. We've been over this. We're about to hit the final month of this campaign. It's going to be several rallies a day, photo ops, press conferences, baby kissing, and who knows what else you and Drake have cooked up for me. On top of that, I still have my obligations in the Senate. This will be my last weekend of R and R for a long while and I'm not giving it up to go on the campaign trail in Godforsaken Kansas for Representative Lester."

Belknap studied his boss. R and R, in Fowler's case should more likely be I and I for intoxication and intercourse. If one moment of indiscretion were caught on camera, their entire campaign would be torpedoed. Belknap had repeatedly stressed that point to no avail. Knowing that Senator Williams' request had set his boss on edge, Belknap chose his next words very carefully.

"Senator, I don't know what you have planned, and I don't want to know. I don't want anyone to know. We all know how hard you have worked and need a weekend off. Believe me, we get it, but hear me out. If we can help push Representative Lester over the finish line, we may just gain the majority in the Senate. If we hold on to the House, then you will have *no* opposition in Washington. Do you know how rare it is for a president to have majorities in both the House *and* the Senate?"

"It's rare, Theron. I know," Fowler said in a softer tone as he assumed a contemplative look.

Theron allowed himself to relax ever so slightly. Fowler hadn't risen this far without being pragmatic. Giving up a weekend of debauchery was a small price to pay to secure his power bid; besides, Belknap was a man of many resources. Arranging for a discreet hotel suite dalliance to pacify his boss on the campaign trail was nothing new for him. Fowler would do the right thing.

"When's the rally for Lester?" Fowler asked with his eyes closed.

"Saturday night, sir."

After a contemplative pause, Fowler spoke. "Fine. Set it up."

"Thank you, sir. You're doing the wise thing. And regarding the Senator Williams request?"

Fowler cursed. "The governor can have HUD. She's a former big city mayor. That should be right up her ally."

"That may not fly, sir. Williams said it was to be a top-level cabinet position."

"HUD is what I'm offering, Theron. Tell Williams he can take it or leave it. And he, for sure, better keep up his end of the bargain!

Nobody goes near our Russian friend!" Fowler said in hushed tones. "Small busts are fine to make it look good, but that's it, and he is to tell that FBI Assistant Special Agent in Charge to find someone else to go after!"

"Yes, sir."

"And, if Williams decides to press the issue, let him know that I know about his son's predicament."

That answered a question further down Belknap's list. He decided to give his boss a minute to calm down. While he waited, he opened up his phone and tapped off a quick text.

Chapter 39

Atlanta, Georgia

Special Agent Javier Gomez purposefully strode down the hall. His leather-soled shoes clicked loudly against the hard-tiled floor. He was average height with a lean athletic build. A former college soccer player who still played in several competitive leagues, his athletic build and youthful face helped him look twenty years younger than his actual age, which was closing in on forty. Gomez was normally, happy, and outgoing; however, today, the fierce anger on his face, along with his tense pace, caused people to part before him as he strode down the busy hall. He reached the office of the Special Agent in Charge of the Human Trafficking Task Force and knocked on the open-door frame.

"Javi!" Special Agent Katie Huggins beamed as she looked up from a desk laden with files. "Come in! To what do I owe this pleasure?"

Gomez stepped in and closed the door. He and Huggins went way back. He had served with her in his early years before jumping ship to Organized Crime while she moved on to Human Trafficking. They remained friends and played together in a co-ed soccer league. Katie having played college soccer at Vanderbilt, was still a competitive force on the field while being a mother of three in her mid-forties. A very perceptive woman, she immediately picked up on Gomez's disposition and the fact that he closed the door.

"I take it you're not here to discuss soccer. What's up?" She asked.

"Clay Whitmore just handed us Victor Tupolev on a silver platter and Winkelman just told us it's a no go."

Andrew Winkelman was an Assistant Special Agent in Charge in the FBI's Atlanta Field office and Gomez's superior. Gomez didn't care for the man. In Gomez's assessment, Winkelman was a career-minded ticket-puncher who put his career aspirations ahead of the mission. He had befuddled past investigations with his meddling and called off other investigations for suspect reasons. Gomez had caught on to a pattern in regard to the Tupolev organization but could never prove it. Today's wave off was the icing on the cake.

"Did he give a reason?" Huggins asked.

"Yeah, same one as always. He says there is a coinciding investigation with another organization and that we are not to get involved."

"Javier, I know he's not your ideal superior and I think he's a bit of a creep myself, but maybe that's really all it is."

"I don't think so," Gomez shook his head. "I've been watching Tupolev and his lackeys for years. He just keeps growing his organization and expanding his territory while we avoid him and take down his adversaries. On paper, it looks like we are helping him."

"Okay, but why are you coming to me? I'm in another division and outside your chain of command."

"Because I don't know how far up the chain this goes. I don't know who else I can take it to. *And* because it involves a human trafficking ring."

Huggins sat up straight. "You have my complete attention, Javi."

"Clay was hired to find a college girl who went missing last week. The trail led straight to Tupolev."

"Why am I just finding about this now?" Huggins asked sharply.

"Easy, Katie," Gomez calmly replied. "Clay just came to me with this yesterday. It involves the Tupolev organized crime syndicate. It's within our purview and I gave it its due diligence. Now that I'm hitting a brick wall, I'm bringing it to you. I wasn't trying to keep you out of it."

"Fair enough," Huggins responded with a nod. "Have a seat and tell me what you know."

Huggins pulled out a fresh legal pad and picked up a pen. Gomez spent the next several minutes bringing his colleague up to speed on what he knew, which was precious little, he had to admit. Huggins listened without interrupting while she took notes. When Gomez was finished, she looked up from her legal pad with her eyes narrowed.

"And Winkelman told you to stand down on this?" Huggins voice began to rise again.

"Yep," Gomez nodded with a tight-lipped expression. "He said the stand down order came from higher up and that it was due to a coinciding investigation."

"Yeah, you said that. *Which* organization?"

"He wouldn't say."

"And this isn't the first time this has happened?" She asked.

"Nope. I can think of several times we've been pulled off an investigation or not given approval. Every one of them involved Tupolev's mob. I'm starting to smell a rat."

Huggins stared across her desk with pursed lips as she processed the information.

"I do to. Rescuing those girls is a priority. I can't see the logic in a stand down. The question is who is behind this? Is it Winkelman or does it run higher?"

"Exactly," Gomez said in agreement. "And you're in a better position than me to figure that out."

"Well, the key is SAIC McPherson," Huggins spoke. "If I go to him with this and he tells *me* to back off, then we know it's either him or someone higher up the ladder. If he approves it, then we know Winkelman is compromised."

Special Agent in Charge McPherson was the head of the Atlanta Field Office. If the person in question was above McPherson, then the problem was in Washington. Huggins prayed that wasn't the case. Lord knew her beloved organization had been through enough controversy over the past several years. By and large, the FBI was made up of dedicated men and women who put in long hours, at great personal expense, to get the job done. A few corrupt people at higher levels had tainted the Bureau's reputation, something she considered terribly unfair to the amazing people she worked with. If she could root out a corrupt leader, she would do so; however, three girls were missing and being subjected to who knows what kind of indecent horrors. They would have to come first.

"Does anyone know you're coming to me with this?" She asked.

"No."

"Good. Let's keep it that way for now, Javi. I'll reach out to Clay, personally. I want to help him secure those girls first. I'll figure out a way to include McPherson after the fact and see where that leads. Thank you for coming to me with this!"

"In all honesty, Katie, I wanted this case, and I hate that I can't trust my superiors enough to run an end around like this, but something has to be done."

"I agree. This isn't over, Javi. Oh, do we know where that airplane is headed?"

"The flight plan has them heading for Key West, but Clay is wary of that and I have to agree."

"Clay was an exceptional agent when we all worked together," Huggins nodded. "Good instincts. I'll see if we can track the plane. Keep your head down but let me know if you learn anything else."

"Thank you, Katie," Gomez said as he stood and opened the door. "I'll see you at practice."

Gomez strode back down the hall. The scowl was still present but slightly less harsh.

Chapter 40

Lawrenceville, Georgia

" That is one cold-hearted woman," Ramsey remarked as he and Joe walked out of the garage.

They had spent the last hour interrogating the two Russians. Neither had given them any actionable intel pertaining to the three girls of interest. The guy, Igor was his name, would not break. He either truly did not know where Tupolev's plane was heading or he was able to endure the pressure points and water boarding that were inflicted upon him. Joe was leaning toward the latter. He recognized a unit tattoo on the man's arm. Igor was former Russian special forces - known as *spetsnaz* - and well trained to resist enhanced interrogation. Both Joe and Ramsey had no problem using such techniques to obtain life-saving information, but they drew the line at permanently harming or disfiguring anyone. They would have to find another way.

The woman, Elena, broke after a few minutes and spoke plainly of their human trafficking operation. Devoid of conscience, she nonchalantly described how they abducted and enslaved the girls. She confirmed the auction for Tracy Courtnall but stated it was abruptly stopped before a buyer was determined. She personally helped Igor and Sergei put the girls on the airplane. Unfortunately, she had no information pertaining to where Courtnall and the other girls were being flown. She didn't think Igor knew either. Joe wasn't sure what to believe but hoped Whitmore and his team were getting better results.

They walked into the kitchen from the back porch and saw Whitmore peering over Chuck Springer's shoulder, studying a computer screen. Looking up, he saw Joe and Ramsey. His eyes brightened.

"Please tell me you have something for us, Joe."

"Not what we're looking for, Clay." Joe said shaking his head. "We were able to confirm the girls are on the plane along with their identities and how they were abducted, but nothing about where they're headed. I'm sorry. How about you?"

"Not much better here. We're beating every bush but coming up empty."

"Anything from the FBI?" Joe asked as Ramsey's phone began to ring.

"Nothing. My contact texted back and told me the investigation is still shut down."

"Even with our new evidence?" Joe asked in bafflement.

"Yep. Doesn't make sense," Whitmore said shaking his head. "My contact is a solid guy. He would help me if he could but, for some reason, the higher ups have seen fit to put the kibosh on it and there is nothing he can do. We'll keep at it. Something will pop loose."

Joe had to admit, he liked Whitmore's energy and enthusiasm. He was a problem solver. The kind of guy who would tackle a problem forty different ways until he fixed the issue. Not unlike what he was trained to do as a Navy SEAL officer.

"Clay, I've got an update," Ramsey announced as he pocketed his phone.

"Something good, I hope."

"I wish," Ramsey answered. "No, it was my buddy, Big Dave. No trace of Tupolev's plane."

"Well, I guess we saw that coming. Alright, that's one place we don't have to look. So let's figure out where they could have gone. Rod?" Whitmore asked looking at his IT guy on the computer screen.

"Clay, I don't have information on a new flight plan just yet, but their last known position put them over the gulf West of Tampa about forty minutes ago. Where they went from there? We can only speculate but, an educated guess says they weren't heading back into U.S. airspace. That specific Cessna Citation has a maximum range of 3500 nautical miles which could get them to South America, Central America, or anywhere in the Caribbean. Unless they went somewhere close in the Caribbean, they're likely still in the air. Now here's where it gets interesting. Every flight entering or departing the United States is required by Customs and Border Protection to submit an APIS."

"Is that an Advanced Passenger Information System report?" Whitmore asked.

"Precisely, Clay," Roderick Boulware answered in his steady baritone. "The APIS includes a manifest listing all passengers and flight crew for customs purposes. They are usually submitted by internet prior to departure, but in exceptional circumstances, can be submitted by radio if the flight plan is altered."

"So what's the interesting part?" Whitmore asked.

"This flight was filed as a domestic and private flight. They didn't have to provide that information, only the number of people onboard."

"Does that mean they have to stay domestic or can they fly to another country?"

"Technically, they're required to file a flight plan and report a manifest, but the main party interested is the nation they're flying to. They all have varying customs regulations."

"So do we know where they're headed?" Whitmore asked.

"No, sir."

"Do we know how many are on board?"

"Our count is eight, which includes the two pilots."

"Do we know the names of those onboard?"

"No, sir."

"You're killing me, Smalls!" Whitmore spouted in exasperation.

"*Sandlot* references aside, sir, I can only provide the information that is available. I'm sorry, Clay."

"I know, Rod, and I appreciate what you're doing. We're just up against the wall here and the longer it takes to figure out where they're heading, the greater the chance of losing them. Is there a way you can search likely airports to see where they may be arriving?"

"We're working on that, Clay but, due to the number of airports within their flight radius, it will be like looking for a needle in a haystack. And that's *if* they have real time data we can access; furthermore, we're not dealing with your garden variety gangbangers here. We are talking sophisticated, powerful people with access and means. They likely have friends in the right places who can hide their arrival or the identities of those on board. I'll do my best, Clay but it will be extremely difficult."

"I hear you, Rod. Just do what you can. There are three girls whose lives depend on us."

Whitmore looked up at Joe and Ramsey with a grim expression.

"I'm open to suggestions, guys. How would the Navy handle this?"

"We would scramble a couple of F/A-18's to go force them to land," Joe answered. "We also have airborne radar and satellite tracking capability."

"Well, I don't have any aircraft at my disposal and, as good as Roderick is, I can't ask him to hack into the Department of Defense system to use their satellites."

"What about their phones?" Ramsey asked. "Surely either Igor or Elena have one of their bosses on speed dial. Can't we track them that way?"

"We've got Sergei Petrenko's phone but it's not showing up anywhere. He must have removed the SIM card, knowing we would try to track him. Neither of those two had anything for Tupolev that we could find. We're gonna have to hope Sergei turns his phone on wherever they land and work from there."

"Don't they have a transponder we can trace?" Joe asked.

"Not if they turn it off and fly at low altitude, sir," Roderick answered through the computer screen.

"Okay, once we do locate them, what then?" Joe asked.

"If they're in another country, we contact the U.S. Embassy and lead them to the location."

"Can they do anything with the scant evidence we have, Clay?" Joe asked skeptically. "Forgive me for not having a lot of faith in the State Department, but I don't see some career bureaucrat putting his reputation on the line with little to go on. We're going to have to go after them ourselves."

Whitmore studied Joe and Ramsey for a brief moment. The serious look in their eyes told him they weren't joking. *They're freaking serious!* He thought to himself. He had no idea how to conduct such an operation in, what might be, a banana republic with corrupt officials. They would be in alien territory and performing without a net. Failure could get his men killed. Failure would also get those girls killed. *But so would failure to act, Clay.* Eventually. Not before they were ruthlessly abused and mentally destroyed by those dirtbags. *This is way out of my league!*

"Just so we're clear, guys, you're talking a rescue operation on foreign soil. We won't have any backup."

"That's right," Joe answered while Ramsey nodded next to him.

"We don't even know where they're heading and it may be to the heart of the lion's den," he cautioned.

"We're aware of that," Joe agreed. "We need to have a plan in place the moment we learn anything. I'm talking logistics, comms, weaponry, personnel, escape plan, medical care. That takes planning and we need to get everything in place and ready to go. We'll need a private jet. Do we even have access to one? Otherwise, we're hosed."

"I think I can get us a plane," Whitmore said in deep thought. "But I'm not sure about the other things. And I'll mount up with you, but I can't ask any of my men to risk their lives. They didn't sign up for that."

"Screw that, Clay, I'm in," Gary Lee spoke from behind Joe and Ramsey where he had been listening in.

"Gary, I can't ask you to do that."

"And you also can't tell me I can't do it either, Clay." Lee said as he stepped around and looked at Joe and Ramsey. "Gentlemen? Are you SEALs okay with an old Marine going down range with you?"

Joe sized the man up. Lee stood a little over six feet and looked to be a solid 200 pounds with muscular arms and a trim waist. He looked to be in his upper thirties, around Chief Ramsey's age.

"What'd you do in The Corps, Mr. Lee?" He asked.

"Infantry. I was a squad leader with the 1st Marines in Iraq early on in 2004 and 2005."

"Fallujah?" Joe asked.

"You know your history, Lieutenant Commander. Yes, sir, my company stirred up quite a bit of dust in that hellhole. We took our hits, but we gave out a lot more than we took."

"I'm sure you did," Joe said appreciatively. "If you're willing to go outside the wire with us, we'd be glad to have you."

"I'll second that," Ramsey said giving Lee a fist bump. "I was up in Afghanistan when you Marines were sweeping through Fallujah. I know several guys who were there, and they spoke very highly of you Marines. Good to have you on board."

"Thanks. Well, I think I'll leave the planning and load out to you guys. Since Clay is working on the location and transport," Lee said, nodding over at Whitmore who was engaged in another conversation on his earbuds, "I'll see to those girls and figure out what to do with them. We need to get them somewhere where they can get help."

"I might be able to help you with that, Gary." Joe said glancing at his watch. "My girlfriend volunteers in a shelter for abused women. They handle a fair number of victims of human trafficking. She works nights but will be up in a little while. I'll call her and see if we can get them in there."

"Do they provide medical care and counseling there?" Lee asked.

"Yes, along with addiction treatment and long-term placement if needed."

"Perfect. These girls have been through hell. They're going to need a lot of help."

Joe looked into Lee's living room. The girls had all showered and put on clean clothes. One of Whitmore's associates had gone out and purchased some clothing and basic necessities. The girls sat motionless with the ten-thousand-yard stare that reminded Joe of what was often seen in veterans returning from brutal combat. Sunken cheeks and sallow complexions betrayed the drug abuse and malnourishment that underscored the physical and emotional abuse of their enslavement. When he was young and innocent, Joe would have been horrified to think that one human being could treat anyone so cruelly. That was then. Joe had seen too much evil around the world to be shocked anymore. That didn't quell the rage that welled up inside him. This was outrageously intolerable. Human trafficking victimized millions of women around the world. Joe knew he couldn't stop it all, but he could at least track down this organization. They would rescue those girls and they would either bring Tupolev and his organization to justice or put a bullet in their heads.

"We've got em'!" Whitmore spoke excitedly from across the kitchen.

"You found them?" Joe asked. "How?"

"I'm on the phone with another FBI contact of mine. She's got a tech guy tracking their ADS-B signal."

"Any idea where they're heading?"

"They're heading south-southwest towards the Yucatán Peninsula of Central America. Could be Cancun, Mexico City, Belize City, or anywhere around there. They're only halfway over the Gulf of Mexico so it's tough to tell."

"Any report of a new flight plan?" Roderick's voice boomed out of a computer screen.

"Katie, can your guys contact the likely airports and see if there is a new flight plan?" Whitmore asked into his earbud.

He looked at Rod on the screen and shook his head as he listened. Joe turned to Ramsey and Lee and spoke quietly.

"I know I don't have to tell you this, but Central America is cartel territory. Handguns won't be enough. We're going to need a full load out; rifles, comms, packs, ammo, and more. We should be ready to be wheels up the moment Clay secures a plane."

"Clay is well funded on this one," Lee spoke. "The father of the Courtnall girl will finance anything we need. We just need to make a list."

"Making out a list will be the easy part," Joe said. "It's filling it that won't be easy."

"I know a few people," Lee nodded reassuringly.

"We've got a weapons guy too, Joe," Ramsey reminded.

"That's right, Rammer! Thanks," Joe said as he wrote out a list of items on a small pad.

"Gary, I think we can handle the weapons, ammo, and a lot of the tactical gear. Can you get any of these items?" Joe asked as he handed over the list.

Lee quickly perused the list. "Yeah, I should be able to handle this."

"Good! Let's split up then. Rammer and I will head out to see our gun dealer if you don't mind taking care of that list," Joe said.

"Got it, but you're gonna need a company expense card wherever you're going," Lee explained. "Hold on."

"Clay," Lee said as he gently tapped his boss on the shoulder.

"Hold on a second, Katie," Clay spoke before looking up at Lee. "Yeah, Gary?"

"Under the presumption that we will soon be heading toward Central America, the door kickers and I are going to procure some supplies. We're splitting up to save time. They need the Suburban and can they use your credit card?"

"Actually, I sent Isaiah and Diaz out to get O'Shanick's truck while he was working over the Russians. It's out front," Whitmore said as he pulled his credit card out and handed it over.

"Have you worked out a way for us to get down there, Clay?" Joe asked.

"I think so," he answered. "That's going to be the next call I make."

Chapter 41

Charlotte, North Carolina

The top floor of Courtnall, Clark and Leeman was a bustle of activity and excitement. A big sell-off had begun on Wall Street and the phones were ringing with worried investors. Charles Courtnall and his two senior partners stood near each other in "The War Room." The War Room was a large windowless room with a half dozen high-speed computers, each with three large monitors. Lining the walls of the room were several large flat screen televisions, each tuned to different news or financial stations. A few displayed what was on some of the computers, which were high tech graphs and charts operating in real time.

The overall mood was upbeat. The Courtnall, Clark and Leeman Group was faring quite well despite the sell-off. Their algorithmic software, much of which Courtnall had written himself, had predicted the sell-off in ample time for the group to sell key stocks before they tanked. They had come out way ahead and their investors would be pleased when they checked their earnings reports. The fun now was watching individual stocks and funds and buying when they bottomed out. Other stocks were rising as a result of the massive sell-off and the group was speculating and buying these as well. Charles was in his element. His leadership position involved a lot of press fleshing and meeting with clients but days like this – watching his programs do what they were created to do, strategizing with his two close friends and trusted partners, mentoring their younger partners and interns, moving ahead of the trends – this was what he loved about his job. A day like today was like pitching in the World Series for Charles.

Unfortunately, he couldn't enjoy the moment. He was able to keep his head in the game, but his heart was heavy as thoughts of his precious Tracy were always circulating in his head. It had been days. Whitmore had picked up a scent on the trail, but there was no confirmation and she certainly was not out of harm's way. Charles couldn't help but wonder where she was. What was being done to her and by whom? Was she suffering in pain? Scared? He didn't even want to consider it but was she even alive? With each passing day, the agony of that terrible thought became more prevalent. The substantial wealth gains and successes of the day that his firm and their clients were gaining would normally be cause for great celebration but today he was numb to it. Wealth could not measure up. Tracy was priceless. His entire family was priceless and losing Tracy put everything in perspective.

Courtnall wasn't experiencing the regret of a neglectful parent who prioritized work and pleasure over his family. As careful as he was a financial investor, he and his wife had, even more so, meticulously invested their time and focus into their family.

Time.

Time was the key element. In the grand scheme of things, time was infinite; however, in one's lifetime, time was a limited commodity. No amount of wealth could purchase additional time. Particularly time with family and loved ones. If wisely invested in one's family, it could produce tangible and intangible dividends, but it could not be extended. Even if one were to get ninety years of life it would, at best, end in a bed and the only thing that mattered was who was present at the end. Boats, houses, bank accounts, and cars would not satisfy when the hourglass ran out. Memories, people, and love would be all that mattered. Try as he might, Courtnall could not suppress the ominous thought that their time with Tracy may be up.

He was jolted out of his thoughts when his phone began to vibrate. He retrieved it from his Brooks Brothers suit coat and looked at the screen. It was Clay Whitmore. His current mood made him hesitate as he looked at the screen. Would this be good news, bad news, or more of the same? He took a breath and opened the call as he stepped out into the hall.

"Hello, Clay."

"Mr. Courtnall. Am I catching you at a bad time?"

"Not if you have an update for me."

"I do and I know how valuable your time is, so I'll get right to it."

Under more pleasant circumstances, the irony of Whitmore's statement using the word *time* would have amused Courtnall.

"Please do," he spoke.

"The good news is that we have confirmed your daughter is alive and we know who she's with."

"Well thank God she's alive, but I noticed you're *not* telling me where she is," Courtnall pointed out. "Is that to say you still don't have an exact location?"

"That's partially correct. She's currently in a private jet over the Caribbean. Where they are taking her is another question. One we are trying to figure out."

"Can you expand on that, Clay?

Whitmore spent the next several minutes bringing Courtnall up to speed on the events that transpired over the past eighteen hours.

"So once you figure out where they're landing, you're going to look for them in that location?"

"That's correct, sir."

"Okay and I trust you, Clay but I have a few concerns. Even if you find them, I'm wondering how you plan to get them back. I don't think this Tupolev fellow is just going to hand them over. You won't be in the United States, so you won't have federal or even local authorities to make that happen. This will require a hostage rescue scenario which I *know* is *not* part of your purview. Don't we need to think about hiring a team of professionals to conduct a rescue?"

"We're covered. I happen to have two active duty Navy SEALs helping us out on this one and two retired Marines with combat experience."

"How did you get two Navy SEALs on board?"

"It's a long story, sir. The short version is, they were also looking for the girls and we bumped into them at the first apartment building.

They volunteered to ride along with us and handle the rescue. They're the ones that conducted the raid of the second location."

"And you're confident, your team can pull this off?"

"Once we locate the girls, we will assess the situation and coordinate a rescue operation as fast as possible before her captors know what hit them. They won't be expecting us. If it seems they are better protected than we expect, then we will maintain surveillance while we get more help. The bottom line, sir, is we have to get eyes on ASAP if we want to recover your daughter and the other girls."

Courtnall quickly pondered this information. His analytical mind kicked in as he considered risks and probabilities. The honest answer was this was out of his knowledge sphere and he didn't have the capability to protest what Whitmore was telling him. Two Navy SEALS was impressive, and also having two Marines was good as well, but would they be enough? He would prefer an entire team of SEALs but that wasn't possible. Were there mercenaries he could hire? Probably, but it would probably burn considerable time trying to find some, not to mention putting such an effort in motion. Whitmore was on the trail and had a plan. Courtnall would go with Whitmore's team but hedge his bets and work on a mercenary team as fallback.

"Okay, Clay, I'm trusting you with my daughter's life. This is your area of expertise. Do what you think is best."

"We will, Mr. Courtnall."

"Do you need anything from me?"

"Yes, sir. My team is out procuring weapons and supplies for this mission, but we're going to need to charter a jet. There are several services here in Atlanta. I was going to ask your permission to..."

"I'll do you one better, Clay," Whitmore interrupted. "I'll be down there in ninety minutes with our corporate jet."

"I think that'll do, sir."

Chapter 42

Duluth, Georgia

T hwack.

Joe saw Ramsey standing in his peripheral vision, sporting a grin of contentment. Joe returned the grin and turned his attention back to the rifle. He sighted in the target at the far end of the range. He took a slow, controlled breath in and let half out while applying gentle pressure to the trigger.

Thwack.

Both shots were in the x-ring. That was to be expected with their skill level at this range. What had Ramsey smiling was how little sound the shot made.

"Not bad for a civilian setup," Joe remarked with a matching grin.

TV shows and movies tended to over-exaggerate the quietness of a suppressed rifle. The reality was most firearms still made a relatively loud sound when suppressed. The three main components contributing to the sound of a gunshot were the exploding gasses at the muzzle, known as the muzzle flash, the mechanical action of the rifle or pistol, and the sound the bullet made when it broke the sound barrier. When Joe and Ramsey expressed their need for a capable yet quiet sniper rifle, Critter didn't bat an eye. Within minutes, he assembled a Remington Model 700 SPS AAC-SD rifle in .308 caliber, with an AAC suppressor and subsonic .308 rounds. The sturdy bolt action rifle removed the sound of the action since it required a manual clearing. The subsonic round did not give off the loud crack of a hypersonic round and the suppressor significantly muzzled the sound of the muzzle flash. The result was a sound similar to a single moderate clap of the hand.

"I thought you boys would like that," Critter remarked.

They were in the range alone and he allowed them to shoot without hearing protection to get an accurate assessment of the quietness of the weapon.

"I've been using this as demo, so the scope is already zeroed in. Let me give it a quick cleaning while you try out the other weapons and it'll be good to go. I'm sending you with both subsonic and hypersonic rounds for this bad boy," he said as Joe handed him the rifle. "Now as far as handguns go, what I have in stock that'll work is the Springfield XDM. Nine-millimeter; holds twenty-two rounds and it comes with a threaded barrel. *And* I just so happen to have two suppressors for those, which I use for demos, and can let you borrow."

"Wow! That's fantastic, Critter! Thank you!" Joe exclaimed.

"I've got suppressors for the AR-15's as well. Those are a hotselling item. The only problem is they cost a lot and there's a waiting period before you can take them home with you. That would deter a lot of sales but once people try my demos, they want 'em. You're welcome to try them out, if you like."

"Can we?" Joe asked.

"Yep, I'll be right back. Go ahead and give those Springfields and AR's a once over while I go get them out of my vault."

"Good thing he's Christy's neighbor," Ramsey commented after Critter left the room. "Otherwise, we'd be going downrange armed with sling shots and broomsticks."

"I hear ya, Chief," Joe said as he donned his hearing protection. "We'll have to hook him up when we get back."

Ramsey nodded as they both inserted magazines into their AR-15 rifles. The two men set up on their targets and began to fire. Both finished with a tight grouping on their targets. They changed out the rifles for two additional rifles and repeated the process. A few minutes later, they had thoroughly tested all of the rifles and handguns they had purchased. Critter walked back in carrying a box of suppressors and had the Remington 700 slung on his back.

"You boys want to try these out?" He asked.

Joe glanced at his watch. "We would but we really need to get moving, Critter. If you tell us they work, then that's good enough for us."

Joe removed his front pocket wallet, pulled out Whitmore's credit card, and handed it to Critter.

"We really appreciate this," he said. "That's Clay Whitmore's expense card. He said to call him for authorization, if you need to. I can give you the number."

Critter looked the card over.

"I'm supposed to, but I'm sure it'll be fine. I know where to find you," Critter said followed by a chuckle.

"What's so funny?" Ramsey asked.

"I was just thinking," Critter said as he tapped the credit card into the palm of his hand. "Between all your weapons, ammo, tactical gear, and load out, we're going to tickle this guy's credit limit today."

"Really?" Joe asked astonished.

"Maybe," Critter said with a mirthful shrug, "but just tell him I gave y'all my veterans' discount. That oughta smooth things over."

Ramsey grinned through his goatee as he watched Critter walk back out to the main part of the gun shop. He held his grin as he turned to look at Joe.

"We'd best get to cleaning these bad boys, Joey-O."

"Roger that, Chief," Joe said as he picked up one of the rifles and began to field strip it.

Fifteen minutes later, they were nearly finished cleaning and lubricating their newly purchased weapons when Joe's phone began to ring. He looked down on the table where it lay and saw it was Christy calling. Before he could pick it up, Ramsey snatched it up and opened the call using the speaker.

"By the grace of God and the ingenuity of Mr. Alexander Graham Bell you have reached the hallowed phone of Lieutenant Commander Joseph O'Shanick. For whom does the bell toll?" Ramsey spoke in mock seriousness.

There were a few seconds of silence before Christy finally spoke. "You're a hot mess, Matt Ramsey. Are you aware of that?"

"I heard the word *hot*, ma'am. That's good enough for me. I'll take it."

"Yes, I'm sure that's what you *did* hear! Now can you put Joe on, please?" Christy said in an amused tone.

Ramsey handed the phone over to Joe. "It sounds like some crazed banshee woman, Joe. I strongly recommend hanging up."

"Matt Ramsey!" Christy's voice spilled loudly out of the phone as Joe laughed pulling it up to speak.

"I'm sorry, Christy. I can't control him when we're off duty."

"You can't control him when you're *on* duty!" Christy laughed. "I just woke up and saw you texted earlier. What's going on?"

"Well the abridged version is we are getting ready to fly out of the country," he answered nonchalantly.

"Are you serious?" She asked. "Where?"

"We're not sure yet."

"Okayyyy," Christy said slowly drawing out the word. "How about we try the unabridged version?"

Joe spent the next several minutes explaining what had transpired since that morning. Christy listened calmly, without interrupting, as if allowing a patient to give a comprehensive history of their illness. Joe concluded only to be met with a brief silence on the other end.

"And here I went bed thinking you were just going to look at a sailboat."

"Well, we *did* go look at the sailboat," Joe offered.

"But then you and Matt decided you needed to get a little froggy," Christy responded. "Honestly, Joe, it's never a dull moment with you."

"I'm sorry, hun, but Clay Whitmore called, and we *did* agree to help him if he found the other girls."

"Joe, you don't have to apologize. I'm not mad. I just woke up and you caught me off guard. I'm just giving you a hard time because you're not here."

"Really?" Joe asked.

"Yes, Joe. *I'm* the one who dragged you into this mess. It wouldn't be fair to be angry. I just didn't think it would escalate into something like this. That's all."

"I hear you. Neither did we," Joe answered. "But we can't back out now either. Those girls need us."

"I get it, Joe," Christy answered quietly. "Isn't there somebody else who can go instead? Someone in a more official capacity? And more adequately manned?"

"Not within the time frame this needs to happen," Joe said with a sigh. "I'm concerned *we* might not make it in time."

"This could get dangerous, Joe," Christy said, her voice still quiet.

"I know, babe. We're taking every precaution we can. You know how we operate."

"I know a *little* of how you operate, but I also know you need to do this. And I know this is what you do, and you are quite good at it. If I was one of those girls, you're exactly who I'd want coming for me," Christy said as her voice grew a little in intensity.

"I think I remember doing that once," Joe said trying to lighten the tension.

"You most certainly did. And, actually, it was twice," she said in a softer tone. "But this is still dangerous, and I want you to promise me you'll be careful."

"I will; I promise."

"So who all is going?" She asked.

"Me, Rammer, Clay, and one of his guys. They're both Marines with combat experience," Joe added.

"That's it?"

"Well, Clay will probably have a couple of his computer guys along as well, but they won't go outside the wire with us," Joe answered.

"Assuming you rescue those girls, they're likely going to need medical care. And, God forbid anyone in the rescue party gets injured, they will need medical care as well. *Advanced* medical care!"

"Rammer and I both have combat medical training," Joe offered.

"That's not enough, Joe. You need a doctor trained in trauma and critical care," Christy spoke sharply, the concern evident in her voice.

"Yeah, that'd be great, but we don't have one," Joe responded.

"Yes, you do," Christy answered sternly. "I'm coming with you."

Chapter 43

Lawrenceville, Georgia

"Thank you, Ryan. I'll text Chip and let him know you're filling in for me. I hope it's a reasonable shift."

"No worries, Christy. I'm grateful for the hours. Thanks for thinking of me. I hope everything goes well down there. If I don't hear from you, I'll just plan on working your shift tomorrow night too."

"I'll let you know one way or the other. I really appreciate it. Bye," Christy signed off and thumbed the end call button on her steering wheel.

She gave a quick prayer of thanks that Ryan was willing to take over her night shift with little notice. He was a great guy in a desperate situation. The former emergency department director of a nearby hospital system who lost his job when a large corporate medical group underbid his group's contract and took over. The large corporate mega groups were gobbling up many a hospital contract and not in a good way, in Christy's opinion. Far too often, their physicians were reduced to cogs in a large medical machine, known only by their spread sheet numbers. Those spread sheets focused heavily on production numbers as opposed to the quality of care given. It was a growing problem in corporate medicine, one Christy, so far had been able to avoid. She was extremely grateful to be part of a small democratic group that only served two hospitals. Each partner had equal say in their practice. More importantly, they were adequately compensated and able to focus on delivering good care.

The job market for emergency medicine physicians had been wide open when Christy finished her residency in Augusta, Georgia; however, in just a few short years, the market had tightened up considerably. A major expansion in the number of emergency medicine residencies over the past few years had led to a rapid rise in the number of physicians available to work, many of them young, in high debt, and willing to work under lousy conditions for low pay. This played right into the CMG's hands. Similarly, there had been a sharp increase in online nurse practitioner programs which were cranking out the mid-level providers in droves. Nearly all hospital and medical systems were turning to these lower salaried providers in an effort to reduce staffing costs. As a result, Ryan Caughman found himself out of a job and desperately trying to earn a living in a now tight job market. It wasn't fair. He was a good physician; one Christy's group would gladly hire full time if they had an opening; instead, he kept his foot in the door by making himself available to fill in any shift when needed. Still working to pay off her loans, Christy worked sixteen to twenty shifts a month and didn't give many up. This was a rare occasion, but she was glad it would help Ryan out.

Christy drove down Buford Drive as fast as she would dare. She wasn't a lead foot by any means, but she knew time was tight and didn't want to be responsible for delaying the flight to wherever they were heading. Joe had initially protested her joining them. His reasons were valid but chivalrous. He expressed concerns for her safety as well as this being a mission he and Ramsey volunteered for and did not want Christy to feel obligated. Christy countered with valid reasons of her own and, in the end, Joe relented.

Christy smiled gently. That was the closest they had ever come to an argument. Joe hadn't gotten overly emotional or angry. He simply expressed his concerns while listening to Christy present her reasons. No drama, no selfishness. It was refreshing in this day and age. Furthermore, Christy knew Joe's main opposition to her coming along was rooted in love and concern. That was a good test in their developing relationship. He was a keeper, but she already knew that.

Christy's main concern was to be present and provide medical treatment should it be needed. However, she begrudgingly admitted that part of her reason was also rooted in anger and guilt. Guilt that she pushed Joe and Ramsey into this. Anger because this prostitution ring caused the death of her patient; an amazing young woman who had had a bright future. Lindsay's life was callously snuffed out in the interests of someone else's power and money. If she could just, in some small way, help Joe and Ramsey rescue those other girls, it would be something. It wouldn't bring Lindsay back, but it would save the lives of three other innocent victims.

As an emergency physician, she often saved lives. That would never grow old; however, far more than often medicine was, in many ways, damage control and simply trying to slow down the inevitable progression of disease and mortality that many people brought upon themselves through poor lifestyle choices. Christy often told people that wellness was a destination. In order to reach that destination, one had to walk the path his or herself. No one could walk it for them. Physicians simply provided the information and therapeutic interventions to enable their patients to walk the path; however, if the patient chose not to walk the path, their lives would be marked with a growing list of debilitating medical problems. Sadly, fewer and fewer people were choosing to walk the path to wellness. She saw it every day. Christy could count, on one hand, the number of patients she saw in a year who were physically fit and lived a healthy lifestyle. Their healthy immune systems fought off illness. They rarely suffered from mental health issues and most certainly avoided, or at least deferred for years, medical problems such as hypertension, diabetes, and poor diets that led to more complex problems such as strokes, arthritis, and heart disease. Yes, age and genetics factored into the equation, but why open the door and allow those problems to set in earlier?

Christy shook her head and decided those were problems for another day. To help Joe and the others rescue these three girls would make a positive impact on three young and promising lives and *that* was worth pursuing. The thought jarred her memory and she pressed the steering wheel button to initiate a call to Stacy Morgan.

"Hey, Iron-girl!" Stacy answered.

"Wow!" Christy exclaimed. "I didn't expect you to answer. I hope I'm not interrupting anything. I know you're in clinic. I was just gonna leave a message because I'm driving and can't text."

"No, it's okay. You caught me between patients. What's up?" Stacy asked in her usual upbeat mood.

"A couple things. I'm gonna have to bail out on our run later this afternoon. Joe and Matt are flying out of the country in a half hour and I'm going with them."

"WHAT?!" Stacy's voice was a mix of excitement and concern. "You're not eloping, are you?"

"No! Oh my gosh, no, Stacy. Nothing like that."

"Good! As much as I hope to see wedding bells in your future, if you run off and get eloped without bringing me, I'll chop your legs down until you're my height!"

"Duly noted," Christy said with a laugh. "No, it's nothing like that. They're helping an investigator track down some girls who were abducted into a prostitution ring. I'm going with them to provide medical care for the girls when they find them. Which is the other reason I called. They've already rescued three girls. They're in a safe house in Lawrenceville. If I text you a contact, can you get ahold of Linda at Samaritan's Shelter and see if she has room for them? I'm almost to the airport and I won't have time to coordinate that."

"Of course I can. Just tell me one thing. Does this have anything to do with the girl you treated last night who was shot?"

"It has everything to do with her," Christy said solemnly. "I promise I'll fill you in as soon as I can, but I'm almost to the airport and we are running behind. I'm sorry I can't say more right now."

"No apologies, Christy. Just promise me you'll be careful. I need you around here, my friend."

"I will, I promise; besides, I'll be with Joe and Ramsey."

"I know and I can't think of two better guys to be with, but they're drawn to danger like a moth to the flame. Please be careful and tell them to be as well. I'm rather fond of both of them."

"I am too..." Christy's voice trailed off in thought until she saw the turn off for the airport. "Alright, I'm pulling into the airport now.

I have to go. I'll text you a contact. His name is Isaiah and he will help you get the girls to the shelter."

"That works. I'm not on call tonight, so I will take them there myself. Okay, I'll let you go. Call me as soon as you can and let me know you're alright!"

"Will do, Stacy, and thanks. Bye."

Christy found the parking lot Joe had described in a text and turned in. She immediately spotted his pickup truck. She could see him standing in the bed handing plastic totes and other items down to Ramsey, who then stacked them on a pushcart. Two SUV's were parked beside them with other people unloading items onto another cart. Through a chain link fence, she saw a sleek white Learjet with black and teal trim rolling to a stop.

Christy pulled up alongside Joe's truck. She looked over at Joe as he handed the last item to Ramsey. He stood up and removed his navy-blue ball cap, mopped his forehead with his short sleeve, and fit it back onto his head. He wore khaki tactical pants with a black tactical polo and dark sunglasses. His broad shoulders tapered down to a narrow waist, giving him an imposing look. He looked over at Christy, flashed a disarming smile and waved. Christy waved back. *It's always an adventure with you, Joe O'Shanick.*

Chapter 44

Lawrenceville, Georgia

*C*hristy hopped out of her Highlander. Joe placed his sunglasses on top of his head and vaulted the side of his truck, landing in front of her.

"Well, hey there, pretty lady!" He said still sporting his charming grin, his green eyes lighting up his dark rugged features as he wrapped her in his muscular arms and pulled her in for a hug.

Despite being nearly six feet tall, Christy had to look up Joe to kiss him. Joe bent forward and rested his forehead on hers, allowing him to look directly into her emerald green eyes.

"If I came off as not wanting you to come with us, I'm sorry," he said. "This is *not* how I planned this day to go and, as much as I know you can take care of yourself, I still worry about your safety."

"Belay that, sailor, you're stuck with me," Christy kissed him once more and then gave him a shove. "Now help me unload this stuff."

"Hey Matt!" She waved to Ramsey who greeted her in return as he wheeled the cart in their direction.

She walked to the back of her Highlander and opened the hatch. The rear cargo hold contained several plastic totes. Joe reached in and grabbed one.

"Geez, what do you have in here?" He asked as he lifted a heavy tote. "Rocks?"

"Just medical supplies. That must be the one with all the IV bags and medications. Would you like me to get that for you?" She teased.

"I'm good," he grunted as he turned and carried it over to the cart.

They transferred a few more containers to the cart and then Christy shut the hatch. She retrieved a backpack out of her backseat and locked her vehicle. Joe did the same with his truck.

Whitmore gave a shrill whistle, and Joe and Ramsey looked in his direction as he pointed to the Learjet. Whitmore, accompanied by Chuck Springer, Marco Diaz, and Gary Lee, started out toward the tarmac. Ramsey did a 180 with the cart and followed them out along with Joe and Christy. An average build, middle-aged man with thick premature gray hair, well dressed in a charcoal gray suit bounded off the plane and greeted Whitmore's group.

"Mr. Courtnall, I'd like you to meet Lieutenant Commander Joe O'Shanick and Master Chief Matt Ramsey," Whitmore said as Joe, Ramsey and Christy stepped up.

"It's an honor, gentlemen," Courtnall said as he shook their hands. "I am forever in your debt for your willingness to help me find my daughter."

"Think nothing of it, sir," Joe replied. "This is what we do for a living."

"And who might this young lady be?" Courtnall asked, offering his hand to Christy.

"This is Dr. Christine Tabrizi," Joe answered. "She's board certified in emergency medicine and volunteered to come with us to provide medical support, if needed."

"It's an honor to meet you, Dr. Tabrizi," Courtnall said appreciatively.

"Christy," she said as she shook his hand.

"Well let's not waste any time," Courtnall said taking a step back and addressing the group. "I'll help you get your gear stowed away and we'll be off as soon as the ground crew is done refueling. Do we have a destination yet, Clay?"

"I believe we do, sir," Clay answered as he hefted a laptop and a go bag. "Based on their current flight path, they appear to be about forty-five minutes from landing in Belize City."

Joe glanced over at Christy who stared directly back, her eyebrows raised. Joe shrugged and grabbed one of their plastic bins.

"Dr. Tabrizi? If you would follow me, please," Courtnall said as he led Christy up the steps and into the plain.

Joe stepped aboard the aircraft, behind Christy, and marveled at what he saw. They turned right into a small kitchen galley that appeared well stocked. He then stepped into the lavish main cabin complete with large leather swivel seats, a long couch lining one side, and facing a large flat screen television on the other side. Behind this was another seating area with several large leather chairs seated facing each other. In the tail section was an enclosed bedroom with a double bed and a private lavatory complete with its own shower. Everything was well appointed. The spacious cabin was big enough that Joe didn't have to stoop to avoid hitting his head on the ceiling. Courtnall led the way toward the rear of the jet.

"There's a storage compartment through a sliding door in the back of the rear lavatory," he announced over his shoulder. "Anything you don't need during the flight can be stored there."

Dr. Tabrizi?" He asked as he stopped in the bedroom.

"Yes, sir? And please call me Christy," Christy answered.

"Christy it is then," he nodded in a polite gesture. "Why don't you set up shop in the bedroom area? I know it's not much, but it should give you a little privacy and some room to work without people walking past you. If you need more beds, every seat onboard this aircraft flattens out into a small bed. Will that do?"

"That will do just fine, Mr. Courtnall," Christy answered. "I hope we won't need any of it."

"I share your optimism, but if I'm to refer to you as Christy then you are to refer to me as Charles or even Chuck," Courtnall smiled as he gently patted her on the shoulder and he stepped back into the center of the cabin.

"Everyone, if I can have your attention for just a second," He announced.

The cabin became quiet as everyone's attention focused on Courtnall.

"I want to thank you all, again, for your personal involvement in helping recover our daughter, Tracy, and these other girls. What you are doing is above and beyond the call of duty and I am immeasurably indebted to you. Please make yourselves at home. I think you will find this aircraft quite comfortable. The galley is fully stocked with snacks, sandwiches, and refreshments so please help yourself. Once we are in the air, if I could have Mr. Whitmore, Mr. O'Shanick, Mr. Ramsey, and Mr. Lee join me in the back, there are a few things I'd like to discuss with you. Again, make yourselves at home and please accept my family's deepest thanks."

Courtnall nodded to everyone, removed his suit coat, and then stepped off the aircraft to help carry the team's items aboard. Joe and Ramsey followed suit. Once everything was onboard, Courtnall stepped into the cockpit while Joe grabbed Ramsey and headed aft.

"I was thinking, Rammer. By the time we land, those guys could be long gone. Clay may be able to track Petrenko's cell phone but if they unload the girls, the trail will grow cold in a hurry. We need some eyes on. Which platoon is covering the coast of Belize?"

"I believe it's Charlie Platoon," Ramsey answered.

"Do you happen to know who their Chief is?"

"Yep. That'd be Senior Chief Lennon. Good guy and a solid operator."

"Is he that big guy with the cleft chin?"

"That's the one."

"You wouldn't by any chance have his number, would you?"

"Yeah. Don't know if he'll answer," Ramsey shrugged.

"Try him anyway. I'll beat down some other trees and see if we can't get someone to hightail it to the airport for some eyes on. Tell him we'll pay."

"Will do," Ramsey replied as he sat down and opened up his phone.

Joe sat down as well and began to work through his list of contacts until he found the number for the Officer In Command (OIC) of Charlie Platoon. He dialed the number and it went immediately to voice mail. *Not good.* He dialed a second time, hoping it would break through a Do Not Disturb setting, but it went right back to voicemail. Joe left a message requesting an immediate callback as soon as possible to discuss an urgent matter. He ended the call and began racking his brain for the platoon's Second in Command (2IC). *What is his name?*

"We're set, Joe!" Ramsey exclaimed from the chair across from him. "Lennon said he has two operators monitoring the airport for cartel planes. They are there now and will keep an eye out for us."

"That's great!" Joe responded. "Did you give them the flight information and the tail number?"

"Man you really do think us Minnesotans are just a bunch of ice-eating, cow-tipping hicks with hockey sticks, don't you? Of course I did."

"Alright, alright, Rammer," Joe said with his hands in the air laughing. "I was just double checking is all. I knew you had it."

Ramsey smiled as he flashed Joe a one-digit salute.

"Lady and gentlemen, this is your captain from the flight deck. We have been cleared for takeoff. If you could all take your seats and buckle up, we will begin our taxi immediately."

"Yeah, Joe! Buckle up!" Ramsey chided as he fastened his seat belt.

Joe found his seat belt and began to fasten it as Christy appeared from the back and took the seat next to him. She looked all business wearing navy blue scrubs with her long dark hair pulled back in a ponytail.

"Mind if we join you?" Courtnall appeared with Whitmore and Lee in tow.

"Please do," Joe said gesturing to the empty chair facing Christy.

Courtnall took a seat in the chair. He sat immediately next to Ramsey and the two of them faced Joe and Christy. Whitmore and Lee took the two opposing seats on the other side of the narrow aisle. The nearly soundproof cabin allowed the six of them to hear each other clearly without having to raise their voices.

"Everybody comfortable?" Courtnall asked as he fastened his seatbelt.

"Yes, sir," Joe answered as the aircraft began to taxi. "What kind of plane is this, if you don't mind me asking?"

"Not at all, Mr. O'Shanick. It's a Gulfstream 700."

"Well it's very nice. I've never flown in anything close to this," Joe said looking around.

"Well, thank you. I hope it doesn't come off as ostentatious, but it belongs to the company and we actually do use it quite a bit. As much as we have to travel to meet with clients, we might as well make it convenient and pleasurable."

"I'll say," Ramsey agreed." It sure beats sleeping on a fold down bench on a C-130."

"That's beyond my experience, Mr. Ramsey, but I should think you're right. You'll find this aircraft not only far more comfortable, but it will also outperform the C-130 and the C-17 and C-5 for that matter. She has a top speed of Mach 0.95, a cruising altitude of 41,000 feet and a range of 7500 nautical miles. Quite convenient. Wouldn't you agree?" Courtnall said looking around as the others nodded while the aircraft began to accelerate down the runway.

"Which brings me to my first question," he continued. "As fast as this aircraft is, we will still be about two hours behind the other aircraft. What is your plan to catch up to them?"

Knowing Whitmore's plan of tracking cellphone signals was a little flimsy, Joe decided to jump in first. "We're taking a multi-pronged approach, Mr. Courtnall. Clay's tech guys are working on tracking their cellphones while we have reached out to some boots on the ground who are already at the airport and will follow them for us until we arrive on seen."

Courtnall nodded his approval. Joe was positioned to see Whitmore along with Courtnall and saw him calmly nod as if he knew what Joe and Ramsey had, just minutes earlier, arranged.

"How in the world do you have people at the airport already?" Courtnall sounded astonished.

"We caught a break," Joe answered. "As soon as we learned where they were headed, we called down to some folks we know in the area."

Joe silently willed Courtnall not to press further. He really did not want to get more specific and reveal the presence of an operating SEAL platoon. They were doing him and Ramsey a big favor as it is. Maintaining OPSEC (operational security) was a priority. Courtnall either knew this or was satisfied with Joe's intentional vagueness as he simply responded with a thoughtful nod. Joe sensed it was the former. Courtnall was no idiot. The high-tech luxury aircraft they were flying in was evidence of that.

"As Joe said, my tech guys are working on several methods to track them electronically," Whitmore added. "Marco Diaz is currently reaching out to local authorities on the ground for assistance. We're trying to get their customs officials to hold them on the runway until we get there."

"Could it be that simple?" Courtnall asked in a hopeful manner.

"In a perfect world, yes," Whitmore answered. "However, we are dealing with powerful entities here in a third world nation. We hope it's that simple, but we are preparing for all scenarios."

"What scenarios would you consider likely?"

"They could refuel and take off for another destination, they could drop the girls off to a local buyer..." Whitmore abruptly stopped as he seemed to swallow his words. "I'm sorry, I didn't mean to say it like that, Mr. Courtnall."

Courtnall waved him off. "It's alright, Clay. This is no time for sugar coating. I appreciate full candor. Continue."

"Thank you, sir. Yes, they could offload the girls to somebody local, they could take them somewhere else by land or water, or they could be meeting someone with their own airplane who will take off with them for another location. We hope the local authorities will help us out and at least stall them until we arrive. In case they don't, we are trying to get the flight control people to eyeball what's happening while Joe's associates do the same."

"And presuming we do locate them, what then?" Courtnall asked.

"We'll assess the situation, devise a plan, and get them back," Joe said in a serious tone.

Courtnall met Joe's serious gaze with one of his own. Joe saw a man, who was used to making things happen, but now struggling to trust total strangers with the life of his daughter. It was probably the most difficult thing the man had ever dealt with in his life. Joe thought of Christy and his sister, Marina, who had been abducted at the hands of the mafia a few months ago. Joe had been ready to die to get them back. How much more so must a father feel that way about his daughter?

"I cannot imagine the pain and the anguish you must be feeling, sir, let alone the difficulty you must be experiencing trusting us to get your daughter back. But, know this; this is what we are trained to do, sir," Joe said gesturing towards Ramsey and himself followed by Whitmore and Lee. "This is what we do for a living."

"I know that, Mr. O'Shanick. I just have a hard time trusting other people with my daughter."

"That's understandable," Joe replied. "May I ask you a question?"

"Please."

"Do you ask people to trust you with their hard-earned money? Their retirement accounts?"

"Yes, I do, and it motivates me to work doubly hard managing their wealth and resources."

"Good," Joe responded. "Then I should think you will be able to understand that we will be equally motivated to live up to your trust."

"Thank you, Mr. O'Shanick. That means a lot to me. I do trust you."

Joe responded with a nod of gratitude. Courtnall nervously drummed his hands on the padded leather armrests of his seat.

"Well, gentlemen, and lady," he said with a polite nod to Christy, "I'll get out of your way and let you get on with what it is you do.

"Sounds good, sir," Whitmore said as he and Lee got up out of their seats. "We'll be up front if you need us."

"I'm gonna grab some rack time," Joe said. "No telling what to-night may bring."

"I'm gonna do the same," Ramsey added. "I'm told these seats stretch out?"

"They do, but one of you can take the bedroom right there and the other can stretch out on the couch up there," Courtnall gestured with his thumb over his shoulder.

"No, sir," Joe politely declined. "This is your plane. We'll be fine in these seats. Believe me, we've managed to rack out in far worse."

"No. I won't hear of it. You two gentlemen are heading into harm's way on behalf of my daughter. You'll take my bunk and the couch, and that's the end of it. I insist."

"Very well. Thank you, sir," Joe said before looking across at Ramsey. "Rock, paper, scissors for dibs?"

"Best of three," Ramsey nodded.

They threw down three times and Ramsey won the tiebreaker on the third throw. He punched Joe in the chest, stood up, and announced he was taking the couch. Joe protested, knowing Ramsey was being polite, but Ramsey had already stepped around Courtnall and was already on the couch before Joe had finished.

"Well, we had an exceptional trading day and I powered straight through lunch. I think I'll head up to the galley and fix a little something. Would either of you care to join me?" Courtnall said looking between Joe and Christy.

"No, thanks. I'm good, sir," Joe said. "I really do need to hit the rack."

"I'll grab something in a little bit," Christy replied.

"Alright then. I'll leave you to it. Like I said, please make yourself at home," Courtnall said as he rose from his seat and walked up the aisle.

Christy turned to Joe and quietly spoke. "Does anyone on this plane know about you and me other than Matt?"

"No, and we should probably keep it that way, I would think," Joe answered. "I'm trying to earn that poor guy's confidence. It's probably better off if he doesn't think I could be distracted with you onboard."

"That's a good thought," Christy said with a thoughtful nod. "Go hit the rack, as you say, and I'll see you when you get up."

Joe started to rise but Christy grabbed his left forearm, pulled him down, and leaned in close.

"But I *do* want to hear all about the sailboat you and Matt went to look at. Only you could go look at a sailboat and end up with all of us on a plane to Belize chasing human traffickers, Joe O'Shanick!"

Joe gave a slight shrug and a smirk in acknowledgment. Christy playfully punched him in the shoulder, made sure no one was looking and gave him a quick peck on the cheek.

"But I love you. Now, go on!" She said with a hand gesture shooing Joe away.

Joe stepped around her and into the aft cabin. He unlaced his tactical boots and pulled them off. The shades were down on all the portholes. Upon closing the sliding door to the main cabin, the aft cabin went completely dark. Joe climbed into the bed, immediately impressed with how comfortable the mattress felt. He mentally set a wake-up time for two hours from now. That would allow ample time for a sit-rep from Whitmore as well as Charlie platoon's men at the airport. They would begin mission planning then. When he woke up, it would be all business. He closed his eyes and quickly drifted off to sleep. His last thoughts were a semi-dream of sailing across Lake Lanier in a Hunter 33 with one hand on the wheel and the other around Christy.

Chapter 45

Philip S.W. Goldson International Airport Belize City, Belize

"Call," Tracy said as she tossed four chips into the center. "What do you have, Daddy?"

"Two pair. Kings and twos," Charles Courtnall said proudly as he laid his cards on the table.

"Beats me," Jane Courtnall said tossing her cards face down.

Tracy's brothers, Charles IV and Scott, had already folded. Everyone looked at Tracy as she studied her cards as if in confusion.

"Kings beat queens, don't they?" she asked.

"They do indeed, T-bear," Charles replied with one of many nicknames he had for his daughter.

"But not three of them!" Tracy squealed excitedly as she revealed her hand holding three queens.

Jane sized up the considerable pile of chips in front of Tracy. "I think little Miss Money Bags is the big winner."

"Awe, Mom, we've got time for a few more hands," Scott protested.

"She's right, son," Charles spoke gently. "We all agreed that the last deal would be when Captain Coonts announced our approach. I think your mother is right. Tracy took us all to the cleaners."

"Yay!" Tracy exclaimed. "That means I get to pick what we're having for dinner!"

"Great," Scott said with a roll of his eyes. "We get to have dinner picked by a ten year old."

"Dad?" Charles, the oldest son spoke up.

"Yes, Charles?"

"Now that we're almost there, can you *please* tell us where we are going?"

Tracy felt her dad's warmth as he leaned over her and looked out the Gulfstream V's porthole. She excitedly looked with him but saw only clouds. It was the first day of Christmas break. Tracy was sure they were going skiing. They went every winter. Plus, she had been secretly spying on her mom packing and saw winter clothes being packed.

"It's gonna be Utah," she said knowingly which caused her father to smile.

"I hope it's Breckinridge," Scott replied.

"You guys are both dunces," Charles countered from across the table. "Haven't you been paying attention? We left Charlotte ten hours ago. It has to be Europe. Maybe the Swiss Alps."

"I'll tell you what," Courtnall said. "Everybody, look out a window. The first person to correctly guess where we are landing gets to have pop with their dinner tonight! But is has to be before we land, or it doesn't count!"

Scott jumped up and hopped across the aisle to the empty seat across from their mother. He kneeled on the seat and peered out the fuselage window while Tracy and Charles did the same. Daddy was always running contests. Mom said it was exercise for their minds. Even the family poker games were meant to sharpen their minds. Tracy just thought they were fun. They didn't play for real money but there was always a prize for the big winner or "big wiener" as Scott like to say. She glanced at her tiny wristwatch. It really had been ten hours. They played Trivial Pursuit, which Daddy won as usual, and poker the entire time. It went by so fast. Maybe Charles was right? Could they be spending Christmas skiing the Swiss Alps? *I'll bet it's even prettier than Breckinridge!* She thought as she pressed her little button nose against the plexiglass window and looked out.

The plane dropped below the clouds. What Tracy saw made her gasp. Instead of rugged snow-covered mountains, she saw the bright sun rippling across dark blue water that transitioned to turquoise waters and white sandy beaches which, in turn, quickly gave way to sharply rising mountains covered in deep green vegetation. She recognized this!

"Kauai!" She shouted in excitement! "That's Kauai!"

"You're right, sweetheart!" Tracy's mother replied. "How did you guess so quickly?"

"It looks just like the poster hanging in my room. That's where Bethany Hamilton lives! Do you think we'll get to meet her?!" Tracy asked jumping up and down with excitement.

"I don't know about that, sweetheart. She may be away for a surfing competition, but Kauai isn't that big, so you never know."

"Wait," Charles spoke up. "We're spending Christmas In Hawaii?"

"That's right, son. You sound disappointed."

"No, not really. I've always wanted to go to Hawaii it's just, it's just weird, I guess. We've always spent Christmas skiing or snowboarding somewhere."

"Well, you guys are all aces at skiing and snowboarding. Your mother and I figured it might be time for a challenge. Maybe something like surfing? What do you think?"

"Yes!" Tracy and her brother enthusiastically answered in unison. "Thank you, Daddy!"

"Don't thank me. Thank your mother. It was her idea. She even found us a beautiful resort on Poipu Beach that has its own surfing school. You guys will be riding the waves in no time!"

Tracy and her brothers all went over and hugged their mother followed by their dad. Captain Coonts announced their final approach and asked them all to take their seats and buckle up in preparation for landing.

Tracy stared out the window in anticipation. Bethany Hamilton was her hero. A few years ago, at the age of thirteen, Bethany had been on her way to becoming one of the world's best surfers when her left arm was bitten off by a tiger shark. She didn't let that hold her back. After recovery, she got right back in the water and learned how to surf with only one arm. She was now back on top competing with the best surfers in the world and winning. Her amazing story was captured in the 2011 film *Soul Surfer*. Tracy's parents took them all to see it when it was in the theatre last year and, ever since then, Tracy had been a Bethany Hamilton fan. Like Bethany, Tracy was an athletic, adventurous, little blond with two older brothers of whom she tried to outcompete in nearly everything. Tracy soon had posters of Bethany and Kauai all over her room. Now she and her brother were actually going to learn to surf in Bethany's home island of Kauai, Hawaii! This was going to be the best vacation ever! Her excitement grew as the island loomed closer. They were nearly on the ground when the runway suddenly appeared underneath them.

The gentle landing awakened Tracy from her dream with a startling jolt. The pleasant diversion of her dream faded as the harshness of her reality came rushing back. The rapidly decelerating airplane confirmed they had just landed. Where? She had no idea. Her head had been covered with a dark pillowcase immediately after boarding the plane.

After taxiing for a minute, the airplane came to a stop. She heard the engines whine down and felt a blast of warm humid air as she sensed the cabin door open. She couldn't hear it because noise cancelling headphones had been placed on her ears before they took off. A large hand suddenly gripped her left arm and pulled her to her feet. She was then forced to walk a short distance until she was stopped. The headphones and pillowcase were removed. Tracy looked around and realized she was in a small lavatory with a large man standing in the open doorway, blocking her view of the rest of the plane. He pulled out a key and unlocked one of the clasps on her handcuffs.

"You have one minute," the large man said in a thick Russian accent.

Tracy briefly thought about trying to get past the man but quickly discarded the thought. He was well over six feet tall and his shoulders were wider than the door. He wore an ill-fitting dark suit which matched his large nose that had obviously been broken so many times it no longer fit his face.

It had been hours and Tracy's bladder was full. She quickly answered nature's call while the large man looked on. After almost seven days, Tracy was becoming immune to being leered at, even when she used the bathroom. Her dignity was giving way to a mind-numbed indifference. Her bigger concern lay in what was in store for her. For nearly a week now, all the girls around her had been beaten, raped, and prostituted. One had been shot right in front of her. They had just flown her somewhere for a reason. It couldn't be good. Was she being held hostage? Had they discovered who her father is and they were holding her for ransom? Was she being sold to ISIS to become an object of animalistic recreation for a bunch of jihadists? Tracy had heard about that. She couldn't understand how their religious zealotry would allow for violent sexual deviancy and rape but, if killing innocent civilians through acts of terror was acceptable, then surely they found justification in raping innocent women. Young American women in particular, she imagined. Her captors were Russian. Did they have ties to ISIS? Syria? Yes, she followed world events enough to know the Russians were in bed with certain Syrian elements. Maybe she was simply being sold as a sex slave. She had definitely been kidnapped by a human trafficking ring. Was she being sold or traded? The possibilities were endless and all frightening to one degree or another. She longed to return to sleep where she could escape this nightmarish reality. Perhaps with another dream about a past family experience? The dreams were the only pleasant experiences she had had over the past week.

Tracy stood up and reached to turn on the sink. The large man quickly snatched her wrist and tugged down. He snapped the other handcuff back on. He slipped the pillowcase back over her head and led her back to her seat. He left the headphones off allowing Tracy to hear but the airplane's cabin was relatively quiet. Tracy heard similar commotion and guessed the other two girls, Darcy and Rebecca were getting their moment in the lavatory. As Tracy thought about it, she realized that, for Darcy and Rebecca, these past few hours in the air had been the only thing close to peaceful they had experienced since being kidnapped. No sooner did she think of this when she realized they had been getting regularly injected with heroin and could actually be experiencing the excruciating misery of withdrawal. Tracy thanked God that hadn't happened to her, but she worried that it was only a matter of time.

Her thoughts were again disrupted when another large hand grabbed her arm and yanked her up onto her feet. She heard the same being done to Darcy and Rebecca. The three were marched off the airplane with their pillowcases still on. Tracy picked up on the cavernous sound and the echoing clank of a wrench and guessed they were inside an aircraft hangar. They walked a short distance and were roughly lifted into the back of a cargo van. Tracy struggled to sit up on the hard floor while the door slid shut with a loud boom at the end. She found her way to a bare metal wall on the side but lost her balance and fell to her side when the driver accelerated the van out of the hanger. As if in defiance, she worked her way back up into a sitting position only to tumble forward when the driver took a hard left. Frustrated, Tracy resigned to simply lay in the floor. She had no idea where they were going. No idea how long they would be in the back of this hot van and no idea if the ordeal would ever end. Nearby, one of the other girls began to cry.

*****

Senior Chief Petty Officer Jeremy Lennon sat in the driver's seat of an aging Ford Explorer as he watched the main entrance to the airport hangers. He was ostensibly helping two of his men track a drug shipment; however, after getting Ramsey's sit-rep, he decided to hightail it out to the airport. His men would act as spotters, and he would be able to follow any would be suspects, should they make an appearance. The Explorer was one of several vehicles they used, on a rotating basis, for insertions and surveillance. It's age and cosmetic flaws made it blend in with every other vehicle in the area.

"Charlie Three this is Charlie Six," the voice of SO1 Antonio Flores came through his radio earpiece.

"Go ahead, Charlie Six," he answered back.

"Tres amigas were just frogmarched into a white Chevy panel van. I'm sending pictures your way. ETA your position, one mike."

"Good copy, Charlie Six. Tres amigas in a white Chevy van."

Lennon watched as the white van appeared from around the hangers. It turned onto the main road and accelerated away. He felt his phone vibrate, signaling the incoming pictures, as he put the Explorer into gear and followed from a distance. They came to a traffic circle and the van took a right turn.

"Charlie Six, this is Charlie Three, I have eyes on target. Target just turned onto John Smith Road. Maintaining eyes on. Charlie Mike."

"Roger that Charlie Three, Charlie Mike. Good hunting."

Lennon continued to follow from a distance. The van followed the road for several miles through mostly mangroves until it ended on George Price Highway. It turned left and headed North toward the coast and Belize City. Lennon took his time turning left, careful not to draw attention but all the while keeping close enough not to lose the van. He followed them through an S-curve and watched as they turned into a marina. Lennon drove past the marina for a tenth of a mile and doubled back. He turned into the other entrance, parked his vehicle pointing toward the exit, and got out.

Lennon was dressed to blend in. He wore khaki cargo shorts, an athletic gray t-shirt, navy blue baseball cap, and sunglasses. He quickly walked down to the docks and assumed a slow pace as if he were admiring the boats. There was a collection of fishing boats, off-shore boats, and sailing catamarans. He scanned across the basin and spotted the white van parked close to the docks on the opposite side. The doors opened and two men got out. The driver was a very alert looking Hispanic man. Lennon quickly pegged him as former military by the way he carried himself and monitored his surroundings. *I'll bet he's Los Fantasma Guerreros,* Lennon thought. The other man was tall and athletic with close cropped hair and a well-trimmed beard. He matched the picture of Sergei Petrenko which Ramsey had sent him. *Hello Sergei!*

Lennon pulled out his cellphone and began snapping pictures while feigning he was taking pictures of a nearby fishing charter. Petrenko opened the sliding door and a ridiculously large man appeared. He had classic Russian features. *We'll call you Ivan the Terrible.* "Ivan" turned back into the van and began gesturing. A red-headed girl appeared, and the Hispanic man wrapped his left arm around her and began to walk her toward the dock. He appeared to be holding a gun in his right hand, but it was difficult to tell. Sergei followed behind with a taller blond girl, and then Ivan with a petite blond girl. Lennon was ninety-nine percent certain she was the girl in the picture Ramsey sent. All three were walked down a gangplank and onto the transom of a large sport fishing cruiser. Lennon managed to snap dozens of pictures before the girls were taken below. He lingered a bit longer with his phone making sure to get pictures of the boat's registration and the name on the back. Satisfied, he wandered over to a waterside restaurant and walked in. It was half full with the early dinner crowd. The bar was busier with a mix of tourists and local fisherman. Lennon found a spot where he could watch the fishing cruiser without being spotted. He pulled out his phone, composed a text, and pressed the send button.

Chapter 46

41,000 feet over the Caribbean Sea

A quiet hum permeated the Gulfstream's cabin. Having slept most of the day in preparation for another night shift, Christy was wide awake. She tried to use the time to catch up on her continuing medical education by listening to this month's EM:RAP podcast. Try as she might, her thoughts were elsewhere and after over an hour, she realized she couldn't even recall what had been covered. She closed the podcast and removed her ear buds.

Standing up for a stretch, Christy felt her stomach growl and decided to head up to the galley for a snack. On her way, she passed Whitmore and his team, who were clustered up front working on their computers and quietly talking amongst themselves. Christy found the small galley to be well stocked with a variety of items. She selected a banana, some Greek yogurt, and a peach Snapple iced tea. She was heading back to her seat when she noticed Courtnall seated across the aisle. His laptop was open, but the screen appeared to have timed out as he absently stared out the window. Christy knew that look. Following an inner prompting, she leaned in and gently tapped his shoulder.

"Mr. Courtnall, if I'm bothering you just tell me, but I just wanted to see how you're holding up."

Courtnall turned away from the window and looked at Christy.

"Holding up as best as can be expected, I guess," he said with a weak smile. "I appreciate your concern. Have a seat."

Christy sat down in the seat facing Courtnall and placed her snack items in the adjacent seat. She studied the man before her. His stately appearance was marred by the sallow complexion of one who hadn't slept in days. His forehead was wrinkled from an involuntary furling of self-doubt. Before her sat an accomplished man, one who was normally confident but not arrogant. His face betrayed a level of concern mixed with self-doubt and exhaustion.

"You know, one of many skills we ER physicians develop is guiding a patient and family through frightening and often life-threatening ordeals," Christy spoke softly with a gentle smile. "I cannot imagine the grief and anxiety you must be experiencing, but I'd like to help if you'd let me."

Courtnall cracked a gentle smile as he looked back at her. When he finally spoke, his voice cracked. "This is all so foreign and overwhelming to me. I wouldn't even know where to start."

"How about telling me what you're feeling right now," Christy coaxed.

Courtnall stared at Christy. His eyes darted back and forth as if searching for something. After a contemplative minute, he spoke.

"I'm scared. Scared for my baby girl. Scared of what might be being done to her right now. Scared of what's been done. Scared we may never get her back. Scared I may have to return home and console her mother when I can't even console myself. On top of all that, I'm furious."

"It's perfectly normal to be scared during a situation like this," Christy acknowledged.

"Not for me it's not," Courtnall countered. "I'm the logical one. I don't get emotional. At least not much. I've always been able to stay the course no matter what was going on around me. My family depends on me. My investors depend on me. I feel helpless on this one and I'm trying to keep my wits about me, but I've never dealt with something like this before. Now I find myself in a position where I am having to depend on others to get my daughter back for me."

"There's nothing wrong with that. We all have to depend on other people to perform tasks they are better qualified for. Joe was right, earlier. People depend on you to manage their money and retirement."

"True."

"We're trusting your pilots to fly this airplane. Aren't we?"

"Yes, and I would bring a sick family member to see you rather than pretend I'm a doctor. I understand your point, Dr. Tabrizi. I'm just having a little trouble accepting it all. All these doubts keep creeping up."

"Doubts," Christy nodded. "We all can have those. Anything in particular?"

"Well," Courtnall began, while steepling his fingers together under his chin. "I know those two guys are SEALs, but it's still hard to trust people you don't really know. Take your profession. There are excellent physicians and there are some, shall we say, not so good physicians. Wouldn't you agree?"

"I do, but let me tell you about those two particular men," Christy said with a slight gesture of her head over her shoulder. "I happen to know them both quite well and I would, one hundred percent, trust them with my life. In fact I have. On more than one occasion."

"You have my complete attention," Courtnall responded as he shifted in his seat.

Christy spent the next ten minutes detailing the events of her personal experiences with Joe and Ramsey, first during the compromised rescue mission in Honduras and more recently during a run in with an organized crime family in Niagara Falls. Courtnall listened intently, occasionally speaking words of incredulity. When she was finished, Courtnall leaned back in his seat and quietly looked at Christy.

"I knew the name, O'Shanick, sounded familiar," he spoke after a minute of contemplating everything he had just heard. "So that's him."

"Yes, sir, that's him," Christy nodded with a reassuring smile.

"And you're sure he and his friend are up for the job," Courtnall said as a statement rather than a question.

"Yes. I have total faith in them," Christy answered.

"Faith," he grunted as he looked at the backs of his hands.

Christy cocked her head to her side and leaned in a little closer. "I'm sorry. Did that offend you?"

"No," Courtnall shook his head as he looked up. "It's just I keep hearing that word. My wife's been saying it all week. My friends…

co-workers, everyone. Don't get me wrong, I'm a church-going man, raised Southern Baptist. I believe, but...but just having a hard time in the faith department."

"With what in particular, Mr. Courtnall?"

Courtnall's eyes looked up at the ceiling. He took a deep breath and let it out as his eyes settled back on Christy.

"With everything, I guess. If God is real, how could He let these people take Tracy? And those other girls? Any girl! I mean, He's God. He's all powerful and all knowing. He *could* stop these things from happening. But either He doesn't, which makes Him cruel, or there is no God. Either way, our faith would seem to misplaced."

"You say you were raised Baptist?" Christy asked.

"That's right. Southern Baptist."

"Then may I presume you're familiar with Scriptures?"

"I'd say so, yes. My wife, Jane, and I teach Sunday school together. Well, she does most of the teaching," Courtnall grinned.

"Then let me ask you this," Christy started. "Was God cruel when He allowed Jacob's sons to sell their brother, Joseph, into slavery?"

"I'm sure Joseph thought it was cruel at the time, but it worked out in the end. He was elevated to a position of power and which placed him in position to save his family from starving during a famine."

"So God allowed something to happen that led to something that not only saved his family but preserved the entire Jewish line. The line which would lead to the Messiah," Christy prompted.

"Okay, yes," Courtnall conceded.

"What about the First Century Christians?" Christy asked. "God allowed the Romans *and* their fellow Jews to persecute, torture and, in many cases, execute them. Was that cruel?"

"It would seem that way," Courtnall replied, "but I know where you're going with this one. By allowing the early Christians in Jerusalem to be persecuted, they scattered and took the gospel with them to all corners of the world."

"Thereby leading to an explosion of Christianity throughout the world," Christy added. "Do you think that would have happened had they not been persecuted?"

"Not to that degree," Courtnall said shaking his head. "I suppose a few people would have gone but most likely wouldn't have."

"Because most of us tend to want to pursue our own interests, especially when life is good," Christy stated. "So, taking it to the next level, I think we would both agree that God allowing His Son to be beaten, tortured, and nailed to a cross would seem pretty cruel."

"Yes," Courtnall nodded, "but that, ultimately, served the highest purpose. Jesus took upon Himself the punishment for all the sins of the world."

"Including yours and mine?" Christy prompted.

"Yes, including yours and mine," Courtnall answered.

"And, as a result, He can offer us forgiveness and salvation, something we could never achieve on our own no matter how good or religious we might be. Right?"

"What do you mean? We can't be religious enough?" Courtnall's eyes narrowed. "Aren't we *supposed* to be religious?"

"No," Christy answered simply.

"*No?*" He asked incredulously.

"No," Christy responded softly.

"You lost me, Christy."

"Being religious is just going through the motions. It's empty works and rituals in an attempt to please God. The truth is we *can't* please God though our own works and religion. He wants a personal relationship with each of us. That's what pleases Him. He already did the perfect work through Christ. We simply receive what Christ did and enter a relationship with Him. Out of that will flow good works and positive change but it's God doing the work through the change He works in us as opposed to empty religious adherence. If Christ isn't truly in your heart, if you aren't truly living to follow Him, it's all for naught. Just a religious sham. That's why Jesus was so harsh with the religious leaders of His day. He called them *whitewashed tombs.*"

"Now hold on a second," Courtnall said, holding a hand up in protest. "I've been in church all my life. I tithe and donate millions on top of that to all kinds of charities. I teach Sunday School with my wife, conduct my business honestly, I've never been unfaithful, and I rarely ever curse. Are you saying that's not enough?"

"I'm not saying it. The scriptures spell it out. Jesus said it. Those are all good things, but unless you have committed to Christ in your heart, it's all just religious window dressing."

"Where did Jesus say that?" Courtnall asked.

"Well, in Matthew chapter fifteen, verse seven, Jesus said:

"You hypocrites! Isaiah was right when he prophesied about you:
'These people honor me with their lips,
but their hearts are far from me.
They worship me in vain;
their teachings are but rules taught by men.'"

And again in Matthew chapter seven, verse twenty-two He said:

"Many will say to me on that day, 'Lord, Lord, did we not
prophesy in your name, and in your name drive out demons
and perform many miracles?' Then I will tell them plainly,
'I never knew you. Away from me, you evildoers!'"

"You're right, He did say those things," Courtnall admitted. "I just thought they applied to the hypocrites. You know, like the people who go to church but cheat on their wives, beat their children, get drunk all the time. Those kinds of people."

"We're all hypocrites, Mr. Courtnall," Christy said plainly. "Everyone of is guilty of sin and none of us are perfect. We are all equally sinful in God's eyes. The only thing that makes a difference is whether or not we are willing to admit it, accept what Christ did for us on the cross, repent and turn our lives over to Him; otherwise, we are the people Jesus spoke of in those verses."

"I understand what you're saying, Christy, and it is quite sobering to think about, with this perspective. Be that as it may, can I ask a question?"

"Of course. And thank you for calling me Christy."

"You're welcome," he smiled gently. "But my question is in that last verse, Jesus said *'I never knew you.'* How can He say that if He is

God who is all-knowing and personally created each and every one of us? That seems contradictory to me."

"I can see how you would question that," Christy answered, "but when you study what Jesus is saying in its context and in the original Greek language, which it was written, the word *know*, in this case is not referring to a cognitive awareness or familiarity; instead, Jesus was referring to an intimate relationship, as in a man knowing his wife. It's way beyond and much more involved than what we usually think of when we hear the word *know*."

A surprised look of understanding suddenly registered on Courtnall's face. "That makes sense. I get it."

"You do?" Christy asked.

"Yes, I really do," he nodded.

"Then may I ask *you* a question, Mr. Courtnall?"

"Yes, Christy, but you have to call me Chuck."

"Okay, Chuck. Do you *know* Jesus?"

Courtnall's eyes narrowed. His mouth opened slightly but he uttered no words.

"Chuck?" Christy leaned in and looked at him intently. "When you stand before Christ, one day, will He *know* you?"

Courtnall stared back speechless. The question Christy was asking was simple in form but complex in every other way. He completely understood what she was asking but was at a loss as to the true answer. Hadn't he been a Christian since he was a child? Had he simply been adhering to a religion rather than following Christ? A cultural Christian but not a true follower? What if he *was* simply a cultural Christian? Could that really be? What then?

"Mr. Courtnall?"

Courtnall snapped out of his introspection and looked up to see Joe standing in the aisle looking at him. Ramsey and Whitmore were standing next to him.

"Yes, gentlemen?" He asked, somewhat grateful for the interruption.

"We've received an update from our people on the ground," Joe spoke plainly.

Courtnall looked at all three men. He tried to read their expressions but couldn't get a read. He took a breath and exhaled.

`   "Let's hear it," he sighed.

"We believe we have positive ID on your daughter. Our people took pictures of her getting off the plane in question and later being transferred onto a yacht," Joe said as he sat down with his iPhone and began flipping through the pictures Chief Lennon had sent them.

Courtnall's breathing became noticeably loud as he looked through the images. The first few images weren't definitive as all three girls had pillowcases over their heads. Things changed when he saw the images from the marina. His heart sped up when he instantly recognized his daughter. A cloud of emotions rushed over him. Anger, fear, but most of all, relief that she was still alive and walking. He fought back tears as his watering eyes lingered over the still images of his daughter.

"Not to be critical, but was there a reason your people on the ground couldn't rescue them?" Courtnall asked as he handed the phone back to Joe.

"I understand the question and I wish it could have been that simple," Joe replied. "I cannot divulge much but, suffice it to say, the guys who took those pictures are currently working another mission. There was limited manpower and no way to put together an effective rescue mission with the short amount of time they had."

"I understand. I just had to ask," Courtnall answered. "What's next?"

Whitmore spoke up. "Joe's man on the ground was careful to get detailed photos of that yacht. We have the registration number and my guys are working on a link to track their GPS signal. They pulled out of the marina just a few minutes ago."

"Once we track them to their next location, we will quickly assess the situation and plan a rescue," Joe added.

"What about intercepting the yacht?" Courtnall asked. "We know they're on there now. Would that be easier?"

"If they were in international waters, we would have some options including a Coast Guard intercept, but the current situation has us still in the air with no resources we can call. An approach in broad daylight would not only remove the element of surprise but would give them enough time to react and mount a defense. It's a good thought but not our best option. I'm sorry," Joe finished with a grimace.

"Any ideas as to where they might be taking her?"

"Difficult to say but my best guess is one of the barrier islands," Joe replied.

"And what makes you think that?" Courtnall asked.

"A few things," Joe began. "For starters, they went to a lot of effort to move those girls down here on a private jet believed to be owned by LFG."

"LFG?" Courtnall asked with his eyebrows raised.

"*Los Fantasma Guerreros*," Joe clarified. "One of the major drug and human trafficking cartels in Central America."

Courtnall nodded his understanding. "Thank you. Proceed please."

"They moved the girls to a yacht. With them was Sergei Petrenko and one of Tupolev's bodyguards along with an unidentified Hispanic man presumed to be member of the cartel. They are *not* big enough players for Tupolev and Cardenas to hand off the girls to for a pleasure cruise. They're being moved."

"Who's Cardenas?" Courtnall asked.

"Pedro Cardenas is the new head of the LFG cartel. He replaced Fernando Escobar a few months ago," Joe said being careful not to bring up the fact that he and Ramsey led the platoon responsible for Escobar's takedown.

Courtnall nodded his understanding and signaled for Joe to continue.

"Therefore, if they're moving the girls, then one of three scenarios emerges. They could be transferring them up or down the coast, but we consider that to be unlikely. It would be easier and safer to have done so by land. They could be meeting up with another yacht and transferring them over or they could be taking them to one of the barrier islands. That scenario makes the most sense. Many of those islands are privately owned small resorts. LFG owns at least one that we know of but there could be more, or they could even be taking the girls to someone else's island. Regardless, if we can track down their location, we can plan an op."

"I see." Courtnall nodded. "Any idea as to how soon this might happen?"

"Tonight, sir."

Chapter 47

Scottsdale, Arizona

" That's right, Chelsea. With this bill I've introduced, we will fund an additional one hundred billion dollars to the Department of Defense to build better housing and fund improvements for our brave men and women who serve in our armed forces. Additionally, some of this money will be used to build daycare facilities on our bases and fund additional diversity and sensitivity training to help modernize our military and make it a service that matches the ideals of our progressive society."

"To your last point, Senator Fowler, President Galan has vocally criticized your stated policy of implementing social justice reforms and diversity training within our armed forces. He says, and I quote, 'The mission of the military is to kill people and destroy things and anything interfering with that mission not only puts American lives in danger, but it also threatens the entire free world.' What would your response be to that?"

Fowler narrowed his eyes and, theatrically, shook his head while he made a sour face. Inwardly he smiled. The cable news anchor was following the scripted questions to the letter. She was firmly in his camp like the rest of the mainstream media. Not that it surprised him. The media had been an ally since he was a freshman representative many years ago. Chelsea McMann was fairly new. An idealistic Millennial who was rapidly rising in popularity on the left and notoriety on the right. She had been particularly supportive and could always be counted on to follow a script of questions and answers that were determined ahead of time by Theron and his staffers. Fowler could sense her admiration and was certain he could bed her if he ever wanted to, but she was too earthy and tried too hard to appear a serious intellectual, which probably played well for their young progressive viewers but didn't appeal to him in the least. *Where have all the info-babes gone?* He lamented to himself as he looked into the teleprompter and began to read his scripted response.

"Chelsea, just the mere wording of such a deplorable statement should shock us all! Galan is a misogynistic throwback to a bygone era when men forced women to stay home while they went out to fight in wars and rape and pillage other lands. Fortunately, we have evolved. We are an enlightened global society now. Our military must also evolve to serve the humanistic needs of our globalist society. They can't do that if they aren't sensitive to the diverse cultures of the people they serve. I don't want to imagine a nation where we build a military whose purpose is to kill and destroy and neither should decent Americans. We need a diverse military. A tolerant military that builds others up and serves the needs of the oppressed wherever they may be found. This bill is a giant leap forward toward that ideal. A Fowler administration will continue to work toward that ideal and we will not stop until we achieve a kinder and gentler world that celebrates diversity and ends oppression. My opponent would prefer to march us back into the dark ages, whereas my record will show that I have led the charge for social justice and global equity, first as a representative and now as a senator. Well, I've only just begun. I promise you that, on my first day in office, I will take charge in building a military that helps us lead the free world towards equity for all."

"I have no doubt you will," the anchorwoman nodded with a gentle smile. "Senator Fowler, thank you for taking time out of your busy campaign to be with us tonight."

"It was my pleasure, Chelsea, thank you."

"And we're clear," came the announcement from Fowler's media producer.

Fowler stood up and unclipped his lapel microphone. Across the room he saw Theron give a nod and a thumbs up. Fowler nodded in return and quickly walked out of his press room, thanking his staff as he walked by. He returned to his private office and closed the door to the anteroom before his assigned Secret Service agents could enter. They would take up positions outside the door until he reappeared. He walked through his office, stepped into his private bathroom, and closed the door. His Scottsdale office was located in a building he had designed and constructed during his first year as a representative. The bathroom, like his office, was spacious and well appointed. It included a large tiled shower, a jacuzzi, and even a sauna. Ostensibly, these amenities were for his chronic back pain; however, Fowler thought to himself with a grin, many young, aspiring, but most importantly, attractive female interns knew differently.

Fowler opened his phone and fired off a one-word text. He then quickly removed his suit coat and pants along with the rest of his clothing down to his boxer shorts. He carried his clothing into an adjacent walk-in closet and delicately laid them on a dressing table. He turned to an array of casual clothes and selected a pair of khaki shorts, a loose-fitting, flowery Hawaiian "Aloha" shirt, and a ball cap and put them on. He stepped into a pair of boating shoes and hung a pair of aviator sunglasses in his shirt. He checked himself in the mirror. The ball cap concealed his receding hairline. Shocks of graying blond hair protruded all around causing Fowler to believe he resembled a younger version of the singer Jimmy Buffett.

Pleased, he began whistling "Margaritaville" as he walked back into the bathroom and opened the sauna door. He reached under the raised wooden floor and released a latch. He was then able to pivot the floor upright revealing a concealed escape hatch in the floor below. He unlocked the hatch and gently lowered it down. Fowler turned on his cellphone light and directed the beam into the dark hole. A man appeared at the bottom of the ladder and looked up expectantly. Fowler quietly motioned with his hand and the man climbed up into the sauna.

"Good to see ya, Pick!" Fowler whispered excitedly as he clapped the man on the back and led him into the walk-in closet.

The man immediately stripped out of his clothes, folded them, and neatly placed them on a shelf. He then donned the suit Fowler had just laid on the dressing table. He turned to the full-length mirror, worked the light blue tie into an impeccable Windsor knot, and rearranged his hair with a brush. He turned and faced Fowler, who looked him over and nodded his approval. Fowler was looking at himself.

Fowler had been a freshman congressman in the House of Representatives when, as a joke, James Pickering sent him a picture in which he was dressed and groomed to look just like Fowler. Pickering, aka "Pick," a divorced loner, lived in nearby Phoenix where he worked out of his garage restoring furniture. Where Fowler's staff remarked at the uncanny resemblance, Fowler saw an opportunity. Having a double would allow him some freedoms he may not have otherwise had. Fowler discreetly contacted Pickering and set up a meeting where he made a generous proposition. For a man who barely scraped by financially, the prospect of a substantial boost to his income was too good to turn down and he readily agreed to becoming Fowler's double. The two met regularly for several weeks where Pickering learned to imitate Fowler's voice and mannerisms along with accumulating a working knowledge of his personal life and career.

The first trial run had been a lunch outing at one of Fowler's country clubs. Pickering passed the test with flying colors. Not one of the members who were familiar with Fowler had been any the wiser. Over the years, Pickering had stood in dozens of times, usually keeping a low profile but occasionally at a public event and only one person, other than Fowler, knew. That person was Fowler's chief of staff, Theron Belknap. Fowler felt it necessary that Belknap knew as he would be able to run interference anytime somebody got too close or Pickering seemed to be out of his element in a discussion. Belknap would have figured out the ruse quickly enough anyway, but others might not. Even Fowler's wife, Cassandra, had not caught on but Fowler usually had a plan in place to keep Pickering out of Cassandra's proximity.

Fowler had been on the *Los Fantasma Guerreros* cartel payroll for many years. In return for governmental favors and key intelligence, LFG had wielded their money and power to help get Fowler elected to the Senate and were now a major player, behind the scenes, in his presidential bid. Fowler knew that as long as he continued to produce for LFG, he would continue to add to his already substantial personal wealth as well as expand his political power. Conversely, if he ever crossed the cartel or stopped being the goose that laid the golden egg, he would immediately find himself in the cartel's crosshairs. Having a lookalike to take his place in those crosshairs just might come in handy one day.

Up until recently, he had mostly employed Pickering for low key events and appearances; however, once Fowler became a presidential candidate, he was assigned a Secret Service protective detail. Having a protective detail mere yards away 24/7 made it extremely difficult for Fowler to engage in his preferred extracurricular activities, which almost always involved top shelf liquor, a generous amount of cocaine, and at least one woman, if not more. To get around this, Fowler began employing Pickering more often.

"You look perfect," Fowler said as he straightened the lapels while looking over Pickering. "You're heading up to my mountain house in Sedona. I told Cassie I was heading up there tonight and would be working out of my Flagstaff office tomorrow. She's probably already in bed with one of her boy toys so I doubt you'll hear from her. If she does call, don't answer. Send her a text saying you're in a meeting, that you decided to stay in Sedona, and are busy with campaign business. That should be enough. My staff will bring you back here Saturday afternoon. Tell them you need a nap and shut yourself into my office until I get back and we'll switch out then. I've already wired the first payment to your account and you'll get the rest when I get back. Any questions?"

"Yeah. Are we going to keep doing this when you're in the White House? I've always wanted to be the president," Pickering smirked.

Fowler snorted out a chuckle. "That's funny, Pick. Truth is, I'll probably be tempted but fooling the Secret Service and a gaggle of staffers is a completely different ballgame. I'll have to work on it though," Fowler glanced at his watch and looked toward the door leading back into his office. "Alright. You all set?"

"Yeah, buddy," Pickering said using one of Fowler's trademark expressions in a perfect impression.

"Perfect!" Fowler said slapping Pickering on the back as he pointed him toward the door. "Theron is expecting you. He'll take it from there. Enjoy Sedona but keep a low profile. And don't drink all my booze!"

Pickering shot an amused look back at Fowler.

"I'm kidding, Pick. Make yourself at home. I'll see you here Saturday afternoon," Fowler said as he turned back into the spacious bathroom.

He turned out the light and waited until he heard the door to the anteroom shut behind Pickering. Satisfied, he collected a small backpack go-bag and stepped into the sauna. He climbed down the ladder, stopping to lower the sauna floor. After that, he closed the trap door hatch and locked it with a key. He climbed the rest of the way down the ladder and stepped onto the tunnel floor. Using a small flashlight attached to one of the backpack's shoulder straps, he illuminated the tunnel before him.

Over the past few decades, threats of death and violence toward politicians had become more commonplace. As a result, many congressmen and senators had hired security consultants to enhance the safety of their staff and themselves. Mostly themselves. Trap doors, safe rooms, and emergency escape routes had been some of the many safety recommendations, and many politicians had seen to it that these measures were taken. Having designed and built this office building, Fowler had installed two such escape routes. His staff were all drilled in the use of the main escape route but were unaware of this one. Fowler was afraid that an active shooter would go straight for his office leaving no avenue for escape to the main escape route; therefore, in the interest of self-preservation, he saw to it that his own personal escape hatch and tunnel was installed. This one led to a utility room in a building located behind his office building.

Fowler quickly traversed the two hundred feet through the tunnel leading to another ladder at the far end. He climbed the ladder and unlocked a metal hatch that led to a small space behind a wall. He opened an app on his phone which gave him access to a small security camera in the utility room on the other side of the wall. If a utility worker were to be in there when the presidential challenger stepped in through a hidden door, there would be a lot of explaining to do. There was no one there. Fowler released a latch and quietly slid aside a wheeled shelving panel. He stepped into the room, slid the panel back, and locked it in place. An access door led to the side of the building. Fowler switched his app and checked the outside cameras. The alleyway was clear. He donned his sunglasses and pulled his ball cap down over his eyes. He exited the building and kept his head down as he walked to a black Lexus sedan waiting at the curb. Fowler climbed in back and the car sped off.

Chapter 48

Goldson International Airport, Belize

C ourtnall's Gulfstream was parked in a remote area of the airport. The engines were shut down and the door remained closed, but the cabin was refreshingly cool, due to the air conditioning being powered by the aircraft's auxiliary power unit - more commonly known as the APU. A mission planning event was being conducted in the middle cabin area where a long couch lined one side of the aircraft, directly across from a flat screen TV panel on the other side. Joe sat in the middle of the couch with Ramsey to his right, Christy to his left, and Courtnall seated on Christy's left. Chuck Springer and Clay Whitmore stood by the screen as they gave an update on the latest intelligence. An overhead image of a tropical island was currently on the flat panel screen.

"We tracked the yacht's GPS to this island," Springer said as he directed his laser pointer to the screen. "It's a small resort island, known as *Isla Esmeralda,* which was recently sold to an overseas corporation believed to be a shell held by multiple parties, one of which being a dummy corporation owned by Pedro Cardenas, the current head of *Los Fantasma Guerreros.* The island is home to an exclusive resort that caters to celebrities and the wealthy looking for an exclusive getaway. We were able to get a look at the guest records and reservations and noted a trend that appears to block the resort for private use every few months. This is one such week. A comprehensive search of the net has revealed rumors that this island is Cardenas' own version of Epstein Island."

"Epstein Island?" Ramsey interrupted. "As in the sexual playground that scores of celebrities and politicians frequented with underage girls?"

"That's correct, Chief Ramsey," Springer answered. "Rumor has it, Cardenas uses this island for similar purposes as a way of courting various politicians, celebrities, and South American cartel chieftains to gain their favor."

"So you think Tracy and the other girls have been taken there to be this weekend's entertainment," Courtnall stated bluntly.

Springer met Courtnall's eyes with a solemn look. "I wasn't going to verbalize it but, yes, that does seem to fit the picture, Mr. Courtnall. I'm sorry."

Courtnall appeared to fight back a flare of rage as he briefly closed his eyes before quietly signaling for Springer to proceed.

"We're monitoring the GPS signal of the yacht. So far, it appears to be still tied up at the resort's main dock," Springer said circling a small pier at the south end of the island. "Unfortunately, we only have this satellite image and the GPS signal to go by. We have no live surveillance otherwise."

"So you're saying that Tracy and the other girls could be moved by another boat and we would have no way of knowing," Courtnall again phrased this as more of a statement than a question.

"Yes, sir, but logical deduction leads us to conclude that they were brought to this island for a purpose and won't be moved elsewhere. At least not tonight," Springer cringed at the unspoken implication. "I'm sorry."

"I appreciate that, Mr. Springer, but now is not the time for apologies or tip-toeing around my feelings. God knows what those animals have already done to my daughter and the others. If keeping them on that island helps us locate and rescue them, then I'll just have to focus on that and not the nefarious reasons they are on that island in the first place. With that in mind, what are our options?"

"I'm going to defer to our SEAL operators for that part," Springer replied. "Mr. O'Shanick?"

Joe stood up and approached the flat screen.

"Can you pan the image out a little, please?" He requested.

Springer worked his laptop, and the image panned out. A larger and seemingly uninhabited island appeared adjacent to *Isla Esmeralda*. The two islands made up a large group of barrier islands and were separated by a narrow stretch of water. *Isla Esmeralda* was triangular in shape with the apex pointing north and the base south. The base was split in half by a lagoon that angled to the northeast resulting in large and small portions of the island connected by a narrow strip of shore on the northeast side. The smaller side contained two buildings and a helicopter landing pad. The larger side held a dozen buildings all scattered around a central clearing; six beachfront cottages, three large buildings, two smaller buildings, and a central cabana. The western side of the triangular island was a long strip of trees and mangrove running the entire length of the side, with the exception of a very small clearing midway down the shore. Across the narrow straight, to the north, the larger island was nearly all mangrove. A small cut through the western side of the mangrove left a tiny patch of island which caught Joe's eye.

"I think, if resources allow, we should approach by water, preferably using a RHIB."

"A RHIB?" Courtnall asked.

"Yes, sir," Joe replied. "RHIB is short for Rigid Hull Inflatable Boat. Much like the Zodiac style the Coast Guard uses. We use them a lot in the teams for insertions. A RHIB will allow us to maneuver easily around these coral reefs and mangroves. We could take up position behind this tiny patch of mangrove and launch one of the drones. Once we get an aerial recon, we can firm up the op but there are several options to consider."

"Such as?" Courtnall prompted.

"Well, sir, the primary objective is the safe rescue of your daughter and the two other girls. The simplest op would be to locate them, rescue them, and exfiltrate in a stealth manner, preferably without the enemy knowing we were ever there. The problem is the known unknowns. We don't know if there are other girls there. If so, do we rescue them as well?"

"I think we have to. Don't you?" Courtnall responded.

"Agreed, sir. It's the right thing to do. The problem then becomes, if there are others, how many and will we have enough room to rescue them as well?"

"I guess we'll have to cross that bridge when we get there," Courtnall nodded grimly. "I'm here to get my daughter back, but I can't, in good conscience leave someone else's daughter behind. I couldn't live with myself."

"I understand, Mr. Courtnall. Neither could we," Joe said with a nod toward Christy and Ramsey.

"Well, you have a blank check with me. Procure whatever boats you need and more than one if necessary."

"Thank you, sir. With that in mind, we need to plan for every contingency. If there are other girls and we have a large enough RHIB to accommodate them, then we grab them all and get out of there as fast as we can. If there are too many, then we must have an alternative plan. We may have to engage the enemy force and subdue them in order to call in an alternative way to extract the girls. I'm hesitant to have to depend on Belizean authorities. We aren't exactly authorized for this mission and they may not react too kindly to our presence. Not to mention that whoever responds could be on the cartel's payroll. I would just as soon get in and out unnoticed and avoid an international incident."

"Agreed," Courtnall nodded.

"But that also opens another problem," Joe continued. "We have no idea how many enemy combatants are currently on the island. The girls may be heavily guarded in a manner requiring this op to go kinetic, meaning we may have to fight our way in and fight our way out. That's a question we won't be able to answer until we have eyes on and can accurately determine what we are up against and where the girls are, but we need to be prepared for a firefight."

"I hope it doesn't come to that, Mr. O'Shanick, but that's your call. I don't want to ask you to kill anyone under these circumstances, let alone risk your lives, but I'm desperate to get my daughter back and I have no other options," Courtnall had to force the last words out through tears.

"Sir, we are fully prepared to do everything it takes to get your daughter and the other girls back," Ramsey said looking over at Courtnall. "What Joe is getting at, is, if this op goes kinetic, we may have to kill every last one of those dirtbags and leave no witnesses."

"He's right," Joe added. "Conversely, there may be a few HVT's worth capturing and bringing stateside to face trial."

"HVT's?" Courtnall asked.

"High Value Targets, sir," Joe clarified. "They weren't on the yacht with the girls, but if we were to find Tupolev or Cardenas on the island with kidnapped American citizens, bringing them back alive might be the better option. It would give us leverage legally, not to mention the hit it would put on their organizations."

"That sounds good to me. I'm not much for killing anyone, so if we can bring them back alive and let them face justice, I'm all for that. But, if killing them is the only way to get Tracy and the others back, then kill every last one of them, gentlemen," Courtnall said looking at the other men. "They chose their fate. I won't lose any sleep over it. It'll save the taxpayers a fortune in legal costs and prison time."

"Very well, sir," Joe affirmed. "If this goes the way we want, we will be in and out with the girls without anyone ever knowing we were there. If it goes kinetic and we have to eliminate some hostiles, we won't lose any sleep over it either."

"So you need two RHIBs. Anything else?"

"Two would be ideal. We like to build redundancy into every op. Plus we may need the extra room. Other than that, I think we already have everything else we need," Joe answered.

"Good," Courtnall said and then looked directly at Whitmore. "Clay? Have one of your men get online and locate a marina that sells RHIBs. Rent or purchase, I don't care. I can have cash wired directly if that will speed up the process, but I want them ready within the next couple of hours. Will that do, Mr. O'Shanick?"

"That will do just fine."

"So what's your plan from there?"

"Well, again, I would like to approach from the larger island and hole up in this cut between the mangroves. We launch a drone, firm up our recon, and finalize the op plan," Joe glanced over at Ramsey.

"Rammer, jump in anytime, but I'd like to put one of us up on this building here as overwatch," Joe said pointing to the building by the helicopter pad.

"I'll take that, Joe," Gary Lee spoke up.

"You sure, Gary?" Joe asked. "That's going to entail sniper duty as well."

"No problem," Lee answered.

"Just so you know, the best approach for that would be to drop in offshore and swim up on the far side of the island rather than try to move through the main compound."

"Can do," Lee answered with a nod.

"Alright. That frees Ramsey up to help me locate and rescue the girls. Clay," Joe said with a glance toward Whitmore, "We'll leave you with the RHIBs concealed in the mangrove, while Rammer and I swim across the strait. It's all trees and mangrove on this side so it's the best approach. We'll make this the primary extraction point," Joe said pointing to the small clearing in the mangrove, "I'll call you when we are on our way there with the girls, and you keep the engine idling and be ready to come in fast. Can you handle that?"

Whitmore hesitated. "To tell the truth, Joe, I'm not very experienced with boats. I think I would be more useful on the ground."

"I can handle it, Joe," Christy spoke up.

Everyone directed their attention her way, Joe in particular. Joe tried to hide his concern as he looked in her eyes. Christy gazed back intensely.

"What?" She said breaking the silence. "You know I'm comfortable around boats."

"That wasn't part of the plan," Joe answered back without emotion. "We need you back here set up for medical which we hopefully will not need."

"I respectfully disagree," Christy answered all businesslike. "God forbid there are any injured, but if there are, I'll be needed up front with you. Plus, with me behind the helm, that frees Clay up to hit the island."

"I appreciate that, Christy, but this op has a good chance of turning into a firefight and…"

"And it's less likely to do so if you have four men ashore rather than three. I'm not asking to go ashore with you, but I am saying I can help manage the RHIBs and I'll be much more use to you out there than back here."

"She's right, Joe," Ramsey spoke up.

Joe's eyes looked briefly Ramsey and then settled back Christy. Joe knew Christy was not only capable of coxswaining a RHIB, but she could handle herself if things got hairy. It was a combination of her training and temperament. Joe had personally seen her perform under fire on more than one occasion. She was a healer first and foremost but had an inner warrior that was equally impressive. Her competency wasn't the concern. It was Joe's inner sheepdog. His natural instinct was to protect others from danger, particularly those he loves like his family and now Christy. Some of the best trained operators Joe had ever known had met their demise on the battlefield. He didn't even want to consider exposing Christy to such danger. *Los Fantasma Guerreros* are a unique cartel comprised of former Mexican special forces operators. If the bullets started flying, nobody would be safe. Not even himself or Ramsey.

Joe looked back at Ramsey. Rammer was not only his best friend but his right-hand man, a most trusted Chief Petty Officer. Having a good CPO was an integral part of a SEAL platoon's success. Even though Joe was Ramsey's commanding officer, Ramsey had taught Joe much about the intricacies of SPECOPS and the art of leading a platoon of SEALs. Ramsey was a frogman's frogman and Joe trusted him beyond measure. The fact that he agreed with Christy coming along was a focus on the mission, not a nonchalance toward Christy. Ramsey thought of Christy as a sister and thus would and, in fact, had laid his life down for her. His agreement that she should come along, led Joe to reconsider.

"Roger that," Joe nodded solemnly. "Clay, that puts you coming ashore with Ramsey and me. You good with that?"

"That's why I'm here," Whitmore answered. "Tell me what you need me to do."

Before Joe could begin, Courtnall spoke up. "I'll drive the other RHIB."

Joe looked back. He could sense it wasn't a request.

"I appreciate that, Mr. Courtnall, but I'm trying to minimize the number of noncombatants. Our mission is to bring your daughter *and* you back to your family."

"I understand and I respect your position, but I have extensive experience handling all types of boats, you need another driver, and this is *my* daughter we are talking about. I'll handle the boat but will otherwise stay out of your way."

"Fair enough," Joe answered. It was hard to say no to the man, considering his daughter was the reason they were here in the first place.

Chapter 49

Duluth, Georgia

D r. Stacy Morgan manipulated the ultrasound probe as she carefully imaged the young girl's reproductive system. The girl's name was Hannah. She was only fifteen. Her pelvic exam was highly suspicious for PID - Pelvic Inflammatory Disease - a complication of a sexually transmitted infection, usually Gonorrhea or Chlamydia, which could cause severe scarring to her reproductive organs which could leave her sterile or at risk for a life-threatening ectopic pregnancy in the future. The current concern was to make sure there was no abscess. An abscess on her Fallopian tubes or ovaries may require surgical drainage or removal. After another minute of careful scrutiny by ultrasound, Stacy was satisfied that there was no abscess.

"Okay, Hannah, everything looks fine on ultrasound," Stacy said as she removed the probe. "Angela will help you get dressed while I take a look at your slide."

One of the shelter volunteers, a junior at Georgia Tech applying to medical school, helped Hannah up while Stacy walked over to an old donated microscope in the corner. She readied the Wet Prep slide, placed it on the microscope, and leaned down to take a look. Using the knobs, she maneuvered the slide giving her incremental looks at each section. Stacy straightened up and gently waved Angela over to take a look.

"What do you see?" Stacy asked quietly as the student peered through the eyepiece.

"Looks like a lot of white blood cells and...some moving cells. That's Trich, isn't it?" The student asked quietly, referring to the sexually transmitted infection known as Trichomonas. She looked up at Stacy for confirmation.

Stacy nodded in response. She then dipped her head in Hannah's direction who had just gingerly climbed back up on the exam table after getting dressed.

"Okay, Hannah," Stacy said softly as she sat down on the examining stool facing the young teen. "The good news is you are not pregnant, and you don't appear to have suffered any significant damage to your reproductive organs; however, you appear to have at least one sexually transmitted infection and possibly one or two more. We won't know for sure until the other labs come back in a few days, but we are going to start you on some antibiotics now which should help reduce your pain over the next couple of days."

Hannah quietly nodded as a tear rolled down her cheek. Stacy fought back her own tears as she looked at the waif-like girl in front of her. Hannah was five foot three inches tall but had only weighed eighty-seven pounds when they weighed her earlier. She was severely malnourished and her medium brown hair, which looked to have been thick and wavy at one time, was now thin and stringy. Even after reassuring her that she was safe and that her nightmare was over, Hannah remained quiet and apprehensive throughout the exam. It was typical. Most of the girls they rescued out of prostitution were so battered and hurt that they were scared of everyone. The psychological damage was going to be the most difficult part to treat. Much more so than the sexually transmitted infection, the malnourishment, or even the opiate and cocaine addictions.

"It's okay, Hannah," Stacy soothed as she gently grabbed Hannah's hand and held it. "We're going to help you with everything you need. You can trust us."

Hannah didn't respond. She simply stared back with a blank expression.

"Hannah? Are you from around here?" Stacy asked.

Hannah gently shook her head.

"Okay, where are you from then?"

"Batesburg-Leesville, South Carolina," her voice croaked.

"Can I call someone for you?"

Hannah simply shook her head again.

"Are you sure?" Stacy asked. "A family member?"

Hannah subtly shook her head again, so subtly as to be nearly imperceptible. Stacy had seen this before.

"Can I ask why?"

Hannah slowly nodded. Stacy waited patiently for Hannah to summon up the will to tell her story. The student, Angela, sat down in an adjacent chair.

"Because my mom's in prison and my dad is dead."

Stacy closed her eyes briefly in shock. She opened them and gently spoke. "Oh, Hannah, that's terrible. I'm so sorry. May I ask what happened?"

"They were both Meth addicts," she started. "They weren't always, though. Daddy was the high school quarterback and Momma was a cheerleader. Nanna Jean says he was good enough to play college football, but he got into Meth with his friends and dropped out before he graduated. He got Momma into it and then she dropped out. Before long, they done had me. We lived in trailers, shared apartments with people, and sometimes lived in Daddy's car. I sometimes stayed with Nanna Jean. She was good to me. Bought me clothes, took me to her church, and cooked all the time. I cried when Momma come got me. Didn't want to leave."

"How long ago was that?" Stacy asked.

"I was ten. I knows that cuz Nanna Jean done made me a cake for my birthday. I ain't never seen her since. Momma promised me things were gonna be all better, but they weren't. She and Daddy had a little house out in the country. It was cold in the winter, hot in the summer. We didn't have no water or nothing. Had to go outside and do our business in holes Daddy dug. Most of the windows was busted and the roof leaked when it rained. Daddy cooked Meth out in the shed. I didn't know what it was at first, but I heard them talkin' about it and figured it out when I got older. That wasn't the worst part though. Daddy started beatin' Momma and makin' her have sex with men. Lots of men. Then one day, one of them wanted me. Momma was all drugged out. I tried to run but Daddy whipped me good and made me go in the living room with the man. Pretty soon it was lots of men until the explosion..." Hannah's voice trailed off.

"The explosion?" Stacy asked. "Are you talking about the shed?"

"Um hmm," Hannah nodded. "Momma was passed out. There were three men in the house. They done got scared and ran. I was afraid to go outside so I just watched the shed burn from the window. The cops came and took Momma to jail. I went into a foster home until my Uncle Jimmy come and got me."

"And then what happened?" Stacy asked, afraid she already knew the answer.

"Same thing. Uncle Jimmy and his girlfriend told me they were doing me a favor but didn't have no money to put me up. They said I had to earn my keep. I had to sleep with her and Uncle Jimmy that night. I tried to get away, but they whipped me with a 'lectric cord. Next night, they made me start sleepin' with their friends. 'Til Pitbull came."

"Pitbull?" Stacy skied wondering how many chapters this horror story had.

"Yeah, a big hairy man. I'd seen him before. Always come and make Uncle Jimmy give him money. One night Uncle Jimmy didn't have no money so Pitbull pulled out a big gun and held it to his head. Uncle Jimmy wet himself. I know cuz Pitbull done laughed at him about it. Uncle Jimmy started crying and then he give him me. Pitbull put me in his truck a drove a long time. He pulled over and gave me to Scarface who took me here. I been here ever since."

"How old were you then?" Stacy asked.

"Thirteen."

Stacy held her breath and fought back tears. She had seen a lot in the nine months she had been working at this shelter. Too much. What people would do for sex, money, and power; the level of depravity, it was almost too much to comprehend. She would never have believed it had she not met the victims, the surviving victims that is, and helped try to repair their decimated lives. Nine months and she was nearly devastated. Stacy often wondered how much more she could take. Here was a fifteen-year-old girl whose entire life had been nothing but

misery and horror. *How can I even think of walking out on these girls?*
Stacy asked herself as the tears began to form. She tried to hold back
and appear strong for Hannah. Someone had to be strong for her. She
thought of what Jesus said to his disciples:

"The harvest is plentiful but the workers are few."

Was it ever. She was one of the few workers and she was over-
whelmed. Stacy found herself in a very rare scenario. She was at a loss
as to what to do next. Even in a complicated delivery or in a difficult
surgical case, Stacy could remain calm and work her way through
any scenario. Not this time. She couldn't even relate to this young
girl. How does one establish trust when, other than her Nanna, this
girl has never had anyone she could trust? How does one comfort a
girl that has never known comfort? *God, I can't do this without you. I
want to run away from this like your prophet Elijah did after defeating
the false prophets. But how can I? I am simply hearing it. She has
lived it! Please give me the strength to help this young girl and all the
others. And please protect Joe, Matt, and Christy as they step into the
battlefield tonight to rescue even more. Give them your protection and
victory. Help us all. Please save these lost angels.*

Stacy quickly transitioned back into the methodical problem
solver. Her emotions were held at bay while she and Angela helped
Hannah comprise a list of known relatives and where they lived. That
list was pathetically short. The truth was, Hannah wasn't sure what
Nanna Jean's last name was or where she lived. Hannah thought she
might be in North Carolina but wasn't sure of the town. Hannah was
pretty sure Nanna Jean was her father's mother. It would take some
detective work, but Stacy vowed to get started on it right away. The
shelter would also use their resources to track down a next of kin, but
Stacy wouldn't settle for anyone other than Nanna Jean, if she could
be found. No one else could be trusted.

With Angela's help, they administered a shot of Ceftriaxone,
which would cover for Gonorrhea, followed by oral doxycycline for
Chlamydia, and oral metronidazole for Trichomonas. They handed
her over to the shelter staff and then performed similar intake exams
on the other two girls Joe and Ramsey had rescued. Their stories
were similar and equally horrifying. All three had been trafficked

for a lengthy amount of time and all three would be fighting addictions. Neither of the other two seemed to have Pelvic Inflammatory Disease but Stacy would follow their cultures and treat any disease that grew out.

A few hours later, Stacy said good night to Hannah and the other girls and promised to be by to check on them the next day. All three were fairly numb and shell shocked, a far more apt term than the more clinical PTSD in Stacy's opinion, but Hannah had actually stood to her feet and given Stacy a long tearful hug. Hannah wouldn't let go. Stacy eventually had to sit down in a rocking chair with Hannah in her lap. Willing herself to be strong for Hannah's sake, Stacy stifled her emotions while she rocked the young girl of a teenager to sleep. A teenager deprived of a childhood.

After placing Hannah's light frame into her bunk, Stacy bid the staff goodnight and slowly walked out to her SUV. She took a deep breath and exhaled, willing the toxic emotions to escape. She hopped in her vehicle and started off toward her condominium on the north end of town. She so wished Christy was with her so they could decompress together.

Her streaming radio service began to play over her Bluetooth. *Some music will be good,* she thought to herself. The U2 song "Mothers of the Disappeared" began with its unique mechanical intro that sounded like a distant storm approaching. A minute later the mournful melody kicked in. Stacy felt a pit begin to rise into her chest. She knew what this song was about. She reached for the button to advance to the next song but froze. Something inside her told her she had to experience the emotions. Another minute passed and Bono began his soulful mourning of the missing children in Central America. The tears began to flow. Stacy cried herself to sleep later that night.

297

Chapter 50

Belize Barrier Islands

A canopy of stars shone brightly overhead on the moonless night. A warm, tropical breeze floated out of the east as it nudged the waves along. The waves in turn emitted a gentle yet hypnotic roar as they crashed onto the barrier reef a short distance out to sea. Conversely, the large uninhabited island blocked out the wind and the waves resulting in a dead calm on its leeward side. A quiet symphony of birds and insects broke up the relative silence on this side and continued unabated as a dark intruder quietly floated by.

Joe leaned forward on the starboard side forward inflatable gunnel, maintaining a low profile as he gently paddled the Zodiac in unison with Chief Ramsey, who paddled on the opposite side. They hugged the western shore of the island for additional concealment. It was likely overkill as they were approaching the resort island from downwind and from its tree-lined mangrove shore, but Joe wasn't taking any chances. They had turned off the twin 250 horsepower outboards about one kilometer behind them and quietly paddled the rest of the way.

Despite Mr. Courtnall's vast resources, the limited time left them only able to procure one RHIB. It was a nice one, however. A Zodiac Pro 850. The spec sheet reported it to be capable of carrying up to twenty-five occupants, but there were only three bench seats in addition to the large center console. Additionally, the equipment they were carrying took up much of the deck floor. They'd be lucky to carry fifteen. Joe wished they could have brought two but, as it turned out, they were fortunate to have even obtained this one. Even that required Courtnall offering a fair amount over the list price to purchase the demo at the only marina that was still open. He had insisted on coming along for the rescue. Joe tried to talk him into staying behind but didn't push too hard. How could he? Nobody would be able to keep Joe behind were it his daughter that had been abducted into a prostitution ring.

As they rounded the south end of the island, they entered the narrow cut between the island and a small crop of mangrove. The cut was just wide enough to allow the Zodiac unimpeded progress. Joe looked around to make sure everyone else was crouched down low as they approached the opening on the far end of the cut. The tiny resort island came into view. It was very close, roughly 150 yards away across a narrow pass. As their recon revealed, the clearing and its structures were all concealed by the tree-lined mangroves on the nearby western side of the island. Joe and Ramsey lowered their night vision goggles and studied the shore. A few soft glows of light were faintly visible beyond the mangroves but there was no sign of any human forms along the shore. Joe had to remind himself that these weren't run-of-the-mill cartel thugs they were up against. They were well-trained and well-equipped former special forces operators. They knew how to conceal themselves. They should also be wise enough to watch all sides of the island, including the difficult approaches like this one. After studying the shore for another minute, Joe nodded to Ramsey and they slowly backed the RHIB behind the small mangrove until they could no longer see the resort island.

Ramsey opened a hard-plastic case revealing a small drone. Within a couple of minutes, he had the drone readied and launched. Joe sat beside him and studied the display screen with Lee, Whitmore, Courtnall, and Christy watching from behind. Ramsey deftly worked the controls on the remote, being careful to approach the island from downwind. The drone had a very low sound profile, but they weren't silent and, if anyone of the island spotted it, the mission would be compromised before it began.

The drone camera had Forward Looking Infrared (FLIR) technology which allowed them a fairly high-resolution overhead view of the island. The human profiles could be seen with enough detail to distinguish male from female which was exactly what was needed.

"I count two armed males by the pier on the south end and two more up on the beach," Ramsey quietly spoke as he pointed to several male profiles carrying rifles. Joe couldn't make out the type of rifle definitively, but they appeared to be of the M4 variety and, no doubt, automatic, considering who was carrying them.

"Agreed," Joe said. I see four more in this building which I would guess is their quarters. It looks like we have four non-combatants in this building cooking and cleaning. Kinda late but it is a resort. Let's check the bungalows."

Ramsey panned out with the camera and then refocused on the beachfront guest quarters. Two were occupied. On the far right, several men could be seen lounging on a bungalow porch, smoking as they looked out over the Caribbean. Joe guessed they were the VIP's. He wished the camera would allow him to get a good enough look to learn their identities but that wasn't possible. Opposite of them, on the side closest to where Joe and the team were positioned, the figures of three females appeared to be laying on beds in their bungalow. Normally the FLIR camera would not be able to penetrate a roof to obtain such a clean image. Joe guessed the roofs must be made of woven palm leaves and thin enough to allow the infrared heat signatures to be seen. That was a huge break. The lone figure of an armed male appeared to be seated on the porch, likely keeping watch over the bungalow's occupants.

"Bingo," Ramsey commented.

"Please tell me that's them," Courtnall whispered.

"Looks like it," Joe said as he studied the screen. "They were courteous enough to keep them in one place, but we'll have to neutralize the two beach sentries and then that guard," Joe stopped and looked out to their right.

Out of nowhere, the sound of a rapidly approaching helicopter was heard off to their right. Due to its approach from downwind, it wasn't heard until it was close in and beginning its approach to the island. Before Joe could mouth the words, Ramsey quickly maneuvered the drone out of the helicopter's flight path but kept it in the air to observe the new development.

"Probably not the hired help," Ramsey commented.

"Nope," Joe agreed. "Likely the VIP guests. That'll complicate things."

The helicopter flared out over the far side of the island and softly touched down on the landing pad. The passengers waited for the pilot to shut down the engine before they got out. There were only two, both men, with the taller man carrying a backpack slung over his right shoulder. Neither appeared to be carrying a rifle but Joe could not discern whether or not either had a concealed handgun. They were met by an armed man driving a golf cart. The two hopped onto the cart and were whisked around and over the narrow strip of land connecting to two halves of the island. The cart stopped to drop the men off at the other occupied bungalow. The men who were seated on the porch stood, stepped down from the porch and greeted the new arrivals. The group then began to walk around the bungalow toward a larger round open-air shelter in the center of the compound behind the beachfront bungalows. Joe could see a few of the staff members heading that way with a pushcart, likely bringing refreshments for the new guests. After greetings were exchanged, the men settled down into chairs while the staff arrived and attended to them.

"Rammer, I think we need to strike soon while the girls are all in one place and the VIP's are eating and drinking," Joe commented while studying the screen. "If they take the girls into separate bungalows, we'll have to cover more area."

"Roger that, Joe. How do you want to do this?"

"Gary? Are you sure you're good swimming to the far end of the island and taking overwatch?" Joe asked.

"Yeah, no sweat."

"Alright then. Gary, you'll swim around and insert on the southeast side then take up position over here on overwatch," Joe said pointing to what looked like an outbuilding by the landing pad. "Clay, you're with me and Rammer. We'll wait for Gary to get in position and then we will insert on the near shore where we have concealment. We'll move through the trees to the clearing by the first bungalow. Here's where we run into a problem. There is a guard on each end of the beach and one on the porch of the first bungalow, guarding the girls. There's no way we can take this guy out without the guy on the porch noticing. He'll sound the alarm and then the mission will be a goat rope. I think we have to take them both out at the same time. I see no other option. What do you think, Rammer?"

"Yeah, I know we'd prefer to get in and out without firing a shot but that's not an option with their guards spaced apart. From what the drone is showing us, there is no back door on those bungalows, making the porch entrance the only option. Won't be easy sneaking up on a trained guard. It's the right move," Ramsey concluded.

"Okay," Joe continued. "That leaves the guard on the other end of the beach. I'm hoping he won't be alerted when we take the bungalow, but we need to be ready in case he reacts."

If this were an actual SPECOPS mission, Joe would have the overwatch sniper take the other guard out when they were hitting the other guards; however, this was an unauthorized civilian mission and Joe did not want to ask a civilian like Gary Lee to kill anyone unless absolutely necessary.

"Therefore, once we neutralize the guards, I'll move into position by the porch to guard the far side of the beach while Clay watches our six. Rammer, you'll rescue the girls out of the bungalow while we cover you."

"That'll work," Ramsey nodded.

"Gary, I need you to monitor the area and let us know if anyone is heading our way."

"I can do that, Joe, but may I offer a suggestion?"

"Shoot," Joe answered.

"If that other guard gets wind of your presence, you *will* have a goat rope on your hands. Why don't I take him out so that doesn't happen?"

"I can't ask you to do that, Gary," Joe said looking up at Lee.

"Yes, you can," Lee answered back. "Clay and I are here to get those girls back just as much as the two of you. We're both combat veterans and, as far as we're concerned, these dirtbags deserve to be drawn and quartered and then fed to the sharks. I'll have no problem putting a bullet in their heads and, in my humble opinion, doing so will increase the odds of mission success. It's a no brainer."

Joe looked over at Whitmore who nodded his agreement.

"Alright, then. I was going to try to keep your hands clean and keep you in reserve, but it will be better to have you play a more direct role. That'll actually help a lot. Keep in mind that the VIP's may notice. If they react, we may have to take them out as well."

"I sure hope so," Lee growled.

"I hear you, Gary," Joe responded with a nod. "But they could be armed too, and you can bet they will most certainly sound the alarm bringing the rest of the guard force into the arena and I'd just as soon avoid that. On my command, we will all shoot at the same time. Christy?"

"Yes?"

"When you hear me say *execute,* that will be your signal to bring the RHIB in hard and fast to the primary extraction point here," Joe said pointing to the small clearing on the mangrove lined side of the island. "If that falls apart, secondary extraction point is the near end of the beach and tertiary extraction point is the boat dock on the south end of the island. If it all falls apart, we'll have you pick us up offshore about 100 yards off the beach. Are you good with all that?"

"I'm good," Christy nodded.

"Mr. Courtnall, if you can handle it, we need you to monitor the drone feed with Christy. Keep us up to date on what's happening on the ground. We're leaving it in a stationary hover that will give us a view of the entire island. We'll each have infrared strobes blinking so you can distinguish us from the bad guys. Any major changes or movement, let us know."

"Will do," Courtnall affirmed. "I can handle the boat and free Christy up for medical care if needed too."

"Thank you, sir, but, if this goes as planned, I'd prefer to have you freed up to help your daughter on board."

Courtnall was speechless. Were it not for the near darkness, the tears in his eyes would have been clearly seen. He swallowed hard and managed a solemn nod towards Joe and the rest of the team.

"Alright, we need to get moving," Joe said. "Rammer, give Christy and Mr. Courtnall a crash course on how to fly the drone while we gear up."

Within a few short minutes, all four had donned combat vests, tactical gear, and swim gear. They tested their inter-squad radios. Christy and Courtnall also wore helmets complete with radio headsets and NVGs - night vision goggles. Due to the need for stealth, using the RHIB's navigation or docking lights was out of the question. Christy and Courtnall would have to use the NVGs to operate the RHIB. The green-hued images could throw them off along with the significant loss of depth perception the user experienced with NVGs. Joe had them use them on the ride over to get used to the difference. It was far from ideal, but it would have to do. The four men inspected each other to make sure there were no shiny objects or loose objects that could make a noise and give away their position.

Having to swim a longer distance, Gary Lee entered the water first and swam away. After a few minutes, Joe nodded to Ramsey and Whitmore and they quietly slipped over the inflatable gunnels and into the black water. Through the dark, Joe and Christy locked eyes. They bade each other a silent farewell, both fighting the urge to embrace on the deck as the enormity of the situation descended upon them like a dark cloud. Joe took one last look at Christy and slipped over the side into the dark water.

Chapter 51

Belize Barrier Islands, Belize

Christy watched Joe silently disappear under the water. She stared out over the water but only saw Whitmore's head as he quietly swam into the darkness. Joe and Ramsey could not be seen or heard as they swam their combat sidestroke. Soon, even Whitmore was no longer visible. She silently prayed for their safety and then sat down at the center console where she could monitor the drone's camera display.

"How long have you two been together?" Courtnall asked quietly.

"Excuse me? What?" Christy asked in an equally hushed tone, startled by the question.

"You and Joe," Courtnall prompted. "How long have you been together?"

"How did you know?" Christy asked.

"In addition to being a financial analyst, I'm also a tournament poker champion. I've gotten pretty good at reading people's faces over the years. I picked up on something between you two on the plane, but you just confirmed it for me a minute ago."

"I'm sorry," Christy apologized. "We tried to keep it strictly professional for this mission. I can assure you, Joe is the consummate professional. His mind is in strict operational mode right now."

"I have no doubt. I find him very impressive. Chief Ramsey as well."

"They are. Trust me. If anyone can get your daughter back for you, it's those two. Joe saved my life twice."

"But that *is* how you met him?" Courtnall asked. "That issue in Honduras with the cartel? The one for which President Galan awarded him a medal in the Rose Garden ceremony?"

Christy briefly looked up from the video display. "Yes, our world's collided when their team came to rescue us. They lost half their team that day. The cartel captured me and then Joe when he came after me. He figured out a way to escape and we eventually got away, but here we are dealing with the same cartel. They just seem to keep crawling out from under their rock," she sighed.

"Tell me again how you got away?"

"We were being held captive on an island similar to this, just a little south of here, actually. Joe was able to break out of a pair of handcuffs, killed two armed men in the room and then we swam to a nearby island where we found a big cruising sailboat that we used to escape."

"Impressive," Courtnall commented.

"Yes,. Joe is quite resourceful and a highly-skilled and respected operator, but I also think God had His hand in it as well."

"See, there's where you lose me," Courtnall bristled. "Just like we talked about on the plane. God could have prevented you from being captured in the first place. Why do you think He would allow you to be captured just so He could save you?"

"You just gave the answer in your question," Christy answered.

"Come again," Courtnall responded with a confused tone.

"You said *allowed*. And you're right. God *did* allow it."

"Alright," Courtnall said spreading his hands apart, "but *why* did He allow it? That's my question."

"Because there was a purpose," Christy replied while studying the video screen.

"No offense, Dr. Tabrizi, but that answer is vague and nonsensical."

"Is it?" She asked without looking up.

"Yes, it is. What possible purpose could be responsible for allowing something evil to happen to you? Or to my daughter?"

"So what you're asking is what is God's purpose?" Christy asked as she looked up at Courtnall.

"Yes, exactly."

"It's the same purpose that led Him to create the universe. The same purpose that led Him to create the stars, the planets, the laws of nature, life and, ultimately, us."

"Okay and what *is* it?" Courtnall asked in exacerbation.

"To know Him and to help others know Him. You see, God is relational. He created us to have a relationship with us. To know Him like what a husband and wife know each other."

"Yes, you explained that on the plane, but it doesn't explain the evil that He allows."

"Sure it does. He chose us, but He also wants us to choose Him. Love is a choice. It's not something that can be forced. In order for us to be able to choose to love, He had to give us free will; however, that also allows us the free will to reject Him and reject His moral standard, replacing it with we think is right or desire to do. That's where sin comes in. We are all sinful and fall short as it says in Romans 3:23; therefore, we will do bad things. Some more than others but we are all sinful to one degree or another. Now God may and probably does prevent a lot of bad things from happening, but He still has to allow some bad things; otherwise, He would have to kill all of us or, at the very least, take away our free will. But here's the point: He is still sovereign. His ultimate will of reigning with us in His eternal kingdom *will* be accomplished. Nothing will stop that from happening. That's His sovereign will. Having said that, there is also His permissive will. By giving us free will, He has to permit bad things to happen; however, He doesn't abandon us, but rather works in the midst of the bad to make good things result as He spoke in Romans 8:28 where He said *For God works all things together for the good of those called according to His purpose.* In other words, His permissions have a purpose."

"And what good came out of your ordeal last year?" Courtnall asked skeptically with a tilt of his head and his arms crossed.

Christy looked up from the screen. "Where would you like to start? There are several high-ranking cartel members facing justice. Many more who are dead and will never hurt anyone ever again. That *ordeal*, as you described it, led me and several other people to get outside of our comfort zones and serve in ministries that combat human trafficking. We help a lot of people regain their dignity and start a new life. I also met the man that I am one day going to marry and raise a family with. That *ordeal* began a process in that same man transforming him from an atheist to a man of God. There will also be a ripple effect of good things that transpire from here on out. Don't get me wrong, it was a horrible thing to endure, but my life and the lives of many others are far better off, and I wouldn't change a thing."

"Well you're certainly optimistic, Dr. Tabrizi. I'll give you that. But do you really think something good will result from what's being done to my daughter?" Courtnall asked accusingly.

Christy sighed. It was not out of frustration. She was completely sympathetic to this man's pain and skepticism. How would she feel if she had a daughter in a similar situation?

"Mr. Courtnall, what's been done to your daughter and family is absolutely criminal and evil. Joe, Ramsey, and Whitmore's team are here to right that wrong. I don't know why this happened, but I do know God is real and He does not lie. If He promises us, He will make all things work together, then He will," Christy paused as a thought came to her.

"Have you ever heard of the surfer, Bethany Hamilton?"

"Have I? She's one of Tracy's heroes. A remarkable young lady…" Courtnall paused for a moment as the revelation hit him. "Ah, okay. I see where you are going with this. Yes, what happened to her when that shark bit off her arm was tragic, but Bethany's story and Bethany in particular has inspired and given hope to millions of people."

"That's right and when asked if she could go back in time and not have surfed that day when the shark attacked her, she said she wouldn't change a thing because of what came out of it."

"Yep," Courtnall nodded. "In fact, Tracy's favorite line from *Soul Surfer* was when Bethany told the reporters she wouldn't change anything because it allowed her to embrace more people with one arm than she ever could with two arms."

"That was my favorite line too," Christy smiled gently.

"You know, Tracy surfs," Courtnall spoke with a slight smile as he looked at Christy.

"Really?" Christy asked.

"Yep. After seeing *Soul Surfer*, Tracy became a Bethany Hamilton fanatic. Wanted to learn how to surf and everything. One year, her mother and I surprised the kids with a trip to a surfing school in Kauai. She and her brothers were hooked. We ended up buying a beach home in the Outer Banks where some of the best waves on the East Coast can be found. We're actually supposed to go there when they're home for fall break..." Courtnall's voice trailed off.

"They'll get her back, Mr. Courtnall," Christy reassured.

"Charles," he said with a softer voice, gently patting her shoulder. "And I'm sorry I gave you a hard time. I'm afraid I'm not handling this as well as I should. I admire your faith. Will you pray for me?"

"How about I pray *with* you instead?" Christy said as she grabbed his hand.

Chapter 52

Isla Esmeralda, Belize Barrier Islands

An array of tiki torches illuminated the compound revealing palm branches which gently swayed in the breeze to the rhythmic dull roar of the waves crashing onto the beach. In the center of the clearing stood a round open-air structure constructed of bamboo and the obligatory palm thatched roof. A soft, inviting light emanated with the sounds of laughter from within. Inside, a well-stocked bar occupied one end facing several round tables, only one of which was occupied.

Seated around the table, a notorious who's who of world power brokers were present either in person or by proxy. In addition to Cardenas and Tupolev, some of the more notable were Ali Nazari, the deputy minister of defense for the Islamic Republic of Iran, Zheng Wu, special assistant to the president of The People's Republic of China, and Ernesto Valdez, chief of staff to the president of Venezuela. Cardenas clinked his champagne flute with a knife and stood. The casually dressed men stood around the table with glasses extended toward their host, as he led them in a toast.

"My friends, this is truly a momentous occasion. We gather on the precipice of victory. A victory all but certain and one that each of us has made possible. Each one of us has contributed in a meaningful manner and each one will soon reap the benefits in ways we cannot measure. But there is still work to be done, my friends. We must continue to push our mutual friend across the finish line. We must see to it that he has friends in his Senate and House of Representatives whether by election or by other means. We must see to it that he has judges to support and further his agenda. Our agenda. The days of the incompetents are over. With Senator Fowler's election to President, *we* will show the world what true consensus is through our alliance and what true leadership is through our power. But it is also a bittersweet occasion. For as our victory is all but assured, we will not be able to gather together to celebrate when that day comes. In fact, we will not be able to gather again until long after our valued friend steps down from the presidency. We will have the next eight years to work hard and establish a new world order. When that day does come, and it will, my friends, we will gather together and celebrate what we have accomplished; therefore, let us take this time to celebrate what we have already accomplished and what we will soon accomplish. To victory," Cardenas said as he held up his champagne flute. "And to the next president of the United States, our president, Robert Fowler!"

A round of acknowledgments sounded out followed by the clinking of champagne flutes.

Cardenas drained his glass, along with the others, and sat down. Two servant girls quickly refilled everyone's glasses while others began to lay out steaming bowls of food to be served family style. Cardenas looked at the men seated around the table and grinned.

The "alliance" had been his brainchild. The idea began to grow legs when *Los Fantasma Guerreros* had risen to power under then chief, Hector Cruz. An ambitious visionary, Cruz had quickly warmed to Cardenas' idea when it was presented to him. So much so that Cruz provided a long-distance jet and a security detail to travel around the world in his proxy to build this alliance. The alliance was more of a tangled web of world powers working together and serving each other to build their influence and world standing in a mutually beneficial manner. Each member was carefully chosen for their ability to contribute to the cause as well as control their region. Iran had the ability to control oil production and exert it's influence over the Middle East but needed buyers for their oil and wanted nuclear arms capabilities. China needed oil and resources and had the cash to fund many of the other players in the alliance. In return, the Chinese wanted open access to western markets and unrestricted control of their region and the South China Sea. They also relied on the export of fentanyl in its raw form which they sent to the Mexican cartels to move into the United States. Russia was also oil and mineral rich and needed buyers for their product. Tupolev was proxy to the oligarchs representing their interests but also needed a steady supply of drugs and sex trade workers from Central America and freedom to operate his underworld in the southeastern United States. Russia, if allowed to export its oil and natural gas to Europe and Asia, would have the military and economic might to control much of Europe and northern Asia. All three nations had been working to establish a presence and control in the South American nations. There were resources, land, a drug trade, and people to exploit. Iran had, so far, had the most success with their radicalization of Lebanese Shi'a expatriates living in South America. China and Russia wanted their piece of the action as well.

Enter Venezuela. In addition to their oil rich resources, Venezuelan government officials were actively involved in the drug trades, international crime, and human trafficking, and had the military to assist with these endeavors. Cardenas saw the Venezuelan government as the gateway to South America.

Cardenas had studied the geopolitical situation of these nations and the world as a whole and saw an opportunity. Each nation, oligarch, and power head could bring something to the table to meet each other's needs. Cardenas had spent the last three years carefully developing relationships and building a consensus. He had eventually gotten everyone on the same room to hammer out their differences and broker some deals. In fact, many deals were brokered. The interdependence was so complex, the cartel's IT specialist had to track it all using special software.

The key to the entire matrix was the United States. Access to be precise. Access to her borders, access to her markets, and access to her lawmakers. China, Iran, Venezuela, and the rest of South America needed someone to get their drugs into the United States. Cardenas had that access. The same nations needed to get their people and their sex slaves across the southern U.S. border. Cardenas could offer that. Iran used Cardenas' coyotes to get their sponsored terrorist organizations, groups like Hezbollah, into the United States, which, again, depended on a soft border. China, Russia, Iran, and Venezuela needed reduced sanctions and open markets to sell their products. Cardenas and the cartels wielded great influence over many politicians, some by intimidation, most by incentive. Cardenas already had two Supreme Court justices in his back pocket, both of whom had been past guests to his island. Owning the president would be the final piece, the master key to it all. Once he had leverage over the Executive Branch, the other branches would fall in line, especially if the House and Senate were of the same party.

Cardenas began building the alliance a year after the last presidential election. He had hired a marketing firm and investigators to scout out likely presidential candidates and look for weaknesses to exploit. Within several months, their search had landed on Senator Fowler. He was ambitious enough to crave the presidency, well connected, a wealthy Washington insider, and a darling of the media. He was also a philanderer. There had been rumors of this, but they were quickly dismissed by his admirers in the press and within his constituency. A deeper investigation revealed that Fowler was more of a perverted sex-fiend than just a simple bed hopper. When Cardenas raised the idea of exploiting Fowler and riding him into The White House, Hector Cruz took Cardenas into his confidence and revealed that Fowler had already been on their payroll providing key government intel, money laundering, and fighting for open borders. It was simply a matter of further cultivation and a few well-placed honey traps to secure his loyalty. Dangling the presidency in front of him won over his cooperation.

The key to the success of *Los Fantasma Guerreros* and, more specifically, to that of Cardenas' success was getting the United States to keep the borders open while going soft on the other nations in his alliance. The key to the United States was Fowler and the key to Fowler was his ego, greed, and power. Salting it all by appealing to his sexual appetite was the icing on the cake.

The men all ate lightly and were soon finished. All, that is, except for Zheng Wu. Unlike the majority of his countrymen, Zheng was a fat and happy communist pig by Cardenas' assessment. All of those present had been guests here many times over and knew what to expect. They ate lightly because their appetites were for other things. Right on time, Alejandro Lopez, Cardenas' second in command appeared along with Sergei Petrenko. Lopez nodded at his boss. Cardenas surveyed the table, took a large swallow of his tequila, and stood.

"Well, my friends, as usual, we have some *special* entertainment in store for each of you. If you would like to follow Señor Lopez and Señor Petrenko, they have some special companions from which to choose. Take two if you think you can handle them," Cardenas said to their amusement. "There will be more food and refreshments here when you need to recover. Enjoy, my friends!"

The men all stood and followed Lopez and Petrenko out of the meeting hut. Tupolev lagged behind, gently grabbing the man before him by the arm to hold him back. Cardenas approached the man.

"Senator Fowler, if you will follow us, Señor Tupolev and I have a special gift for you."

Chapter 53

Isla Esmeralda, Belize
Barrier Islands

O n a sunny day, the crystal-clear water around the island was a pleasant turquoise blue. Unfortunately, the moonless night made it a near inky dark. Joe hated that. Having trained on Coronado and the San Diego Bay, and more recently the beaches and inlets of Virginia Beach, he was used to it, but he still didn't like it. One never knew what creatures lurked just beyond what could be seen, especially around mangroves and coral reefs. The swimming creatures would usually get out of the way. It was the non-swimming creatures that concerned him. Particularly sea urchins. The little creatures were armed with dozens of sharp needles that could penetrate the sole of a shoe and make walking a miserable experience for weeks. Such a mishap would certainly screw up this mission before it even began. Joe was relatively certain his tactical boots would protect his feet, but he had heard sea stories. He didn't care to find out.

As they neared the island, Joe sensed the bottom approaching and cautiously placed a foot beneath him. Sand. That was a relief. Keeping low with just his eyes above the water, Joe planted the other foot and remained still. He studied the shore through his night vision goggles, looking and listening. Ramsey and Whitmore remained about thirty yards behind, waiting on Joe to give the all clear. The artificial green hues of the tree-lined shore revealed no signs of hostiles. Joe signaled the all-clear and kept watch with his AR-15 rifle while Ramsey and

Whitmore swam up to his position. They quietly removed their swim fins, clipped them to their sides and slowly advanced out of the water. Once inside the tree line, they hid their swim gear while Joe took a knee and checked in over the radio.

"Echo Base, this is Echo One, passing Dirty Harry," Joe quietly spoke into his microphone.

"Good copy, Echo One, passing Dirty Harry."

Joe suppressed a smile when he heard Christy's voice over the radio. The use of call signs and mission codes was probably not necessary considering they were infiltrating a resort island and using encrypted radios, but they were still dealing with former special forces operators and he wasn't taking any chances. Tonight's mission codes were all names of different characters Clint Eastwood had portrayed in movies. Christy had a small writing tablet where she was keeping track of their location while keeping watch over the drone with Courtnall.

"Echo Four, this is Echo One, sit-rep, over."

Joe's call to Gary Lee went unanswered.

"Echo Four, this is Echo One, sit-rep, over."

Silence.

"He should have made it by now," Joe whispered to Ramsey and Whitmore. "You sure he's a good swimmer, Clay?"

"Yes, he swims with the Masters Swim Team at the Y."

"Alright. We'll give him another five minutes, but we may have to carry on without overwatch so let's plan for that contingency."

After a few minutes, Joe keyed his radio microphone in attempt to raise Lee.

"Echo Four, this is Echo One, sit-rep, over."

His call was met with two rapid clicks of the microphone. Lee was letting them know he was in a position where he was unable to verbalize. Ramsey and Whitmore kept watch while Joe listened intently.

"Echo Four, do you require assistance?"

Lee responded with two clicks signaling he was okay. Joe waited intently. They may be engaging sooner than expected. It was time to get into position. He tapped Ramsey and Whitmore on the shoulders and signaled for them to move out. Ramsey led them on point as they began to quietly move through the trees. A few methodical minutes later, Ramsey dropped to one knee and held up a closed fist signaling the others to stop. Joe and Whitmore both dropped onto a knee. Ramsey turned allowing Joe to see him point to his eyes and hold up one finger signaling he had one enemy hostile in sight. Ramsey signaled for Joe and Whitmore to form up on him. As they did, Lee called in over the radio.

"Echo One, this is Echo Four, I've reached Gunny Highway. Sorry about the delay, I had to neutralize a target."

"Echo Four, are the tangos aware they have company?"

"Negative."

"Very well, Echo Four, Charlie Mike."

That didn't take long. Joe was impressed that Lee was able to kill one of the guards in a manner that didn't raise the alarm; nevertheless, they would have to move fast before the others discovered one of their own was missing.

Christy's voice came over the radio, interrupting Joe's thought. "Echo One, we have a problem."

"Go, Echo base," Joe responded.

"We're seeing a bunch of people that just came out of one of the main buildings. I count four men, two of them armed and what looks like ten females."

"Are they heading our way?" Joe asked.

"Negative. Two of the men are heading to the meeting hut. The other two are lining the women up."

"Echo One, this is Echo Four, I confirm. Four hostiles and ten female friendlies. They just came out of the big structure and it has a tiled roof. Probably why we didn't see them on the drone, sir."

"All units, hold what you got. Let's figure this thing out," Joe said as he took a breath and collected his thoughts. "We now have thirteen females total. Likely all being held against their will to entertain the guests. Our priority is the three we came for but without a positive ID we don't know whether they're the three being held in the bungalow or if they're being held with the others. Ideally, we need to rescue them all anyway. Echo Four, do you have a shot at the tango on your side of the beach?"

"That's affirmative, Echo One, he's just perched in a beach chair having a smoke."

"Very well. Do you also have a shot at the two tangos with the women?"

"Affirmative again, sir. Your orders?"

Joe was quite impressed with Lee. He hoped his shooting was equally impressive. They were going to need it. Joe keyed his mike.

"Okay, here's the plan; on my command, Lee, you take out the tango on your end of the beach, Rammer will take out the guard by us, and I'll take out the guard on the bungalow porch. Use head shots. I want them down without a sound. Clay, you and Ramsey will sweep the hooch and remove the girls while I post rear guard over the compound. If those are the girls we came for, call out "Jackpot" and get them to the beach head for extract, while I provide cover. If not, call "lost angels," get them to extract, and then form up on me and we will push back to the compound for the others. Lee, once we have the girls aboard, I'll signal you to start neutralizing targets. Start with the two guarding the women then look for anyone carrying a weapon, except for us," Joe called each person out by name to avoid any confusion with the new hastily laid plan.

"Roger that," Lee answered.

"Christy, when you hear me say "execute," make haste for the secondary extraction point at the beach head."

"Roger that."

"Once you have the girls on board, head around to the primary extraction point and be ready to take on fourteen of us."

"Got it," Christy answered over the radio.

"Clay, I'll have you stick with me when we push back into the compound. Rammer, I want you to flank through the trees."

"Got it, boss," Ramsey answered.

"Alright, let's move into position," Joe commanded.

"Echo One, hold what you got," Lee called out over the radio. "The party just broke up in the meet house and you've got three males heading your way."

Chapter 54

Isla Esmeralda, Belize

"Say again your last," Joe spoke into the microphone.

"You've got three fighting-age males heading towards the hooch in front of you," Lee repeated over the radio.

Joe looked in their direction as he quickly ran through a list of options. Through his night vision goggles, he saw the green spectral images walking toward the bungalow. They were nearly there. He couldn't see rifles, but the men could still be armed. Regardless, it was too late to assault the bungalow and get out before they got there. To act now would require killing the guards which would alert the three newcomers, possibly resulting in a firefight but definitely drawing the attention of the other cartel soldiers. Once again, Mr. Murphy of *Murphy's Law* had chosen to insert himself at the precise moment of inconvenience. Even the best laid plan doesn't survive the first shot of battle. *We haven't even fired a shot yet!*

Joe toggled his microphone. "All units, hold what you got. Let's see what they do."

The three men passed on the far side of the bungalow, briefly passing out of sight. They reappeared in front and climbed up onto the porch. Joe instantly recognized Victor Tupolev and Pedro Cardenas but the third man wore a baseball hat and couldn't clearly be seen. Not that it mattered. They were entering the bungalow where three kidnapped women were being held as sex slaves. It was obvious what was about to go down. Time to act.

*****

Tracy stared at the faux palm leaves of the slowly spinning ceiling fan while laying on the plush, king-sized bed in a beautifully decorated Caribbean beachside bungalow. Most people would consider this tiny tropical resort to be a paradise. To Tracy, it was just another chapter in a continuing nightmare.

The Russian man, Sergei, and the slick little Mexican man had forced Tracy, Darcy, and Rebecca to change into the skimpiest of see-through lace lingerie. There was very little left to the imagination. It was better than being completely naked like she had been for the first few days, but not much. She felt exposed and vulnerable.

To her right was Darcy, curled up in the fetal position, rocking back and forth crying from the sharp flu-like body aches and chills of heroin withdrawal. Her tear-filled face was a pale vision of misery. Conversely, Rebecca was sprawled across the foot of the bed. She didn't seem to be in withdrawal. She didn't seem to be aware of much of anything.

Tracy wrestled with her thoughts as she continued to stare at the ceiling fan. No one had molested her...yet. She feared that was about to change. The Russians had gone to great lengths to move her and the other girls to this tropical island. It wasn't to give them a vacation. She was pretty sure they were going to be room entertainment for someone. She tried to take her mind off of it by reliving past memories. Pleasant memories, but they wouldn't come. Her daily escape into dreamland was elusive.

She toyed with the idea of looking for a way of escape. She snuck a glance out through the porch opening and saw their guard was still watching them. Tracy had gotten off the bed earlier to have a look around and he immediately came in, twisted her arm behind her, and forced her back onto the bed. Maybe if she could get Darcy and Rebecca to jump him when he came in, they would have a chance, but neither seemed up to it. She racked her brain trying to think of another way out, but the ceiling fan wasn't offering any suggestions.

The sound of footsteps drew her attention back toward the porch archway. Three middle-aged men appeared and stepped inside. There was a muscular man with short graying hair and sharp blue eyes standing next to a stocky Hispanic man with dark menacing eyes. Another man stood behind them wearing a ball cap. The dimly lit room and ball cap shaded his facial features, but a tuft of graying blond hair stuck out from under his cap and she thought he looked vaguely familiar.

*****

Senator Fowler peered over Cardenas' shoulder and surveyed the three scantily clad women before him. He found all three appealing and instantly began to feel his senses heightening as his lust began to engage. He savored the feeling. Life as a prominent politician demanded so much self-deprivation and proper manners in order to keep up a public persona. Infinitely more so now that he was a contender for the White House. Twenty hours a day of endless campaigning, photo ops, posing and press appearances didn't leave much time out of the power suit. Ironic that he, a self-admitted hound, craved ultimate power even more than women, yet despised the trappings of the very power he craved. Little matter. Power brought money and more women. Case in point, here he stood with two of the most powerful criminals in the world and they were cozying up to him with women and money as offerings.

Tupolev and Cardenas were not only powerful but dangerous. Between just their two organizations, Fowler estimated they likely accounted for thousands of deaths, either ordered or by their own hands. Despite that fact, Fowler ditched his security detail to travel down here and stand among these high-priced thugs without the slightest concern for his safety. Tupolev and Cardenas needed him. As did Iran, China, Russia, and many more. They had a lot invested in his future presidency. Nothing would happen to him. Once he ascended to the presidency, he would be *their* power broker.

"I'll take all three!" Fowler half-joked, to Cardenas and Tupolev's amusement.

"You may have all three, my friend," Cardenas quietly spoke said as he slapped Fowler on the back, "but the blond one in the red is a rare jewel. A virgin. Certified pure, complements of Victor here. She is our special gift to you."

Fowler's interest peaked, causing him to burn on the inside as his lustful desires began to consume him. The other two girls suddenly faded from his vision as he focused on the perky-looking blond. A virgin would be a first for him. His past conquests were too numerous to count but, all had been experienced. Some professional, some coerced and most, he vainly assumed, helplessly overcome by his stature and magnetism, but all had been experienced. He had not expected this. A rare and precious gift indeed.

"Are you serious?" Fowler asked, mystified as he looked at Tupolev.

"Only the finest for you, Mr. President," Tupolev smiled. He then lowered his voice. "I regret now that I didn't have my people dress her in one of those Stars and Stripes bikinis. It would be quite symbolic, don't you think?"

"Why? Because she's American?" Fowler asked not picking up on Tupolev's implication.

"Because what you are about to do to her, you will soon be doing to your country," Tupolev said breaking out into a hearty laugh with Cardenas.

Fowler responded with a half-smile as he processed what Tupolev said. He finally got the joke and began to laugh along with the two drug lords. Tupolev had a point. The laughter subsided and Tupolev eyed Fowler with a mirthful smile.

"My people tell me that little pixie can be quite a handful. I can have her sedated if you don't think you can handle her," he said in an amusing form of a challenge.

"Oh come on, man!" Fowler replied with a confident laugh. "I've tamed many a shrew in my day. I can handle her."

"I'll bet she wears you out!" Cardenas teased.

"Not a chance," Fowler said as he began walking toward the bed. He cast a glance over his shoulder and grinned, "I'll be ready for the redhead in an hour!"

*****

"All units, on my command, we proceed as before. Lee, take out the tango on your side, Rammer, you've got the one on our side and

I'll get the guy on the porch. After that, Lee, continue with overwatch. Rammer and I will take the room. Clay, you follow us in once we've cleared the room. I want these guys alive if we can do it but, if they're armed, they don't get a shot off. Christy, on my mark, gun it and hit the beach fast. Everyone acknowledge."

"Roger that," came the replies.

Joe checked down-range at the center of the island to make sure no one else was heading their way. He shouldered his AR-15 and sighted in on the soldier standing watch on the porch.

"Stand by to execute in three...two...,"

The sound of a woman screaming emitted from the door as Tupolev emerged carrying a redhead girl over his shoulder. True to the stereotype, the feisty ginger continued to scream as her legs flailed in the air and pounded her fists into Tupolev's back while he laughed it off. Cardenas followed behind carrying a blond girl. Her long hair splayed out as it hung down nearly to the backs of his knees. She was either unconscious or decided not to put up a fight. Joe briefly wondered if that was Courtnall's daughter but quickly dismissed the thought. By Courtnall's description, Tracy was a sweet girl but a fierce competitor and would likely put up a fight. *Unless the fight had been taken out of her by sedation or terror.* Joe couldn't see her face and was unable to determine whether or not it was Tracy Courtnall. Not that it mattered. They were here to rescue all three... and now the roughly dozen or so that just materialized in the center of the island.

"All units stand by," he spoke.

Joe quickly reassessed the situation. They remained undetected and still had the element of surprise. He was tempted to shoot the guards and then take out Tupolev and Cardenas before they were even aware but, with the girls slung over their backs, a shot like that would be too risky with an M4. He could accidentally hit the girls just as easily. That would be an epic fail.

"What do you want to do, Joe?" Ramsey asked.

"Looks like Tupolev and Cardenas are taking those girls to their hooches. I say we wait for them to settle in then we spread out and hit all three at once. Catch them with their pants down, literally. It'll require a little coordination and it'll also mean we hit each hooch solo, Clay included, so I'm open to other ideas."

"It's the best option, Skipper," Ramsey replied. "All three of us hitting them one at a time may alert them. There's only one of them in each hooch, preoccupied and likely not holding a weapon. That gives us tactical advantage while keeping the element of surprise. Let's roll with that."

"Clay?" Joe asked. "Are you up for it?"

"Can do," Whitmore responded.

"Good," Joe was as equally happy to hear Whitmore's response as he was to know Ramsey agreed with his plan. "Clay, you take the first hooch. Rammer, Tupolev just went into the second hooch so you take that one. I'll take Cardenas. He looks like he's heading for the last hooch."

Suddenly, a woman's terrified screaming began to emanate from the first bungalow, followed by a guttural male bellow and a loud slap. Joe saw Cardenas briefly turn back to the sound before proceeding to the last bungalow. The sounds of a violent struggle began to intensify. Joe hoped Courtnall couldn't hear what was going on but sound travels well across water.

"Clay, you better let me handle the first hooch. You take Cardenas down at the end. Move fast as soon as we drop the guards. Rammer and I will neutralize our tangos and be right behind you."

"I'm good, Joe," Whitmore answered. "Once a Marine always a Marine."

"Very well. Heads on a swivel, boys. Lee, we don't have time to let them settle in. We need to move now. You ready with your shot?"

"Roger that," Lee answered.

"Very well. Everybody, stand by. On my command…"

Chapter 55

Isla Esmeralda, Belize

*J*oe controlled his breathing as he sighted in on the man guarding the porch. The cartel soldier sat upright and seemed to listen with amused interest as Tracy's screaming intensified. Her distress made Joe want to act immediately, but he fought off that urge and focused on the task at hand. He listened to the surf's rhythm. He gauged it to be loud enough to, hopefully drown out the sound of their suppressed rifles. Even with a suppressor, the semi-automatic action of the AR-15's would still make a metallic clacking sound that would be easily recognizable by the seasoned *soldados* of the cartel. Joe timed his command to coincide with the crash of the next wave. He moved his index finger to the trigger and gently applied pressure. He sensed the surf begin to build and spoke into his microphone.

"All units, execute on my mark and three…two…one, Execute!"

Joe gently pulled the trigger and felt his rifle recoil as the 5.56 millimeter round shot out of his rifle at 3100 feet per second. His round entered the man's head just above his ear resulting in a pink mist. Joe squeezed the trigger once more hitting in the same area before the first round's momentum could knock the man out of the chair. Joe leapt out of the bushes and sprinted toward the bungalow, covering the thirty yards in mere seconds. He flew up onto the porch and launched through the entrance with his rifle up in the shooting position.

Joe, habitually, scanned the room for threats before zeroing in on the objective. A shirtless man with mussed graying hair was positioned on top of Courtnall's daughter. He snarled at her in a menacing tone while he clamped his left hand over her mouth, muffling her screams. Tracy kicked and struggled under his weight while his right hand fumbled with the button on his shorts. Her hands flailed at his face, but he shrugged off the blows, steadfastly trying to remain on task. Tracy kept at it, making contact with her right hand and dragging her fingernails across his face. The man screamed in rage and open hand slapped her with his right hand followed by a punch to the side of her head.

"Get on the floor!" Joe yelled.

The man looked up, startled and angry, as he faced Joe who was staring at him down the barrel of his rifle. Joe did a double take. Before him, in a near state of undress, attempting to violate Tracy Courtnall, was presidential candidate Senator Robert Fowler.

"Hands up and on the floor now!" Joe persisted.

"Easy, son," Fowler said as he slowly got off of Tracy and stood up with his hands in the air. "Put the gun down and let's talk this through."

"Negative, Senator," Joe replied. "Get on the floor and put your hands behind your back."

"Good!" Fowler responded with confidence. "You know who I am. Then you should also know that's not going to happen. The only thing that's going to happen is you're going to hand over that gun, right now."

"Negative, Senator. On the floor now," Joe growled.

"Or what?" Fowler asked with a pompous smirk. "You'll shoot me? Son, I'm a duly elected member of the United States Senate. A member of the Senate Armed Forces Committee and, very likely, the future president of the United States. That means you take orders from me and I'm *ordering* you to hand your gun over and stand down!"

Joe didn't move. He remained motionless with his rifle trained on Fowler. He quickly ran through his options. Shooting a known cartel member would have been explainable, especially under these circumstances, but shooting a senator? Particularly *this* senator? The man was caught attempting to rape a kidnapped United States citizen. He was a guest of a notorious cartel leader and Russian mobster. On the other hand, this was not an official operation. It wasn't even law enforcement. Joe, Whitmore, and Ramsey were acting as private citizens. They had no legal authority here. The simplest thing to do would be to kill every last one of them, rescue the girls, and never talk about it again. Ever. But they couldn't do that. Not everyone here was guilty. Some of the workers were simply that, workers. Joe didn't kill innocent people. Especially people who were probably too scared and powerless to stand up to the cartel. For that matter, there was record of them just having landed in country. A paper trail showing purchase of a RHIB and the authorities knew about Courtnall's missing daughter and the Tupolev organizations involvement. It wouldn't take a genius long to piece it all together. Fowler seemed to be reading his mind.

"Do you have any idea of the amount of trouble you're already in, soldier? Threatening a United States senator with deadly force? Put down the gun before you do something to make it worse. Something you will regret. Do it, right now, and I'll see to it you get a lighter sentence."

"That's not gonna happen, Mr. Fowler. You're in bed with the Russian mafia, the cartels, and God knows who else, and now you are literally in bed trying to rape a kidnapped *American* citizen. Rather symbolic of what you've been trying to do to *our* country. I swore an oath to protect and defend our nation. Even if it means I end up in prison, I'm taking you down with me. Now get on the floor, you treasonous scumbag!"

Fowler smiled smugly, held up his middle finger and shook his head.

"Nope," he said, amused. "Look behind you, Captain America."

Suddenly, a shout came from behind Joe. "*Suelta el arma! Manos en la cabeza!* Drop your weapon! Hands on your head!"

Chapter 56

Isla Esmeralda, Belize

"Drop your weapon! Hands on your head!" Barked the accented voice, racking a rifle for emphasis.

Joe refused to take his eyes off of Fowler but saw the source of the voice circling around on his right, holding an AR-15 pointed at Joe as he repeated the command.

"Last chance, gringo! Drop your weapon!" Pedro Cardenas ordered as he moved in next to Fowler with his weapon trained on Joe's head.

Joe considered his options. Other than complying, there weren't any. Cardenas had the drop and he was positioned far enough away to be out of striking range yet so close as to not miss. Joe slowly lowered his rifle to the ground.

"Now your handgun and your knife, gringo," Cardenas spoke while holding his rifle in the firing position.

Joe upholstered his FN High Power 9mm and slowly placed it on the ground followed by his Ka-Bar combat knife. He stood with his hands raised and looked at Cardenas.

"Good, now move over to the wall, turn around, and get on your knees facing me with your hands on your head."

Joe did as he was told. When he turned around, he saw Chief Ramsey standing in the room with his hands on his head. Behind him stood Victor Tupolev with Ramsey's AR-15 pointed at his back. Joe and Ramsey made eye contact. *What the actual flip just happened?*

Joe asked silently. Ramsey stared back, grim but determined. Both men knew each other wouldn't go down without a fight. They were both actively studying the situation, looking for an opportunity. Any opportunity.

Where was Clay? Joe asked himself. The fact that Cardenas and Tupolev were both here was not reassuring. Had he gotten away or was he already dead?

"You," Cardenas said gesturing with his rifle toward Ramsey. "On your knees, next to your friend. *Vamos! Ahorra!*"

Ramsey moved over under the watchful eyes of Cardenas and Tupolev. Cardenas kept a safe distance and then moved to cover both Joe and Ramsey. He studied the two of them for a minute, seemingly puzzled. Suddenly, his eyes went wide with recognition.

"*Jota de Picas y Diez de Picas!*" Cardenas spoke in satisfaction.

Joe spoke the translation out loud. "Jack of Spades and Ten of Spades?"

"*Si, gringo,*" Cardenas grinned maliciously. "Or should I say Joe O'Shanick?"

"Wait!" Fowler spoke up. "What did you say?"

"You don't recognize your own countrymen, Senator Fowler?" Cardenas asked. "This is Joe O'Shanick and Matthew Ramsey. The leaders of the SEAL team that have been disrupting our business and killing our men. They captured Hector Cruz and Fernando Escobar who *still* sit inside your prisons. They've been on our kill list for some time now. We have a deck of cards much like your military did during their pathetic war on terror. O'Shanick is the, how you say, Jack of Spades and Ramsey is the Ten of Spades."

"Why, yes! Joe O'Shanick! I *do* know who you are!" Fowler spoke gleefully.

"Of course you do, you dishonorable hack," Joe replied. "Escobar had the Niagara Falls mafia come after me and my family and you were all over the news trying use it to score political points against President Galan. Until the truth came out. Amazing how that story went away so quickly."

"Yeah, well, what can I say? It's quite helpful having the media believe in my cause," Fowler replied smugly.

"I wonder how they'd react if they knew the cartels and organized crime also believe in *your* cause?" Joe nearly spat the last words out as he inclined his head toward Cardenas and Tupolev.

"What makes you think they don't?" Fowler smirked. "Many of my benefactors own much of the media. The important players are on board. The rank and file may not know but they are one with the cause."

"Does it not bother your conscience to know that your entire campaign is based on deception and that you use a once trusted entity of information as a propaganda arm to deceive the people?" Joe asked, desperately trying to buy some time as he searched for an opportunity to take out Cardenas and Tupolev.

"Why should it? The ends justify the means and my cause is worthy of those ends."

"Your cause?" Joe spoke with sarcasm. "Your cause ascending to the highest seat of power by whatever means necessary, which in this case appears to be empowering drug and human traffickers, reckless spending that our grandchildren will be forced to pay for, a weakened economy and a weaker America. Let's be honest here, Senator, the only cause you are after is your own and to hell with the rest of America!"

Joe continued to look for a window of opportunity, but Cardenas was well trained and wasn't giving anything. He maintained a safe distance, covering Joe and Ramsey while he listened in with an amused look on his face.

"Now that's not true, Joe. You know we are *Building a Better America*," Fowler said in a patronizing tone as he quoted one of his campaign slogans. "And *Better Days are Just Ahead.*" Fowler completed his campaign's catchphrase sharing a laugh with Cardenas and Tupolev.

Joe's legs were coiled in preparation to jump up. In his mind he willed Cardenas to look over at Fowler as they laughed. Being on his knees, Joe knew he would have a slim chance to overtake him, but a slim chance was better than no chance. Besides, it might be enough to allow Ramsey to take down Cardenas and get the drop on Tupolev. Joe was willing to risk it if it allowed Ramsey a chance to escape with

Tracy Courtnall. Joe looked over at her. Fowler's retaliatory strike had knocked her unconscious and she was just now beginning to show signs of life. Unfortunately, Cardenas wasn't letting his guard down. Joe had to keep buying time.

"Better days," Joe said with disdain. "Your policies will lead to higher inflation, unemployment, government debt, and dependency. How will that lead to *better days?*"

"I don't have to answer to you, *Lieutenant.* You're the hired help. Cannon fodder, if you will. You do what you're told without questioning your superiors, which I am, and soon will be your commander in chief. Only I'm not impressed with you and I don't think you're fit to serve under my command. So, what to do? What to do?" Fowler feigned being deep in thought. "I guess I could have you dishonorably discharged and brought up on charges for treason but that could take years and cause unwanted distraction keeping me from doing what's best for the American people. On the other hand, I could just have Señor Cardenas see to it that you suffer the same fate as your teammates did last year in Honduras. A pity you weren't on that helicopter with your other teammates when they were shot out of the air. It would have saved us so much trouble over the past year, now wouldn't it have? I must say, I was impressed that you survived your plunge over Niagara Falls and your involvement with the mafia *did* provide me with yet another issue to attack that idealistic fool of a man who currently resides in the White House. Yet, here you stand, or kneel as fate would have it, and it is I who will determine your fate, just as I did your team last year."

Joe felt his blood begin to boil. "Are you saying…"

"That I had your team blown out of the sky? Why, yes, Mr. O'Shanick," Fowler flashed a sadistic grin. "You see, I have that kind of power. Your team was interfering with my loyal friends here and it was time for some retaliation. We have a greater mission, a global mission, one men like you and Jorge Galan are too idealistically simple to appreciate, which leads to people like you getting in our way."

"Uh-oh. Did I just confess to something that could incriminate me?" Fowler asked with a feigned expression of shock. "Why, I believe I did. I guess that means we won't be able to let you two live to tell about it. But then you're both smart enough to know I wouldn't divulge such information for no reason. As Pedro sends you off to eternal torment, I want to send you off in a state of despair and rage to fuel your fires."

"Kill them, Pedro," Fowler commanded without emotion.

Cardenas raised his rifle from the low ready position to firing position. Knowing he had seconds to live, Joe scrambled to his feet to mount a desperate attack. He knew it was likely futile but so was doing nothing and he'd rather go down with a fight than just accept the bullet. *Never out of the fight.* Ramsey, being of similar character and ethos, did the same thing. Joe prayed to remain Cardenas' target, thus giving Ramsey a fighting chance. As Joe rushed to his feet, the adrenaline surge to his brain created an extreme heightening of his senses to where everything around him dramatically slowed down into a surreal slow-motion scene. Joe watched as Cardenas' rifle rose to meet his eyes. His senses were so enhanced that he could actually see the subtle changes to Cardenas' index finger as he applied pressure to the trigger. With laser focus, Joe began to veer left as he charged Cardenas. If he could get his right hand on the rifle's muzzle before Cardenas fired, he might have a chance to deflect the shot and follow through with a disarming technique; however, Cardenas was a former special forces operator and, wisely, kept a considerable distance for just such a reason. The slow-motion scene continued to unfold as Joe's body, seemingly on autopilot from years of training, pressed the forward motion of his attack.

However, in Joe's mind, a different scene began to play. What Joe saw in the course of a nanosecond he perceived like a thirty-second video. Vivid images of himself with Christy and three young children, two girls with Christy's silky long dark hair and a young boy with short dark hair, swimming in the river at his parent's house on the Niagara River. Their children. Joe knew that without question as he saw them squealing with delight as they jumped from the dock into his or Christy's arms only to swim back to the ladder to climb out and jump again. Joe had heard of people describing their life flashing before them in a near fatal moment of peril, but what was this? Was this some kind of flash forward of what might have been? A wishful dream of regret playing out before him within a fraction of a second before a bullet took his life?

The vision disappeared as quickly as it appeared only to be replaced by the startling sight of Cardenas's head exploding in a pink mist. His index finger reflexively squeezed the trigger causing his rifle to fire a round that passed within an inch of Joe's right ear and through the wall behind him. Everything began to speed up as Joe hurdled Cardenas collapsing form with the intent of taking out Tupolev who was just beginning to bring his rifle to bear. Joe grabbed the muzzle, deflecting it away with his right hand and delivered to quick jabs to Tupolev's nose with his left. In a flash, his left hand reached over the top of the rifle, grabbed the magazine, and rotated the rifle out of Tupolev's grip. He then jumped back as he flipped the rifle around and pointed it at Tupolev.

"Get on the floor!" Joe shouted.

Instead of getting on the floor, Tupolev, in a rage, lowered his head and charged at Joe. Joe sidestepped and hammered the rifle's buttstock into the side of Tupolev's head, sending the Russian mob boss crashing to the deck. The blow did not render him unconscious but only served to fuel his rage. Tupolev immediately tried to get up on all fours but Joe smashed the buttstock down onto the back of his head and jumped on his back.

"Secure his arms, Rammer!" Joe said, looking around for Fowler while pinning the still struggling Tupolev's head to the ground.

"Shoot! Where's Fowler?" Joe asked looking around the room.

"He was just here," Ramsey grunted as he pulled Tupolev's wrists tightly together with a set of flex cuffs. "He must have squirted!"

Joe stifled the first word that came to mind and keyed his microphone. "Lee! We've got a squirter out of the first hooch. Do you have eyes on?"

"Affirmative, Joe. One male squirter running away from your position, up the beach. Do you want me to take him out?" Lee replied cool as ice.

"Negative, Lee. That's an HVT. We need him alive," Joe answered. "Keep me informed of his location. Oh, and nice shot, by the way! Your timing is impeccable."

"That dude needed killing," Lee stated. "You guys good?"

"Yeah, for now. Cover us. We're gonna sweep the other hooches for Clay and the girls," Joe spoke as he got up off of Tupolev. He picked his rifle up off of the floor and slung it on and then replaced his sidearm in its holster. "Christy, are you in position?"

"Affirmative," she responded immediately.

"We'll be there in fifteen seconds!"

"I'll get Tupolev, Joe. You grab Tracy!" Ramsey said as he pulled another flex cuff tight around the mobster's ankles.

Joe turned his attention to Tracy Courtnall and, for the first time, realized she wasn't wearing any clothes. He quickly looked around the room but only saw her discarded lingerie on the floor. Picking it up, he realized both pieces were torn. *Fowler probably ripped it off of her, the animal,* Joe surmised as he looked around the room for something to cover her up with. He was *not* going to hand her over to her father in a state of undress. They deserved better than that. Nothing else materialized. Joe improvised by covering her with the bedspread.

"Tracy?" He asked. "Your safe now. I came here with your dad to rescue you. Do me a favor and wrap yourself up in this and I'll carry you to him."

She was still loopy from Fowler's punch but with it enough to follow Joe's instructions although she didn't seem to react to the news that her father was here. Likely in shock or disbelief, Joe guessed as he slung her over his shoulder. He followed Ramsey out the door who was dragging Tupolev by the collar.

"Lee? Are we clear to exfil?"

"You're clear."

"Good copy. Let's go Rammer!" Joe said as he leaped of the porch and began to sprint across the beach.

As Joe approached the extraction point, the dark outline of the RHIB began to materialize.

"Red!" He called out.

"Barchetta!" Christy answered back completing the pass code.

Joe ran up to the bow of the RHIB where Courtnall stood waiting. Christy stood watch with the extra AR-15 in the high ready position. She had proven a quick learner during their shooting range sessions over the summer. *She's a jewel,* he thought to himself with a grin. The grin broke into a smile when he handed Tracy over to her father. With open sobbing, the man took his daughter in his arms and cradled her tightly.

"Daddy?" Tracy asked, the groggy confusion plainly seen.

"It's me T-Bear," Courtnall could barely form the words through his sobbing. "I'm here. You're with me now. It's over."

Chapter 57

Isla Esmeralda, Belize

" S he took a good punch to the side of her head which knocked her out," Joe said to Christy as Courtnall carried his daughter to the stern where he gently placed her on a bench seat.

"Any other injuries?" Christy asked.

"Nothing obvious. I *did* notice some bruising on her backside but, other than that, I have no idea."

Ramsey arrived with Tupolev. Joe helped hoist the Russian mob boss into the RHIB. He noticed Ramsey had stuffed the discarded lingerie into Tupolev's mouth to gag him. Unfortunately, there was no time to appreciate the irony. Ramsey jumped into the RHIB, pulled a length of parachute cord out of a belt pouch and tied Tupolev's wrists to one of the seat frames. Once he finished, Ramsey grabbed Tupolev's face and got up close and personal.

"You try anything while I'm gone, *Victor*, and I'll tie you to the bottom of this boat and drag you over a coral reef when I get back!" Ramsey growled as only a salty chief petty officer could before hopping out of the RHIB. "Ready, Joe!"

Joe began pushing the RHIB into the surf. "Meet us at the far end of the beach. We're going back for the others," he said as he spun the RHIB until the bow was pointing out toward the waves.

Joe keyed his microphone, "Lee, we're gonna start working our way down the beach."

"Good copy, Joe. You're still clear."

Joe made his way back onto shore as Christy guided the RHIB out through the breaking surf. Reaching the shore, he and Ramsey broke into a sprint for the second bungalow. They quickly ascended the porch and cleared the room. No one was there. They methodically worked their way down through the next two bungalows which were also empty. Joe expected this but the prudent course was to clear their way down. The mission had already gone sideways. They didn't need another surprise. They found the other blond, Rebecca, Joe remembered that being her name, in the next bungalow. She was passed out but still dressed. Ramsey scooped her up and slung her over his shoulder. They ran her down to the RHIB and handed her over to Christy and Courtnall then turned back to the next bungalow. Both knew this was the bungalow where Whitmore went after Cardenas. They hadn't heard from him since.

Joe and Ramsey ascended the porch and, like the other rooms, used a standard two-man clearing technique to enter the bungalow. There were no hostiles, but they found Whitmore laying on the floor with the red-headed girl seated next to him, crying, her back against the wall, holding his head in her lap. She looked at Joe and Ramsey and screamed.

"Shhh!" Joe cautioned. "You're okay now. We're here to take you home, ma'am."

Darcy was speechless. Her tear-filled face was a mix of fear and relief. Joe slung his rifle and knelt down next to Whitmore as Ramsey covered the door.

"It's Darcy, right?" Joe asked. "Darcy Kerrigan?"

"Yes," she answered, barely getting the words out.

"Is he okay to move? Tell me what happened," Joe said as he began to assess Whitmore using the MARCH algorithm of combat medicine.

"The Mexican man tackled him, and then he took his gun and knocked him out with it."

Joe saw a large area of swelling on the back of Whitmore's head but no bleeding. His helmet was laying on the ground and must have been knocked off before he took the blow. He was breathing and had strong pulses. The assessment was done. Time to get him out of there.

"Help me get him up," Joe said as he sat Whitmore up while supporting his head and carefully positioned him over his left shoulder. "Can you walk on your own?"

"Yes," she said slowly getting to her feet.

Like the others, Darcy was barely dressed.

"Grab that cover off the bed so you can cover up and follow us. Lead the way, Rammer!"

"Echo One, you've got four hostiles heading your way!" Lee's agitated voice came over the radio.

They poured on the speed and quickly crossed the beach down to the surf-line where Christy and Courtnall were waiting in the RHIB. Ramsey jumped in the bow and, with Courtnall's help, quickly lifted Whitmore into the boat. They carried him toward the stern and then Ramsey hopped back out.

"He took a bad blow to the head and was knocked unconscious," Joe told Christy, breathlessly, as she helped Darcy into the boat. "We've got company coming, so you need to move now! Once you shove off, I need you to head back around to the primary extraction point but maintain position on the opposite shore with the engines running. Be ready to come in when I call you!"

"Shore, opposite primary extraction point. Got it!" Christy spoke with an urgent nod.

"Good! Now get moving!" Joe said as he and Ramsey pushed the RHIB off the beach and pointed it back out to sea.

"Where are they at, Lee?" Joe asked as he keyed his microphone.

"They split around the two hooches closest my position. I got one before they split but there's still three of them approaching your position."

"High tide line, Joe!" Ramsey urged in hushed tones.

Ramsey was right. There was no time to seek cover. They were totally exposed on the beach. Together, Joe and Ramsey dove into the sand, Ramsey to Joe's right, and belly crawled up the gently sloped beach to the high tide line which would provide the only cover they could find on the beach. It wasn't much but the dark night and their low profiles might give them a slight advantage. Both flipped down their night vision goggles and waited. They didn't wait long. The green silhouettes of men appeared between the bungalows, two on the left and one to their right, rifles up and searching for targets. Joe and Ramsey fired simultaneously. Joe dropped the first man with three rounds on target while Ramsey did the same with the man on the right. The second guy on Joe's left returned fire and receded out of sight, behind the bungalow.

"Two more down, Lee! There's one more who just fell back, do you have eyes on?"

"Negative. He must be between the structures. I'll let you know if he pops up."

"Roger that." Joe responded. "Any more hostiles approaching?"

"Negative."

"Copy. Lee, be advised, I'm gonna flank him around the second hooch. Rammer, cover me!"

Ramsey fired three shots into the gap where the last shooter just was. Joe jumped to his feet and sprinted up the beach to the opposite side of the second bungalow. Once there he brought his rifle up and quietly moved towards the back of the bungalow. Rifle up, he quickly turned the back corner and crossed along the back side of the bungalow and keyed his microphone.

"I'm in position, Rammer. Distract him with three more shots."

Joe waited for the third shot and then dashed around the corner. He came face to face with the cartel soldier who immediately grabbed Joe's rifle and thrust the muzzle to the side while he sent a heavy fist into Joe's jaw, stunning him. The night vision goggles over his eyes put Joe at a disadvantage in this close up fight. He let go of his rifle and let it drop on its sling. His opponent threw another punch at Joe's face, which he didn't see coming but instinctively circled his left arm up and over his attacker's arm and locked it into place. Joe then thrust his right arm out and clamped down on the man's trachea, squeezing for all he was worth. Gaining just a slight advantage, Joe pushed the man back on his heels and swept his legs out from under him. The man used his free arm to land several kidney punches on Joe before the priority for breathing took over and he began to try to pry Joe's hand off his throat. Sensing, his opponent was losing strength, Joe let go with his left arm and unsheathed his Ka-Bar knife. With a controlled but swift thrust, Joe plunged the knife into the man's throat, severing his trachea. He then placed his weight on the hilt and plunged the knife back through the spinal cord.

As the paralyzed cartel soldier slowly died underneath him, Joe keyed his microphone. "Tango is neutralized."

Chapter 58

Isla Esmeralda, Belize

"Move up on me, Rammer," Joe spoke over the radio as he rolled off the dead cartel soldier.

"We going after Fowler?" Ramsey asked as he ran up.

"Not yet," Joe answered. "We need to get the remaining girls off this island first. Then we'll get that worthless political hack."

"Well then, let's work fast. I don't want him getting away. That treasonous piece of excrement just admitted to blowing the op that got half our platoon killed last year!" Ramsey said furiously.

"I hear you, Rammer. We'll get him. I just want the rest of the girls out of harm's way first. That's what we came here for. Let's Charlie Mike and finish this thing," Joe said giving his chief a fist bump.

Ramsey bumped him back and nodded. "You're right. Let's do this."

Joe keyed his radio mike. "Echo One to Echo Base, I need a sit-rep on the drone feed."

"Stand by, Echo One," came Courtnall's voice over the radio. "Echo One, state your position."

"Both of us are beside the outermost bungalow."

"Very good, Echo One. You have six enemy combatants set up around the largest building in the compound. I don't see any of the civilians so they must be back under the roof. I count three more over by Lee, none of them appear to be armed."

"Lee, you got them?" Joe asked.

"Affirmative, Echo One. One of them is your squirter. He's pretty insistent that the other two go find and neutralize you. Want me to take them out?"

"Negative. We need the squirter alive. I need your eyes on the large building. That's our main target. We're gonna flank them through the woods and come up behind them. Hold your fire until I say so. Keep us apprised of any changes."

"Roger that," Lee spoke with his cool drawl.

"Echo Base, is there anyone else around the beach area or in the woods?"

"That's a negative, Echo One."

Joe backhanded Ramsey's arm. "Let's roll!"

Joe turned and ran them down to the beach where they would be partially covered by the bungalows and the high tide mark. They double timed their way to the wooded mangrove. Upon entering the mangrove, they slowed their pace to a stealthy creep as they made their way around the back end of the island. It took several minutes to move what was a little more than 100 yards. The thick vegetation was difficult to penetrate, and the ground was covered in treacherous plant roots which could roll an ankle or emit a telltale sound. Joe and Ramsey used their night vision goggles to navigate their way as they carefully and slowly made each step.

The edge of the mangrove actually touched the back corner of their target building, the one in which they assumed the girls were being held. There were two men alongside the building, both armed with rifles. They couldn't have been more than forty feet from Joe and Ramsey's current position. Their rifles were at low ready and they were up against the outside wall. They we're definitely alert. Joe slowed his pace even more. He wanted to get behind the building in order to allow him and Ramsey to hit both sides at once. Hitting just one side would alert the other side and take away the element of surprise.

Head on a swivel, Joe alternated his attention between the cartel soldiers a mere dozen yards away and the ground in front of him. Joe glanced at the ground and gently set his foot down while turning his attention back to the cartel soldiers.

Snap.

A small unseen twig snapped beneath Joe's right foot. Both soldiers immediately pivoted toward Joe and Ramsey's position with their rifles raised. Joe froze. He fought the urge to drop to the ground. The human eye was more attuned to movement in the dark as opposed to actual perception. Joe willed himself to look like a tree and knew Ramsey was doing the same. Joe blinked the sweat out of his eyes as he stared down his rifle barrel at the two men searching in their direction. He thanked God the soldiers weren't using night vision devices. He and Ramsey would have been spotted immediately.

The soldiers continued to peer intently into the woods. It was obvious they were certain they heard something man-made. They were trained SPECOPS like Joe and Ramsey and they were in their natural environment. Joe kept a slight amount of pressure on his trigger, anticipating the situation going sideways in a split second. The only way he and Ramsey would survive it was to shoot first with perfect accuracy. A miss would not only be fatal for Joe and Ramsey but also for anyone inside the building were they to be on the other side of the thin wall where the bullet struck. No room for error. Joe ignored the sweat stinging his eyes as he controlled his breathing while a few more tense seconds ticked by.

Suddenly, the unmistakable sound of glass shattering emanated from the tiki bar in the center of the compound. Both soldiers redirected their attention to the sound. A second crashing sound of glass rang out which led the soldiers to move to the front corner of the building. Joe and Ramsey took advantage of the distraction and quietly crept the few remaining yards to the back of the building. Both leaned into the wall keeping watch over opposite corners.

"Hope that got you two frogmen out of that Mexican standoff. No pun intended," Lee calmly spoke over their unit comms.

"Your timing is impeccable," Ramsey replied. "First round's on me."

"Won't be in the tiki hut," Lee quipped. "I just shot two of Pedro's finest bottles of Don Julio. You two in position?"

"Affirmative," Joe answered. "Echo Base, give us a sit-rep on the enemy positions."

"The camera just blacked out, Echo One. The battery was blinking low charge. We held on as long as we could, I'm sorry," came Courtnall's panicked voice.

"Lee, you're our only eyes. Tell us what you see."

"Two on each side. I can't see the far side completely, but my side has one facing into the clearing and one watching the woods behind you. I'm assuming a similar situation on the opposite side. There are two more inside the door that I know of. Not sure how many beyond that."

"Alright, here's the plan," Joe quietly spoke into the microphone. "On my mark, Lee, take out the rear-facing soldier on your side and then any hostile you see in the door. Rammer, you clear the rest of that side and I'll clear my side. Christy, you'll make for the primary extraction point. Everybody clear?"

All answered in the affirmative. Joe and Ramsey already had their rifles up ready to fire as they inched toward their respective corners.

"Very well. On my mark. And three...two...one...execute!"

Joe quickly turned the corner. His extensive training led him to immediately spot and sight in on his target, firing three quick bursts from his rifle. The soldier was only a few yards away; therefore, all three of Joe's shots found their mark and the soldier crumpled to the ground before he had a chance to react. Joe was already onto his next target before the first soldier had completed his fall. Joe fired three more times; two to the back of the man's head and one in center mass, in this case his back. His head exploded in a pink spray that looked like a green mist on Joe's NVD's.

"Two tangos down, but there's at least one more inside," Lee called out over the comms.

"This is Echo Two, one tango down, approaching the front corner," Ramsey spoke.

"Copy Echo Two, I have two tangos down and approaching front as well," Joe responded.

Like a finely choreographed dance, both Joe and Ramsey smoothly walked, heel to toe, knees slightly bent, rifles up and searching for targets. Both reached their respective front corners, searched the open area for hostile targets and, seeing none, raised their rifles to high ready and turned toward each other. They stopped on each side of the door. Ramsey prepped a flash-bang grenade and tossed it through the door. The grenade exploded in a blinding and deafening fashion which was automatically muted by the headphones Joe and Ramsey were wearing. Joe turned first, lowering his rifle to firing position and pivoted through the door. He leaped over the body of the fallen cartel soldier and turned right looking for a hostile target. A man stood with his hands over his ears and a M4 hanging down on its sling. Joe immediately dispatched him with three shots and began looking for another target. He heard Ramsey do the same.

"Clear!" Joe yelled first after seeing no other hostile targets.

"Clear!" Ramsey answered in kind.

The room was a bunkhouse of sorts. Likely for the hired help or, in this case, the weekend's entertainment. Like an old Quonset hut barracks, a row of bunk beds lined each wall separated by an aisle down the middle. Joe and Ramsey cleared their room by fast walking down the aisle, rifles raised, looking for any additional hostiles who might be hiding amongst the dozen or so very young-looking women laying on their bunks curled up holding their ears. Several were crying.

Joe reached the last bunk on his side and found a scantily dressed, young Hispanic woman, a young teenager more likely, curled up on the floor. Hidden behind her, under the bed was a pudgy man with dark brown eyes, a full gray beard, and a balding head. He clutched the girl closely to him as Joe pointed the rifle at him. He was unarmed.

"I've got an unarmed middle-aged male over here, Rammer! Looks Middle Eastern to me."

"That makes two except mine is a little further east. China, if I had to guess. Also unarmed," Ramsey answered back.

"Probably heavy hitters but I don't recognize either one of them," Joe commented. "Let's cuff em' and get the girls out of here. We'll come back for these two and our friend."

"You!" Joe said pointing his rifle at the bearded man on his side. "You speak English?"

The man just glared back. Hatred emanating from his dark brown eyes.

"Let her go," Joe commanded gesturing with his rifle.

The man pulled the girl in tighter as he continued to glare back. Joe sighed, slung his rifle over his back and took out his side arm. He squatted down, grabbed the older man's ring finger, and forced it back. The man cried out in pain.

"*Arrrrgh!* Infidel puppets of the Great Satan!" He yelled. "Let me go!"

"Sounds like a great death metal band," Ramsey quipped as he freed a young girl from the Asian man.

"At least we know he speaks English," Joe replied, still holding pressure on the man's finger. "Let go of the girl and you can have your hand back, old man; otherwise, I'll snap it all the way back!"

The man responded by spitting an expletive at Joe. "You have no idea who you are dealing with, you fool!"

"From what I can tell, I'm dealing with a cowardly pedophile who hides behind young *girls!*" Joe said, snapping the man's finger back for emphasis.

The man howled in pain and released the young Hispanic girl.

"*Mueve amiga, alli*" Joe spoke gently to the girl, encouraging her to move out of the way.

The young Hispanic girl scurried off the floor and huddled with the other frightened girls near the entrance. Joe could tell they were all unsure what to do. Speaking in Spanish, he calmly informed them that he and Ramsey were here to rescue them and asked them to wait inside the door.

Joe turned his attention back to the man under the bed. He grabbed him by the shirt collar and dragged him out into the open. He removed his iPhone from its holder on his tactical vest and took a picture of the man's face. Joe then placed a knee on the man's back and secured his wrists with flex cuffs followed by his ankles. Ramsey did the same with the Asian man. Neither was saying much but Joe decided to gag them anyway. Using his knife, he cut a bedsheet into smaller pieces. He tossed one to Ramsey and they both stuffed the rags into their captive's mouths.

Joe and Ramsey stood up, holstered their sidearms, and unslung their rifles. They moved to the door. Ramsey began to calm the frightened girls and organize them in preparation for their run to the shore where Christy and Courtnall were waiting with the RHIB. Joe counted twelve girls. They were all relatively small but adding to their number was the three other girls, Christy, Courtnall, Tupolev, the equipment, and the four of them. There may not be enough room. They would have to cross that bridge when they got there. Time to move out. Joe keyed his radio.

"Echo Four, this is Echo One, we're set to move out with twelve friendlies. You got a sit-rep?"

No reply.

"Echo Four, this is Echo One. Come in."

Silence.

"Echo Four, if you're compromised but can hear me, acknowledge with two clicks."

Silence.

Chapter 59

Isla Esmeralda, Belize

"That's not good," Ramsey commented.

"No, it's not," Joe answered as he moved to the door and scanned the compound.

"I don't see any movement, Rammer, so here's the plan; I'll provide cover while you lead them to the extraction point. Once they're all out, I'll cover our six. Then we'll recover and go find Lee."

"Roger that," Ramsey said as he finished lining the young women up. "We're ready, Skipper!"

"Let's go!" Joe said as he led the procession out of the sleeping quarters.

Joe stepped out onto the small terrace and kneeled behind a decorative wooden piling. He carefully scanned the compound for hostiles while Ramsey quickly led the train of young women toward the nearby shore. Joe rose to his feet after the last woman filed out. As a precaution, he peeked his head back into the sleeping quarters to make sure all of them were out. Huddled in the corner sat a tiny, dark-haired, young teen. Her face was a look of abject terror as she sat with her knees pulled up to her chest, shaking in tears.

"Echo Two, this is One, we've got one too spooked to run. I'm gonna help her out. Charlie Mike," Joe updated Ramsey over the unit comms, instructing him to continue with the mission.

"Copy that, Echo One," Ramsey answered back.

As Joe approached, the girl tried to retreat even more into her corner. Who could blame her? She had likely been taken from her home by force if not sold by her parents which was actually quite common, if not well known. She looked barely old enough to be in her pubescent years and yet she had probably been beaten, raped, and forced to perform sexual acts more times than she could remember. Just a few minutes ago, Joe and Ramsey had stunned the entire room with a flash-bang grenade and killed two men in front of her. Now these unknown men who had violently entered her already dark world were trying to take her elsewhere and she was supposed to just trust them? *Yeah. Who can blame her?*

The expedient thing would have been to scoop her up, get her to the RHIB, and let Christy do what she does best. Joe couldn't bring himself to do that. This little girl had suffered enough trauma, physical and emotional. Joe removed his helmet and knelt down in front of her. Speaking in Spanish, Joe began to try to alleviate the worst of her fear.

"Como se llama, amiga?" He spoke softly, asking her name, as he gently placed a hand on her hand.

She looked up. She had long, silky dark hair, with bangs that hung just above her eyebrows, framing a soft oval face with lonely, dark eyes. Despite his dark, rugged features, Joe's bright Irish green eyes twinkled as he gently smiled back at the waif-like young girl before him. She seemed to relax, just a bit.

"Yoana," she spoke, barely above a whisper.

"Yoana, my friends and I are from the United States. We came to rescue you and the other girls from these men and all they have been doing to you. Will you come with me?"

"Won't you just hurt me too?" Yoana asked looking directly in Joe's eyes. "Every man always does."

"I'm so sorry, *mija*," Joe soothed. "You have been around some very bad men. I'm not like them. My job is to find bad men and stop them. That's why I'm here."

Yoana looked over at the dead cartel soldier's body on the floor, not ten feet away, where Joe shot him.

"You killed him," she stated as a matter of fact.

"Yes," Joe said after giving a quick glance in the cartel soldier's direction. "He was a bad man and I had to stop him so we could help you."

Yoana stole another look at the dead cartel soldier before returning her gaze to Joe. Joe looked into her eyes and sensed a mix of fear and distrust battling an urge to be hopeful. What she must have endured, at such a young juncture in life, to have no ability or reason to trust any man but rather fear what they would do to you. Joe had an idea. He keyed his radio.

"Echo Base, this is Echo One. Christy, do you read me?"

"I read you, Echo One. Where are you?" Came Christy's hurried voice.

"I've got a scared little one here who could use a friendly female voice to convince her she can trust me."

"Roger that, put her on."

Joe removed the earpiece from his ear and held it for Yoana to see.

"My friend, Christy, is on the boat waiting to take us away from here. She's a doctor in America. She came down here to help us rescue you and she wants to talk to you."

Yoana nodded. Joe placed the earpiece in her ear and adjusted the microphone. He then showed her how key his radio when she wanted to talk. Yoana keyed the mike and hesitantly spoke.

"Hola?"

Joe watched as her dark eyes darted around while Christy spoke to her over the radio. She nodded along, verbalizing an occasional word without keying the mike. Joe mimicked pressing the button by way of a reminder. After another minute, her features softened and she enthusiastically nodded. Joe keyed the mike for her as she answered.

"Si! Si! Gracias!" She concluded before reaching for her ear.

Joe helped her remove the earpiece and replaced it into his own ear.

He keyed the mike. "We good?"

"Yes! She'll go with you. Now please hurry!"

"Echo One, this is Two. All friendlies are on board. I'll be at the edge of the woods covering your exfil," Ramsey chimed in.

"Good copy, Echo Two. I'm on my way. Be there in fifteen seconds," Joe said as he stood and donned his helmet.

He offered a hand to Yoana, who responded by jumping up into his arms and clinging to him like a koala bear. She was so tiny; she couldn't have weighed eighty pounds. Joe flipped down his night vision goggles and carried her to the door. Looking out, the only image he saw was Ramsey's at the edge of the clearing. Joe slung his rifle over his back, pulled out his 9mm sidearm, and took off for the extraction point. Two rifles immediately opened up on full automatic behind him. A round struck his right arm just before he passed behind the cover of a smaller building. Ramsey waited for Joe to pass and then began to return fire. Joe ignored the pain in his arm and kept running. Up ahead, through the pass, was the waiting RHIB. Bullets whistled all around making contact with the trees and foliage on both sides of him.

As he neared the RHIB, he immediately saw that it was extremely overloaded. Some of the girls were forced to saddle the inflatable tube that ringed the craft. He and Ramsey might be able to squeeze in but that would be it. There was no room for Lee and definitely no room for the Fowler, let alone the others.

Joe reached the RHIB and handed Yoana over the bow to Christy who immediately noticed Joe's bleeding arm.

"Joe! You're bleeding! Were you hit?" She asked in shock.

"It's minor. I'm fine. You guys need to get out of here!" He replied as he began to push on the bow.

The overladen RHIB did not budge. Courtnall and Christy had beached it with a much lighter load. A dozen more souls were onboard and, although they were all relatively small, their collective weight was causing the bow to hold firm to the sand.

"Charles!" Joe yelled. "Throw it in reverse and give her some throttle!"

Joe squatted down low and began to lift up on the bow while driving with his legs as Courtnall increased the throttles in reverse. His right arm now searing in pain as if a hot fire poker was jammed in his triceps muscle. The RHIB rocked but she still wouldn't budge. The bullets continued to shriek by as Ramsey returned fire. Joe had an idea.

"Rammer! Pop smoke and meet me at the RHIB!"

"Roger that! Popping smoke," Ramsey replied acknowledging that he was tossing a smoke grenade to provide some cover.

A few seconds later, Ramsey came running up.

"They're weighed down, Rammer! Help me get them off the beach and then climb aboard!"

"What about Lee?" Ramsey asked as he slung his rifle and began to push.

"We're not leaving him! Just get on. I've got an idea," Joe grunted as he pushed on the bow and drove with his legs.

The RHIB finally began to give way as the gunfire increasingly grew louder. The smoke provided temporary cover, but it was also a signal informing their attackers right where to pursue. The RHIB settled down low in the water as it backed away from the beach. Joe and Ramsey swung the bow seaward and then both slung a leg over the gunnel and pulled themselves onboard.

"Everybody, get down!" Joe yelled loudly in Spanish as he and Ramsey dropped down into the boat and unslung their rifles. "Charles! Take us about 200 yards out and then circle southeast around the island."

"You got it!" Courtnall replied as he gunned the engine and turned away from the beach.

The RHIB was so crowded they had little room to maneuver. Tracer rounds began to emanate from the shore they had just left. A round struck the starboard engine causing the engine to cough and sputter. Their speed dropped but the port side engine seemed to hold up. Joe and Ramsey returned fire and the tracers briefly stopped before restarting. The RHIB began to gently pitch in the small swells as they moved further away from shore. The bow was riding rather low causing Joe to be concerned that it could submarine in larger chop. The RHIB was extremely buoyant but swamping the boat would not be an easily workable problem. Crossing back to the mainland would be an issue.

Joe stood six feet four inches and carried 220 pounds on his lean, muscular frame. Ramsey was about the same size. Joe calculated that would be 440 pounds less as his plan began to solidify in his mind. He watched as the tracer rounds receded in the distance. Time to get on with it.

"That's good, Charles! Now circle us around, please."

"What are we doing, Joe?" Christy asked, her concern ever apparent.

"Lee's missing!" He answered back. "Rammer and I are going back for him."

"Do you think he's even alive?" She shouted over the roar of the twin outboard engines.

"I don't know, but we can't leave him. No man left behind."

Through the dark, Joe saw Christy nod solemnly. He knew she didn't want him to go back but she knew the code and she would never tell him not to go back for Lee.

"Charles!" Joe called over to Courtnall. "Once we are due south of the island, Ramsey and I are going to drop in over the side. Maintain this speed. Once we drop into the water, I want you to hightail it back to Belize City. Tie up at the Coast Guard station and explain what happened."

"Joe! We can't leave you guys!" Christy protested.

"She's right!" Courtnall agreed. "We'll wait offshore and come get you!"

"I appreciate that, but you can't!" Joe yelled over the roaring outboards. "This boat is overloaded as it is and now one of the engines is dying! You'll never make it across with all of us, but you'll have a chance once Ramsey and I are gone."

"Joe, I'm not sure that we can trust their Coast Guard!" Ramsey shouted. "I think we should have them go back to the marina. Senior Chief Lennon said he will meet them. I just texted him a sit-rep and he responded."

"Christy!" Ramsey yelled. "I just texted you the number for a SEAL buddy of ours. His name is Jerry Lennon. Get ahold of him right now and explain the situation. Have him meet you guys at the marina and take you to the U.S. Embassy in Belmopan."

"Why don't we drop everyone off and then I will come back for you?" Christy asked.

"It's too risky and we don't know how much longer this RHIB will hold up," Joe answered as he and Ramsey climbed up onto the inflatable pontoon away from the shore. "Ready, Rammer?"

"Ready!" Ramsey said holding up a thumb as he and Joe laid forward while straddling the pontoon.

"Joe!" Christy pleaded. "Do you have a plan on how you will get back?!"

"I'm working on it!" He flashed Christy his mischievous grin and rolled over the side.

Chapter 60

Isla Esmeralda, Belize

The sound of the engines began to fade as the RHIB trailed off in the distance. The loud staccato gunfire ceased and was replaced by the gentle lapping of waves against the shoreline. Sergei Petrenko cursed out loud as he ejected another empty magazine from his rifle.

"It's okay, my friend," Alejandro Lopez soothed. "We tried our best. We still have much to do."

"*Pizdets!*" Petrenko cursed again. "They have my boss! They have Mr. Tupolev! We have to go after them!"

"We can't!" Lopez countered.

"Why not?" Petrenko shot back. "We can take the big cruiser boat we came out here on. We can catch them if we leave right now. Let's go!" Petrenko said as he started to stand.

Lopez grabbed his colleague by the arm and pulled him back down. "Think this through, Sergei. We *could* try to get him back, but we don't even know if he is alive. Also, they are a little boat and we are in a big boat. They would see us coming way before we get to them and make for the shallows. They are also armed, and we would have no advantage. It's a fool's mission compared to what must be done."

"*Must* be done?" Petrenko asked skeptically.

"My friend," Lopez continued. "I have lost my boss too. You saw what's left of him on the floor of that bungalow. Nothing we do will change that. But, if we do what *must* be done, right now, we can preserve what our bosses have worked so hard to put together."

"Wait a minute," Petrenko spoke with realization. "You just became the new head of *Los Fantasma Guerreros!*"

"That's right. Although I do not welcome the circumstances in which it happened," Lopez shook his head feigning remorse. "Pedro and I served together in *Fuerzas Especiales de la Marinas* before we helped build and run this most powerful cartel. He is my friend and my brother. I will miss him, but I will not let everything we have worked for be taken from us. You shouldn't either. You might be the new head of your organization. Our networks are still in place, but we could lose them quickly if we do not get Senator Fowler back to *Los Estados Unidos*. The Iranian, the Venezuelan, and the Chinaman are less important but, if they are still here and still alive, it would serve us well to get them out of here as well."

"Then everything will continue," Petrenko said nodding his comprehension. "The open borders, the movement of drugs, humans and weapons…"

"That's right, Sergei, and either we can oversee that or we can stand by and watch as it is all ripped away from us."

"I'm with you. How would you like to proceed?" Petrenko asked as he rose to his feet.

"Let's go see if the VIP's are still with us and, if so, get them and Fowler out of here before the authorities come find us."

Chapter 61

Isla Esmeralda, Belize

The dark waters were calm on the leeward side of the island. The island blocked the gentle trade winds coming from the west, leaving a quiet serenity in the warm tropical night. Thirty yards off the leeward shore, two dark shapes silently broke the surface.

Joe and Ramsey flipped down their night vision goggles and turned them on. They studied the surrounding area for a minute and, satisfied the area was clear, began to slowly wade in to shore. Unlike the northeast side of the island, this side was bisected by a small lagoon lined by landscaped shore on both sides. The right bank fronted the helicopter pad and the large building where Lee had been on the roof keeping overwatch. Two men could be seen walking toward the helicopter, neither was armed. Joe was pretty sure one of them was Fowler. The left bank led to the main compound. Joe and Ramsey agreed that the smart move was to clear the compound of any remaining hostiles and work their way to where Fowler had run, secure him and find Lee. Joe reached the left bank and quietly climbed up while Ramsey did the same. They lay prone on the edge of the bank and scanned the compound. They saw one person out by the beachside bungalows but that was it.

Joe and Ramsey quietly stood and kept to the edge of the clearing as they worked their way around to the last known location of their attackers. There was no one there. They checked the small building in front of the extraction point and found it empty. They then entered the large building where they had left the Iranian and Asian man. They were no longer there.

"I'll bet the VIP's are about to be flown out of here on that helo," Joe whispered.

No sooner did he say that then the telltale whine of the helicopter beginning its startup reached their ears. Their eyes met in instant recognition.

"Let's go!" Ramsey said as they both turned for the door.

"Blow through, Rammer. There could still be hostiles on this side."

"Roger that," Ramsey said as he peeked out the door and quickly worked his way to the next structure.

They quickly conducted a "blow through" in which they checked all potential hazards for hostiles while hastily working their way toward the objective. They reached the end of the beach where the narrow strip connecting the two halves of the island lay and they rounded the bend. The helicopter rotors were now rotating at a high rate of speed. It was about to take off. The green silhouettes of four armed men were still on the ground. As Joe rounded the bend, the landing pad floodlights turned on and lit up the entire half of the small island, rendering their night vision goggles useless. Joe and Ramsey maintained their fast pace as they flipped up their goggles. The large building, which turned out to be an elevated bungalow, loomed ahead blocking their view of the helicopter. Suddenly, two automatic rifles opened fire from the porch. The cartel soldiers were hidden in the shadow while Joe and Ramsey were now lit up by the landing pad's elevated floodlights. Joe and Ramsey immediately ducked behind a small outbuilding perched on the edge of the eastern shore's mangrove. The incoming rounds churned up the sandy path beneath their feet, but both men made it to safety unscathed. Joe quickly peeked around the corner of the building and fired off two controlled bursts before ducking back out of sight. Glass windows shattered and wood splinters flew all around as incoming rounds began to slam into the little building.

"We need to dispatch these tangos and get to that helo before it takes off!" Joe yelled over to his teammate. "If you can keep them occupied here, I'll duck into the mangrove and flank them!"

"I got it!" Ramsey said, clapping Joe on the right shoulder a little too close to his gunshot wound.

Joe winced in pain as he used the cover of the outbuilding to move into the mangrove. Between the roar of the helicopter and the unsuppressed cartel soldiers' gunfire, there was no need to remain quiet so, keeping low, Joe quickly moved down the tree line and snuck up on the soldiers' flank. He raised his rifle and fired multiple times until both men were down and out of the fight.

"Clear!" He spoke over the radio. "Two tangos kilo. You good, Rammer?"

"I'm good!"

No sooner did he say that when gunfire opened up again, this time from the far corner of the bungalow. Joe and Ramsey immediately began to return fire. With both sides well concealed, the firefight continued on as they each exchanged gunfire. Joe concentrated on the corner and waited for the cartel soldier to inch around and open up. The tip of a rifle appeared and Joe aimed six inches inside the corner. He couldn't see anything but the shooter's rifle but that meant the shooter couldn't see him either. Joe opened up with several rounds and the rifle disappeared. There was no telling whether or not Joe had hit him. Ramsey fired several rounds in the shooter's direction.

"Last mag and then I'm Winchester!" Ramsey called over the radio, informing Joe he was down to his last magazine of ammunition.

"I may have gotten him!" Joe yelled. "I'm not sure though but there is still at least one more back there. I counted four, originally."

Suddenly, gunfire opened up from the corner closest to Joe. Several rounds whizzed past his head as he ducked down and returned fire. Joe moved to his left and opened fire again. His rifle locked open signaling another empty magazine.

"Reload!" Joe yelled as he ejected the magazine and fished another one out of his vest. It too was his last magazine. "Last mag then *I'm* Winchester!"

"I'm on your side of the building, Joe! He's focused on you. Stay low!"

The automatic gunfire continued to rip the mangrove trees around Joe as he hugged the ground. A few metallic clacks came from behind

Joe as Ramsey opened fire with his suppressed rifle. The enemy rifle suddenly went silent. Joe could see the cartel soldier sprawled in the floodlights.

"He's down, Rammer."

"That makes three tangos kilo and one unaccounted for," Ramsey commented.

The helicopter's sound began to grow in intensity.

"They're about to take off!" Joe yelled. "We can't let Fowler get away! Cover me, Rammer!"

Joe leapt out of the mangrove and sprinted to the near side of the bungalow. He hurdled the dead cartel soldier's body as he continued toward the rear of the bungalow. He saw the fourth cartel soldier as he reached the back. The man was shielding his eyes from the sand being stirred up by the helicopter's rotor wash. Joe took no mercy and dropped the gunman with three rounds.

"Fourth tango down!" Joe yelled over the noise as Ramsey ran up behind him. "We have to disable that helo!"

Joe and Ramsey both opened up aiming for the helicopter's engine and rotors. The pilot was an unknown. He could have been an innocent man hired to pilot the flight. Shooting him was not an option. The helicopter slowly began to lift off the ground as Joe and Ramsey continued to shoot.

"Winchester! I'm out!" Ramsey yelled as he dropped his rifle and reached for his handgun.

Joe fired two more rounds and then his weapon locked open after the last round was fired. Joe threw down his weapon and, in a fit of rage, ran directly at the rising helicopter.

"Joe! What are you doing?!" Ramsey yelled after his teammate and friend.

Undamaged from the gunfire, the helicopter was over six feet off the ground and was pointed almost directly at Joe, giving the pilot a full view of the camouflaged man sprinting in his direction. Realizing what Joe was about to do, the pilot compensated by banking left at the last second allowing the aircraft to absorb the weight shift as Joe leapt into the air and grabbed ahold of the starboard landing skid. He allowed his momentum to swing his legs upward where they wrapped around the skid. The helicopter rose just above the bungalow's roof and dipped its nose as it began to move out over the island. Joe wasted no time. He quickly shimmied down the skid and reached up to the passenger compartment door handle. Pulling himself up into a sitting position, Joe pulled out his handgun and transferred it to his left hand. He then opened the door and stood up on the skid, leaning into the compartment with his handgun out in front.

Rather than go for altitude, the pilot spun his aircraft to the left hoping to lose Joe off the side. Joe felt the maneuver begin and managed to brace himself through the turn. On the far side of the compartment, the Iranian pulled out what looked like a Glock 43 and leveled it at Joe's head while Joe did the same. The pilot spun to the right just as both men fired. The sudden spin caused both me to miss but Joe quickly regained his edge and put two rounds into the Iranian man's head resulting in a massive spray of blood and brain tissue in the compartment. The Asian quickly tried to retrieve the gun off the floor and Joe shot him as well. Seated closest to Joe, Fowler tried to kick the gun out of Joe's hand but Joe absorbed the blow and followed it up with a viscous blow to Fowler's kneecap with the gun's handgrip. Fowler bellowed as he clutched his knee, while Joe pointed the gun at the pilot.

"Put it down, right now!" Joe yelled.

The pilot went full Ricky Ricardo, responding in a tirade of Spanish as he threw the helicopter into another spin. The compartment door slammed into Joe as he simultaneously was spun to his left, nearly losing his footing. His wounded right arm burned in pain as he desperately held on. It was dark below them. They were out over the water now. He felt his arm begin to weaken. He couldn't hold on much longer. He would either have to jump not knowing how high they were or pull himself into the cabin. If he were to attempt to climb into the cabin, he would need his left hand to pull that off. His holster was on his right side. There was no way he would be able to holster his gun using his left hand.

He should just shoot Fowler and be done with it. Fowler deserved to die. He had betrayed Joe's teammates resulting in the deaths of his entire second squad. Fowler was a sell out and a traitor to their nation. Joe would have no trouble putting a bullet in his head. It would result in a life sentence for Joe but that was preferable to letting this scumbag traitor get away. No doubt Fowler had an escape plan where he would disappear and assume a new identity with plastic surgery and end up on a beach somewhere sipping margaritas, all funded by offshore bank accounts. No, Joe would not let that happen. He shifted his aim, leveling his handgun at Fowler's head.

"Tell him to land this thing!" Joe yelled.

The pilot fishtailed to the right and Joe's right hand gave way. Out of desperation, Joe dropped his gun, causing it to fall out of the aircraft while he clutched for anything he could grab hold of. His hand found Fowler's shirt and he gripped it with everything he had. Joe desperately tried to pull himself into the aircraft but the spin caused his feet to slip off the skid. Another fish-tail and Joe felt himself begin to fall. Fowler had not bothered to buckle himself in. The combination of his momentum and Joe's weight caused the two men to tumble out of the aircraft. Twisting together, they fell toward the dark void below.

Chapter 62

Isla Esmeralda, Belize

The impact was jarring. Joe felt like he had just fell off the thirty-foot-high tower at BUDS and landed flat on his back in the sand. As he plunged into the dark water, he had a vivid flashback of a similar plunge over Niagara Falls just a few months ago. Joe quickly regained his thoughts, oriented himself, and calmly headed for the surface. A quick head to toe self-assessment revealed no new injuries. He broke the surface and saw the helicopter heading west toward the mainland and gaining altitude. The pilot was likely eager to put this incident behind him. Joe briefly wondered what would result with the two dead foreign nationals before turning his thoughts to Fowler. He was nowhere to be seen.

Joe reached up and turned on the tiny flashlight mounted to his helmet. He scanned the water around him and saw no sign of Fowler. They couldn't have landed very far from one another. Joe briefly considered leaving well enough alone and swimming to shore but he couldn't do it. Taking a deep breath, Joe dove below the surface and began to search for the politician.

He quickly saw a silver-white trail of bubbles reflecting in the light as they rose to the surface. Joe swam deeper and followed the bubbles to their source. They lead to Fowler's body, which was slowly rising to the surface. Joe swam up to him, grabbed his shirt collar with his right hand, and began to kick and stroke to the surface. His right arm continued to hurt but it was a dull ache compared to a few minutes ago. They broke the surface and Joe settled into a rescue swim, pulling Fowler behind him as he began to swim to shore.

Fowler began to cough and gasp for air. After a minute, he regained control of his breathing and began to thrash about trying to wrestle away from Joe's grip. Every time the man moved, a bolt of searing pain shot up Joe's arm. Joe tried to ignore the pain as he swam along, but Fowler would not let up. Then Fowler began to speak.

"You let me go right now, Joe O'Shanick! You have no idea what you've gotten yourself into!"

Joe kept swimming to shore.

"Do you have any idea who you're dealing with! I will have you rotting in a prison cell for the rest of your life! That's if something unfortunate doesn't happen to you first! Are you hearing me?!"

Joe had had enough. He pulled Fowler up, rolled onto his right side and wrapped his left arm around Fowler's throat from behind.

"Listen, you worthless political hack!" Joe said as he clamped his arm down into a light choke hold. "I could have just left you to drown back there! You had half of my team killed last year, you traitor! Half my team! Five of those men had wives! Three of them left children behind! And for what?! So you could further your political career while lining your pockets with the taxpayer's money? Drug money? Money made from sex trafficking?! Several innocent girls were abducted and brought here just to serve your perverted power trip! How many more have been sacrificed on your all-important altar? Huh, *Senator* Fowler? How many, you spineless piece of snake excrement?" Joe emphasized those last words by tightening his choke hold.

Fowler tried to reply but Joe wouldn't let up and he couldn't get the words out. Joe didn't care what the hack had to say. He was a career politician. Not a statesman. A career pandering, power-hungry, self-serving hack, who didn't care who he trampled on his way to the top. Lying was his native language. Fancy suits, sound bites, and photo ops were the imagery that formed the deception he portrayed to fool the electorate into voting for him and fawning over him. Men like this lived for power and the adulation of others.

Joe knew he had crossed some lines in capturing Fowler. He should have been content to rescue the girls and turn over what he knew to the authorities and let them sort it out. But it wouldn't be enough. Fowler would skate. High-ranking politicians like him always did. The media had picked their man and Fowler was it. This story would be buried within a weak without a trial and that's if it even saw the light of day. How many times had Joe and his SEAL brothers had missions blown by the loose lips of fat cat politicians like Fowler? Power-hungry, self-serving politicians the world over had to impress people by showing them how they were in the know, how they wielded the levers of power, and they always wanted everyone at the cocktail party or in the hotel room to know.

How many good men and woman were killed in the line of duty because of people like Fowler? Joe could name several dozen. More when one considered the ridiculous rules of engagement he and his fellow warriors were often forced to follow when confronting an enemy that had no honor and no code. All so the politicians could pacify the media and play their power games in Washington while real men and women lost their lives in battlefields all around the world.

Joe would do everything in his power to make sure this spineless cretin stood trial. That his level of corruption was exposed, at least to the people who cared. Joe knew quite well that, even if he stood trial, the powers that be would circle the wagons, the media would play it down or run other stories, and far too many people would be more concerned about the latest episode of *The Voice* or the latest trending video on TikTok to even notice.

But there were those who did care. People like his brothers in the Teams, Charles Courtnall, Clay Whitmore, Gary Lee, Joe's family, and Christy. People like the Cajun Navy; regular hard-working Americans who would leave their families and jobs to organize a hurricane response by trailering their aluminum john boats to hurricane flooded areas to spend countless hours rescuing those who were stranded. People like Saved in America, a volunteer organization comprised of some of Joe's retired Navy SEAL brothers and special investigators, who put their lives on the line to locate and rescue young women from human trafficking rings. Police officers, firefighters, paramedics, and all of the men and women in the armed forces. That was the America Joe identified with. Those were the people who loved their country enough to care enough to know how political hacks like Fowler were trampling their Constitution and selling their nation to the highest bidder. Even if Joe had to tell the tale from a prison cell or the witness box, he would do everything to see that the people who cared knew. That was the right thing to do and that was why he had decided to pull Fowler to shore rather than let him drown.

"Joe!"

Joe looked over his shoulder and saw the red and green running lights of a small Boston Whaler approaching. Chief Ramsey pulled up alongside and put the outboard engine in neutral.

"Get in, Joe. I've got him," Ramsey said as he used a boat hook to grab Fowler by the shirt. Joe swam around to the opposite side so as not to place too much weight on one side. He climbed in as Ramsey pulled Fowler aboard. Ramsey then pushed Fowler to the deck, placed a knee in the man's back and fastened his wrists with a set of flex cuffs. He turned Fowler over and leaned him up against the forward bench seat. Joe sat down on the bench next to Ramsey and exhaled loudly. Ramsey put the engine in gear and pushed up the throttle. The light boat pitched up briefly before it planed out at speed. He looked over at Joe and smiled.

"You really are one bullet proof, buttoned up, watertight frogman!" He joyfully exclaimed. "I saw you fall out of that helo and I thought your ticket was punched this time for sure!."

"Yeah? How high up were we?" Joe asked.

"I'd say at least eighty feet," Ramsey answered. "I'm not kidding, Joe. I really thought I was coming out here to find what was left of you! That was your mom's prayer covering over you, brother. I want in on that!"

"She loves you like one of her own, Rammer. She's been praying for you for years. All of our team for that matter. You really think it was eighty feet?"

"At least that," Ramsey said as he lowered the throttle and began to approach the island's main dock.

"It's a miracle either one of us survived," Joe said nodding his head toward Fowler.

"Cockroaches like that can crawl out from under a rock after a nuclear detonation," Ramsey spoke with detest as he and Joe stood to grab the mooring lines.

"You may want to consider that," Fowler spoke. "I just might weather this storm better than the two of you. Play your cards right and I might just see about keeping you two out of prison. I know people. A lot more than you two. They can be persuaded to help you."

"Is that so?" Ramsey asked sarcastically as he lifted Fowler up using both hands and dropped him face first on the dock. "Well, I don't think I want to know the kind of people that would associate with the likes of you. Oh! Sorry about the dock, Senator. Did that hurt? It looked very painful!"

Chapter 63

Isla Esmeralda, Belize

An eerie calm hung over the now deserted island, replacing the loud chaos of the firefight that took place less than thirty minutes ago. Despite the gentle trade wind, the smell of aviation fuel and cordite lingered. Ramsey had quickly secured Fowler by flex cuffing his wrists to one of the dock cleats. They were in a hurry to find Lee. No one had heard from him in nearly an hour. Both were now presuming the worst but refused to give up hope and the urgency of finding him took precedence.

They double timed it to the other side of the island. Along the way, they stopped to grab a few magazines off the dead cartel soldiers. Both stuffed the magazines in their vests as they ran to the bungalow. Joe picked up his rifle that he had dropped before running for the helicopter and slung it over his back. The island was deserted and it was probably unnecessary but the helicopter pilot could be a cartel member and have already called for help.

Joe led Ramsey to the porch where they pulled themselves up onto the roof via the overhang. They scaled the gently sloped peak and saw Gary Lee's prone body on the far corner. He wasn't moving. Joe reached him first and quickly confirmed he had been killed. Lee had been shot multiple times in his right torso and head. Together, they rolled the former Marine now turned investigator over. His eyes remained open.

"You and I would both be dead had he not taken Cardenas out with that shot earlier," Joe commented as he gently closed Lee's eyes.

Ramsey stood and looked over to where they had been when Cardenas had nearly shot them. He cocked his head in curiosity and walked up and over to the front side of the roof. Joe watched with curiosity as Ramsey moved about, studying the bungalows and then lay prone on the roof. He popped back up and walked back to where Joe was tending to Lee.

"Joe, it's nothing short of a miracle that he even made that shot!"

"Really? Why's that?"

"There are four other bungalows between here and there. That hooch we were held up in can barely be seen and the window through which he made that shot could only be seen from the front of the roof. Had Cardenas been anywhere else in that room, or had Lee been anywhere else, that shot wouldn't have happened. We shouldn't be alive right now," Ramsey finished somberly.

"But instead he's the one who gets his ticket punched," Joe added.

"You're right," Ramsey replied. "Doesn't seem right when you think about."

"It's never right, Rammer," Joe said sorrowfully as he studied Lee's now serene face. "Semper Fi, Marine."

Joe stood up and removed a body bag from Ramsey's Molle Pack. Together they worked Lee into the bag and then gently lowered him off the roof using a length of paracord. They climbed back down, picked up Lee's bag, carried him back to the dock, and placed him down below on the cruiser. Ramsey cut Fowler loose from the dock and lead him onboard the sport fishing cruiser, a Hatteras GT 65 Carolina. Joe climbed up to the flying bridge and began prepping the engines for startup. Ramsey secured Fowler down below by sitting him on the floor next to Lee's body bag and securing his cuffed wrists behind him to a stainless-steel stool pylon in the main salon. Ramsey stood and looked down.

"The man in that body bag came here and put his life on the line to rescue innocent girls he never even met. Girls who were ripped from their livelihoods to serve the sadistic cravings of scumbag perverts like you! He gave his life to save those girls and he ultimately saved our lives as well. That man has more honor in his pinky toe than you will ever have in your entire life, *Senator!*" Ramsey said unsheathing his Ka-Bar knife.

"If it were up to me, I'd cut your arms and legs to ribbons and then drag you behind this boat as chum bait for the sharks until there was nothing left of you. But that man up there," Ramsey said using his knife to point upward to where Joe was on the flying bridge, "that man, has more restraint than I have. He saw to it to spare your life when he could have let you drown. *That* man, whose team he commanded, was killed at *your* hands! *That* man whose family was brutally attacked by surrogates acting on behalf of *your* cartel associates and with *your* knowledge and encouragement! *That* man chose honor and mercy to spare your life and allow you a trial in a court of law when *you* would not give him, his family, or his teammates an ounce of quarter but rather chose to eliminate them like squashing a bug. You're a disgrace to our nation. A disgrace to those who have served and a pathetic pile of human waste. The next time you see me after today, I'll be wearing my dress blue uniform complete with my Silver Star, my jump wings and, most importantly, my Trident. It will be *my* honor burn you on the stand!" Ramsey said placing emphasis on the last point by throwing his knife down with practiced proficiency.

Fowler screamed out in fear as the knife stuck into the teak deck mere inches from his groin.

Chapter 64

Western Caribbean Sea

The RHIB plodded along as Courtnall piloted it through the mild swells. The second engine had begun to sputter shortly after the first engine died. Courtnall worked it as best as he could but it was clearly in its death throes and they weren't even halfway to Belize City.

Christy tried not to think about it as she continued to check on all of the boat's occupants, whom she now considered her patients. All seemed stable. The girls all had various bruises but no immediate medical issues as far as she could tell. Their individual mental health would be another issue entirely but that was not something she could address nor was it her specialty. Whitmore would need attention. Although still drowsy, he had regained consciousness and seemed fairly alert but his head injury still warranted a CT scan to evaluate for internal swelling or hemorrhage.

Similarly, Tracy Courtnall had shown a fair level of awareness but somewhat drowsy ever since Joe brought her on board. Christy decided to check on her again. She stepped up to the center console where Courtnall was piloting the RHIB. Tracy had both her arms wrapped around her father's left arm and was leaning into him with her head on his shoulder.

"How's she doing?" Christy asked just loud enough to be heard over the sputtering engine.

"I think she's asleep," He answered looking down at his daughter. "Poor thing cried herself to sleep. Kept telling me she was sorry.

I kept telling her she had nothing to be sorry for, that those animals are to blame," he said trying to force back a sob. "What in the world would cause her to say such a thing? What could they have possibly done to her?"

"I can't even imagine, Mr. Courtnall, but it could be extremely bad. What she has endured is nothing short of traumatic. We will need to get her better looked at physically but she will also need extensive counseling. It's not uncommon for victims to assume guilt which is why she may have been saying those things, but I'm only speculating."

"We've got a long road to recovery ahead of us, don't we?" He asked.

Christy chose her next words carefully and formed a gentle re-assuring smile. "From everything you've told me about Tracy, she's a resilient fighter. With the right support, I'm confident that she will heal up just fine. What she needs more than anything else is the love and support of her family. Especially her father and brothers to reaf-firm what a real man is; a safe haven, a source of unconditional love and protection. The fact that you moved heaven and Earth to find and rescue her will go a long way toward that end. That's something to build on."

Courtnall acknowledged Christy's words with a quick glance and a quiet nod and then looked back out in front. The engine emitted a loud cough and began to sputter more severely.

"I hope we make it back," Christy said looking back at the engine.

Her voice remained calm and professional just like the demeanor she maintained at the bedside of a crashing patient. Inwardly, her concerns were growing. Whitmore and Tracy seemed stable but they would need further evaluation, and soon. If either had intracranial bleeding, they could quickly become unstable. There would be very little she could do for either one of them miles from shore. She was also concerned over Joe and Ramsey. They had swum back into a hos-tile situation. Could they have been captured? Or, dare she consider it, dead? Christy didn't think so. Those two were very good and re-sourceful. They were trained for mission success, but one never knew. Her thoughts were interrupted by the sound of the engine sputtering it's last and then giving up its ghost. The already slow moving RHIB settled down even lower in the water and drifted to a stop. The silence was overwhelming.

"Well, I guess that answers that question," Courtnall said as he tried to restart the engine. The metallic ring of the starter went unanswered after each attempt.

Courtnall looked at Christy and sighed in resignation. "I think we're going to have to take our chances with the Coast Guard."

"Are you sure?" Christy asked. "There's got to be some other way. Matt really didn't think we could trust them not to have someone on the cartel's payroll. What if we try paddling?"

"I like your spunk, Christy, but we are miles from shore and even further from our destination. We either take our chances with the Coast Guard or we pray for a miracle."

"That's not a bad idea," Christy said grabbing Courtnall's hand. "Let's pray."

Together, they bowed their heads. Christy waited to see if Courtnall would lead them but, when he remained silent, she stepped in.

"Heavenly Father, we thank you for helping us rescue Tracy and all these other girls tonight. We thank you for their deliverance and protection and we pray for a complete healing for each and every one of them, physically, mentally, and spiritually. Help us to minister to them and send others to do the same that each one may rebuild their lives. Restore what the enemy has taken for them. We also ask that you protect Joe and Matt as they risk their lives once again for others. Jesus, you said; *Greater love has no one than this, that he lay his life down for another.* As Joe, Matt, Clay, and Gary have done so tonight, help them to finish what they started in a victorious manner and guide them to safety. Now we pray that you will help us find a way back to safety. To get each of these girls to a safe haven and for us to get back home. It's in your name we pray. Amen."

Christy raised her head. Courtnall not only kept his head bowed but grabbed Christy's hand tighter and tearfully began to pray out loud.

"Lord, I'm in no position to bargain or ask anything of you. You have blessed me beyond measure while I have given you little more than lip service. I have claimed to serve you yet I don't truly know you. And now you've shown your grace to me once again by delivering my daughter back safely into my arms. All the riches in the world couldn't measure up to that, but that just shows me how much you gave to have your one and only Son die for us to pay the penalty for our sins. So here and now, I acknowledge my sinfulness, my stubborn pride, and my need for you as a Savior. Please come into my life and help me finally know you and live for you from this day forward. And I thank you for this amazing young lady you used to boldly look into my heart and reveal what I've needed to know for my entire life. Please answer her prayers, bless her, and place her back in the arms of the man who I now know you sent to rescue Tracy. Thank you for sending these… these warrior angels to redeem my Tracy, these other girls and even me from my pride. Thank you for these forces of redemption. Amen."

Courtnall looked up with tears in his eyes. Christy met him with tears of her own and a deep hug. With a start, Christy broke the hug and stood bolt upright.

"Was that the radio I just heard?" She asked.

"What?" Courtnall asked. "I didn't hear anything."

"I could swear I just heard the radio crackle," Christy said with conviction as she began looking around the console. "I thought I left it up here."

Suddenly the metallic sound of a muffled voice followed by a brief static hiss of a radio sounded from the stern.

"Now, I definitely heard that!" Courtnall spoke excitedly. "We're on a remote encrypted network. That *has* to be them!"

"That's right!" Christy exclaimed as she walked back to the aft bench seat. "I set the radio down back here when I was checking on Clay and Yoana. Here it is!" She said, pulling it out from her medical bag.

"Echo base, this is Echo One, do you read me?"

Christy broke into an excited smile as she keyed the radio. "Echo One, we read you loud and clear. It's good to hear your voice."

"Yours too. What's your status?" Joe asked over the radio.

"Both engines are out and we are adrift miles from shore."

"Roger that. Is everyone okay?"

"All are stable but several in need of better medical care ashore," Christy answered.

"Well it just so happens we can help in that department," Joe responded sounding a little more upbeat. "I've got your radio signal on GPS. We'll be at your position in five mikes. If they're not already on, turn on your navigation lights so we'll see you."

"They're on!" Courtnall called from the helm.

"They're on!" Christy spoke into the radio.

"Good copy. See you in five."

Chapter 65

Western Caribbean Sea

The twin diesels emitted a hypnotic baseline to the melodious sound of the water washing off the hull as the sleek sport-fishing cruiser cut through the gentle swells. Joe savored the warm breeze washing over his face as he gazed forward and marveled at the canopy of stars. The moonless night seemed to enhance the brightness of the countless celestial bodies overhead. Joe inhaled the tropical air and sighed. For just a moment, he blocked out his feelings of anger and sadness over Lee while allowing his mind to decompress as the adrenaline wore off. Overall, the mission had been a success. Lee's loss was tragic and they would help Whitmore deal with it, but, for now, there was nothing Joe could do but allow his mind and body to relax and recharge as he piloted the cruiser back to port.

Alone up on the flying bridge, Joe was able conduct a private after-action report in his mind: processing his thoughts, what went well, what went wrong, and put the mission behind him. He glanced behind the cruiser to check on the RHIB which trailed behind the cruiser on it's tow line. It was pulling along just fine. He wondered what Courtnall would do with it. Several of the rescued girls sat on the deck below. They huddled together but no one spoke. Some had their eyes closed and others just stared at the water as it went by. More sat down below. He and Ramsey had moved Lee's body bag into one of the deck wells so as not to shock the girls when they came aboard. Tupolev was tied up in the main salon next to Fowler; meanwhile,

Ramsey and Courtnall were helping Christy settle the girls in. The yacht was loaded with snacks and beverages which the three immediately began to distribute among their shocked passengers. Fowler and Tupolev would have to be satisfied with the rags he and Ramsey shoved in their mouths. *Screw em,'* Joe thought. They were lucky to be alive. He smiled when he pondered how they would like prison food compared to that which they enjoyed from their personal chefs and favorite restaurants.

Joe was looking out over the water when a familiar presence quietly sat down next to him. Joe looked over to find Christy leaning in for a kiss. Joe withdrew slightly resulting in Christy forming a mock look of sternness.

"Aren't we still keeping things under wraps?" He asked.

"Nope," she grinned. "The cat's out of the bag on that one."

"Really? How did Courtnall find out?"

"A lucky guess," Christy answered evasively.

Joe raised an accusing eyebrow.

"Okay, if you're gonna sweat it out of me, Charles and I had a little heart to heart while you guys were on the island," Christy said with her eyes mirthfully looking upward.

"I worry about you, Christy," Joe said playfully as he slipped his arm around her slender waist and pulled her in. "You fold too easy under questioning."

"Only for tall, dark, and handsome SEAL officers," she said as she allowed Joe to pull her in for a lingering kiss. "I brought you something," she said as she pulled away and held up a stainless-steel travel mug.

"I hope it's something with caffeine," Joe said reaching for the mug. He suppressed a wince when a jolt of pain shot up from his gunshot wound. "Rammer and I have been up since before sunrise and now the post-op fatigue is settling in."

"You have to guess," Christy teased using her long arms to hold the mug out of Joe's reach.

"It's coffee," he replied, reaching out, "I can smell it from here."

"Not just any coffee," she smiled, her eyes twinkling in a manner Joe found irresistible. "Guess!"

"I don't know. It's the cartel's boat. It's probably some fancy Columbian blend where the beans were handpicked by some guy named Juan with a donkey."

"Nope," she answered before reconsidering. "Well, it might be, but it was brewed special by a guy named Matt."

"Ooohhh!" Joe said happily. "Chief made his secret chief's brew? I'm all over that!"

Christy took a sip before handing it over to Joe. "That *is* good, but I still liked yours better last year."

"The stuff I made on the sailboat?" Joe asked perplexed. "That was adequate under the circumstances but it can't compare to Chief's brew."

"Those *circumstances* were a scary and perilous time, Joe O'Shanick, but that's how you and I met. I was cold, wet, and scared when you handed me that coffee and you helped calmed me down with that simple gesture. That will always the best coffee I ever had," Christy said leaning in for another kiss. "I'm glad you're back safe."

"I'll drink to that," he answered carefully transferring the mug to his left hand.

"Now let me have a look at that wound," Christy said as she pulled a small medical pouch from behind her back and placed it on the console. "Tell me what happened."

"I think I took a round when I was carrying Yoana to the boat. I'm pretty sure it went through and through."

"I'll be the judge of that," Christy said rolling up his sleeve.

Joe stared straight ahead in silence as he piloted the large cruiser across the water. Christy inspected the two small wounds with a penlight. Satisfied, she conducted a thorough exam of his strength and sensation in his arm as well as the strength of his ulnar and radial artery pulses.

"It looks like it went through part of your triceps but that's it. We just need to clean it and put a clean dressing on and it should heal up fine," she said as she opened a small bottle of Betadine and poured it over a small container of gauze pads.

Christy went to work cleaning the wounds. The Betadine stung for a minute but Joe didn't utter a sound. He continued to pilot the cruiser while watching Christy out of the corner of his eye. She truly is one in a million. Intelligent, competent, and compassionate, not to mention beautiful. Add inspiring to that. There weren't enough adjectives to adequately describe her. Just being around her made him want to be a better person.

Exactly one year ago, he had been an agnostic, self-confident man who attributed his success and accomplishments to his own talent and work ethic. He was raised in a Christian family and, as much as he loved his family, he had wanted nothing to do with their God. Not based on his own interpretation of the world. Last year, Christy dropped into his life on that blown rescue mission in Honduras that had killed half his team. The mission Fowler had just bragged about blowing. At first, he was put off by Christy's very evident faith. Annoyed might be a better word. But he quickly learned that it wasn't some religious pretense with her. Her faith was indeed genuine and he later learned not at all pretensive or baseless. She had patiently and lovingly shown him that her faith was not some blind belief in some mysterious god but an actual trust in the One whom the evidence led her to believe in. As such, Joe saw an inner quality in Christy that transcended her many other admirable attributes. That intrigued Joe enough to the point where he willingly engaged her in discussions of her faith with an open mind which soon led him on a journey of discovery and his eventual acceptance of Christ as Lord and Savior.

He didn't turn into some wild-eyed, peace-loving weirdo like he thought he would. Rather, his life took on new purpose and meaning, much like that of Christy and his family. What he did as a SEAL, what they did earlier tonight, that was meaningful. They were protecting others, even redeeming them, so to speak. Killing people was never desirable, but in a justified war or in the defense of self or others, it was not sinful. He understood that better seeing it through God's eyes and it helped. Joe had racked up a sizable body count over his several years of combat. Even the most hardened of SPECWAR operators could sometimes wring their hands or lie awake with guilt when mentally processing the lives they had taken, no matter how justified they had been. Experiencing the forgiveness of Christ and having a biblical worldview had lifted that burden of guilt-ridden angst in a very tangible manner. There was an incredible peace with that. A peace like he felt right now on a beautiful tropical night, piloting a large cruiser with this amazing woman by his side.

A woman who had seen something in him that he had not seen himself. Yep, that *had certainly been* some good coffee. Christy was right. That experience had been life changing. *She* had been life changing. He couldn't imagine his life without her now.

What was it his mother always told him?

"Don't marry the person you can live with; marry the person you can't live without."

Was he really to that point.? Was it too soon to think about marriage? Joe didn't think so. True, they had only officially been a couple for not even three months, but that relationship had been forged over the past year. And what about that vision he had seen earlier? A vivid glimpse of them playing with their future children? Where had *that* come from? Was his subconscious trying to tell him something? Was God?

Talk to her you moron! Joe told himself as he continued to watch her work on his arm. She was very open and reasonable. It wasn't like he had to pop the question. But maybe he would anyway? No, Christy deserved better than that. She deserved to be swept off her feet. Nevertheless, past conversations had alluded to a possible future together and it would be good to get things out in the open and, perhaps, get an idea of where they were headed.

"Penny for your thoughts," she prompted as she finished wrapping Coban around his dressing.

"Huh?" Joe said, caught off guard as he turned his eyes to her. *Does she know what I'm thinking?*

"You have that quiet contemplative look you get when you're thinking about something important," She replied looking at him with her eyebrows raised in a curious expression.

Man, does she know me! Joe thought as he gazed back, speechless.

"Joe?" Christy cocked her head with an amused expression.

That's right, you moron! She does know you. What are you so afraid of? Now's your chance. Just talk to her, you idiot!

"Yeah, I, uh…umm…I was wondering, well more like thinking… umm…"

"Joe, what is it?" Christy asked, her amused expression still present. "I've never seen you so tongue tied before."

Joe decided right then that he was going to do what he does best and kick down the door. He was going to ask Christy to marry him. They had met on this sea in nearly the exact same location. He may not have a ring on him but he knew she wouldn't care. This was the time and this was the place. He took a breath and began to speak.

"Christy, would you…"

"May we interrupt?" Courtnall's voice materialized behind them.

Joe and Christy looked over and saw Courtnall's head peeking up from the ladder well.

"Yeah, sure," Joe said exhaling with mixed emotions. "C'mon up."

"We wanted to come up and thank you both, personally," Courtnall said as he climbed up onto the deck and helped Tracy who followed him up.

"Well, look who's up and about!" Christy exclaimed as she stood and gave Tracy a hug.

Christy stepped back and surveyed Tracy with her physician's eye. "How are you feeling, Tracy?"

"I'm much better, ma'am, thank you. Just a little headache. I asked Daddy to bring me up here so I could thank you all."

"I did very little," Christy replied as she turned and extended a hand toward Joe who was half turned in their direction as he continued to steer. "This is the man who led the team that rescued all of you. Tracy Courtnall, I'd like you to meet Joe O'Shanick."

With tears in her eyes, Tracy padded up to Joe, wrapped her arms around his midsection and hugged him tightly. She was clad in the t-shirt and shorts Christy had found below in one of the cabins. Her head only came up to Joe's chest. She looked like a blond pixie next to Joe. Joe felt her deflate as she began sobbing. He wrapped his free arm around her and shared a smile with Christy and Courtnall.

*****

Tracy leaned against her father as he piloted the cruiser. She inhaled a refreshing lungful of the salt air and savored the moment. A moment she had dreamed about but had thought would never come. Dr. Tabrizi had excused herself to head back down to check on Mr. Whitmore. Mr. O'Shanick, "Joe" he had insisted she call him, had only been too happy to relinquish the helm to her father. Joe, still clad in his tactical gear, had stretched out on the flying bridge's starboard bench and fallen asleep almost instantly. Tracy drifted in and out of a light sleep. Her ordeal of the past week made her wary of falling asleep. Part of her feared this was another dream and she really wasn't safe in Daddy's arms, but for the most part she was comfortable that all of this was real and her ordeal was over. And what an ordeal it had been, although not as bad as what the other girls had been put through. Nevertheless, she had never experienced such fear and humiliation not to mention having been nearly raped by…

With a startling realization, Tracy looked down at her left hand. The platinum ring was still there. A shining symbol of a promise that had endured. A promise mutually made by Tracy with her family. Mutually made and mutually kept. She ran her fingers over it, tracing the outline of the heart. Tracy held her left hand up before her father, the tiny diamonds glimmering under the stars.

"They didn't get to me, Daddy. The promise endures. Thank you."

Chapter 66

Gwinnett County Airport Lawrenceville, Georgia

The Gulfstream G700 slowly rolled to a stop and the engines immediately began to wind down. Special Agent Javier Gomez stood on the tarmac waiting. Next to him was Special Agent Katie Huggins. Both sipped coffee Gomez had picked up at a nearby shop as they waited quietly. The first rays of sun were just beginning to peak over the eastern horizon. The morning air was a relatively cool sixty-one degrees. It was a perfect morning for a run, Gomez thought to himself, somewhat remorseful over missing his early morning run. It was supposed to get up to eighty-eight today and by the time he got in a run it would be sweltering. If he got in a run. This was shaping up to be a rather long day. But a good one.

The aircraft door popped open and extended down to just above the tarmac. Chuck Springer stepped off first followed by Clay Whitmore who was being helped off by two of his associates. Gomez and Huggins walked up to them and exchanged handshakes.

"Where's Tupolev?" Gomez asked looking beyond them toward the airplane.

"He'll be off in a minute," Springer explained. "I wanted to talk to you both first. We've been on Tupolev's trail for a week now and we've gotten nothing but resistance from your office. We rescued over a dozen girls from a cartel human trafficking network but we lost one our teammates in the process and nearly lost Clay. As it is, he needs to go to the hospital so I'm stepping in on his behalf. Clay tells me I can trust you two but I'm not confident I can trust those above you. I need your assurance that you will see this through."

"Sir, I will personally vouch for Special Agent Gomez and SAIC McPherson," Special Agent Huggins spoke up. "Strictly off the record, we have an agent we are concerned about but we will get SAIC McPherson in on this right away."

"That's what I need to hear, ma'am," Springer answered. "This is *way* bigger than the Tupolev organization. They're just one cog in an international crime syndicate that involves some big-name players."

Springer removed a backpack from his shoulder and handed it over to Gomez. "This contains cellphones, tablets, and laptops we collected from the Caribbean island we rescued the girls from. It's owned by the LFG cartel through a few shell corporations. They killed one of my men last night and nearly killed Clay as well. We have facial pics of all those who were there. It appears the Iranians and Chinese are also involved. It turned into a bloodbath but the men with us fought them back and prevailed, including taking out the head of LFG, his number two and Tupolev's main pimp, Petrenko. They not only captured Tupolev alive but caught a much bigger fish."

"Bigger than Tupolev and Cardenas?" Gomez asked incredulously.

"Way bigger," Springer answered. "Which is why I need your assurance that this will be handled with the utmost care. We cannot let this one skate."

"Who are we talking about, Chuck?" Huggins answered.

Springer turned toward the plane, let out a shrill whistle and waved the occupants out. Gomez and Huggins watched as Ramsey led a cuffed Tupolev out first. Joe followed with Fowler.

"You've got to be kidding me!" Gomez exclaimed dumbfounded.

"I wish I was," Springer spoke quietly. "Here is the list of his charges. DO NOT screw this up!"

Gomez and a couple of his agents took custody of Tupolev and Fowler. Gomez took personal charge of Fowler and began by placing him in formal handcuffs.

"Senator Robert Fowler, you are charged with attempted rape, two accounts of accessory to commit murder, violation of the National

Security Act, and treason. You have the right to remain silent. Anything you say…"

"Can it, fella," Fowler snapped, sounding annoyed as he interrupted Gomez. "I'm an attorney and a United States senator. I know
my rights. I want to see the Special Agent in Charge immediately!
This is an egregious mistake! I want these men charged with murder and for assault, unlawful restraint, and kidnapping a United States
senator! Did you get all of that?"

"Yes, sir. You wish to speak to Special Agent in Charge McPherson. Right away, sir," Gomez said as he pulled out his phone. "I'll just
need you to get into this vehicle first, sir."

"I'll do no such thing. I'm standing right here while you get
McPherson on the phone!"

"I'm sorry, sir, but as long as you're under arrest, you will do
what I say. Now please get in the vehicle," Gomez replied as he gently
placed a hand on Fowler's back.

"Do you have any idea who you're dealing with, son?" Fowler
snapped. "Get your greasy hands off of me right now or I'll have your
badge!"

"Whatever you say sir," Gomez said as he placed his hand on top
of Fowler's head and forced him into the dark SUV.

Fowler went into a loud tirade of profanity ridden threats which
were muted out when Gomez slammed the door.

Chapter 67

Atlanta, Georgia

The sun was overhead when Joe walked out of the FBI Headquarters. He spotted Christy and Ramsey across the parking lot. They were in a shaded area of the parking lot, sitting on the open tailgate of Joe's truck. All three were still in their green and tan camouflage tactical clothes.

"You all done there, Joey-O?" Ramsey asked as Joe walked up.

"Finally," Joe answered. "Special Agent in Charge McPherson came down and questioned me personally. He's a good guy and he was meticulous with his questions. I basically had to walk him through it every step of the way from Wednesday night on. He's doing the same thing with the Courtnall's right now. Tracy scratched Fowler's face when he was forcing himself on her. They scraped under her nails for a DNA match. Gomez and McPherson are dotting every i and crossing every t on this one."

"Good," Ramsey grunted. "They're gonna have to. You know Fowler is gonna have an army of lawyers trying to get him off."

"Yeah, it's gonna be a goat rope," Joe nodded as he leaned on the gate next to Christy. "At least his political career is over. Just think how screwed this country would have been to have that clown sitting in the White House."

"He would still be in the race had you guys not volunteered to go find those girls," Christy added.

"Yeah, I didn't think about that," Ramsey nodded thoughtfully.

"So how did everybody turn out?" Joe asked Christy.

"Fine," she answered. "Both Clay's and Tracy's CT scans were negative. They suffered mild concussions but nothing more from a physical standpoint. Tracy will need some counseling as will the other girls. Darcy has already left with her parents and Rebecca's parents are on their way. Both were showing signs of opiate withdrawal and will need help with that as well. I just hope the girls we left at the shelter in Belize City will be okay..." Christy's voice trailed off.

By the time they had docked in Belize City, the consensus was to get everyone on board Courtnall's jet and return to the United States. Christy had contacted a parent ministry she volunteered for that establishes and funds shelters for woman escaping human trafficking gangs. They gave her the number for one such shelter in Belize City and they were able to drop the Central American girls off there where they would get help with recovery and ultimately be able to return to their families.

Little Yoana had clung to Christy's side from the moment they stepped off the cruiser. When it came time to leave the shelter, Yoana tearfully clung to Christy, refusing to let her leave. Only fourteen years old, Yoana was from Costa Rica where, growing up, she had been beaten and molested by her father for years before her mother sold her into prostitution when she was just twelve. Yoana begged Christy not to leave her. Christy tearfully considered bringing Yoana with her on the plane until she was warned by the staff that there would be major immigration issues and that Yoana would be better off with them where she would be properly looked after. After considerable anguish, Christy relented and tried to console Yoana while the staff literally pried her off of Christy.

"You're thinking about Yoana, aren't you?" Joe asked sympathetically as he rubbed her forearm and grabbed her hand.

Christy nodded silently as tears began to roll down her cheeks.

"Christy," Joe spoke softly, "I know you want to help her but what the staff at the shelter said made sense. It would have been an immigration fiasco under the circumstances and she may have ended up in federal custody. She's *much* better off being looked after by that ministry."

"She needs a family, Joe!" Christy stated emphatically. "She's never had one! She just needs someone to love her! A place where she can feel safe, valued, and cherished! I could give her that!" Christy finished by gently crying with her face down into her hands.

Joe was silent. What could he say? Joe vividly recalled trying to convince Yoana to head to the RHIB with him. Yoana bluntly stated that she had never met a man who didn't abuse her. How sad. How pathetically sad. Christy was right. Yoana needed a family. A family with a father. A good father that would love her and show her what a good man was all about. A man whose arms were not a threat but a haven of protection. He looked over at Ramsey and subtly motioned with his head, asking Ramsey to give them a moment.

"I'll be back in a minute," Ramsey awkwardly stammered. "I have to go, um, be somewhere else."

Had Joe not been so laser focused on his thoughts, he would have smiled at Ramsey's awkward exit. He nodded to his friend and squared himself, facing Christy, standing before her as she sat on the tailgate. She looked up.

"I'm sorry, Joe. I didn't mean to snap at you. I'm tired, emotionally spent and feeling guilty that I could have done something more for Yoana. Something life changing and meaningful. She needs that."

"It's okay, Christy," Joe said giving her thigh a reassuring rub. "I knew that wasn't directed at me. I know how much this upsets you. And you're right. Yoana does deserve better. But that would be a huge undertaking for you.

"I can do it," Christy stated confidently.

"I have no doubt you can," Joe answered, "but Yoana also needs a father-figure in her life. And you and I both know that parenting is a two-person job."

"I'm not arguing that, Joe, but what I could provide her would still be better than spending the rest of her teenage years in an orphanage somewhere."

Joe's eyebrows narrowed slightly as he stared at her in thought.

"Okay, let's pump the brakes for just a second," he said as he formed the timeout sign with his hands. "You're the most level-headed, right-brained woman I know, but you've been through a lot in the past forty-eight hours. I just want you to stop and think this through. Are you *sure* this is what you want to do?"

"Yes," she answered quietly. "While you were sleeping on the plane, I was wrestling and praying about this."

"You're sure? Because this is life changing. Not only for Yoana but for you as well."

"I know it is," Christy nodded seriously. "But I feel led to do it. I want to do this. Besides, Daniella will graduate Teen Challenge in a few months. She'll have her GED and will come live with me and start nursing school while she works in my ER as a CNA. She will be a big help with Yoana. They're both from Central America, both rescued from the cartels and human trafficking."

"That's true, she will be a big help," Joe agreed staring off in thought.

"What's wrong?" She asked. "You've got that look. Are thinking this is going to change things between us?"

"You don't think it will?"

Christy took a contemplative breath and spoke softly. "Oh, Joe. I just realized I haven't even stopped to consider where you stand on all of this. I haven't even asked your opinion. Please forgive me. I don't want this to come between us. Maybe we *should* take some time to think about this. Together."

Joe stopped looking off into the distance and looked into Christy's eyes. "No. I think this needs to happen. You're right, Yoana needs a family. Daniella too. You and I have been blessed to have come from great families. We could do the same for them."

"Really? Wait," Christy's brows creased as she looked back at Joe, "did you say we?"

"Yes," Joe replied.

"Joe O'Shanick, are you saying what I think you're saying?"

"Yes."

Chapter 68

Atlanta, Georgia
One day later

The soft sound of footsteps broke though the cool morning air. A squirrel darted off the cart path when a man materialized from around the bend in light morning mist that hung over Chastain Park Golf Course. He ran by, a moderate sheen of sweat, mostly caused by the humid air, dripped from under his Atlanta Braves baseball hat. Nikolai Sivakov glanced at his Garmin watch and saw that he was maintaining a seven-minute mile pace. It was slower than he normally ran but exactly what he had planned on for this morning.

Former Russian Spetsnaz, Nikolai had a near genius IQ. Furthermore, he could completely separate his mind from his body, focusing on complex mental tasks while running at a sub six-minute mile pace or running up a steep mountain carrying a twenty-kilogram rucksack.

This morning he was running, what was for him, a light pace while working out a simple algebra problem in his head. It was the classic one car overtaking another car traveling at a distant speed equation. Only in this case he was calculating what pace he needed to run in order for another runner to pass him at a preselected location. By observation and experience, he knew roughly how fast the other man was running. He also knew the distance between them and the distance to the location. His computer-like mind computed his pace and he was right on it.

With a half mile to go, Nikolai began to focus in on his surroundings. The sun was just beginning to rise and, as such, there were no golfers out this far. Other than himself and the other runner, there was no one else around. He was actually surprised. Buckhead was a trendy upscale location, popular among the younger crowd, who tended to still maintain a fair percentage of fitness enthusiasts. The golf course was an ideal place to get in a morning run. It was a pretty area with paved cart paths away from the city traffic. Perhaps they prefer their trendy gyms where they can socialize and spend their money on expensive protein drinks? It didn't matter. Nikolai was just glad they weren't here.

With a quarter of a mile to go, Nikolai heard the runner's footsteps as he slowly closed the distance between them. He could hear the man's rhythmic breathing as he trotted along at a six-and-a-half-minute mile pace. Not bad for a man in his mid-forties.

A patch of trees loomed up ahead. They lined both sides of the cart path and their branches intertwined overhead creating a short tunnel. The golf course stretched out to the right and a multi field baseball complex lay not a hundred yards to the left on the other side of the trees. Nikolai maintained his pace as he followed the cart path through the trees. The other runner was just behind him and starting to pass on Nikolai's left.

"Nice pace," Nikolai commented as the man passed by with his legs pumping in an admirable stride.

"You too!" The man answered with a wave as he gently eased back in front of Nikolai.

Nikolai quietly reached into his runner's pouch and retrieved a small Glock 43 9mm pistol. He picked up his pace slightly to keep from losing his prey as he retrieved a suppressor and quickly screwed it onto the specially made threaded barrel. He raised the suppressed handgun and pointed it at the base of the man's skull. He gently squeezed the trigger and a sharp metallic thwack sounded that was quickly absorbed by the thick stand of trees. The single round hit its mark and the man dropped to the ground, skidding to a stop. Nikolai stopped briefly to ensure his mark was dead and then detoured through the woods. By the time he reached Lake Forest Drive Northeast, he had already disassembled his handgun and replaced it inside his pouch. There was no one about. He jumped into the old Honda Civic he had stolen and drove off.

Chapter 69

Buford, Georgia

"*I*s Ina here?"

Joe looked up from the kitchen island cooktop stove. Christy was standing in the doorway to her bedroom with a surprised expression on her face. She was wearing an oversized, gray University of Tennessee t-shirt that reached halfway to her knees. Her long, dark hair hung loosely around her shoulders.

"You just wake up?" Joe asked.

"Yes," she answered as she crossed the great room to her kitchen. "I woke up to this heavenly aroma. I thought your mom was here. This is *you*?"

"Yes," Joe said as Christy stepped up and kissed him. "Are you surprised?"

"I would say yes," Christy started as she wrapped her arms around Joe and nestled in against his chest, "but then I remember Ina telling me that she taught you how to cook. So what are you making?"

"Slow-cooked Chicken Adobo, coconut rice, and Lumpia. And, yes, they are all traditional Filipino recipes that were handed down to me by the one and only Maria O'Shanick, better known as *Ina* to those of you within her inner circle," Joe stated proudly. "Everyone's gonna love it!"

"Everyone?" Christy stepped back and looked up at Joe.

"Well, Rammer's still here and I invited Stacy," Joe said nonchalantly.

"Joe O'Shanick!" Christy exclaimed with her eyes going wide. "Did you really?"

"What?" Joe said feigning innocence. "I just figured you two would want to catch up. You know, fill her in on all your adventures from the past two days."

"Yeah right!" Christy laughed as she began poking Joe in his abdomen. "*You're* playing matchmaker! Admit it! Admit it, Joe!"

"I can neither confirm nor deny that accusation," Joe said with mock seriousness.

"Don't give me that Navy-speak, Joe O'Shanick!" Christy said is she began tickling him. "You're playing matchmaker! C'mon! Admit it!"

Christy knew Joe was extremely ticklish and kept at it. In defense, Joe pulled her into a tight bear hug, pinning her arms to her side.

"I admit nothing other than I was just playing wingman to what you already started last week," Joe teased. "But I *did* think that if anyone can get that salty pipe-hitter to come to church with us tomorrow, it'll be you and Stacy."

"Hmm, I don't know if I completely buy that, but it's good thinking," Christy said as she broke out of the bear hug and stepped back, glancing at her Garmin watch. "When's dinner?"

Joe checked the timer for the rice. "It'll be ready in about fifteen minutes."

"Oh," Christy's eyes registered a surprised look. "When is Stacy getting here?"

"She's outside."

"With Matt?" Christy looked pleasantly surprised.

"Yeah, they're out on the patio," Joe said nodding toward the back yard.

Christy cast a quick glance through her screened in porch before heading out of the kitchen. "Then I better get a shower in before dinner's ready!"

Joe watched her lithe form as she walked with athletic grace back to her bedroom and closed the door. He longed for the day when he would be able to follow her into the bedroom, but that day was still a ways off. Hopefully not too far off though. Their conversation yesterday was a big step toward that goal. Life changing, actually. They were not formally engaged, but both had enthusiastically agreed that marriage was definitely in their future, and soon. They had also agreed to pursue adopting Yoana; additionally, they would mentor and house Daniella when she returned from Teen Challenge. Joe smiled. He was amazed at how quickly he had warmed to the idea of an instant family. *With teenagers no less. Girl teenagers!* Was he really ready for this? Yes. The truth was Joe was very family oriented. One of five children of a very tight family with role model parents. If he was half the dad to Daniella, Yoana, and someday his and Christy's own children, that his dad was to him, Joe knew he would be just fine. His SEAL platoon had been like a family to him as well. Now that he was being rotated out of command would be the perfect time to take it to the next level.

He couldn't think of a better person to share that experience with, to have by his side, than Christy. What a literal gift from God. During a time when Joe saw his operating days as an elite Navy SEAL quickly coming to a close, Christy appeared into his life. Looking back, Joe clearly saw God's hand in all of it; the changes He had worked in Joe's life through her, the way He had woven them together and now an exciting new adventure to enter into as he stepped away from his brothers in the Teams. God's timing was perfect. Yes, Joe was ready. It would be a challenge but one he was excited to face. He was now glad his spur of the moment plan to propose to Christy had been thwarted by Courtnall's appearance on the flying bridge. Even if she had said yes, he would have regretted not pursuing her hand in a more honorable manner.

That was about to change. While Christy was at work last night, Joe and Ramsey spent a great deal of time by the fireside with Critter and Stubber. They hammered out a workable deal for their tactical course which they agreed to work out on paper with an attorney in the upcoming weeks. During that time, Joe would resign his commission and Ramsey would end his enlistment. Earlier in the day, Joe placed a deposit on Mr. Wilhelm's sailboat. Once everything was up and running, Joe would sneak away and pay a visit to Christy's father to ask for her hand. It would be done right and honorably. She deserved all that and more.

Chapter 70

Buford, Georgia

A soothing crackle emanated from the fire pit as the flames began to consume the recently added oak log. The early sliver of a waxing crescent moon hung low in the peaceful early night sky.

Joe savored the smoky aroma of the cool evening air as he re-clined in an Adirondack chair. Christy sat close-by on his right as she conversed with Stacy on her other side. Ramsey sat to Stacy's right flanked by Critter on the other side. Joe was content to let them all talk while he quietly enjoyed a perfect evening with good company. Now that Ramsey was committed to moving this way, Joe hoped evenings like this would become a regular occurrence. A good fire by the lake was a comfortable place for him, having spent many a similar evening at his parents' house on the Niagara River.

"…anyway, the social worker is trying to locate her grandmother. I hope she finds her. Otherwise, Hannah will end up wherever the state places her and you know how that can go," Stacy concluded giving everyone an update on the three girls they rescued from the apartment two days earlier.

"Any idea where she lives?" Christy asked.

"Last she knew was somewhere near Batesburg-Leesville, South Carolina," Stacy sighed.

"I've heard of it," Christy replied. "It's about an hour away from Augusta where I did my residency. We occasionally got patients from there. It's a small town so hopefully someone will know where to find her," Christy added in a hopeful tone.

"What about the place Daniella is at? Teen Challenge?" Joe asked. "Could she go there if you don't find her grandmother?"

"It's a consideration, Joe, but she really wants to be back with her grandmother."

"Hey guys," Critter spoke up, a look of concern on his face as he looked intently at his cell phone. "You're not going to believe this!"

"What is it?" Ramsey asked.

Critter began to read from a newsfeed. "The body of a man found earlier this morning at a local Atlanta area golf course has been identified. The man has been identified as FBI Atlanta Field Office Special Agent in Charge, Special Agent Cliff McPherson. His apparently slain body was found on a Buckhead golf course. Preliminary reports indicate Special Agent McPherson died of multiple gunshot wounds to the head. His body was found on a cart path at Chastain Park Golf Course. Although foul play is presumed, no suspect has been identified. Assistant Special Agent in Charge, Andrew Winkelman has been named interim Special Agent in Charge. A full investigation is underway."

"Whiskey Tango Foxtrot," Ramsey spoke slowly.

"Good copy there, Rammer," Joe spoke. "That seems *way* too convenient."

"You think this has something to do with Fowler?" Critter asked.

"I wish it didn't," Joe began, "but McPherson was the one heading up the investigation on Fowler's charges. The FBI agents we met thought very highly of him. He interviewed all three of us yesterday. Seemed like a straight shooter. Clay Whitmore seems to think that there might be an agent or two who are politically motivated and taking orders from someone way up the food chain. Someone from the Field Office rejected Clay's request for assistance in rescuing those girls from the Tupolev organization. Went so far as to tell him to stand down and that the orders came from higher up. Springer was adamant that Gomez go straight to McPherson with Fowler. The timing is certainly suspect."

"Why don't you give him a call, Joe?" Ramsey suggested. "See if he knows anything."

"Good idea," Joe said as he pulled out his iPhone and dialed. "I'm calling Springer though. Clay might still be a bit loopy."

Springer picked up on the second ring.

"Chuck, it's Joe O'Shanick. Have you seen the news?"

"Seen it?" Springer answered. "I'm watching it right now. I feel like I'm living in an alternate universe. This is an absolute sham of a justice system! That self-righteous, treasonous hack is gonna skate!"

"You think Fowler will skate just like that?" Joe asked incredibly. "Just because McPherson got schwacked? Gomez and Huggins seem like good people. You don't think they can handle this?"

"Aren't you watching this?" Springer asked.

"No. Why?" Joe replied. "What are they saying?"

"Go turn on the news. Right now, Joe. Any news. Then call me back," Springer ended the call.

Joe pulled himself out of the Adirondack chair and stood. A tangible heaviness descended upon him.

"Joe? What's wrong?" Christy asked.

"Springer says we need to go turn on the news, right now," Joe said with grave concern as he started towards Critter's house.

The group stood and followed him in. Upon reaching the great room, Critter picked a remote control off the coffee table and turned on Fox News. A live press conference was underway. Standing at the podium was none other than Senator Robert Fowler. The headline at the bottoms of the screen read:

Presidential Challenger Senator Robert Fowler cleared of all charges.

Fowler wore a charcoal gray tailored suit with a white collared shirt, a sharply knotted light blue tie, and a dark scowl. He spoke with an inflamed rhetoric.

"...It is inconceivable that a sitting president, a man sworn to uphold the Constitution, could even consider, let alone actually send his personal hit squad to assassinate the challenger to his presidency. A United States senator, no less! The fact that Galan would have any American citizen savagely killed to preserve his reign of power should be immediate grounds for his arrest but at the very least grounds for impeachment. I call upon my fellow citizens in the House of Representatives to open an inquiry into Articles of Impeachment immediately! It is their patriotic duty to act. Never, in all my years of service

to the American people, have I seen such egregious and unconsciona-
ble act come from the White House! Jorge Galan claims to be fighting
the cartels of Central and South America? He is more tyrannical, more
criminal than all of the cartel leaders combined!" Fowler emphasized
his last point by pounding his fist on the podium.

"Look," he said switching to a more somber tone as he leaned forward on the podium. "This is not the way we do things. We are Americans. We are just and we are fair. This, what these men have done,
what Galan has done, this is a tremendous black eye on our nation's
history. These are dark days...dark days, but as president I promise I
will lead us into better days. That's not just a campaign slogan, people.
It's a promise. Now...I'll take your questions."

A flurry of questions arose from the press. Fowler pointed at a
reporter off camera and called her name. "Yes, Joanne."

"Senator Fowler, in your statement, you alluded to the president's
hit squad. Could you be more specific and what exactly did they do?"

"Thank you, Joanne. Yes, I did refer to Galan's hit squad. Whereas
I cannot tell you just how many people are on this hit squad or who all
they may be, I *can* tell you that I was personally attacked and assaulted
by two Navy SEALs personally known to the president. I personally
witnessed them brutally kill, in cold blood, several high-ranking foreign nationals. We are all familiar with these two men. They have
found their way in and out of the press on several occasions over the
past year, often for very sketchy reasons."

Joe felt his blood begin to boil as he shared a glance with Ramsey.

"I'm talking about Navy SEALs Lieutenant Commander Joseph
O'Shanick and Master Chief Petty Officer Matthew Ramsey."

The screen briefly changed to side by side images of Joe and
Ramsey's official service pictures. It was readily apparent that the
press had been briefed ahead of time. This was no spontaneous press
conference.

"As you may recall," Fowler continued as the screen returned
to his live feed. "Lieutenant Commander O'Shanick made the news
a few months ago after being rolled up in a multiple murder arrest
with a known drug and prostitution ring. He somehow got out of the
charges but the exact details of the incident and those regarding his

involvement have been kept hidden from the public. A year ago, O'Shanick and Master Chief Ramsey were personally awarded medals for their involvement in an incident with the cartels in Central America. It doesn't take a genius to connect the dots and realize that O'Shanick is Jorge Galan's personal henchman much like Heinrich Himmler was to Adolf Hitler in Nazi Germany. This man personally smashed my knee with a gun, shot two foreign dignitaries inside a flying helicopter, attempted to shoot me, and then pulled me out of the helicopter to fall from a height of over a hundred feet. After realizing I survived the fall, he then tried to strangle me in the water. His accomplice, Chief Matt Ramsey, threatened to throw me off a yacht in the middle of the Caribbean before narrowly missing me when he hurled a knife in my direction. I have personally spoken to the acting Special Agent in Charge of the FBI's Atlanta Field Office Andrew Winkelman regarding these incidents and he is in the process of having these two rogue Navy SEALs arrested and prosecuted as we speak."

Christy and Stacy turned to look at Joe and Ramsey. Their faces registering concerned looks of alarm. As if on cue, the sound of sirens could be heard in the distance. Joe looked back at Christy as the sirens grew louder. He could hear Senator Fowler continue to bloviate but the words no longer registered. Funny how the press didn't ask Fowler what he was doing surrounded by cartel thugs and abducted American girls on a resort island owned by the cartel. Ramsey cursed at Fowler's smug image on the screen to which Critter added his agreement.

Christy approached Joe with tears in her eyes. "This is all my fault. I'm so sorry I ever got you involved in this!" She blurted out emotionally as she buried her face in Joe's chest and began to sob.

"It's not your fault," he soothed. "Rammer and I chose to go. It was a good op. We'd do it all over again."

Joe held on to her as he and Ramsey traded looks of concern. They were out of their element. It was one thing to engage the enemy on a battlefield where Joe and Ramsey led a team of highly trained apex predators. They were now fully engaged with a different enemy on a different battlefield. A battlefield controlled by crooked establishment politicians who did not play by the rules. A battlefield where perception was reality and that perception was shaped by an increasingly deceptive establishment in collusion with a sympathetic media. A new battlefield with a new enemy. Or had they been fighting this enemy all along?

The End

About the Author

J ohn Galt Robinson is a practicing emergency medicine physician. He weaves his experiences from the exciting, tragic, and sometimes humorous world of emergency medicine into a much larger story with intriguing characters who tackle relevant social issues in a fast-paced adventure. John grew up just upriver from Niagara Falls on Grand Island, New York. He earned his medical degree at East Tennessee State University after a previous career as a Certified Athletic Trainer. He lives in South Carolina with his wife and family where he is an active sailor and triathlete.

His first two books, *Forces of Redemption* and *Power City* have been well received.

Author's Note

Dear Reader,

My first novel, *Forces of Redemption*, was intended to give the reader a glimpse into the horrors of human trafficking. In *Lost Angels* I attempted to delve much deeper into the domestic aspect of human trafficking. In reality, the horrors are far worse and far more widespread than can be explained in the context of a novel. Human trafficking is an enemy that must be fought on a grand and individual scale. Nations and states must rise in defense of those who cannot defend themselves but we, as individuals, can contribute as well. Neighborhood awareness, serving in a ministry or shelter and community involvement are a great place to start. Donating time or resources to a ministry or charity that fights these battles is another great option. While conducting research in preparation for *Forces of Redemption*, I learned of an organization, made up of volunteers who locate and rescue victims of human trafficking. They are retired Navy SEALs, private investigators, law enforcement investigators, and other servants. Their organization is named Saved In America. If you would like to learn more about them or financially support them, please visit their website www.savedinamerica.org.

In each novel, I have referred to an organization named Adult and Teen Challenge that really exists and has scores of treatment centers nationwide which serve to rehabilitate and train people who have walked the path of addiction or a troubled lifestyle. Adult and Teen Challenge houses and trains people to leave their troubled past behind them for good. Please strongly consider financially supporting this vital ministry. For more information, please visit their website www.teenchallengeusa.org.

One final note, I hope you have enjoyed reading this novel as much as I have writing it. As I write this, I am hard at work with the next novel in this series. Joe and Christy will be back in a new and different adventure along with some familiar friends and some new villains. As Christy learned, what she does matters. May this be said of each of you.

Thank you,

John Galt Robinson

Forces of Redemption

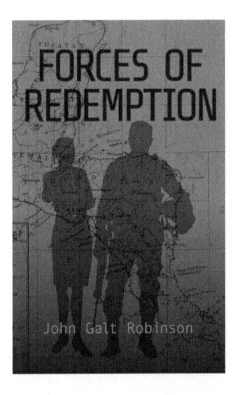

During a hectic Emergency Department shift, Dr. Christine "Christy" Tabrizi rescues a young Honduran girl from the gang that has been prostituting her and discovers the horrors of human trafficking tracing all the way back to the cartels in Central America. Christy volunteers for a mission in Honduras, to help rescue as many young girls as possible from the Cartels that control them. Joe O'Shanick is part of a Navy SEAL platoon deployed in Central America and finds himself in the midst of hostile territory when the President of the United States, a man of Mexican American heritage who sympathizes with the human condition in Central America, declares war on the Cartels. In the middle of a tense hostage scenario, Christy and Joe's paths collide, and they must rely on each other and their respective skills to escape with their lives.

Power City

A man is mysteriously swept over Niagara Falls. The city of Niagara Falls, nicknamed The Power City, finds itself in the shadow of a new power broker, the Catalano organization. This resurgent mafia family's rise to power leaves a trail of death and corruption in its wake. Navy SEAL Joe O'Shanick is their next target for execution, but the sinister reach of the Catalano organization extends beyond O'Shanick to his family and physician friend, Dr. Christy Tabrizi; however, this criminal organization forgot one thing: Navy SEALs leave no man behind. Power City explores the dark world of organized crime while weaving a story of faith and the selfless love of one's family and friends in a roller coaster ride of crime, medicine, military action, and suspense.

KCM Publishing
a division of KCM Digital Media, LLC